THE STORYTELLER FROM BALINCIA

THE STORYTELLER FROM BALINCIA

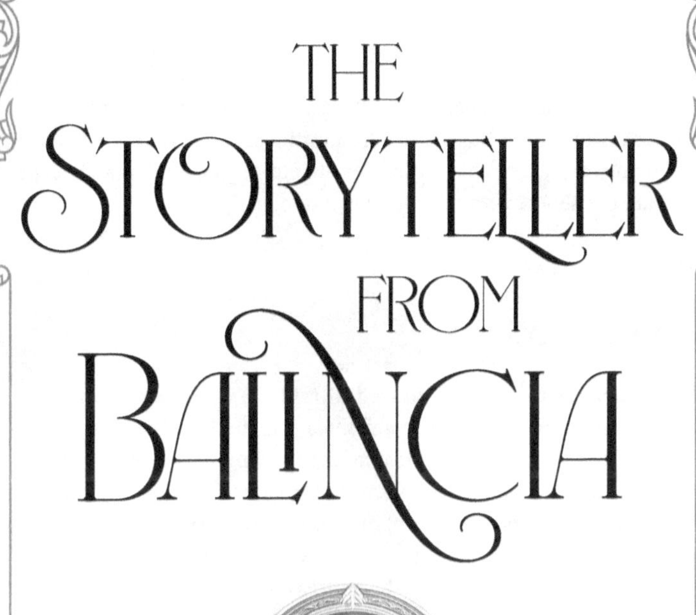

BOOK ONE OF
THE *DRIFTSTONE* SERIES

S.W. KENT

This is a work of fiction.N ames, characters, places, and incidents are either a product of the author's imagination or are used fictitiously . Any resemblances to actual persons, living or dead, events, or locales are entirely coincidental. Except for Giants, they are entirely real and live hidden among us.

Belquis and Martel Publishing LLC
1209 Mountain Road Pl NE Ste R, Albuquerque, NM 87110

Cover Illustrator: Miles Smart
Cover and Interior Book Design: Jess LaGreca, Mayfly book design
Appendix Illustrator: Yornelys Zambrano
Map Design: Inkarnate

Library of Congress Control Number: 202491683
Paperback ISBN: 979-8-9915807-2-4
Hardcover ISBN 979-8-9915807-0-0
Jacketed Hardcover ISBN: 979-8-9915807-3-1
eBook ISBN: 979-8-9915807-1-7

Contact author @swkentbooks.com

*Dedicated to all those who, as children, never found reflections
of themselves in the pages of a Fairy Tale.*

CONTENTS

Part Two

Part Three

PROLOGUE

In the hush of night, a solitary figure emerged from the lake under the lavender and blue moons. Cloaked, the old woman stepped onto the sands of a vacated beach on the island, her wet footprints stolen by the receding waters, leaving no trace of her arrival.

She had sought this hideaway for ten thousand annual cycles around the sun. Breaching its barrier had come at a cost. The trip took its toll on her faculties, leaving her mind struggling to regain its bearings. This was a clever enchantment—unsurprising, knowing the casters.

Still, it was a feat to fool so many for so long.

Clutched tight in her frail black hands, she carried a beaten, leathered book. This tome held the key to the destiny of two witches, lost to time, and a young man in their charge, who led her here. She wasn't a sentimental woman, but even she felt sorry for the string of events she and the boy were about to set in motion.

Whether the twins were prepared or not, she had a contract to fulfill.

She needed to find the Storyteller. Only he wielded the power to read the prophecies hidden within the book. Fate demanded it.

Taking her first cautious steps into the island's wards, the old woman made her way to the Inn. Not ready to reveal herself, she checked the concealment crystal, ensuring it still hung on her neck. The last thing she needed was an alert to be sent to the witches before making contact with the boy.

Satisfied, the old woman closed her eyes and held her breath. "This had better be worth it," she grumbled.

Part

ONE

THE PALACES OF CHAOS AND ORDER

At the heart of Balincia, two magnificent floating islands hovered. A giant scale over Crystaline Lake. Detached from land and water, they were visible from every corner of the realm. Inhabiting these isles was a pair of twin witches. Edi, the slightly elder, resided on the right in the Palace of Order; on the left, Pan, the somewhat younger, made her abode in the Palace of Chaos.

Edi, shorter and rounder than her sister, had raven black hair, shoulder-length, and every strand meticulously placed and sensible. Every tunic, cloak, or dress she owned was form-fitting and flattering, never deviating from shades of black, white, or an occasional ceremonial palette of red. When she walked, it was with grace. When she spoke, it was precise and deliberate—every hand gesture, smile, or movement of her eyes was intentional and measured.

The Palace of Order's pristine white marble reflected its master's clean constraint. Two domes adorned the palace's roof, made from hand-carved faerie glass and framed in black sapphire. The interior boasted a grand entry hall with marble floors etched with black diamonds and two ornate obsidian staircases leading to the resident wings on both sides.

Manicured hedges and sculpted trees provided borders for walking paths in the front gardens, sprinkled with strict rows of white and black orchids. A black ornate iron fence circled the property, closing at the front moon gate. Guests, always received at the witches' dock below, levitated up in a wrought iron box with black leather benches.

In contrast, her sister, Pan, was tall, with gangly limbs and long, windswept red hair. Sporting colorful loose robes, oversized trousers, and ill-fitting cloaks, her wardrobe was always an afterthought. Her movements were considered clumsy, distracting, and unpredictable. When she spoke, it was either too loud or too soft, too verbose or too mute. Her eyes darted, observing, telling stories if one was able to read them.

The Palace of Chaos, taller than the Palace of Order, displayed six turrets varying in length where one least expected them. Long ivy curled around alabaster, and grey stones cobbled together. Doors, gatehouses, and walkways were blended with red cedar and oak, complemented by rusted iron bindings.

Some turrets held enormous windows with stained glass; others were open, allowing birds and black squirrels to dive between them. Some held no windows at all, creating surprising pockets of light and shadow across the property.

Guests didn't visit the Palace of Chaos. It wasn't conducive to receiving them.

Due to this, the aesthetic centered on a breathtaking exterior instead of an opulent interior. The surrounding gardens were left wild, covered with climbing roses and hydrangeas. Honeysuckles and trumpet vines stretched like arms, reaching for the waters below.

An unkempt garden grew around the palace by way of overgrown grass and trees with arched branches, allowing rabbits and field mice a

space to flourish and play. Lavender and witch's balm were grown in the garden for teas, while enchanted snapdragons and star lilies were always in bloom for spells.

A cottage-sized range of granite ran the length of the back border, mimicking a miniature mountain landscape. Water roared continuously up from beneath the stones, originating from no identifiable source, plunging over the exterior side of the island, and dissipating into mists that blew across the realm. On the granite's interior side, the water that didn't escape would roll into a stream, weaving through the garden and disappearing underneath the palace.

An ivory bridge wrapped in wisteria vines served as a symbolic connection between the two islands.

In the front courtyards, stood imposing statues of the twins, further emphasizing the importance of their bond. Positioned opposite each other, Pan's likeness was positioned in front of the Palace of Order, while Edi's was placed in the gardens of the Palace of Chaos. This arrangement allowed them to gaze upon their sister from their windows when they were apart.

A reminder of their reliance on each other.

On each new day at the break of dawn, the witches would make their way to the docks. Edi, in her enchanted iron box with no strings, made a gentle descent, while Pan would scurry through her wooden moon gate, proceeding down the floating spiral staircase crafted from stones and stumps.

Exchanging affectionate kisses and taking their twin's hands, they'd welcome the start of each new day with a ceremonial routine.

"Our differences are our greatest gift," Edi would lead.

"When we're in harmony, the land is in balance," Pan continued.

"Balance is essential to the land's survival."

"Balance is essential to our survival."

"One of us can't survive without the other."

"As it is written."

"As it is pledged."

"Our Magic."

"Our Lives."

"Forever connected."

Clasping their hands together, magic would ripple across the lake's surface, and they'd conclude the spell: "May the scales *always* remain balanced."

TWO

BALINCIA

There are precisely 7,700 citizens in Balincia—never more, never less. When one soul departs, another is born in adherence to the fifth law. Whether it required an unexpected mother with an empty womb or an unborn yet carried to term, a healthy baby always arrived when another soul slipped away.

This came as a surprise when the tailor's wife, thought to be too old, went to bed with nothing but a belly full of stew and rose the following day, ready to give birth to her seventh son.

In reverse, when a soul is born, one must also depart, as in the case of the angler, who was excited to witness the birth of his first granddaughter, only to have his heart give out as she drew her first breath.

Luckily, these incidents only occurred in the early days. The citizens today were more prepared due to their education in the land's magic and their understanding of its practicality. It had also helped that the witches had fine-tuned their magic over the years, settling into more routine and predictable outcomes.

Elderly individuals were limited to living a generous one-thousand-year cycle. Once they reached the end, the witches would help them conduct a peaceful and ceremonial conclusion to their lives. The sisters agreed that death shouldn't be messy, painful, or sad, and preparation helped everyone with the process.

Arranged pregnancies were carefully aligned with this cycle, and the ability to bear children without permission and magical intervention became impossible. And while not planned, it didn't hurt that infants were a great strategic distraction to help accelerate the period of mourning for the recently deceased.

In truth, the influence and enforcement of legislation in Balincia was simple. There were only six laws to follow and remember, *at least known to citizens*, all of which benefited the welfare of the people. Edi believed the key to order was simplicity; *one should never have to think about too much.*

After their morning ritual, the witches visited a different township every day to survey the land, gather census data, and meet with their subjects. These outings helped provide opportunities for the twins to identify and correct any defects in their magic. Given the multiple islands scattered across the lake and the additional villages surrounding the borders, the method of travel to accomplish these missions became an issue.

Traveling by boat was impractical. The fastest vessel took three days to cross the lake's diameter, and the witches needed to return to their palaces each evening. Ships were too large and cumbersome to navigate the busy trade and fishing waters, and the additional time required for docking also needed to be considered.

Unable to fly or transport themselves, they required a more efficient mode of transportation.

Portals weren't an option. They required immense magic to maintain. One needed to consider sustaining safe passage, predicting the arrival location, and, most critically, impeding unsanctioned users. The upkeep and risks were too burdensome, pulling their already strained resources from more important efforts.

The sisters agreed an enchantment of mechanical invention was the only viable solution.

Creating two thrones from the cherry trees in Pan's Garden, they

attached the chairs to their docks side by side. Edi's was built a bit higher to maintain the appearance of similar height when next to her twin, and Pan's extended its arms to match her prolonged appendages. A long iron rod connected to the base of both thrones was positioned between them, serving as a guidance system.

Once seated, they'd strap on thick, bottled-lens glasses and secure themselves with a leather strap. Edi always navigated the steering while Pan whispered incantations into the air. Once detached from the dock, the water would rise and bubble, creating a thrashing wave of white water around them.

They rocked, shook, and settled until they'd catapult into the open waters.

The spectacle, always amusing and alarming, became a favorite pastime for Balincians. It was considered a sign of good luck if you spotted Pan's long curls bouncing behind her in a trailing flame. "Witches on Water"—a phrase coined by the sailors—alerted other craft of their often speedy incoming.

Maneuvering around the ships was now easier, and smaller docks were built for their visits to quicken boarding and disembarking. What once took days of sailing was now accomplished in minutes or hours, depending on the destination.

After resolving their travel issues, the witches turned their focus to the agenda of their visits, centered around Balincia's six laws.

When it came time for a Balincian citizen to be born, divinations were scheduled with the new parents. During these visits, the witches would determine the child's future role in society, adhering to the first law: *Every Citizen Has a Purpose.*

Edi believed identifying one's purpose in life eliminated anxiety about the future. It also eliminated the pesky need for broad-based education, which she considered an impractical distraction. Her approach allowed every citizen to prioritize and focus on their innate specialized skills—maximizing prosperity.

Pan sprayed each newborn with moon mist and swung a crystal

pendulum over the baby's head. Depending on the child, some results were instantaneous, which was often the case if their role matched their family's lineage, as it frequently did with bakers, farmers, fishers, and tailors. The divination took several more minutes if a role was more specialized and deviated from the rest, such as healers, beekeepers, or future township leaders.

Occasionally, a few children were born with the honor of dedicating their lives to the witches. Due to the delicacy of this news, those sessions often required more than an hour of focused meditation. Those born in service to the twins were asked to sacrifice their township and the pursuit of family, but gained royal privileges, including a relaxation of the law of provision, *to keep everything in balance.*

In Balincia, everyone was given equal access to necessities to avoid envy, reinforced by the second law: *Every Citizen Would Have All They Needed.*

Currency wasn't required because every good and service was made for and by the community. No titles or roles were more important than any other, and extravagance was frowned upon.

The witches excluded, of course. There were appearances to maintain.

Each household was given equal monthly portions of trade for food and supplies, ensuring no one would be in need or take more than their fair share. Every citizen received two acres of land and enough resources to build their dwelling, *which helped achieve order.* They were also allowed to develop and design their homes however they wished, *allowing for a bit of chaos.*

Every township was equipped with a tailor, baker, and healer, along with a town hall provided by Edi to encourage *consistency.* Pan provided random storefronts dedicated to honey, tea, or pottery, requiring citizens to travel, trade, and interact.

Edi ensured every township received the perfect balance of weather to maximize the success of harvests. To build resilience and flexibility, the citizens could also rely on random hailstorms, blizzards, or scorching temperatures for three days every six months, courtesy of Pan.

The third law required the witches to gift each citizen a talent based on their potential discovered from their divination; *Balincians were solely responsible for refining them.*

Encouraged to share their gifts in the markets and streets of Capital City, various forms of expression in dance, art, music, and craftsmanship brought joy and inspiration to the broader community, enhancing their overall well-being.

The fourth law—the most prohibitive—*and the one the witches would rather not dwell on*—banned the teaching of reading and writing.

These talents were exclusive to the Storyteller, falconers, and the Royal Guardians. Aside from the books in the palaces, any attempts to create, distribute, or obtain reading materials were forbidden. After all, the citizens needed to be protected from the potential dangers of interpreting and disseminating information meant to threaten Balincia's tenuous balance.

Balincians never probed to understand or define these potential dangers, just as they didn't question the fifth law controlling their life expectancy. Nor did they challenge the outcomes of their divinations or demonstrate an interest in expanding their talents beyond their assigned gifts. In fact, their intentional lack of curiosity *was* their most distinct characteristic as a society.

If one were to ask a Balincian about the origin of their land or the construction of their laws, no one would be able to share anything of substance except to acknowledge it always existed.

Admittedly, they also shared no desire to investigate it further.

It was meaningless to question what was—*when what is*—is all one would ever need to know. Balincians were granted provision and purpose, so they were willing to do anything to protect the peace that came with it, including being intolerant of thoughts disrupting its current state.

Curiosity only led to questions. Questions might lead to discomfort, and that lead to confrontation. Confrontation might upset balance, and balance was everything. For this was the sixth and final law: *The Scales Must Always Remain Balanced.*

THREE

THE STORYTELLER

Birk yawned as the first morning sun filtered through the curtains of his cottage on the Royal Isle. Stretching his taut frame, he matted down his ginger locks, anticipation bubbling. *Or maybe it was his stomach growling.* He'd been too excited to eat the night before.

In two days, the streets of Capital City would come alive for the grand celebration of the witches' ten thousand-year reign. This would be the largest crowd he'd ever performed in front of, and he was nervous about debuting *"The Thirteen Foxes,"* a fable selected by his aunts, new to Birk's portfolio. This one would be extra tricky due to its incorporation of marionettes.

After a quick bath, Birk fumbled, throwing everything he required for the performance and his travels into two trunks. Collecting the hand-painted wooden foxes he'd finished the night before, he tossed them onto his emerald dress cloak, a change of trousers, and a collection of teas Pan had gifted him. He was running late. *Again.*

Talbot, the Captain of the Royal Guardians, would soon be there to help him to the loading docks. Growing up, Talbot was the closest thing he had to a father. Stoic and disciplined, he took Birk under his wing and helped wrestle the energy out of him when his youthful energy became too much to handle for the witches.

Drawing upon his military training, Talbot employed strict routines and martial exercises to channel Birk's boundless vigor. From drills at dawn to swordplay lessons, he tamed Birk's impulsive nature and instilled discipline in him, mentoring him like one of his young soldiers. Over the years, they drifted as Birk's interests shifted more towards books than brawn.

Talbot had always been a bit gruff on the outside, but as of late, he'd become even grumpier. He was pulling away from Birk and putting an even further distance between them. The last thing Birk wanted to do was start the day by adding to the man's agitation.

Birk lived across from Talbot on the Royal Isle, which lay behind the two floating islands on the lake's surface. The island's only residents, the Royal Staff, utilized the space during their off-shift. His recent residency made his best friend, Ravenshire, jealous, who was still too young to move into his own cottage, even though he was only a year behind him, *a fact he consistently reminded Birk of.*

The community on the island, along with the witches, was the only family Birk knew. Dubbed the Royal Circle by outsiders, their small group was unique. Every one of them identified as orphans, *or so they'd been told.*

Unbeknownst to anyone except the witches, they'd been taken from their families at birth and raised by the island's previous generation to serve a higher purpose for Balincia. In exchange, their parents were gifted a covert spot at the front of the birthing list to bear a new child, helping to fill the loss of the one they'd offered to the twins.

After the divination results were delivered, the parents were administered tea created by Pan and lulled into an undisturbed slumber. Once asleep, Edi, with care and precision, would block lingering memories of the procreation, carriage, and bearing of the child, eliminating any mental or emotional suffering. To complete the spell, on the first night

after the birth, a warm, gentle breeze blew through the windows of every Balincian, removing any lingering thoughts or additional recollection of the couple's pregnancy.

This was heavy and emotional magic, both in practice and intention, not to be taken lightly.

Edi and Pan did everything possible to make it painless and minimize disruption. However, the decision was always heartbreaking and unavoidable. Despite their secret guilt, they were driven by the belief that this difficult path was the only true course of action for the greater good.

The children, for their part, were too young to remember. They were raised in the palaces and on the islands, filled with happy memories. Growing up with an affection for the sisters, as adoptive aunts, the staff perceived the women as benevolent and generous caretakers.

Birk, in particular, reserved a special place in their hearts, and under their tutelage, he learned to embrace the craft of his divination—*storytelling.*

Edi emphasized that the art of sharing stories was a rehearsed methodology, sculpting his foundation around detail and careful structure. And while she wouldn't admit it, she also delighted in having someone to share her vast library of forbidden books with, who appreciated them as much as she did.

Pan, more playful, encouraged him to let his imagination run wild and allow his stories to soar. Spending hours together, amidst dandelions and ladybugs, they'd lie on their backs and stare into the clouds, forming a deep and unspoken bond. She believed the most important lessons in life were found in the world around them, *not buried in Aunt Edi's books.*

"Nature, Birk, shares the secrets of life through its chaos," her eyes smiled at him. *"You have to learn to appreciate the unpredictability; when you do, you'll understand the definition of real magic."*

"What does unpredictability mean?" young Birk asked.

"Hmm . . . let's pretend a rainstorm spoils our fun on this perfectly sunny

day," she said, lowering her voice to sound scary. She threw her fingers into the air and wiggled them in front of his face, summoning a dark cloud to appear above them with blustering wind and a downpour of rain.

"Booooo!" he yelled, secretly delighted. He loved watching Pan use her magic.

Covering them both with her blanket, they giggled and huddled together to stay dry. "Let's look at the old oak tree, the largest in my garden; its bigger branches are bowing, defiant to the wind, refusing to break. However, some of its weaker limbs are tearing free and tumbling to the earth. Those branches and leaves still have purpose, though, because they'll scatter seeds and erode into the soil."

Waving her hand across the ground, peonies emerged, and tree saplings escaped the soil's captivity.

"The roots and core of the tree are strong and resilient, but it carries the weight of branches it no longer needs. By shedding them, he renews the earth around him, making room for something more beautiful to grow."

Pan realized, by the scrunch of Birk's face, this might be a lot for a young boy to understand. Laughing, she pinched his ivory cheeks.

"If it helps, remember this: We must all give up the urge to control everything. Sometimes life's biggest miracles occur when we accept the storm." To further illustrate her point, she plucked one of the pink peonies from the ground and placed it in his hand.

Pondering this, Birk leaned against his aunt.

"Then why do we have so many rules? Rules are awful and make me do things I don't want to do. I'd rather be a storm," he protested, matching her scary voice.

"What a grown-up question, and Edi will be the first to tell you I shouldn't be the one to answer it. I'm such a stinker at rules," she poked him in the ribs, making him laugh. "As you age, you'll start to see the wisdom in some rules, like I have. We can't live in constant chaos; imagine if it were always storming, you'd never be able to play outside. That's why balance is important."

"I don't know." Birk twisted his face. "I still think they're awful. Aunt Edi has sooooo many rules at her palace. I have more fun with you; I can do what I want over here."

"When you get older, you'll be able to use your judgment to decide which rules are better to follow and which ones are meant to be broken. Remember, though, no matter what you choose, you must always be responsible for your decision. Until then, you'll have to trust your aunts know best." She emphasized the point by tickling his belly. "Now, enough of this seriousness; these are big conversations for such a little boy."

"But," Birk pleaded, tugging her sleeve, "I have one more question."

"FIINE! I surrender, but this is the last one for today," Pan exaggerated, rolling her eyes and making him giggle.

"If I break a rule, will you still love me?"

Pan noticed his eyes fill with the worry of disappointing her, the woman he loved most. So, she did the only thing she could do. She swept him into her arms and covered his head in kisses.

"I will love you even more."

Gazing out his window, Birk noted the second sun was in the sky. He'd wasted too much time reminiscing. Talbot was already at the door, ready to collect his trunks. The Royal Isle was over a full day's sail from Capital City, and it was vital they set sail soon.

Arriving at the boat, Edi stood on the dock, impatient to receive them.

Dressed sharply, she modeled a fitted white dress with polished black buttons, draping it with an immaculate ivory cape. Her hair was pinned tight under a wide-brimmed matching hat, black ribbons circling its diameter. "Running a little late, aren't we?"

She never missed the opportunity to address Birk's punctuality.

"Sorry, Aunt Edi. It's my fault. I became lost in my thoughts," Birk kissed both her cheeks. Somewhere behind him, Talbot, still dragging his trunks, grunted in agreement.

"Understandable to be filled with a bit of nerves," Edi replied.

Using her hands in the same manner as a conductor, she quickly levitated his trunks into the boat, buttoned his tunic where he missed a loop,

and straightened his hair. Birk referred to this as her "magic mothering," the constant and unconscious need to straighten, fix, and repair anything out of order, particularly when it came to him. He considered her fussing a demonstration of love.

"I've ensured you'll experience calm and smooth sailing," she informed him, handing him his leather satchel. "The breeze will be warm and at your back through the night, ensuring you arrive on time. Talbot, don't worry about keeping guard all evening; I've enchanted the boat to reach its destination, avoiding any obstructions you may encounter. I want *both* of you to have a good night's sleep. You need to be at your best when you arrive. Remember, you are our representative."

"Saffrona packed some snacks for you in your satchel," she said, leaning into Birk's ear. "I've included some of your favorite books to pass the time. Don't lose them or allow anyone else to see them when you're in the city. I've also packed you some soap I expect you to use at the Inn. No one wants the waft of a ripe Storyteller during his big performance."

Gleaming with pride, she tugged on his vest and gave him a look over.

"Thank you, you're always thinking of everything." Amused, Birk went in for a hug and settled for her hands, patting him on the back. She was always less demonstrative and uncomfortable with affection compared to her twin.

"The others will leave at the set of the third sun and be on time for tomorrow evening's festivities. Pan and I will be taking the thrones, for expediency. Now, off you go; I won't have you pick up your Auntie Pan's habitual tardiness issues."

Clasping her hands at her waist, she smiled, pleased with her ability to keep everything running tight and on time.

"Birk," she called out as he boarded the ship, "I'm proud of you."

Smiling, Birk watched his aunt spin around and march back to the iron lift—never one to linger and always on the move.

FOUR

Capital City

When Birk arrived at the Capital City docks, the air buzzed with lutes and children's laughter. Heading toward the city center, he caught the smell of roasting boars on spits. The third sun was rising, and vendors were already setting up across the marketplace. Fishers displayed their bounty of fresh seafood, farmers showcased their harvest of herbs and spices, and the perfumed aroma from the baker's storefronts promised hot "witchberry" pies.

Blue and lavender moon blankets spun from silk moths were among the most in-demand items. Considered a luxury, they glowed under the moonlight, resembling stars, and, despite their fine material, they carried the same amount of insulation as three times their weight in wool. Jewelry from the faerie mines lined the market stalls, offering a rare decadence for the Balincians. Homemade remedies and bottled elixirs were passed out by healers.

Baskets, woven for the occasion, were gifted to each household to fill with as many goods and treasures as they could carry. Since it was a special occasion, the township leaders had voted to relax the provision laws, allowing the citizens a day of excess. To show support, the witches, with a sprinkle of enchantment, ensured no vendor would run out of product or supplies, and the Inn would expand to accommodate every guest without lodging.

Balincians took pride in honoring the sisters and dressed for the occasion.

The borderland townships wore colorful tunics and dresses celebrating Pan. Children put on masks of ravens, foxes, and bears, and the women braided their hair with the season's brightest flowers. The islands honored Edi, donning formal attire of obsidian, ivory, and silver. The women pulled their hair tight, and the men paraded their clean-shaven faces.

Birk and Talbot wove through the crowds, pausing to bow to young women or take a knee for the children to whom they were familiar. Losing himself to the sweet smell of cinnamon, caramel apples, and honey-infused tea, Talbot promised Birk they'd satisfy their cravings after they checked in at the Inn. Both men were in good spirits and enjoying the break from palace duties.

An old woman followed the pair through the crowd, monitoring Birk, nervous about his dormant magic.

Would he recognize her? Or would her wish magic hold?

She eyed the man with him. He might be a problem; he was a soldier, an escort sent from the palaces to protect the boy. She'd need to ensure they were separated when she approached.

She sighed. *Did her concerns really matter?* At this point, there were no other options. She was obliged to do what must be done and was left with nothing else to do but follow them and wait for the opportune time to approach.

Patience was everything, and introductions must be perfect.

Paper lanterns of various colors and sizes, paired with emerging fireflies, cast a romantic glow over the city streets. When the blue moon appeared in the sky, Birk took his cue and went to work setting up the marionette stage while the crowds meandered into the outdoor theater. Families were huddled under their new moon blankets, warming their

hands around hearthstone mugs filled with *Honey Kisses*, a Balincian concoction made from warm milk, lavender, and vanilla, topped with a drop of golden honey. Talbot was enjoying his with a splash of rum.

Scanning the crowd, Birk was staring into the heavens when the blankets started to shine and glow. His nerves twitched and tumbled inside him; when a hand tapped him on the shoulder, he jumped like a wizwart toad.

"Boo!" squealed a familiar voice. Pan grinned behind him, delighted at startling him. "I wanted to sneak down and wish you luck or twist a witch's ankle or whatever we're supposed to say at these things."

Birk hugged her and laughed. "I can't believe the wild witch from the floating islands decided to grace us poor peasants with her presence tonight."

Pan blushed, "I know, *I know!* It's been too long since I've been out; it's been good to walk the streets again. I've forgotten how yummy the dipped donut cones are; I'm not ashamed to say I've already snuck two behind Edi's back."

"Where is Aunt Edi?"

"You know your aunt; her hands must be in everything. She's overseeing the setup of the luminaspectras she brought to surprise the townships. I'm sure Talbot is pulling out his hair. I believe she cajoled him into setting them off after your performance. Everyone else is here. Feeona and Feigh are picking silks for new dresses. Ravenshire is in the stands, wearing the silliest fox mask. He made it himself to honor your big debut, *so you must compliment him on it*, and I lost Saffrona in the seafood market." Pan stood on the tips of her toes to see if she might catch a glimpse of the giant woman peeking over the crowds.

"I can't believe you're all here! I hope you take the time to have some fun. The citizens adore seeing you and Edi outside your everyday *witchy* duties."

Pan kissed him on the forehead, grabbing his hands. "Of course, we're here. Isn't this whole festival celebrating *me*?" exaggerating her face, she feigned mock humility, fanning herself with her hand. "In all seriousness, everyone's here to support *you*. I'm so proud of you, Birk.

There's nothing that brings me more joy than watching you captivate an audience with a story."

"I learned from the best," he beamed back at her.

"Alright, I'll leave you to it. I see Edi waving me impatiently to our seats. Kisses and kisses." Squealing again, she scurried through the crowd, much to everyone's delight. Tripping over feet, sitting in laps, and blowing her skirt up like a balloon on her way to Edi, she riled the crowd as Birk's unscheduled opening act.

He loved her even more for it.

The outdoor theater buzzed while everyone settled into their seats, eager for the show to start.

When a hush finally fell over the crowd, the curtains parted in the castelet, revealing a collection of fox marionettes in an enchanted forest. With a glint in his eye and a crooked hat on his head, Birk stepped forward, his voice echoing across the stands.

"Adults, children, and those of you who find yourself in between, I hope you're prepared to embark on a most extraordinary journey," he declared. "Tonight, our tale unfolds in the heartland of an enchanted woods, where thirteen foxes reside."

In his skilled hands, the puppets came to life, each with endearing traits, charming gestures and distinct personalities. Birk performed the cunning fox as sly and sneaky, while the wise elder fox required a deep voice full of gravitas. The audience loved it.

Each earned laugh motivated his performance more, especially when he took on the role of the funny fox, letting loose a series of hilarious quips. He hid his smile, watching the children double over at his antics.

It wasn't all light-hearted, either; Birk intentionally embedded scenes of suspense to keep the audience on their feet.

When night fell on the forest, his voice took on an eerie tone. Scary shadows crept amidst the flickering candlelight when he described the foxes' encounters with lurking dangers. Leaning forward, he jumped at the audience, frightening four young women in the front row and prompting laughter from the crowd.

Building to a climax, his hands moved with lightning speed. Dancing,

tumbling, and performing breathtaking stunts, the foxes were a stringed aerial masterpiece under his expert manipulation.

Finally, the tale concluded, allowing him to bow and bask in the resounding applause.

Pan was the first to jump and cheer. Edi, always reserved, smiled and gave a tight nod of approval. Feigh and Feeona blew kisses, Ravenshire threw his mask in the air, and Saffrona frightened the guests around her when she loomed over them with her standing ovation.

Hearing the crowd's applause, Birk spied Talbot out of the corner of his eye, lighting Edi's luminaspectras on the beach below. The first spectra soared high above them, a blazing comet of emerald green. Exploding into a shower of sparks, it cast a glow upon the now-upturned faces of the spellbound crowd. The citizens cheered as the embers turned into a gentle rain.

Pop! A burst of sapphire blue, followed by a brilliant orange. The luminaspectras took over the sky, taking on the forms of the foxes from Birk's fable, prancing and posing for the crowd. The show's finale ended in grand theatrics, as a rainbow made from fire shot across the heavens, sparkling and spinning until it transformed into caricatures of Pan and Edi, who bowed to the masses—a raving success and end to the celebrations.

FIVE

A Splitting Headache

The streets were thinning as Birk put the final marionette into the trunk. His royal family had already departed to travel back home. Only Talbot remained. Asleep on a bench under the lanterns, he'd grown tired of waiting for Birk to finish talking to the townspeople.

Clicking the trunk shut, Birk took a deep breath and surveyed the quiet streets. He was about to wake Talbot to help him with his trunk when he heard a cough behind him. Flipping around, he found a cloaked figure waiting for him, her face hidden in the shadows.

"Excuse me, Storyteller. May an old woman borrow your ear?" she pulled the hood from her face.

Composing himself from his initial surprise, he dug deep to find his public-facing grin. Wiping away the fatigue, he replied, "Always; how can I be of service?"

"You gave quite the performance tonight." Her silver hair glowed against her dark black skin. "May I inquire where you learned the story?"

"My aunt, Edi, picked it out for the occasion. She thought a fable reminding the audience of the importance of coming together was relevant tonight, on the celebration of their reign." He smiled politely, "All of my productions are inspired by the books in her library. I hope you enjoyed it."

"I did. I'm familiar with this story," she paused, struggling to find the memory. "From ages ago. I haven't heard it in a long time, so I wondered if it was lost. I'm glad to see it isn't." Pausing again, she added, "Although the version I'm familiar with doesn't have foxes, and it didn't end as nice as yours."

In a subtle raise of her eyebrows, she teased him with hints, testing his appetite.

"I'm sorry. Did you say you've heard it before?" Birk asked, confused. "Tonight was its debut."

"Well, I'm much older than you. I've witnessed the creation of many of the fables you now repeat around fires. Many that *even you* may not know." She said, tempting him again.

"Have we met before?" Birk searched her face. There was a vague familiarity to her. "I can't place you from my travels in the townships."

A quick shake of her head. "No, we've never had the pleasure. I don't travel into the townships." She paused, and in a bold move, she placed her hand on his chest. "It doesn't surprise me you aren't aware of who I am. The important thing is I know who *you* are, Birk. I know *all* about you. You're the reason I came tonight."

"I'm honored my reputation reached your ears," Birk replied, intrigued. Many citizens, whether due to age or inconvenience, never came to see him perform.

"May I ask you a question? Earlier, you referred to the witch, Edi, our beloved Practitioner of Order, as your aunt. Is this true?"

Birk took a step back, uncomfortable with her hand on him. Her intimate informality was unnerving. "Yes, not by blood, but Edi and Pan raised me. We refer to each other as family."

It was time for her to lay the breadcrumbs.

"And what of your parents?" She tilted her head, interested in his reply.

"My . . . my parents?"

Birk tried sifting through his memories. For some reason, he was

unable to connect the word or concept of "parents" to himself. Everyone had parents, *even an orphan*, but he realized the thought of who they might be never crossed his mind. *Shouldn't he have been curious about them at some point?*

Standing there, it suddenly occurred to him their existence or non-existence were irrelevant. He decided he didn't care to think about it, and more importantly, he didn't appreciate being asked about such a private thing.

His face scrunched, betraying him to the old woman. She waited for an answer, which should have been at the tip of his tongue, "I . . . uhm . . . don't know." *And he honestly didn't.*

A dull ache formed in his head. He was struggling to remember if his aunts, Talbot, or anyone had offered him details of his past.

The harder he reflected, the more difficult his thoughts were to sort.

"You've never asked?" she pushed again.

Of course I have. Haven't I? Now, he wasn't so sure, nor did he recall anyone ever asking *him* about *them*.

The more he rummaged through his memories, the more frustrated he became. "I—I've inquired. I just can't remember right now." He gave a weak laugh and raised his fingers to his temple, trying to massage out the pain. "Forgive me. I'm not sure what's come over me. I'm feeling dizzy and out of sorts."

A cold sweat dampened his tunic. Nausea was setting in, and the dull ache in his head was turning into a sharp pain.

"I think I didn't eat enough before tonight's performance," he said, embarrassed and irritated.

"Hmm . . . yes, that must be it." The old woman nodded with ambiguity.

It was definite; his mind had been tampered with. The right questions were triggering shields, as she'd been forewarned.

The twins were stronger than she'd been led to believe. If they were willing to enchant their own nephew, how far did it extend among their citizens, and at what cost?

She had no alternative but to keep pushing.

"May I bother you with one more question? I promise I'll allow you to rest after."

Yes, I need rest. "It's no bother at all." *This was a lie; this conversation was becoming irksome, even if it shouldn't be.*

He forced a smile.

"I'm curious why the witches don't teach others to read instead of filtering what can be shared through your performances. After all, don't you think it would enhance the experience of your audience if they could enjoy watching you bring their favorite books to life?" she poked again.

"Are you trying to take away my job?" Birk joked. The old woman didn't laugh. "I'm honored to do what I do; after all, it's my foretold purpose from birth." Unable to read her reaction, he recited, "Besides, reading and writing are forbidden in the fourth law. It's too dangerous for everyone to have this talent."

"Except for you?" her smile gave way to bemusement. "Have *you* found it dangerous?"

Birk, insulted, straightened his body to defend himself. His lips moved of their own accord, but his words were pulled from the deep recesses of his mind. "To maintain order, people must be guided; otherwise, they can lose their sense of purpose. I've trained with the witches to be a skilled practitioner of this art. I share these stories to inspire, not confuse. We are protecting Balincians from being divided in thought. Balance *is* everything."

There it was—the weed's roots in his mind sown in with the deadliest of weapons: fear.

"And who authors the books in the library where you've been trained to practice? They weren't all written or conceived by your aunts; why would we need to fear *their* words? Who created these nefarious stories causing such harm and division?"

She questioned, following her script.

Birk's discomfort was growing. *Who was this woman? No one asked these types of questions in Balincia.* "I-I don't understand," he stuttered. "The stories have always existed."

"We can infer the books have no authors *from* Balincia, based on the

fourth law. Agreed?" she paused, waiting for Birk to nod in affirmation. "We can also assume your aunts didn't write them, since they've forbidden them, and they wouldn't write anything dangerous for Balincians, since they'd *never* seek to do us harm. And yet, they've collected them and shared them with you. Tales of characters, magical lands, and mythical creatures unknown to us, except, of course, through the imaginations of anonymous, non-existent authors. Are there books with maps and illustrations depicting some of these lands?"

"Yes, although many of those books are locked away in an inaccessible section." After Birk spoke the words, he realized how peculiar it sounded.

It was also information he shouldn't have shared. Edi always explained he should remain focused on fiction when he inquired about the other books. The rest of the library was off-limits and dangerous, not fit for public consumption, *not even for him.*

"Everything has a history or point of creation. Aren't you curious about their origin or their writers?" She gave him time for the question to sink in.

"I always assumed they were created from another form of magic, collected and used by my aunts over the ages. If their origins were important, they would've shared them." Birk turned defensive, "I don't care where they came from. I trust my aunts to keep us safe; they glean what is valuable and pass it on."

The old woman didn't reply. She kept staring at him as if she was expecting something more. For a young man with twenty-three cycles around the suns, he was starting to feel like a fool.

He shifted his feet.

"To be honest, I haven't applied much thought to their authorship. I was preoccupied with enjoying the books I *was* allowed to read," he blurted out, surprised at his admission. "And in all transparency . . . it never occurred to me."

He grimaced, hearing his confession aloud.

"I see," she said.

The foundation was cracking. Her gift would do the rest of the work.

"I encourage you to give it more thought the next time you visit your aunt's library."

Birk nodded, feeling like one of his marionettes, his brain full of sawdust, following the pull of the string. He was growing frustrated and impatient with the conversation, ready for it to end. "Yes, I'll try to do that."

The woman lingered, unsure. "I can see I've disturbed you enough, or maybe it's the lack of food you mentioned," the old woman winked. "I promised to leave after my last question, and I've overstayed my welcome. Let me part by giving you something for your time."

"That's not necessary," he replied, fidgeting.

"I insist. I came all this way to give it to you." The old woman pulled out a parcel wrapped in parchment. Holding it out to him, she urged him to take it.

Hesitant, Birk examined the parcel and the insistence on the old woman's face. Giving in, he unwrapped it in front of her and almost dropped it when its content was revealed.

"A book?" He exclaimed, checking to see if anyone was nearby. He wasn't surprised by what it was but by the illegality of anyone but him owning or obtaining one. "How did you . . . where did you . . . these are forbidden?"

"Yes, why are they forbidden again?" she mused. She raised her ebony finger to her lips, "I promise not to tell if you won't."

Birk wasn't relieved by her willingness to accept culpability. He glanced to double-check Talbot was still sleeping on the bench.

"In any case, this is no ordinary book, Storyteller. This one was made for *you*."

Birk inspected the book. The cover was dark, with golden-brown weathered leather, held together with worn-out straps and a silver buckle. In its center, a waxed seal, burnt orange and forest green, bled into the symbol of a tree. Its branches curved into balancing scales.

Unwinding the strap, he opened it with care. "Its pages are blank," he exclaimed, disappointed and relieved at the same time. It wasn't a book, only a journal.

"That's because *you* haven't authored the story."

"Oh, erm, I'm flattered," he said, attempting to find words. "Sincerely. But you don't understand; I can't author stories; I only read and share them."

"Nonsense. Who told you that?" she held his gaze. "Everyone has a story to share; maybe yours is waiting to reveal itself."

He took her words in, closing the book.

"Thank you. I appreciate the generous gift."

He meant it. Their interaction stirred something in him—something worth revisiting.

"You're more than welcome," she acknowledged. "Rest well, Storyteller. I trust your thoughts will lead you in the right direction in the upcoming days."

What a strange way to part. Watching the old crone slip away, he realized she never introduced herself. He called out to her, "Ma'am, you never gave me your name?"

"No, I didn't. One more mystery you'll have to wait to reveal itself," she said without looking back. "Oh, and Birk, ask your aunts about the mountains the next time you see them."

"The mountains?"

"The ones surrounding you," she gestured in a circle toward the mighty Cosimo Mountains. Confused, Birk stared into the distant peaks.

THE BOOK

After his encounter, Birk's mind floated adrift. Detached from his surroundings, his movements went unregistered.

He remembered neither tucking the book into his satchel nor waking Talbot to escort him back to the Inn. Nor did he recall Talbot's grumbling and griping about the weight of his trunk of marionettes. Absent-minded, he undressed and slipped into a hot bath, exhausted. He scrubbed his body with the lye soap, desperate to peel off whatever was sticking to him.

An hour later, he found himself standing naked and dripping in front of the mirror.

What was he doing? How long had he been standing here?

Birk shook the questions away; his body's heaviness was prioritizing his need for sleep.

In an onerous task, he wrangled into a clean pair of braies and tumbled into the bed, listening to the crackle of the dying fire.

Giving into the pleas of his body, he allowed himself to sleep.

He was standing in an unfamiliar bedroom. Paintings depicting battles of warriors with hair colored in various shades of blue hung on the walls. A large canopied bed was draped with velvet orchid brocade. A silver vanity saddled its side.

A woman of black and umber skin, around his age, sat at the vanity, lost in contemplation. Her eyes were violet, and twisted tresses of dark hair clung to her neck and wrapped around her shoulders.

She was beautiful.

A connection pulled him closer. She appeared regal, like a princess. Their eyes locked in the mirror, and she gestured to the floor beside her. Watching her, the ground beneath them shifted like a mechanical clock. Sections of the floor rotated until hidden panels unlocked and moved apart, revealing a secret staircase. The young woman stood, motioning for him to follow.

Taking a step forward, he was intercepted. A white flash of fur darted in front of his feet. A frantic fox stared at him, pawing at his calves, stopping him. Bending to pick up the vulpine creature, his hands disappeared into a foot of snow.

The fox and the floor had vanished, now replaced by a blanket of white. His bare feet stung, being submerged in the new, icy, wet foundation. A vista of snow-capped mountains emerged around him, cascading waterfalls gracing the distant peaks. The scene was tranquil and hypnotic.

His surroundings continued to alter. Black clouds crept over the mountains, covering the hills in an ominous mist. The once serene peaks turned dark, and their shapes grew grotesque. The heads of beasts with fiery red eyes and tangled antlers surfaced from the shadows. Mutated, they took perverse and macabre shapes.

Frozen winds whipped around him, filled with the sounds of anguished wails, a mixture of men and beasts. Birk fell to his knees, covering his ears. The screams grew louder and drew closer. The ground underneath him trembled, and the sides of the mountains shook. Giant boulders dislodged themselves, and the summit crumbled.

With nowhere to retreat, he covered his head and cowered. The earth opened and swallowed him whole.

Birk jolted awake, his heart pounding against his ribcage. Clammy palms, drenched in perspiration, clung to the moist sheets. Slowing his breath, he attempted to anchor himself.

Dread pumped through his body. *The screams . . . the creatures . . . the dark mountains.* He'd never experienced dreams this realistic or vivid. *What were those things?*

He'd never read about anything that terrifying in his books, and he doubted his subconscious was skilled enough to conjure them.

Who was the young woman? Why did he feel drawn to her and obliged to follow? Where was she leading him?

Steadying himself, he put his feet on the ground. The fire, almost dead, barely lit the dim room. He spied his leather satchel, tossed indiscriminately in the corner. Peeking out of it was a book, the old woman's gift.

The old woman!

He'd forgotten about her. *Was she the reason he was having trouble piecing together the end of his night? Was she responsible for his dreams?* No, that wouldn't make sense. That implied the involvement of magic. The only ones with magic were his aunts.

Yes. The only ones capable of magic are your aunts.

The sensible thing would be to share his visions with Pan when he got back home. She'd know how to interpret them and probably say it was a side effect of nerves and poor eating—the old woman, an eccentric, having a bit of fun at Birk's expense.

Still, the more he reconfigured the conversation, the more he realized how disconcerting it had been. She'd probed and picked at the scabs of his parents' identities. She questioned the legitimacy of Balincia's laws and the origins of his books.

He'd been nauseous, his faculties hindered.

He paused; *why had the conversation agitated him?* Her questions were perfectly reasonable. *No, they were intrusive and out of line.* Weren't they?

What did the old woman say when she departed?

The stranger's voice crawled under his skin, urging him to scratch. He leaned against the wall, and another onset of vertigo crept over him.

His thoughts wheeled and spun, pushing him to retch. He tried to rein his mind in, urging it to stand still, but its resistance left his stomach churning. Grabbing his temple, he gritted his teeth and begged for it to stop.

There was a sudden and violent snap inside his head . . .

He stood straight. Relief.

Was he imagining things, or were the colors and the sounds in his room sharper? His mind was stretching and expanding, a muscle awakening from sleep.

The mountains!

The stranger encouraged him to ask his aunts about the mountains—the Cosimo Mountains surrounding Balincia—the ones from his dreams. There was no way their connection was a coincidence.

Falling to his knees, Birk pulled the leathered book out of his satchel.

He wasn't sure why the blank book intrigued him; nothing was in it. He guessed he hoped it would provide clues connecting the cryptic stranger and his recent nightmare. Cracking the cover, he gently ran his finger down the front page, wondering how anyone wrote on such ancient parchment without destroying its fabric.

The sheet radiated with a faint glow, coming to life under his touch. Inked lines materialized, curving and intertwining. Two words scripted themselves in dark ink on the center of the page: *The Driftstone.*

His hand trembled. *This was some sort of magic, but if it wasn't his aunts, did the old woman enchant the book?* He assumed only his aunts carried this sort of power.

A sketch of a map began to take shape, faded contours gaining clarity with every stroke. A giant lake spread across the page, with islands

sprinkled around and within the water. Forests grew at the northern borders of the lake, while mountains rose, surrounding everything.

Birk was staring at Balincia. *Why would the book draw a detailed map of his home?*

In answer to his question, words formed at the bottom of the parchment, appearing to possess a consciousness eager to communicate with him. When the sentence formed, he read it aloud, *"THE WORLD AS YOU KNOW IT."*

Anxious, he flipped the page and ran his finger down the blank canvas again. This time, the words unfolded all at once, bold and centered: *"WHAT IF THERE WAS MORE?"*

SEVEN

TALBOT'S TALE

The waters of Crystaline Lake mirrored the muted colors of the sky above, offering a momentary respite from the night Birk endured. Memories of his nightmares remained in his mind, along with the riddled messages from the book. Hoping it would reveal more, he made several attempts to communicate with it until he accepted it had nothing else to say.

At least for now.

The old woman implied the story would reveal itself when the author was ready. This did little to quell his overactive mind. Plagued with questions, he stayed awake all night.

Listening to the rhythmic clapping of the waves against the hull, he focused on his surroundings. Circling the perimeter of Balincia, stretching as far as the eye could see, the boundless caps of the Cosimo Mountains grabbed and held his attention.

The book was right; his entire world existed inside the mountains' embrace. It was the only world he knew—the only world every Balincian knew.

The peaks enclosed Balincia, and according to the map, there were no marked paths into, out of, or through the summits, making it hard to imagine anything existed beyond them.

But that was ridiculous, he'd read fictional stories of lands bigger than Balincia.

The real question was: why did he insist on these geographical limitations in the first place? Why did anyone?

The Cosimos were Balincia's most defining feature. Every island, shoreline, and home offered a panoramic view. How could a society cradled in their midst never utter more than a passing comment on their beauty or, in their history, venture to explore them?

"Talbot?" Birk called out. The Captain of the Royal Guardians jumped at Birk's voice. "May I ask you a question?"

Talbot, desperate for conversation, turned to face him. "What's on your mind?"

"If I remember, you're about five hundred cycles around the suns, aren't you?" Birk moved from his side of the boat to be closer to him.

"Give or take." Talbot raised his brow, "Why? Am I starting to look my age?"

Birk laughed. "No, years younger," he flattered. Talbot *was* in great shape for a man in the middle of his prime. "Have you been in service to Edi and Pan all these years?"

"Yes, they raised me, similar to you. Believe it or not, I *was* as young as you once," he ribbed, "although Balincians don't age as slowly as the witches. *If your aunts age at all.* Trust me, it's bizarre seeing your face season beyond those who raised you. It'll happen to you someday, too."

Birk cringed, unwilling to imagine himself older than his aunts.

"When you travel to the border townships, do you ever venture into the mountains?"

"No," Talbot answered, quick and definitive. "There's no need to visit them. No one lives in those mountains."

"Some of our villages in the northern forest or the farmlands crawl to their fringes. Have you ever explored their paths or hiked to the waterfalls?"

Talbot eyed him. "My duties are to serve as an ambassador if I'm not safeguarding the witches. I don't have the luxury of exploring."

"Do you know anyone who has?"

Talbot leaned forward, impressing he'd appreciate if Birk would cut to the chase. "Why the sudden interest in the Cosimos?"

"I'm considering checking them out when I have some leisure time. We look at them all day, every day, from a distance. Aren't you curious about them?"

Talbot assessed him before dismissing him. "Birk, I wouldn't do that if I were you. Those mountains aren't safe."

"Why wouldn't they be safe?"

"For starters, you have no experience with wildlife. You'd be defenseless against any wolves or bears."

"The loggers have experience; I'm sure they could teach me the basics to survive an encounter."

"There are no marked trails; you'd get lost and starve out there," Talbot pressed.

"I'll take Ravenshire with me, and we'll keep the townships in view. We could forge new trails for others in the future."

Talbot's patience was straining. "You aren't prepared for the extreme weather; you may run into high winds or blizzards."

"The tailors are capable of making something suitable for the terrain." While Birk was enjoying dismantling every argument Talbot threw his way, he was also becoming exasperated—if not a little insulted. "You're acting as if I'm incompetent. I'm not looking to abandon my post; I only want to spend a few days exploring. You could come with me if you're concerned about my safety."

Talbot remained silent. The creases in his forehead grew deeper.

Birk pushed. "Don't you think it's strange that no one has ever investigated the Cosimos? I'd think there'd be value in knowing the geography beyond our borders after ten thousand years."

"Birk, this isn't your purpose. You're a Storyteller." Talbot was curt, his tone changing.

"Perhaps my purpose includes creating new stories. I imagine people would be inspired and fascinated by a real adventure."

"Your aunts will never allow it," Talbot dismissed, attempting to put a finality to the discussion.

"I won't tell them. I'm allowed my own leisure time," he retorted, looking in the other direction. "I'm not a child who needs his aunt's permission to decide where I go or what I do with my free time."

Even saying it aloud, Birk wasn't sure he believed this, despite the truth behind it. There was little those in service to the witches could do without their knowledge or consent. His self-declared independence wasn't the definition of freedom he thought it was.

Talbot stood. "I'm going to tell you this once, and only once. Abandon this idea. No good will come of it."

"Why?" Birk stood to meet him.

The two men postured.

Standing his post, the Captain of the Royal Guardians reminded himself the young man before him was the little boy he'd carried on his shoulders. The child obsessed with following him around when he was younger—question after question about every tedious thing.

Talbot wasn't angry. He understood the origin of Birk's questions. Better than anyone. He was upset because he hadn't prepared for this day. He assumed Birk, *as close as he was to his aunts*, would be like the other citizens and be blind to the world around him.

He was relieved Birk's mind was his own, but it provided little comfort if the boy didn't learn to rein it in.

No, he wasn't angry; he was frightened that Birk's recklessness and curiosity might endanger him.

He recalled his youth when *he* questioned everything, eager for answers, trying to understand the world. He also remembered the bitter taste of disillusionment when he uncovered the harsh truth behind Balincia's reality, and the loneliness that followed because he didn't have a trusted companion to share it with. He didn't want Birk to travel this same path.

So, he backed down—a decision the Captain of the Royal Guardians had never made.

Sitting on the bench behind him, Talbot buried his face in his palms.

"What I share with you now, I've never shared with anyone," Talbot began. "I'm only telling you this in hopes it will persuade your thinking."

"When I was about your age, there was a young cattle herder and a dairy girl who fancied themselves a picnic in the farmlands. While they ate, the young girl became captivated by one of the waterfalls in the distance, estimating it to be no more than a half-day's hike from the edge of the green hills, and she begged her beau to take her.

The cattle herder resisted the idea; he'd been raised and warned about the dangers of crossing the border. Similar to you, however, the warnings had little effect on the girl. The idea of seeing this waterfall up close grew like a seed inside her mind. The thought distracted her when she milked the cows and fed the chickens and went about her daily chores. Every day and every night, it consumed her.

Eventually, she convinced the herder—as this is the influence of love—a quick day's journey, there and back, wouldn't attract any attention, and she was confident in his ability to protect her. Not only would they be able to fulfill her fantasy of witnessing the waterfall up close, but they would come back with proof the dangers of the mountains were overrated.

Setting off on their little adventure at the first sun's rise, they left with preparations for the day and an expectation to return by the first sun's set.

Except—they didn't return that night. Nor the evening after.

When the township became aware of their absence, a search party was sent across the eastern border. After another day, with no results, the word was sent by falcon, and it was decided Henri, my mentor and Captain of the Royal Guardians at the time, and I would be sent ahead to

assess the situation. Your aunts would follow by their water thrones and meet us on arrival.

When we reached our destination, another search wasn't warranted; the couple had found their way down the mountains. Their stares were vacant, their minds absent. Your aunts were swift to act, and they quarantined them in the town hall. Henri and the gathered citizens followed. I was about to join them until Henri ordered me to keep watch outside the doors.

I wasn't supposed to hear what happened next, but being young and impetuous, I eavesdropped against the door. The young couple gave testimony. They never made it to the waterfall or more than half a mile on the mountain path when they were overcome with disorientation. They couldn't remember which way they entered or which way they were going.

Randomly picking a direction, instead of remaining still, the world around them spun every time their feet moved forward, making them nauseous and dizzy until they were violently ill. Helpless, they lay on the ground, while a breeze rattled the branches around them, carrying haunting voices, warning them to return home. Crawling to each other, they huddled together, terrified.

After several minutes of torture, a parting in the trees appeared, where the sun lit a clear path back to the green hills of home. The cattle herder leaped to his feet, with his lover in hand, and they sprinted until they reached the overgrown grasses with which they were familiar.

They were surprised by the township's reception; they were unaware they'd been gone for days; for them, it had been hours.

It was difficult for me to determine what happened next. Everyone was talking at once. I heard panicked voices from the township—maybe yelling, perhaps crying. I heard Henri trying to calm the crowd, and then . . . it all went silent.

A few minutes later, the doors opened, and the township emerged. Strolling as if on a leisurely walk in the gardens, they smiled at me as they left. Grabbing Henri by the arm, I inquired what had happened. He stared at me, confused, with big, vacant, empty eyes, trying to place my

face. After a few seconds, he snapped out of it, grinned, and invited me to lunch.

Following him to the bakery, I assumed he wanted to speak privately, but no matter how hard I tried to get information from him or how many ways I disguised my questions, he avoided them all.

That's how I felt at the time, but avoidance is the wrong word. He had no recollection of why we were there or what they discussed in the town hall. The more I probed, the more agitated he became."

"I'm familiar with the feeling," Birk uttered, reflecting how irritated he'd become with the old woman's inquiries.

"It wasn't only Henri; it was all the townspeople. Your aunts left for the palaces after the meeting, so I investigated for more information. Everyone, and I mean *every single person*, acted as bizarre and off-putting as Henri."

"What do *you* think happened? Do you think Edi and Pan had something to do with it?"

A moment of silence passed between them.

"I'm not sharing this with you to create distrust with the women who raised us. I want to be clear: I'm entrusting you with this, so it will sway you from pursuing it." Talbot scratched the scruff of his chin. "But, yes, I do believe this. I can't offer any other explanation, but I also believe if they did do *something*, it was in our best interests. Your aunts love this land *and* our people. They wouldn't do anything to harm us."

Birk believed this, too, but the *something* he and Talbot were referring to was a magical alteration to everyone's mind—an extreme violation. There had to be a reason for his aunts to take such drastic measures.

A thought occurred to him, "Why weren't you affected, Talbot?"

"The only thing I've come up with is that they weren't aware Henri stationed me outside the town hall."

Birk noticed Talbot hesitate.

"What aren't you telling me?"

Talbot's eyes were transfixed on the floating islands. "The event I shared with you wasn't the only time I witnessed such an occurrence; I also suspect it wasn't the first."

Birk's stomach dropped. "This has happened multiple times?"

"Rare, but yes. And not *only* because someone wandered into the mountains. Once, it was an inquiry from a council member voicing the benefit of moving beyond our borders, as you did today. Another time, it was provoked by one of our elderly citizens refusing to be termed under our fifth law. There was the baker who aspired beyond the purpose assigned to her at divination, which drove protests from her township, causing everyone to abandon their responsibilities."

"And their minds were altered in the same way?" Birk clarified.

"Following every incident, Edi and Pan would pull the congregation of people involved behind closed doors. Minutes later, everyone reappeared blissful as a dog with two tails. All inquiries, concerns, and conflicts evaporated."

Birk was horrified. "The mountains are one thing, but this is removing free agency. How have you been able to avoid it all these years?"

"By ensuring I *always* slipped out of the room unnoticed. Once you're aware of the signs, it's easy to predict." Talbot faced Birk. "You're the first and *only* person I've shared this with; I believe we're the only ones who have noticed what's going on."

Birk paced the boat. "I can't believe this. I *refuse* to believe it."

"I recognize this is difficult, but remember, Edi and Pan have always done what's best for Balincia. Our crops grow in abundance, and every family has a home. Every citizen is employed and contributes to the bounty and health of the land. We live long lives, our citizens bear children, and suffer no wars. Music fills our streets, and the scenery feeds our senses. What more could we ask for or need?"

Birk understood Talbot's rationale. His aunts did create an entire world where the framework within it worked. The land was thriving, and the people *were* happy.

Or were they only happy and thriving because they were forced to be?

He stared at his trunk of marionettes, once again feeling the pull of strings by a puppeteer.

He acknowledged his aunts carried experience and wisdom the rest of them didn't, but this was unethical. It was also hard to imagine these morally reprehensible actions could be attributed to the women he loved. Every memory with them was now becoming tainted with doubt and disbelief.

Talbot sensed his turmoil. "At your age, I questioned the morality and cost of these actions, as I'm sure you're doing now. With time and experience, I've grown to appreciate what's been built for us. *If* this is what's happening, we sacrifice little compared to the prosperity we enjoy. I've come to peace with what these women do because they do it for us."

Birk looked away, unsure he'd ever be able to come to peace with it.

EIGHT

A Cup of Tea

Pan's kitchen was Birk's favorite room in the Palace of Chaos, an extension of her garden and personality. Unlike the grand kitchen at Edi's, where Saffrona and her staff prepared dishes for the witches, guests, and other residents on the Royal Isle, Pan's space was reserved for her.

The cooking area was lit by a stained-glass arched window, usually open, overlooking the back gardens. Against it, a rustic wooden table lined the wall, covered in plum, red, and teal pottery, mismatched and oddly shaped. Mounted shelves were askew and stuffed with jars of catnip, comfrey, and elderberry, and melted wax from fat-lipped candles dripped over their edges.

Grimoires of fauna and flora were randomly stacked around the room, collecting dust, while mugwort and nettles grew from pots and boxes on the soil-covered floor. Corn dollies hung from the ceiling, and star jasmine sprouted from vines creeping through the window. A cabinet of dried pressed flowers cozied in a corner adjacent to a trunk full of crystals.

When Birk walked in, he found the room empty. An iron cauldron bubbled over the burning hearth. The door to the pantry staircase was open.

"Hello?" he called out.

An explosive crash emanated from downstairs, followed by a plume of dirt and dust through the pantry door. Alarmed, he ran to the opening and began descending the stone stairs, calling out again. "Hello? Auntie Pan? Are you all right?"

"Birk?" answered his aunt's voice, startled but unharmed. "Yes, I'm fine. Please don't come down at the moment. I've . . . made a mess. I'll be up in a second."

Birk halted midway, his curiosity and concern urging him to continue.

He wanted assurance that she was okay, *but* a part of him also wanted to peek at the destruction caused by such an eruption. Unfortunately, he took too long to decide because his aunt met him, winding the corner covered in soot. Grabbing him by his arm, she steered him into the kitchen.

"Here you are . . ." she said in her normal sing-song voice. "I was wondering if I'd get to see you. It's not normal for you to sleep for half the day. Let me take a peek at you." Spinning him around, she greeted him with kisses, stepping back to appraise him. "You look dreadful," she laughed.

"I didn't get in until the middle of the night. I've been having trouble sleeping since the festival," he admitted. Birk was determined to speak with Pan today, hoping she'd connect the loose threads dangling before him.

He wasn't willing to give up faith that his concerns from yesterday had been misplaced. Maybe she could clarify a misunderstanding or provide context that justified her actions. He wanted, *needed*, her to prove his instincts wrong.

Snapping her fingers, she winked at him. "Well, that's something I can fix. Is it your body or mind that's keeping you awake? I can make some tea and send you home with a bag to brew before you sleep tonight. How does that sound?"

Pan's chaos magic complemented her affinity for crafting in the kitchen. Her specialties, teas and scones, ranged from medicinal remedies to enhancing psychic abilities. Some of her concoctions were provided to herbal practitioners trained in the townships. Other formulas required a more careful curation and could only be administered by her skillful hand.

"It sounds lovely. Thank you." His answer didn't matter because Pan was already moving around the kitchen, grabbing the ingredients. Birk was used to her nervous energy; he found it comforting. Always multitasking, her mind occupied several places at once.

Despite this, he learned long ago it was foolish to assume she was moving too fast to be observant.

"It's my mind keeping me awake. I'm distracted."

"I'm not surprised. I ran into Talbot over at Aunt Edi's this morning, and he implied as much." Birk's heart stopped. He stared at Pan, whose back was to him, busy chopping and assembling ingredients. *Was there an intonation in her comment? Had Talbot betrayed his confidence?*

Attempting to decipher any information she may already have, Birk tread slowly and was only able to manage, "Oh?"

"Yes, he mentioned you were drained from the festival and weren't remarkable company on the road." Frowning, she crossed the room to heat the moon water in the kettle. "He said you barely spoke, Birk. I recognize he's a bit of a grump as of late, but I wish you'd get out of your head and try harder."

Birk sighed with relief. "I . . . uh . . . yeah, I was miserable company. I didn't sleep the night before either."

"Edi and I were hoping you'd enjoy some time together. You adored him as a little boy. I know he misses those days. You *both* spend too much time with us and traveling." She stopped at the table, cupping his chin. "It would benefit you to nurture a friendship beyond your childhood. Adult men need friends, too." Her eyes twinkled.

He took her hand, kissed it, and returned it to her. "I'll try to spend more time with him." He paused, "I think we share more in common than I realized."

Delighted to hear his affirmation, Pan sat across from him. "Of course you do! He may not show it, but he's your biggest fan." She leaned in, overemphasizing, "Besides *me*, of course." She laughed. "He loves your performances."

Birk snorted with laughter. "*Really?* I have a hard time believing that. He's always in the back of the audience, arms crossed, looking bored out of his mind. He's never once indicated he enjoyed my shows."

"Nonsense. I think you're reading him wrong. He's a bit more guarded and restrained in his communication, but he was like that as a child." Pan pondered for a moment; crossing her legs, she gave a sly smile. "Don't tell him I told you this, but he requested to step down from his position to be your royal escort once you travel regularly."

Birk was shocked. "When did this happen? This morning?"

Did Talbot want to keep an eye on him after their discussion?

"No, weeks ago. This is why he escorted you to the celebration—a trial run, if you will. He's protective of you. Edi, of course, wouldn't let him step down completely, but she agreed Warrington and Ravenshire could inherit some of his other duties. There isn't much the two of us can't manage alone, anyway."

Standing at the kettle's whistle, she continued, "He'd be embarrassed if you knew, but I've caught him retelling your stories to Saffrona and her kitchen staff. You should see how his face lights, trying to mimic your voices."

Birk continued to be dumbfounded. "I do miss the time we spent together when I was younger, but I'm still not sure I believe you." Stretching his legs, he absently wandered to the pantry door. "What was all that rumpus when I arrived?"

Pouring the tea, Pan paused midstream, overfilling the cup. "You know how clumsy I am," she brushed off. "Nothing to worry about. I knocked over a shelf. There's broken glass everywhere. I didn't want you to get hurt."

"I can help you clean." Birk cracked the door open to peek down the stairwell.

"No, no, it's faster if I do it myself." Pan abandoned the tea and

rushed toward him, closing the entry and shuffling Birk back to his seat. "I need to ensure everything is sorted the right way."

"You never worry about sorting things the *right way*. Is Aunt Edi rubbing off on you?"

She forced a quiet laugh. Gathering the tea mug, she walked it over to the table and placed it in front of him. "Yes, maybe she is." Glancing at the tea and then at Birk, she smiled. "Please, drink. It'll help you recover."

A subtle wisp of steam rose from the oversized mug; Birk eyed it with a hint of skepticism, wondering if something had been surreptitiously added to the brew. "Thank you. I'll give it a moment to cool."

Appearing nervous, Pan changed the subject. "I almost forgot; I've been so scattered this morning. I wanted to ask you a favor."

"Yes, of course," Birk piped up, happy to change the subject.

"The township leaders are coming in for the annual council meeting tomorrow. We timed it this year to be at the back end of the festival so it wouldn't require additional travel for the guests. Everyone loved your recent performance at the celebration, so we were hoping you'd deliver an encore tomorrow evening." She asked, drumming her fingers on the table.

"I'd be happy to help. Did you have something in mind?" he replied, covering his nose at the fragrant aroma of the tea.

"Thank you. Everyone will be delighted. I'll leave the selection to you and Edi. I suspect, due to the timing, there won't be pressure to whip anything elaborate together. She's requested to meet with you at her library tomorrow morning, sharp on the rise of the second sun. Guests will arrive in the afternoon; I believe she's scheduled you after dinner."

"She'll have my full performance planned before I arrive," Birk jested.

On any other occasion, this evoked a smile between them, but Pan remained distracted by the tea.

Reaching out, she took the mug and handed it to Birk. "Drink; it's at its most optimal when it's hot. We want you at your best tomorrow," she urged.

Cornered, Birk lacked a delicate way to decline.

Maybe drinking it would be easier, even if it did result in losing a memory

or two. It had to be better than every future interaction with his aunt wrought with overthinking. A life spent second-guessing every word or action seemed exhausting; he didn't know how Talbot had been able to compartmentalize it for so long.

If he took a sip and confirmed his suspicions were wrong, it would support Pan's maternal investment in his well-being. Deep down, he wanted to believe her love was too strong to deceive or hurt him.

It was her insistence on drinking the tea that caused his doubt.

Or was it his focus on trying to find something suspicious in her actions?

Her past was a mystery; she and Aunt Edi were always so large in their present existence that it never dawned on him to inquire about their past. Balincia had just finished celebrating their ten-thousand-year reign, yet no one paused to think about where they'd been before.

"I want to ask you something," Birk announced, placing the mug back on the table; a flash of irritation crossed Pan's face. "It's been bothering me since the celebration."

Forgetting the tea, Pan switched her focus to Birk. "My darling, what is it?"

"I can't recall you telling me about my parents. I can't even remember thinking about them before—which is concerning." Birk paused when he noticed Pan's eyes glass over. He took her hands and softened his approach; he didn't want to hurt her. "Can you tell me about them?"

"What's stirred these thoughts?" She rested her palm on his cheek and her other on his leg. "Was it your performance of the Thirteen Foxes? We should've been more sensitive about insisting on its selection. It does tend to have one reflect on family."

"Maybe. It's strange, though. I've grown up never wondering about them, and now I can't stop thinking about them. Can you help me?"

"Yes. Of course, I can." Pan stood and busied herself with something in the cauldron. "Why don't you drink the tea while we talk? It'll soothe you. I could use some as well."

"I don't want the tea!" Birk snapped, growing frustrated.

Pan took a step back, affronted. She leaned against the wooden table by the window, clutching its edges. Neither of them spoke.

After an awkward minute, she walked over to the table, picked up the mug and returned to the other side of the room. Raising it to her lips, she drank it, lifting her eyebrow in his direction.

A sheepish half-smile played on his lips, and he cast his eyes to the floor.

"It's natural for children to block memories that discomfort them. Children tend to focus on happier things." Stepping toward Birk, she lowered herself beside him. "And you *were* such a happy child. You've been surrounded by love your entire life; isn't that what matters?"

"I know I'm loved. I don't want you to think I'm ungrateful." Standing from his chair, he took her hands to raise her so they could speak face to face. "You're the most important person in my life. I hope you know this. It's why I trust you enough to ask."

She wiped a tear from her eye. "I'll share what little I can. Your parents faced . . . unfortunate circumstances. In their selflessness, they entrusted you with our care. I'm afraid it's as straightforward as that."

"What type of circumstances? Are they still alive?"

"They . . . are alive." Pan's eyes wandered. "You must know this was a difficult decision for them to make. We took you in under an agreement to never reveal their identity to you or the events surrounding their decision. This was *their* request. I'm attempting to respect it."

Birk couldn't respect it. He didn't believe his parents would abandon him, nor did he understand why he cared so much about it now. Her answers were vague and unsatisfying. Walking to the window, he stared into the gardens.

Pan continued in an imploring voice, "I can see what this means to you, but I urge you to focus on the present, on the memories built with your family at the palaces. Remember what I taught you when you were young; even the storms in our lives have *purpose*. You're here, *with us*, for a reason."

Birk shook his head in disagreement, his temperature rising. "Those decisions were made for me as a child. Whatever *they* or *you* were trying to protect me from may have been relevant at the time, but I'm well past the age where I need a filter for information. I have a right to know."

Pan's patience with his tone waned.

"Why *do* you have a sudden interest? After all this time, why is this a disruption now?" she insisted.

He glared. "I'd like to know that, too. Don't you find it odd that I've never *once* thought to ask? In all these years, my parents *never* crossed my mind. You can't tell me that's normal." Raising his eyebrows back at her, he taunted. "What about the others?"

"What others?" she replied incredulously.

"Talbot, Feeona, Ravenshire, the rest of our adopted family. What about *their* parents? Have you held similar conversations with them? Or have they thought not to ask either? Is the same arrangement made with all the parents?"

"Birk, what are you trying to imply? Are you accusing me of something? I'm starting to feel you aren't sharing something with me."

"Now you understand how I feel," Birk turned to storm out of the kitchen.

"What is that supposed to mean?" Pan cried out to him. "Birk, please sit; I want to discuss this further."

He paused in the doorway. "What's the point? You've told me everything I need to know."

"No, there is one more thing," she whispered as he walked away, never hearing what she had to say. "You're the image of your mother. You were . . . *are* . . . her world."

THE HALLWAY OF DOORS

Birk sat, knees to chest, in his backyard, watching a pair of swans glide across the still water. To his left, the *Driftstone*, which he decided to call the book, lay open beside him, still mute of further revelations. *Appropriate; he was also void of them after his recent interaction with Pan.*

He was ashamed of leaving the way he did; things would now be unresolved and strained between them. He implied she held back truths when nothing confirmed this except his fallible gut. Doubting her intentions, he'd projected his paranoia.

He held more questions than answers when he reviewed the events of the last two days. Laying on his back, he stared into the sky for guidance. Fireflies pirouetted above him. Following the poetic twinkle of their tiny bodies, his eyelids grew heavy, and a breeze blowing the foxtail barley surrounding him created a gentle rustle, lulling him to sleep.

A white fox sat on Birk's chest, flopping his tail from side to side. Tilting its head, it smiled out of the corner of its mouth.

The fox unfurled white, feathered wings from its side and flapped them. The vulpine launched from his chest and circled him, encouraging him to stand and follow.

Leading him into a descending stairwell, Birk followed the fox to a hallway filled with doors. Judging by its cavernous appearance and the clay-soiled walls and floor, Birk deduced he was underground. The walls darkened to a deep ebony at their tips. Speckled with glinting stars, they mimicked a night sky. Three doors on each side stretched out to join an imposing door at the end of the corridor. Above it, a moon painted in silver cast a glow over the passage.

The fox landed on his shoulder. Purring into his ear as if trying to share something, he nipped it playfully and flew up the stairs.

Birk stared at the doors.

Stepping closer, he examined the first door to his left. Made from roughly carved stone, it was jagged and cold. Behind it, Birk could hear a low guttural wind, followed by gusts of whistles and whips, raising the hairs on his arms. No handle or keyhole was visible. Smaller chunks of granite and diorite surrounded the frame. Varying in size and texture, they rattled and knocked against one another when Birk passed.

The second door on the left was made of aged wood wrapped in moss and ivy. Gold and orange autumn leaves peeked from the crevices and cracks. Hovering near the base, a thick fog, redolent of damp earth and pungent flowers, swirled around his ankles.

The final door to his left cast a prism of colors against the cavern walls. On first appearance, he thought it might be crafted from glass or crystal, but with closer inspection, he wondered if it was made of polished diamonds. Sketched across its flawless surface were symbols. The mystical marks came to life when he neared, gliding across the gemstone.

The fourth door at the end of the tunnel was taller and more formidable than the rest. Made from iron, it was covered in elaborate interlocking gears, locks, and bolts. The air around it smelled of leather and polished steel. Emanating a faint blue glow, it crackled with energy.

On the opposite side of the hallway, a door, if one could call it that, was fashioned entirely out of moving water. Glistening droplets poured down the door's skin, forming rivulets; soft palettes of blues and greens refracted in the light. Fleeting images of large shadows swimming past triggered Birk to step back. He was terrified the shapes might suddenly jump into the room.

The sixth door frame was sculpted to resemble vines formed from suspended icicles. When Birk walked by, the door shivered, creating sounds that reminded him of Pan's tinkling windchimes. Crisp, frigid air blew from underneath, carrying a scent of pine and silvered frost.

The last door was molded from fine golden sandstone and had an ivory frame. It emitted warmth. Standing in its entry, Birk could feel the sun shining on him as if a light was waiting on the opposite side. The sandstone carvings depicted people with parchment rolls dripping to the floor.

Without warning, the chamber went dark, all except for the moon, which turned blue and ascended into the night sky. Expanding, it illuminated a forest clearing where Birk now found himself standing. Next to him, the young Black woman from his previous dream was dressed in royal armor, gripping two golden swords made of light. A movement to his left caused him to turn. He jumped at the sight of a massive grizzly bear that appeared to have joined them.

Both the female and the bear looked alert; they stared into the distance.

Following their gaze, he directed his sight to the shadows beyond the trees, and he froze; they were surrounded. The same vile-horned creatures keeping him awake at night moved in the background, growling and gnashing their teeth. Stepping out from the darkness, some of the beasts were taller than the trees, while others wriggled on the ground. They skulked closer to the trio.

The foul stench of decaying flesh permeated the air.

The monsters howled, and the bear lunged protectively in front of Birk; standing on its hind legs, it roared back. The woman took a defensive stance, her back to the bear, urging Birk to do the same. Birk clenched his fists, steeling himself, as the darkness rushed them.

Birk awoke, thrashing in the grass; mud stuck to his face. With a gasp, his eyes opened, adjusting to the ambient light of the stars and moons. Rising from the ground, his body still shaking, he attempted to regain his balance. With shaky footsteps, he approached the edge of the lake. Kneeling, he scooped up some water and washed the dirt from his face.

The coolness allowed him to reorient. He was outside, alone, in the dark. This was the last place he wanted to be.

Scanning the shadows, he gathered the Driftstone and returned to his cottage. Bolting the door, he built a fire to warm up and stared at the magic book abandoned on the floor beside him. Floating embers gravitated toward it, hovering and twirling around its bound cover.

The tree's waxed insignia, once still and dormant, responded to the heat. Stirring with life, its branches stretched and bled across the cover, dripping onto the floor. The flames behind him grew higher.

Birk pulled the book over to him, entranced again by its call.

Slowly opening its cover, he flipped to the first blank page. Running his finger down it, he hoped to elicit the same reaction from his first encounter. The parchment remained empty.

A wayward ember caught his attention, floating in front of him. Hypnotized by the tiny spark, he followed its slow descent to the page. Fighting his instinct to pull the book away, fearing it would burst with flames, he allowed the ember to gently land on it.

A flash pan of blue fire shot across the surface. Almost dropping the book, Birk leaned in to inspect the damage, only to find another illustration. One he was familiar with, still occupying his mind.

A hallway of doors was sketched in exact detail as they appeared moments ago in his dream.

Adrenaline coursed through him.

His eyes darted to the page on the right, hoping for further explanation. Filled with text, Birk read the passage aloud:

In a hidden hall, seven doors reside,
Each tempting with invitations for the traveler to decide.
Boasting rock and stone, the first door is daunting and grim,
Dangers and nightmares lurk within.

Yet if you seek truth, answers it bestows,
To seekers who dare go where their true fate flows.
Love and death are intertwined,
For those unafraid to face these powers combined.

Enchanted wood whispers its sweet plea,
A door where kindred spirits will be.
Talents here are valued and grown
For those who are looking for a home.

Within the forest, travelers will reach their prime,
Shaping a future where love may climb.
The crystal door is frail and cold,
A soul's destiny is uncertain yet bold.

Its Queen may place a shard in your chest,
Or mend what's broken so you can rest.
A decisive choice, to destroy or to mend,
A palace of souls that may break or bend.

Iron door, stoic and strong
This is where a soldier belongs.
Valuable power, locked away with great care,
A history to find, only the worthy can bear.

A key of light, dream doors it unlocks,
The Princess of Iron will reveal all they stock.
Water calls, a gamble it may be,
Fortune's tide is shifting in uncertainty.

If you dive in the waters, your chances swim free,
To be led to multiple possibilities.
Those who enter must offer grace,
This door leads to an unsolved case.

Frozen in place, a forest serene,
Within its chill breath, time's flow can't convene.
If you challenge your reflection and face your true self,
The door of ice will grant its grand wealth.

Skip to the future or witness the past,
Only those grounded in the present will last.
A door of sand stands prophetic and wise,
Dreams separate the truth from the lies.

Step through, Oh Traveler, into the sand,
For learning one's fate awaits in this land.
The sand will reveal what destiny foretells,
And this is where the warden of visions dwells.

Each door will entice you with places to send,
Yet both gain and loss lay at their ends.
Choose wise, dear seeker; your paths lie ahead,
Within this hallway, your options are spread.

Whether it's answers you seek, power or riches,
The doors can only be found in the Palace of Witches.

The last words of the riddle churned in his mind. *The doors can only be found in the Palace of Witches.* There was no mistaking this led back to his aunts, the only witches known to Balincia, both with palaces. The language resonated with his desire for answers, and the Driftstone was guiding him to where he may find them.

The only problem was that Birk was raised in these palaces, so he knew every inch firsthand. Playing hide-and-seek with Ravenshire as a boy, he knew every cranny into which one might crawl. There was no way an entire hallway of doors existed in one of them without him knowing.

Except maybe in the library.

The library, located underneath the Palace of Order, contained a maze of tunnels that were private to Edi and Pan alone. He assumed they were filled with the books claimed to be too dangerous to share. *What if they contained more?*

His thoughts gained speed. Within a few hours, he'd meet his aunt at the library to discuss the council's entertainment. Edi, as she often did, would leave him alone to prepare, busying herself with the guests and giving him ample time to explore.

First, he'd need to find a way to access the library's forbidden section. This wouldn't be a simple task. There were magical protections in place, not physical locks and keys. It didn't matter; he was determined to find a way around them and convinced he'd find the solutions. This was the first time he had direction instead of aimlessly running through conspiracies.

The Driftstone was validating his visions were real, *and* his visions confirmed he was asking the right questions.

Tomorrow, he'd uncover the truth.

TEN

THE FIERCE DRAGON

irk was already dressed when the knock at his door pulled him from his trance. Throwing the Driftstone into his satchel, he straightened his hair and opened it. Talbot, bright-eyed, greeted him.

"Morning, has Aunt Edi sent you to check if I'm on schedule? I promise, I was just about to gather my things and head to meet her."

"No, although I'm confident she'd appreciate your presence sooner rather than later. There's been a mix-up with the guests; instead of their boats arriving this afternoon as planned, they're docking as we speak. I'm sure you can imagine how your aunt is handling the confusion."

Birk could indeed imagine how his aunt, who carefully crafted a strategy for every minute of every day, was handling the situation. It was rare for Edi to be blindsided or unprepared. Seldom did she lose composure; this implied weakness, suggesting she wasn't in control. Instead, if things were out of sorts, her fallback strategy relied on excessive management, inserting herself into the minutest details.

Birk sighed. *This may be a problem.* He didn't need Edi peeking over his shoulder today, of all days. It would be to his benefit to arrive early. If he helped alleviate her stress, she'd step back and remove herself from everyone's hair.

"It'll be a long day, but we have a small window before anyone expects us. I was hoping to catch you before you left; I wanted to speak to you in private. May I come in for a minute?"

"Yes, of course," Birk stepped aside from blocking the entryway.

"Pan informed me she shared my change in responsibilities with you. I apologize; I wanted to deliver the news to you in person. I hoped to share the announcement on our trip back from the festival, but the timing didn't feel right considering our conversation." He paused, "If I were you, I'd have questions on why I initiated this request, particularly in light of our discussion."

Birk nodded.

"Considering my loyalties to your aunts, I'd wager you fear I've betrayed your confidence. The thought crossed my mind of you doing the same." Pausing again, he moved to take a seat. "We're at the crossroads where we must choose to trust each other. This morning, I intend to take the first step in rebuilding this with you as adults."

"The timing did leave me questioning your motives."

"My request to escort you wasn't related to our conversation on the boat, although it reinforces my original reason." Talbot paused, "Entering the second season of your life causes you to assess where you invest your energy. I've been honored to serve my post; however, I've come to view it as performative rather than essential. Balincia exists without conflict, which we should all be thankful for; it shouldn't be taken for granted. With that said, it makes my role obsolete, if not unfulfilling. When I compare my purpose and contributions to the rest of our citizens, it feels small."

"Talbot, you're not obsolete," Birk defended. "It takes a *good* man to be honest and dedicate his life to protecting others. It takes a *disciplined* man to maintain their athleticism and skill, even if their role no longer actively requires it. And it takes a *noble* man to admit when he's wrong and acknowledge when changes need to be made. The role of a good, disciplined, and noble man will *never* be obsolete. I'd be honored to trust such a man with my life as my escort *and* my friend."

Talbot held his composure. "Your words . . . I'm not sure I live up to

them . . . not yet. I've witnessed firsthand where examining our purpose can lead in Balincia."

"Talbot, I—"

Talbot raised his hand; he wasn't finished. "I refrained from sharing my concerns with your aunts because I was selfish; I didn't want to be forced to accept a lie. Even if I were unaware of the coercion, I feared I'd lose a part of myself."

"I can think of no greater torture than being forced to live a life based on what someone else decides for us. No one should be forced into conscious ignorance; we all deserve the right to choose our own path."

"Your arrival in our family changed me, Birk. Feigh and Feeona may have nursed you, your aunts may have tutored you, and Saffrona may have fed you, but *you* followed *me* in your tiny footsteps. You fell asleep in *my* arms in front of the fire after a day of chasing invisible dragons. I was the one who taught you to ride horses, shoot arrows, and fight with swords."

Birk felt a pang in his heart; it had been a long time since he'd reflected on those memories—how effortlessly he'd forgotten them.

"When you grew older, our time together became more limited," Talbot continued. "You leaned into your calling to be a Storyteller, spending weeks at a time tucked away in the library. You discovered a new space—your space. You were transforming from a clever young boy full of energy into a young man full of passionate ideas. I didn't begrudge you. I was proud of the man you were becoming; I loved you as a father. In raising you, *I found my purpose.*"

Birk sat speechless.

"I grew worried when they started to prepare you for travel. I feared your endless curiosity would lead you to the same fates as our citizens, so I stayed close. When you traveled or performed, I made sure I'd be there to step in if you got too close to ideas that could harm you."

"I was under the impression you hated traveling with me. I assumed you found my stories a ridiculous waste of time."

"You'll find, as you age, it's easy to waste valuable time making wrong assumptions. If you're not careful, they'll prevent you from nurturing

meaningful relationships. Watching you perform filled me in ways I never thought possible. It'd break me if the young man I helped raise were prevented from being anyone but himself. I was trying to shield you as long as possible."

"Why didn't you share any of this with me? Why'd you attempt to detour me on the boat?"

"I was convinced the best way to protect you was to keep you silent. I wanted to avoid disturbing our current lives and preserve what we were given. Looking back, I realized I was a coward. If I'm to be a Captain, as fate assigned me, I can't jeopardize our people's welfare only to shield you and me."

"Are you saying you'll help me find the truth?"

"I still want to believe in the intentions of the women who raised us. The more information we have, the more discerning we can be. However, I commit to helping you find the truth; we'll deal with the rest of it as it happens." Talbot paused, reading the hesitation in Birk's face. He placed his hand on his shoulder and leaned forward. "I'm on your side, Birk. I will *always* be on your side."

Birk's hands were trembling. Every lie, every half-truth he'd been fed over the last few days was twisted so tight inside him, he feared he'd break apart. He was desperate for someone to trust.

When Talbot's rough palm settled on his shoulder—warm, steady, unshakeable—something inside Birk loosened. His eyes stung. If he couldn't trust this man, the one who had raised him, who had never once turned his back on him, than there was no one left. He lifted his eyes and opened his mouth, and the words he'd been guarding, the worries eating him alive, poured out of him, until he'd shared everything.

"Thank you for trusting me, Birk. I'll do everything within my power to help you. You're not alone. Now gather your things; they're expecting us at the docks, and we don't want to raise any suspicions. There's a lot for us to do if you're to succeed today."

Throwing the Driftstone into his satchel, Birk surveyed the room for anything else he might need. Satisfied, he turned to follow Talbot out the door. The older man stopped.

"One more thing, I forgot in the commotion," Talbot fished something shiny and silver from his coat pocket. "In my work, symbols and badges are important. They represent an alliance of loyalty and pride."

Opening his hand, Talbot revealed a silver pendant shaped in the mold of jeweled dragon wings. In its center, two dragon feet clutched a book. The craftsmanship was immaculate, designed to give the illusion one was underneath a dragon taking flight and gripping its treasure. Birk didn't know what to say.

"I ordered one for both of us from a jeweler in the southern borders, celebrating our new posts. Similar to a dragon, I will always be your fierce guardian." He swallowed, "I'd be honored to pin it on you."

Birk stood tall, facing the soldier. "Talbot, the privilege is mine."

Talbot fastened the pendant to Birk's vest, close to his heart. Standing back, he appraised Birk. "Right. That's done. Now, let's find your answers."

ELEVEN

A Brush With Chaos

The first voice Birk and Talbot heard as they approached the Palace's loading docks was Porticia Prombey, barking orders at Dupont and Ravenshire, struggling to unload a gigantic stone rooster.

"Careful . . . careful! Reginald is delicate. Be mindful of his beak. This gift for our Practitioner of Order wasn't shipped here only to be broken at the palace gates," she shouted.

Porticia, known as the "Cluckmaster," was one of Balincia's more colorful characters. Serving as the township leader for the Isle of Poultry, she spent most of her day managing a flock of loud fowl. It was suspected she lost her ability, *or self-awareness*, to modulate her voice when she was forced to adapt her volume to be heard over their daily clucking and crowing.

Obsessed with Edi, she stood next to her on the docks, trying to emulate the witch's mannerisms and fashion choices. Attempting to impress for the occasion, she wore an oversized goose-feathered hat draped with a matching white feather boa hanging lopsided from her overly ample bosom. Birk concealed a chuckle when Ravenshire made a face mocking her from the docks.

Edi mustered a strained smile. "Yes, it would be such a shame for such a thoughtful gift and gesture to get damaged."

"Porticia, you've outdone yourself!" Pan squealed, clapping her hands, laughing. Porticia beamed from the approval, the sarcasm zipping past her feathered bonnet. "The rooster even has a name, Edi, did you hear? Reginald! Reginald the Rooster. *I love it!* Reginald will be the talk of your garden. The 'King Cock' of the palace."

Edi shot daggers from her eyes toward her sister. "Perhaps Reginald should take *your* statue's spot in my gardens. I wager it will be an improvement."

Pan's face lit up at Birk and Talbot's arrival. "Boys! I am so glad you're here," she exclaimed, running to hug both of them. To Birk's relief, she demonstrated no sign of tension between them.

"It appears you could use our help this morning," Birk surveyed the bedlam on the pier. Township leaders, ship crews, and palace attendees were tripping over each other to dock and unload simultaneously. The boats spilled over with oversized trunks, full of wardrobe changes, gifts for tribute, and the best bounty from across the lands, all to impress his aunts.

Samuel, the round leader of the farmers, huffed and puffed, clambering to get off the boat. When Lars Axwell, the bearded blonde lumberman, attempted to pull him onto the dock, his cherry cheeks and nose flushed so bright, Birk thought it might pop off his face.

Marching behind a group of frustrated palace men, the petite honey maker, Beatrix Chen, whispered instructions so inaudible they required constant repeating and confusion. Heaving and hauling luggage back and forth in an attempt to follow her orders, Rockwell, Balincia's prime jeweler, was nearly hit when Hawthorne swung a large burlap sack right over his head.

"I'm glad to see you both. We need all the hands we can get this morning." Edi's restraint was reaching its limits. "I don't know how this happened. I sent precise instructions through the falcons. Every ship was assigned an exact arrival time this afternoon to avoid this precise calamity."

"Don't worry. We'll get it under control," Talbot reassured, motioning for Birk to follow him.

"This is *why* I prefer we travel to them," Edi confessed to her sister, shaking her head at the havoc. "The whole palace is out of sorts. We'll be required to feed them lunch now, in *addition* to dinner, and I'll need to repeat the enchantment from the Inn to expand the guest quarters."

"Edi, there's no mess you're incapable of cleaning," Pan flattered. "We only do this once a year, and it means so much to the people. We must maintain good standing in our relationships with the townships. Their support is invaluable."

Edi grimaced in response. "When we started this, I wish I'd had the foresight to predict we'd have to endure this as one of the outcomes of our endeavor."

"Oh, stop," Pan laughed. "There were many things we weren't able to predict, but considering all things, I think we've adapted well. You've never appreciated the social aspect."

"And you've never appreciated the governance," Edi retorted.

"This is why we make a good team," Pan fawned. She stroked her sister's arm, attempting to soothe the fire kindling inside her. "All I'm saying is it's good for you to step out of your comfort zone."

Edi disagreed, glaring at the atrocious stone rooster being dragged up her dock. "People are unpredictable and harder to measure; this has always been your foray," she mused stubbornly.

"Try to enjoy yourself a little. I understand it's against your nature, but a little fun can go a long way," Pan chided.

Edi nodded. With a tiny flick of her wrist, a loose board on the dock's runway rose to intercept Ravenshire's step, sending him stumbling forward. The momentum made him lose his grip on the massive rooster, sending the fowl headfirst into the waters. Behind her, Edi heard Porticia howl as Reginald, her beloved, slipped into the lake's depths.

"Look, I'm having fun already," Edi responded, revealing a subtle, shameless grin.

Talbot partnered with Marina, the fishing and shipping township leader, to help expedite the process. Marina instructed her crews to untangle the boats and moor them in a more proficient procession along the royal docks. Her sculpted arms and olive skin glowed in the sun as she yanked and knotted the ships into order.

Talbot, in parallel, took swift control of the palace attendees and ship crews, organizing them into troops of cargo handlers. Forming an assembly line, they quickly unloaded all the luggage and boxes onto the pier and subsequently into Edi's iron lift. It wasn't long until they were ready to gather in the reception hall.

"Feigh, Feeona, and Jacquelyne will show each of you to your rooms so you may get settled. The kitchen is preparing lunch, as I'm sure you're hungry from your travels. We're grateful to have you with us and eager to discuss your agendas." Edi announced, finishing her arrival instructions as Birk joined them.

Following the guests, Talbot and his crew carried the luggage to their suites. Edi looked to the ceiling and inhaled deeply through her nose. "Birk, I realize we planned to meet in the library this morning, but, as you can see, we're all having to flex. Your help at the docks was appreciated."

"I'm here to help," Birk was anxious to move things along. "Is there anything else I can do?"

"No, I've already taken plenty of your time. I want you to be prepared for this evening. I'll escort you to the library, where we can discuss your thoughts on tonight's performance. I'm sure I can manage the rest."

"Edi, let Birk help you today," Pan interjected, looping her arm into his. "He can help distract and entertain guests during lunch; everyone loves him. Besides, Birk is now an expert Storyteller, so he won't need much time to prepare. Right, Birk?"

His aunts stared at him expectantly. Usually, he'd be thrilled to entertain, but it was rare to be unsupervised in the library. He didn't want to sacrifice his time to search for the hidden hallway.

Showcasing his best smile, he compromised. "It *would* be helpful to have a little time to prepare, but I'm sure I can manage if you can carve the afternoon out for me."

"Really, Birk? You wouldn't mind?" Relief set over Edi's face. "I dread the façade of small talk when entertaining. It would put my mind at ease to have you here with the guests."

Pan squeezed his arm. "What would we do without you?"

The council chamber swept across the backside of the palace and opened to the courtyard, where the panoramic landscape served as a dramatic distraction. Guests were greeted with a sparkling cocktail made from dragon fruit, served by Roux and Jacquelyne, and mingled by the reflection pool. The infinity waterfall's melodious hum chased the morning's energy away.

Xavier showcased his falcon, Millicent, and her aerial acrobats to a small group clustered at the edge of the floating island. A performer and soldier, as much as a falconer, he always attracted a crowd. Tall, with dark black skin and coarse locks of long black hair, his affect was warm and inviting.

Due to the distance between the islands and the shores, falconers were critical to the communication infrastructure. One of the privileged trained to read and write, they announced arrivals, requested trade, and sent word for aid. Raising each multi-colored falcon single-handedly, Xavier also schooled the township falconers, thereby gaining prominence and influence among the leaders.

The Royal Landscaper, Toliver, proudly gave Beatrix and Lars a tour of the manicured gardens while Ravenshire and Hawthorne demonstrated the Guardian's latest swordsmanship drills. Everyone was on full display. Even Feigh and Feeona, Edi's housekeepers, dressed for the occasion. Charged with flattering and fussing over the guests' outfits, who changed to impress for the afternoon's activities, they fawned over every ribbon and every bead, ensuring every guest was given an extra boost of confidence.

Peacocking into the reception, Porticia Prombey proudly flaunted an ill-stretched white dress, wrestling with her body's natural curves. A plume of bright red feathers surrounded her large breasts, creating the

illusion of an accented feathered pillow. Searching the garden, she became dismayed when she was unable to locate Edi.

Setting her sights on Birk, she made a direct line toward him.

"Birk, there you are!" she shouted, startling Roux so badly that she spilled her tray of drinks. Porticia galivanted forward, her arms waving erratically. Bracing, he forced a smile.

"I'd hoped to catch you. Your show in Capital City was *brilliant*, and I was thrilled to hear you'd be performing for us this evening," Porticia's voice boomed.

Everyone within earshot leaned in to listen. "Thank you," he replied, trying to lower the volume of the interaction. "I'm glad you enjoyed the show. I look forward to the encore tonight."

"I hope it's something new," she bluntly responded. Recognizing she was drawing everyone's attention, she was keen to keep the spotlight. "Don't get me wrong; the festival was fantastic, but I was worried after watching some of your earlier performances that our honorable witches may have gotten the divination wrong on you."

Chuckling, Porticia turned to the guests nearby, delighted she was amusing them. No stranger to critics, Birk remembered his Aunt Edi's lessons: Never allow anyone to instigate a reaction. Choosing to laugh along with the others as if in on the joke, he feigned humility. "I appreciate you all suffering while I gained my footing."

"Oh, sweet boy, I wouldn't have even let you perform in front of my chickens. Even they can recognize a bad egg," she taunted, playing to the audience. Birk's cheeks flushed, matching the color of his hair.

"Porticia, I wasn't aware chickens held such distinguished tastes," interrupted a voice behind them. The small crowd parted as Pan made her way across the lawn. "My experience with chickens is that their lives are filled with a lot of pecking, scratching, and clucking until one day their heads are lopped off. Yet, they still run aimlessly, not realizing they've already become someone else's meal."

Porticia's jaw slackened. "No offense, we've never hosted a Storyteller in Balincia *until* Birk came along. We didn't believe it was necessary,"

stammered Porticia, gesturing to the other town leaders, attempting to draw in support. "After all, we've been entertained with dancers, musicians, and artists for years; a Storyteller seemed . . . redundant. Fine for children, not the same caliber for adults."

"Yes, Edi and I should take the blame for not introducing you to more *advanced* arts earlier. When we realized Balincia lacked imagination in its music and craftsmanship, we recognized we'd done you a disservice. Without stories, we lack the skills to craft new narratives or understand experiences beyond our own. Stories inspire our souls, pushing our creativity beyond giant stone cocks."

The entire lawn stood silent. Porticia took a step back, and the crowd closed in.

"You are correct in one thing; it's not of the same caliber as the current talent today because it is *superior*," Pan admonished. "Children are drawn to Birk because they're not limited by the mundane mentality of adults in learning or appreciating something new. If a story or performance seems redundant to you, perhaps it's because you never grasped its meaning to begin with. This is the reason stories are worth repeating."

Noting the crowd's abandonment, Porticia shrank from the public chastisement. Failing to gain the validation she was aiming for, she sulked for penance. "Forgive me; of course, you're right. We all have much to learn from your wisdom," she bowed her head, contrite, "*we* should've never questioned Birk's divination." She glanced at the avoidant eyes of her peers, refusing to take sole accountability for the rebuke.

The subtle change in the guests' body language caught Birk's attention. Their animated conversations fell silent, replaced by fleeting glances toward Pan, who currently held court. Her presence exuded an unsettling aura, and her unpredictability left others on edge.

While generally considered the better-natured of the two, her title alone, The Practitioner of *Chaos*, was intimidating. One moment, her words were laced with honeyed sweetness and charm, enthralling those nearby. The next, a tiny spark in her eyes or a shift in posture transformed her into a more formidable figure, warning others to keep their distance.

No one was ever quite sure what to expect.

TWELVE

CRACKS IN THE TABLE

Every meal served at the Palace of Order was a magical experience. A table constructed of white birch ran the length of the dining area, with wolf fur draped across the attending chairs. A black iron scale, perpetually in balance, adorned the only wall. Every accessory and piece of furniture, whether practical or decorative, was deliberate, invoking both function and mindset.

A crystal fountain flowed with liquid light in the table's center. Cascading across the wood in branching streams, it diverted to each guest, illuminating their plates. Sitting at the end of the table, Edi was dressed in a ceremonial red robe, a hem of sparkling garnets on her waist and bodice.

Lowering her head as she entered the room, Saffrona, Edi's prized Royal Chef, joined the guests.

Always surprised by her stature, many were misled to believe her long limbs and enormous hands made it difficult to maneuver through a kitchen with grace or precision. She delighted in defying their assumptions. Gliding between stations, she would dance around Moreau and step over the diminutive Roux. Her long fingers, quick and nimble, sculpted and plated food with pointed artistry—a display of *true magic*.

Her touch was delicate, her voice soft, contradicting every impression of a culinary master.

Appearing to introduce the first course, Birk brimmed with affection. Knowing she'd preferred to stay in the kitchen, avoiding the gasps and whispers, Saffrona put on a show anyway, a requirement for all of Edi's staff. She nodded at Birk with a cheeky glance.

The first course, an Enchanted Emberroot Salad, was composed of crisp ember-colored leaves of seasonal greens, shards of crystallized moonfruit, and ambrosial nectar from the orchards. The dish shimmered in the fountain's light, its flavors balanced between light and dark, with a crunch of emberroot contrasting with the luscious sweet tang from the moonfruit. Saffrona blushed as guests gushed over her flavors and presentation.

Edi smiled, acknowledging a job well done and allowing the chef to take her exit from the room.

Birk sat at the end of the table opposite Edi, in a position usually reserved for Pan. No excuses were offered for her absence, which was odd since the meal was a formal privilege earned by town leaders. Based on the sideways glances, Birk interpreted he was as an unacceptable replacement.

Wallingford, a tall, ghostly-looking man, sat to Birk's left, a representative from the Isle of Wheat. To his right sat Beatrix, a half-dozen bees buzzed around the honeycomb fascinator attached to her head. He couldn't determine if they were her bees or if she attracted them from the garden outside; either way, she didn't look bothered. Neither guest left an impression they'd care to converse with him.

Samuel, the cherry-nosed farm leader, was the first to speak. "I want to make a toast to our esteemed hostesses, Edi and Pan," he said, raising his glass. Everyone followed suit, looking at Edi and then awkwardly at Birk, who offered a cringe-worthy smile. "After all these years, we are honored to still have you presiding over a conclave of misfits, such as ourselves."

Laughing, everyone clinked and gave cheers.

With the serene smile of a hostess and a quick bow to her guests,

Edi responded, "Thank you, Samuel. I speak on behalf of my sister and myself; governance and leadership are no easy tasks. When we conceived Balincia, we knew it would only be through the ongoing support of our town council leaders and citizens that our mutual vision could grow to fruition and succeed. The honor is ours."

After another round of clinking glasses, a voice rose from the center of the table.

"If I may ask . . . what *was* your vision when you created Balincia?" Porticia leaned forward.

Birk knew firsthand this type of question was abnormal. Porticia's idea to ask it was one thing, but another when she directed it to his aunt in a public forum. To her credit, the inquiry wasn't antagonizing; it displayed a genuine curiosity about Balancia's history. What was odd was that it was a subject Birk had never witnessed surface.

Intrigued, he leaned in, eager to hear his aunt's response. Beyond a quick glimpse of surprise, she seemed unfazed. "What an excellent question, Porticia. Our vision was always to build a society centered on purpose. When we live purposefully, we live a fulfilling life."

"A beautiful philosophy... but... what does it *really* mean? How do we define purpose? Or measure it?" After Porticia's encounter with Pan on the lawn, the poor woman was using all her restraint to measure her tone. Despite Birk's feelings about Porticia, he was impressed with her confidence in pressing forward. "What I'm trying to ask is, if our goal as township leaders is to help achieve *your* vision, how will we identify success?"

"I think Balincia's already successful," Samuel jumped in for Edi. "Our beloved rulers have bestowed us with everything we need to succeed. We *all* have homes, food on our plates, and the ability to start our own families. The land provides everything we could want or need."

The recitation every Balincian knew well. Talbot argued a similar line on the boat.

"I don't disagree, Samuel, but I believe the question Porticia is asking is how we define the purpose, not questioning our provision," Lars interjected. "I won't speak for others, but I think our purpose *is* found in the

work we do to ensure our provision. Without toil and sweat, how else can we appreciate the fruits of our labor?"

Birk heard a few 'here here's from the men's chorus across the table.

"If that's true, Lars, do you consider all our work equal?" Marina probed. The guests shifted in their seats. Marina controlled the largest township in Balincia; when she spoke, people listened. "I don't want to minimize the labor of other townships, but how do we compare the value of goods from our farmlands, forests, and fishing towns to those of honey-makers and jewelers? *We* provide the essentials of food, fuel, and shelter, which sustain our people. Respectfully, how is the value of our work compared to those creating baubles and accessories?"

"What are you trying to imply?" Rockwell squeaked.

"I'm not *implying* anything; I'm pointing out that if our work defines our purpose, shouldn't the work *matter*?"

Beatrix clanged her fork on her plate, pushing her lips into a pout. Not missing the reaction, Edi jumped in to quell the rising temperature in the room. "*Every* good and product offered at this table from our townships provides value to Balincians," she continued. "I don't think there is benefit in analogizing who works harder or what contributions deserve more credit."

"This is *why* our roles are defined at birth; we all have talents built for different forms of labor and contribution," Samuel added, coming to Edi's defense.

"This is the intent of my question," Porticia pressed. "Is our purpose defined by the work we are *assigned* to do? Is fulfillment defined by mastering our divined purpose and talent? Is this our aim for Balincia?"

"I believe fulfillment is achieved through the love and compassion we demonstrate to all living beings . . . *no matter what we do*," Beatrix answered, overemphasizing her last words for Marina's sake. "Keeping bees and making honey may not be essential to our land's survival, but we use honey in our foods to sweeten and amplify their taste. Our healers use it in our medicine, helping to heal our skin and nurture our wounds."

"Beatrix, I'm not trying to attack you or your bees," Marina interrupted.

"You didn't let me finish," Beatrix asserted. "For *me*, our small contributions make life worth living. Similar to honey, we can demonstrate our effectiveness each day in countless ways. The kindness, relief, and support we give to others help define us as a society. Is this not enough of a purpose to drive us?"

"Well spoken, Beatrix," Edi affirmed, addressing the rest of the table. "I'm surprised by the attitudes and ideas of some of our leaders today. We should take a break and pick this up at the council meeting. Besides, I think you'll want to focus your energy on our main course."

Edi waved Saffrona and her staff into the room, hoping a change of plates would change the conversation.

"We don't have dragons in Balincia, of course, and I'm not sure I'd be able to procure one if we did," Saffrona announced, making everyone laugh, "but I was inspired by the mythical beasts from young Birk's stories, hence the name, *Dragonflame Roast*. Each dish is plated with a tender cut of meat from our long-haired cattle, marinated with dragonfire peppers and glisterberry juice, roasted to perfection over cedar flames. Please enjoy."

Bold and fiery scents rose from the dishes as they were plated. A mouthwatering blend of spice, succulence, and textures ranging from crispy char to juicy tenderness left diners spellbound. Talbot and his men stood unblinking at the walls, watching everyone fill their greedy bellies. Birk assumed Saffrona would have hot plates waiting for them in the kitchen, saving the best pieces for her family.

After devouring the decadent meal, guests folded their napkins onto their plates and scooted their chairs back; Lars raised his deep voice over the table. "I want to revisit our conversation. I've had time to think about Beatrix's comments while we ate." Edi gave an inaudible sigh.

"Beatrix, you alluded to focusing on others through acts of love and compassion as a way to achieve purpose. While I agree and align with the nobility of this notion, I'm challenged with the concept of this being our goal as a society."

"Say more," piped Rockwell, rising in his seat and making himself visible to Lars.

"Well, I hypothesize we're neglecting important aspects. Beatrix's argument speaks to values rather than pursuits. If our society aims to grow, why aren't we focused on community achievements, intellectual innovation, or geographical exploration and expansion?"

"Not to mention military defense, we've taken for granted we'll always live in peace. Are we prepared if this changes?" Marina asked.

Eyes narrowing, Edi shook her head. "Why wouldn't we be at peace? *Who* would we be at war with? And why would we need to expand? Our legislation is in place to ensure we don't live beyond our means."

"Edi, our laws have been in place for ten thousand years, with *no review*, only because you and Pan created them." Porticia reminded, once again finding her opening. "*You* created Balincia, and if I may add, wield daunting magic; we're too scared to question what *you* have put in place."

Edi's nails tapped on the birch wood table. Tense and alert, Talbot's attention was glued to her hands.

"That's exactly right," Lars piled on. "Not that we aren't grateful for everything you've gifted us, but let's not pretend our titles hold any weight on this council. We're invited here to report and take orders."

The room went silent, except for the continued tap, tap, tapping of Edi's nails.

Under any other circumstance, Birk would infer he was listening to a typical meeting between council members, hypothesizing and debating the economics, ethics, and governance of the land to which they were charged. Every idea or opinion expressed was reasonable, unoffensive in its aim, *and* long overdue if he was honest. The leaders reminded him of children testing their voices and experimenting with adult conversation.

However, this was Balincia, not one of the stories from his books. Citizens weren't known to wax philosophy, postulate over purpose, and they certainly didn't balk at the hand feeding them. Birk had to remind himself that it was only a few days ago that *he* lacked the imagination or insight to offer the conjecture being served today. It'd be unfair for him to judge the aptitude of those around the table.

It'd also be wrong to surmise Balincians lacked ingenuity or innova-

tive thinking; this discredited their architects, engineers, and artisans. Despite their literacy restrictions, their populations were well-educated, and knowledge was passed down from one generation to the next, both in oral and tactile instructions. Their operations excelled in efficiency, and their culture thrived.

No, it was more accurate to define their curiosity and creativity as limited, restrained by strict boundaries, similar to the borders created by the mountains. Some paths were laid wide open for exploration in their minds; others were forbidden, fiercely defended, herding back the occasional stray woolly sheep.

After his exposure to the book, his mind discovered the key to overcoming these barriers. Still, it was unfamiliar territory for him, and he was cautious about stepping too far, too fast, away from the herd. Unencumbered, his cognitive abilities were growing rapidly, making him acutely aware the questions the leaders circled were unusual.

Based on his limited experience, no one ever challenged legislation or infrastructure, much less leadership. This led him to believe the stretched bands in his mind weren't the only ones snapping.

Recognizing the possible consequences, Birk glanced anxiously at Talbot, who raised an eyebrow in response. Holding their breath, they monitored Edi.

Samuel stood, slamming his fists onto the table, causing Talbot and his men to jump.

"Am I the only one who finds this discussion treasonous?" he bellowed. "With the exception of Rockwell, I carry more years of experience than any of you. In all of my time in Balincia, I've never witnessed such selfish ways of thinking, particularly in front of our Royal Practitioner of Order. You should be throwing yourselves at her feet for all she has supplied you, ungrateful lot. Instead, you dare challenge and insult her?"

"It's all right, Samuel," Edi patted his hand and encouraged him to take a seat. "I don't take it personally, although I confess, this is the first time I've witnessed our council so *inquisitive.*" Standing, she centered both hands on the table, making a point to survey each diverted eye.

"I feel everyone may be a little *off* today," she assessed. "The thoughts and questions are appreciated, albeit peculiar, for this group. I want it known I've heard you," she said, looking at Lars. "And I'm optimistic by this evening, we'll be able to sort it out once my sister joins us."

Birk had a feeling he knew what *sorting it out* meant. He was terrified he'd arrive to perform for a crowd of smiling and vacant faces if he wasn't already included among them. Exiting from the room, Edi left the others to attend to themselves.

The pit in Birk's stomach grew.

Birk turned to see Talbot behind him. "Edi's instructed me to escort you to the library; I thought you might need this," he said, handing him his leather satchel, with the Driftstone tucked inside.

Once the guests left the room, Talbot discreetly pressed his hand against the back wall. The stones behind the large scales shifted into place, opening the entrance to the library. After stepping inside, they waited for the door to close before speaking.

"Something's happening, Birk," Talbot leaned in, "beyond our discussion this morning. It wasn't only the interrogatory behavior during the meal, nor limited to the township leaders. The staff has become more inquisitive, and the guards are more irritable. I think the enchantments are cracking, perhaps as a side effect of whatever is happening between you and the book."

"This may be a good thing. I want people to be curious. We should all be asking questions. The truth *should* come out."

"Yes, but we still don't know the full truth; we must be careful. Incidents similar to today may provoke a strong reaction from your aunts, tempting them to find a more permanent or binding solution. You need to find your answers fast."

"I'll do what I can. Thank you, Talbot."

"You should have a couple of hours while the group breaks into their initial agenda." Talbot touched his shoulder, "Good luck and be careful."

THIRTEEN

THE WITCH'S DOOR

Cozy and warm, the central area of the library featured an opulent fireplace carved from black marble, decorated with a carved tree. Branches and boughs from the sculpted art twisted and spread around the centerpiece, dominating the room's aesthetic. A large, ornate mirror framed in black hung in the wrapped, chiseled timber, reflecting the several lit hallways of grand bookshelves.

Leather mahogany armchairs were scattered across the room, flanking a deep, cushioned couch of the same hue and hide. Edi had left a stack of books on them for his review.

Peeking around the shelves' corners, Birk called out, announcing himself and making sure he was alone. Once confirmed, he set upon the task of figuring out how to access the forbidden section of the library.

Green wrought iron doors, hidden behind the shelves, served as the vaulted entrance. The doors were a work of art, crafted with braided iron ropes stretching across tempered, opaque crystal in their centers. The entrance was adorned with golden brass handles and plates, while three locks were sketched with curling ivy.

Birk loved sitting in front of these doors as a child. In his mind, the dark green suggested an enchanted forest secretly lying beyond its borders. Never able to peek behind them, his aunts only used them when he wasn't around. Based on the illustrations of the hallway in the Drifts-tone, his early fantasy might be closer to reality than he thought.

Excited, he headed toward the locked entrance, eager to uncover their secrets. Despite the situation, he was reliving the daydreams of his youth, living out the life of an explorer—leading thrilling adventures—not just reading about them.

Upon reaching the doors, his enthusiasm wavered. He still lacked a solution to open them. Picking locks wasn't an option; he lacked the skills to do so, and he assumed magical safety measures or alarms were in place to prevent it. Using this logic, damaging or breaking the door would also backfire or, at minimum, give him away.

Running his palm across its face, he probed for a secret button, a disguised latch, or a hidden key. Producing no results, he attempted to use the handle, not wanting to be accused of missing the obvious. He felt foolish when it delivered the expected outcome; *it was indeed bolted shut.*

Perusing the shelves around him, he searched in vain for clues. Flipping through pages and titles, hoping something valuable would reveal itself, soon revealed to be fruitless. He was moving without a compass. Frustrated, wishing he'd been more thoughtful with this part of the plan, he slumped to the floor.

Giving up was becoming more conceivable. Sitting against the bookshelf, stretching his legs, he knocked over his satchel. *Maybe the answers are in the Driftstone.* After all, it led him here.

Pulling the weathered book into his lap, Birk reviewed its contents. Satisfied he didn't miss anything valuable, he flipped to the first empty page. The book was warm but uninterested in sharing anything new. *What if he tried communicating with the book this time? If the Driftstone could talk to him, perhaps he could talk back.*

He set the palm of his hand on the page. Focusing on the green wrought iron doors, he asked the book how to open them. Several eternal minutes passed. Still, nothing.

Clenching his eyes shut, he focused even harder. The warmth of the parchment began to increase beneath his fingers. He withdrew his hand;

the book was reacting. A beautifully detailed replica of the iron doors materialized on the top half of the page. Underneath the illustration, lay another riddle.

Break or bend, plead or implore,
You can't unlock a witch's door.
There is an oath to which it's sworn,
To only open for Magic-Born.

To identify a friend or enemy,
You must introduce your energy.
Magic hands that mean no harm,
Will be given access without alarm.

Birk became fraught. The message indicated the doors would only open for those born with magic; his aunts were the only ones with magic.

His head fell against the shelves behind him, defeated. Maybe Talbot's historical approach of ignoring and avoiding his aunt's actions was for the best. *Who were they to challenge ten thousand years of history?*

Pulling himself to his feet, he deposited the Driftstone back into his satchel and turned to return to the main room, disappointed. *This is for the best.* It was critical to prepare for tonight, anyway. About to leave the doors behind, he paused, glancing back once more.

His mind flashed to the old woman and their conversation. *I know who you are,* she'd told him. *I came tonight for you.* He wasn't gifted the Driftstone randomly; this woman, whoever she was, knew the book would speak to him. Assuming she knew the power of the Driftstone, she believed Birk could do something with what it shared with him.

Surely, it didn't mean . . . no . . . but . . . maybe? Returning to the front of the doors, he raised his palm to their face and focused his energy.

Holding his hand firm, pressing it against the cold metal, he projected his intentions, insistent it hear him.

The door jostled under his touch, alarming him. Keeping his feet planted, he held his position. Determined, he waited until he heard three processional quiet clicks.

He stepped back, too anxious to breathe. Wrapping his fingers around the handle, he gave it a slight tug; the door swung open without resistance.

The door opened— for him. If the Driftstone was correct, it shouldn't unlock for anyone but Magic-Born. If this was true . . .

He raised his hands to his face and stared at them. He was no less ordinary than minutes ago, and his hands looked the same. There was no new energy inside him or raw power in his veins. Shaking his head, he pushed away the thoughts he desperately wanted to chase. There wasn't time to figure out what this meant.

Grabbing one of the lanterns from the walls, satchel slung over his shoulder, he walked through the witch's door. Smiling, he pictured himself, the novel image of a hero, off to meet his destiny.

If he were in a story, the current twist would be an extreme let-down, especially after all his heightened expectations. No enchanted forest or hallway of doors . . . only more books. Row after row after row of books. He couldn't imagine how Edi procured them all, and given his mood, he begrudged her for keeping them to herself.

The floor-to-ceiling shelves were filled with volumes Birk was already familiar with, tales and picture books his aunts often trotted out to teach or entertain him in his youth. It wasn't until he progressed further that the contents became interesting: instructional and informative scripted works, notes on agriculture and biology, spell work to control the weather, and shelves dedicated to medicinal potions.

He wished there were more time; the books begged for future exploration. He considered pinching an alluring title a few times and slipping it into his satchel to read later, but considering Edi's foresight, he feared

anything borrowed might magically trace back to him. Short on time, he ignored the impulse.

Quickening his pace, he trekked rows of tomes and grimoires. Corner after corner, with no ending or beginning in sight, he wondered if the library was a maze. The further he wandered, the sparser the volumes on the shelves became, their titles more concerning.

The "Grimoire of Shadows," a thick book with an obsidian cover and silver sigils, sat alone. Out of curiosity, Birk picked it up and realized it was filled with incantations, summoning forbidden powers and unlocking access to darker spirits. Shuddering, he carefully returned it to the shelf and pushed it far into the back, and out of sight.

The thematic selections continued to grow darker: an entire series on curses and hexes, a journal on transmutation, books on arcane alchemy, and there was even a group of loose pages bound with chains on necromancy. A cold chill ran through him; this wasn't the type of magic his aunts practiced. *Was it?*

Overwhelmed, he wondered if he should abandon his mission and discuss this more with Talbot. He didn't know how much time he wasted wandering or how quickly Edi would return to check on him.

Faint footsteps echoed in front of him, freezing him in place.

Was someone else down here? If it were Edi, she wouldn't be in front of him; she'd be coming from behind. The only other person with access was Pan. *Is this where she disappeared during lunch? What was she doing down here? And why was she ignoring the council on such an important day?*

He crept deeper into the narrow corridor, the dim glow of his lantern his only light. Moving with caution, his ears attentive, he picked up the definitive sound of a door scraping against a stone floor.

She *was* here with him.

His first instinct was to slink back the way he came, hoping she wasn't alert to his presence. He'd wait in the library's main room, review his books, and abandon the mission for the day. This would be the safest strategy.

Leaning against the wall, he debated.

He harbored no fear of Pan; he witnessed the ferocity of her loyalty when she came to his side hours earlier. There was no doubt she loved him. However, neither of them had ever been in a position where they were cornered by the other. Given the several lingering questions about his aunts, it was prudent to acknowledge his ignorance regarding them.

Going against his gut, he moved forward, coming too far to give up. He knew Pan was lurking, but it didn't mean she knew *he* was. If he were careful, he might gather significant intel, even if he was unable to locate the hallway of doors.

Gradually descending, the path's appearance no longer resembled a library. The air was heavier, dense, and stale; shelves vanished from the walls, as did the light. The entire ambiance was contradictory to his perception of Aunt Edi. He anticipated pristine white marble floors, illuminated lavish rooms, and shiny glass cases with books on display. The thought of her maneuvering through shadows and cobwebbed recesses was difficult to envision.

Rounding the corner, Birk entered a circular stone chamber with three closed wooden doors scattered along the borders. Taking a careful step into the room, he jumped at the automatic ignition of an assembly of torches hanging around the perimeter. Mysterious roots dangled from the ceiling, exuding a faint, intoxicating aroma. A table with crumbling scrolls, brittle with age, scattered across its surface lay in the center.

A collection of vials and ingredients was shelved on the walls, surrounded by plants not native to Balincia. Artifacts and what Birk assumed to be magical objects tempted his curiosity: a jeweled dagger, a carved staff, and a mask with eccentric features frozen in a scream. An enormous tome beside the dagger stole his attention. Its title was *"The History of Driftstone."*

Removing the satchel from his shoulder, he extracted his version of the Driftstone. The book tugged upon its release, pulling him to the table. The larger volume summoned the one in his hands. A lunar moth drawn to the moon.

He laid it on the table, side by side, with the record of its history. An electric spark of arcane energy cracked between them. Their ancient

bindings creaked and quivered until a glow emanated from them. The books levitated and their pages fluttered, stirred by an unseen force, until they dropped from the air, smacking onto the table and giving Birk a start.

The interior of the larger tome began to turn rapidly, and the Driftstone synchronized in response. Stopping abruptly, it opened wide to reveal a chapter entitled *'The History of the Thirteen.'* Guided by an unseen hand, the Driftstone opened to its first blank page; the text from the larger volume transferred into it.

Birk leaned in and became mesmerized by the connection between the two, oblivious to one of the doors opening behind him. A shadow drew closer, and the Driftstone's transcription disappeared. Without warning, both books slammed shut, appearing lifeless and dull.

"Birk! What are you doing down here?"

Birk spun around, panicked. Pan, equally surprised, stood before him, her arms filled with heavy books. Attempting to obscure his aunt's view, he positioned his back to block the Driftstone.

"Auntie Pan, I didn't hear you come in." With one hand, he carefully grabbed the book from the table, tucking it into the back waistband of his trousers underneath his cloak. "I'm sorry; I know I shouldn't be back here. I was searching for something to perform for this evening, and I noticed this section of the library unlocked," he lied, counting on her absentmindedness to sell it.

Pan's eyes darted over Birk, the room, and the table behind him. "Birk, this part of the library is off limits for good reason."

"I didn't intend to come this far . . . I . . . I heard someone back here. Forgive me. It won't happen again," he stuttered. Shifting the focus, he redirected her questions, "Why aren't you at the council meeting?"

"Me? I was trying to find—" Pan stopped. "I don't need to explain why I'm in my library." She shifted her weight, shuffling and balancing the books in her hand, she turned the spines so Birk couldn't read them.

She wasn't fast enough, he snuck a peek at one of the titles, *The Gateways of Cyrus*, before she spun it out of sight.

"There's a reason this part of the library is locked, Birk," she repri-

manded. "Do I need to remind you of the dangers? What were you doing at the table?" Pan stepped forward, moving her head to the right and left, trying to look at the contents behind him.

Birk pivoted, directing a question back to her, hoping to benefit from a bold diversion. "What is the Driftstone?"

"*The Driftstone?* Where did you learn that name?" Pan moved to inspect what was behind him. Keeping his back out of sight, Birk stepped out of the way. *The History of Driftstone* remained closed in the center of the table. "Oh, I understand. Birk, I realize you're curious; it's one of the things I love about you, but you've no idea how unsafe some of the information in these books can be."

"Tell me."

Stacking her books on the table, she covered the hefty tome and placed her hand on his chest. "I wish it were so simple. I do, but there is a cost to this knowledge. You aren't ready for it."

He'd been trying to demonstrate contrition for his deceit and intrusion, but her answer irritated him. "I'm exhausted with others making decisions on my behalf. Who are you to judge what I can and can't handle? Why can't you be straightforward and allow me to discern my risks? I thought our relationship was based on trust and transparency."

Offended, Pan removed her hand.

"I'm not sure if this is still about the conversation surrounding your parents or something deeper, but I'm your aunt, who is charged with your well-being. The responsibility of governing what is best for you is *never* relinquished. If you desire transparency, why don't you tell me why you're here? Please don't mistake me for a fool. My patience has its limits."

She was correct; he didn't trust her enough to be honest. He was angry, doubting he'd ever be able to trust her again. He stood defiant to her rebuke.

She shook her head, "Birk, even if I wanted to answer your questions, it isn't *only* up to me, and more importantly, we don't have the time to discuss all of this now." Pan glanced around the chamber, lowering her voice. "Your aunt Edi could come *any* minute. You're lucky I found you. Otherwise, she would have erased—"

She stopped, aware of her slip.

"My what? Go on . . . finish it," Birk demanded, his suspicions confirmed.

"Birk—" she started, trying to assuage her mistake.

Raising his voice, he interrupted her, refusing to hear another lie. "My memories? That's what you were going to say. So, Edi *has* been altering people's minds? And you . . . you knew about it all along, didn't you?" Birk backed away, mortified.

Pan turned mute; her lips quivered.

"Of course you did." Birk's stomach caved in. "You knew because you've done it too."

Pan lowered her head.

Birk understood Edi's nature; It was easy to rationalize her desire to control everything and understand how it might lead to poor judgment. Pan, however, raised him to embrace a sovereign mind. Her participation and approval of this violation corrupted these principles.

"Have you wiped my memories before?" Birk grabbed her by the arm, forcing her to look at him. "Answer me! Have you wiped my memories *before*? Or will it be the first time today?"

Pan raised her hand to his cheek, and he flinched. "Birk, you must believe me; I'd never damage your precious mind."

"It doesn't answer the question, does it?" He swiped her hand away. "You've breached the privacy and free will of others. Why? *For what reason?*" Birk's face flushed with anger. His voice rose, echoing across the chamber, deep into the corridors. "Do you do it anytime anyone *dares* to ask about something you'd rather not answer? Or only when someone challenges or disagrees with you? How many lies are you covering?"

"Birk, that's not fair. You don't understand."

"Help me understand!" he shouted; the books on the table crashed to the floor. Pan took a cautious step back. Catching the distress on her face quenched his fire. He softened and took her hands, lowering his voice to a whisper, "Please, help me understand."

Throwing her arms around him, she cried into his neck. "I will." Breaking the embrace, she cupped his face. "I promise. I *will* help you

understand. *Later*, after your performance. Right now, we must get you back to the main room before Edi finds you here.”

Birk lost any residual fight in him and slumped against her.

“Please trust me.” She redirected her attention to the silver pin on his tunic, she rubbed it between her fingers and smiled. “Do you know what this is?”

“Talbot gave it to me,” he mumbled.

She nodded, “The idea was his; I can’t take credit for the design either; I merely pointed him to it. The symbol goes back farther than either of you realize.” Taking the pendant between her fingers, she kissed it, whispering something inaudible, and patted his chest, “It stands for the *Protection of Truth*. I recognize the irony as I say it.” She gave a sad, soft smile. “Keep it close to your heart at all times. Protect it, and it’ll protect you. Whatever darkness or deceit surrounds you, the truth will always reveal itself.”

The room’s energy shifted. An invisible gust of wind blew out the torches. Flickering back to life, they illuminated Pan’s urgent and frantic face.

She grabbed his arm. “I’m afraid we’re out of time. Edi is on her way.”

Pan loaded her books back into her arms. Scanning the room, she tried deciphering if anything was out of place. “Listen closely to me. I *promise* everything will be all right; no one wants any harm to come to you. Find me at my palace tonight; we’ll discuss this further.”

“But, what should—” Birk was cut off by his aunt’s finger to his mouth.

“Don’t say anything else. Remember this: The leaf that falls from the farthest branch of the tree has the most potential to grow into something new.”

Birk shook his head in confusion.

“Trust me,” she winked.

A scent of citrus and mint trickled into the room, followed by the clickity taps of pointed heels against cobbled stones. Never dramatic or unbent, Edi entered the chamber, assessing the scene before her; the blank stares and silence added to the guilt-infused atmosphere.

Edi inspected them with her eyes. "Pan, what is going on? What is Birk doing here?"

"It's my fault. I left the door unsecured, and he heard me knock over some books. He came to see if I was all right. I was bringing him back to the main room."

Edi nodded curtly. "I see. Birk, you must have the auditory perception of a bat to hear your aunt *all the way back here.*"

Pan stepped in front of him, attempting to draw her sister's attention. "There's no harm done, Edi. He didn't touch anything. He didn't read anything. He was concerned for me."

"Is this true, Birk?" Edi stepped to her sister's side to face him.

Birk hesitated; he shared a lot in common with Pan, but he inherited Edi's tenacity and will. She was fearless and direct, respecting those who met her. If he wanted answers, he'd go to the source. Consequences be damned.

"No, it isn't. I came here intentionally; she's protecting me. I want answers," Birk said, meeting her posture. "I want to know what all this is," he gestured to the chamber around them, "and I want to know why you're both lying to me."

Pan immediately tried to intervene, "Edi, he doesn't know what—"

"No. You were given your chance." Edi cut her off and moved closer to her nephew. "In answer to your first question, *all of this,*" repeating his gesture around the room, "is *private,* and it's an area you knew full well was forbidden. Yet, you *still* felt entitled to break trust in coming here. As for the second question, *please* elaborate on what you think we're lying to you about?"

"Our . . . lives and homes aren't what we've been raised to believe. Pan admitted you're doing something with our minds, keeping us from asking questions and prompting us to forget things."

Edi shot Pan a sharp glare, a warning of future reckonings.

Gaining courage, he continued, "How could *anyone* grow up never thinking about their parents? How can I spend every day staring at mountains yet never wonder about walking amongst them or dreaming about what lies beyond them? How did I read so many books and never *once*

question their author or origin? And why doesn't anyone know anything about your past?"

There. He said it. It was all out in the open.

Edi stood still, her hands clasped together in front of her waist. The slightest signs of a small curve appeared at the corners of her mouth.

"Alright, Birk. Do you want the truth? I'll give you the truth. These thoughts never crossed your mind because I made sure they wouldn't. When this conversation is over, I will ensure they won't again. I'm not sure how your enchantment broke, but it doesn't matter; there is nothing I can't fix. Based on our lunch today, I think everyone requires a little maintenance."

"My enchantment?" While Birk expected this to be the case, he wasn't prepared for her open admission. He realized, then, at that moment, it didn't matter what he said; she would use her "motherly magic" to untangle and iron out all his concerns, leaving no mess behind.

"Yes, *your* enchantment. It is a fail-safe installed in everyone in Balincia, protecting you, me, and everyone you love here."

"Protecting us from *what?*"

Pan interrupted, stepping forward. "It's time," she said to her sister. Pan swept her hand across the air, and images came to life on the chamber walls.

"There was a time before Balincia, Birk, in a world where magic thrived. Your aunt and I, along with our siblings, were the engineers of creation. Mountains, rivers, trees, beasts, and dozens of civilizations, each with their own free will and spirits, were birthed from our collective hands." Pan glowed with nostalgia. "Most of the stories you read are real; they're our history."

"Then the world changed." Edi created new, more sinister images on the walls. The lights of the torches dimmed in reaction.

"There was a division among us caused by greed and ambition for power. Dark and evil magic was introduced to the world, driving us to war. We lost brothers, kingdoms were destroyed, and entire species became extinct. Some of their remnants and artifacts are collected in the corridors you passed through today."

Pan took Edi's hand. This was the first time they'd allowed themselves to speak about these events in ten thousand years.

"Your aunt and I were forced to flee," Edi explained. "We rescued as many people as possible and brought them here. We built this land you call home, in partnership with Balincia's original citizens. A new world that hid us from the old. Those mountains you desperately want to explore are a magical barrier, concealing us from those who seek us harm. Everything we've done, every law we've created, has been to safeguard our people."

"I don't understand why you don't share this with everyone. If this is our history, we deserve to know it. Your people love you. *I love you*," Birk expressed.

"Birk, you saw a small glimpse of how quickly people pivot under their ambitions during our meal today. How fast do you think they'll spin on us or each other, out of fear or panic, if they knew what I've just revealed to you? We haven't even begun to share the real horrors with you," Edi warned.

"You haven't offered them a chance. Explain your motive to protect us. Help them to understand why the laws you crafted are in place. Wiping people's memories or removing their access to knowledge isn't the answer. It contradicts everything you've built. You're weakening us."

"We created your role as a Storyteller in an attempt to share *some* of our history with the people—in small measure. I think it *is* important for us to learn from our past. We don't want significant lessons lost, but the truth must be portioned," Pan explained.

"What gives you the right to decide what portions we receive?" Birk asked, frustrated.

"And whose decision is it? *Not yours.* We're the only survivors of Balincia's history." Edi said, growing tired of the debate.

"Only because *you* have limited our life span under your laws."

Pan reached out to touch Birk's arm. "Even paradise has its limits. We can't outgrow this space. We all want something more, whether it is longer lives, profound love stories, or heroic adventures. We can't grant every wish."

"We gifted you each with purpose; still, you remain unsatisfied, debating and arguing its definition and fulfillment. It doesn't come from responsibilities or talent; we know this. We need something unique to each of us to feed our souls, which is something even magic can't conjure. So, instead, we aimed for peace and well-being," Edi confessed, softening.

"Your honesty and compassion are a testament to the young man we've raised. We're being candid with you because lying serves us no purpose," Pan inserted.

"So, you aren't going to reinforce my enchantment? You'll think about what I said?"

"We didn't say that. I recognize you don't understand our reasons or think us cruel, but we do this out of love, Birk. Your ignorance isn't your fault. You can't comprehend what it means to be both a creator and a caretaker. You've not witnessed the suffering or experienced the devastation fated to others."

Panicking, Birk turned to Pan, "Please don't do this. *This isn't love.* Don't steal my voice; I've only discovered it."

Pan forced herself to look away.

"Birk, I promise this won't be painful," Edi soothed. "The only thing hurting you is your thoughts. It's the reason we *must* do this. If people were allowed to romanticize or minimize the dangers of our past, it would put all our lives at risk."

"You don't know this; you can't know this. Let us surprise you. We might build something stronger together."

Edi shook her head, "Or you might tear it all down. It's not a risk we can afford to take."

"How are you sure it won't hurt me? How can you be confident you aren't taking something important from me?"

"It doesn't operate that way. We can't *read* your mind; we don't remove *anything* from anyone. We don't practice dark magic. Think of it as putting locks on doors. We concentrate on events, people, *or questions* that could endanger you and tuck them away safe and secure. Left in their place are positive nudges, thoughts guiding you back to safer ground. It's only when you resist that you feel agitated or ill," Edi explained.

"I promise you'll feel better when it's finished," said Pan, attempting to assure him.

"It doesn't matter how the enchantment works or if you use love to validate your choices. The truth will always be—you force people to comply," Birk spat bitterly. "The result is the same whether by carrot or stick."

"Birk, hush now. You're being childish. No one can judge what they don't understand. It'll be over shortly." Edi nodded to her sister, "Pan, let's do this now."

Birk stepped back, unaware Pan was standing behind him. Placing her hands firmly on his shoulders, a wave of energy shot through him, numbing his legs. Inch by inch, his body was covered with paralysis, sans his eyes, which were forced to witness their betrayal.

Pan, her face lifeless, joined her sister. "We love you" were the last words he heard her say.

Clasping their hands, they chanted:

In harmony, our words entwine. With our voices united, we sever the line.

Let minds unfold and memories fade, and by magic's touch, let a clean slate be made.

A single tear rolled unnoticed down Birk's face.

FOURTEEN

THE PROTECTION OF TRUTH

Staring into the fire, Birk sat on the couch in the library's study, unaware of how long he'd been sitting there. His attention was drawn to a pile of books beside him. He was supposed to be preparing for tonight's performance.

He leaned forward to grab one and felt an uncomfortable pinching in his lower back. *Something was in his trousers.* Agitated, he reached back, finding another book strapped into his waistband—eliciting confusion. *What are you doing back there?*

The leather binding looked familiar when he placed it on his lap. He opened the cover and read the title page: *The Driftstone.* Flipping through the content, he found it challenging to find a narrative; the book was filled with illustrations and riddles. *This didn't lend itself to his typical performance material. And why was it stuffed in his trousers?* He decided to set it aside and revisit it later.

Refusing to be ignored, the book flipped open, its parchment riffling back and forth. Birk leaned away, alarmed by its sentience. After the shuffling ceased, the tome landed on an empty page, and black ink began to paint across the canvas. Two dragon wings, embracing a book, materialized on the blank space, with text displayed underneath them.

Carried by the wings of dragons, wisdom takes flight.
For in the grip of the protector, the truth is guarded tight.

Clarity struck him—a silver dragon-winged pendant pinned to his chest.

Unconsciously, his hand reached up to touch it. Fragmented memories pieced themselves together. Slow at first, and then a flood, threatening to drown him. Anger. Anguish. Fear.

He was being forced to relive his aunts' actions and lies. He couldn't keep up with the wave of emotions.

Throwing the pile of books to the ground, he raged and kicked some into the fire. Collapsing to the ground, he buried his head between his knees and cried.

The fire popped. The clock ticked. He raised his face.

Wait! He reached for the pendant again; another memory was returning. Something small and discreet. *Pan's kiss.*

She must have woven a protective enchantment into the silver talisman. *She saved his memories.* Birk's anger simmered. Pan, in her flawed love, kept her promise.

Okay. Now what?

He didn't have time to sit around feeling sorry for himself. The enchantment was fading, and the gravity of his predicament was setting in. He was trapped in the library with no straightforward escape, *not without being seen.* He wasn't prepared to face Edi in his current state. He also didn't want to risk pretending to be under the spell's influence in front of an audience.

Pan told him to meet her at her palace.

First, he needed to find a way out.

Considering his options, he paced the floor, his fingers nervously tracing the carving of the tree on the marble mantle. Maybe Talbot was posted outside the entrance; would he be able to get his attention without

drawing notice? If Talbot could help him reach the Palace of Chaos, he could hide there until Pan arrived.

No, he didn't want to draw Talbot into this. He didn't want to put himself or any other guests at risk of a similar fate. He stopped; he wouldn't let his mind go there. Talbot was smart; he kept himself safe for centuries.

His memory flashed back to his conversation with Pan in the chamber. Her words replayed in his mind: *"The leaf that falls from the farthest branch of the tree has the most potential to grow into something new."* When she said it, he chalked it up as another metaphor she always used to teach him. It was unhelpful in the moment and out of context. *What if she was trying to tell him something?*

If she had the foresight to use his pendant as a ward, what if she also predicted he'd be trapped in the library? *Maybe she was providing him with the solution.*

He lifted his hand from the carving of the tree and inspected the fireplace. A long branch stretched across the mantle, filled with budding leaves. Following the bough's length, he found chiseled foliage falling and drifting from the limb at its end, frozen in its float to the ground. One solitary leaf rested aloof, protruding from the floor, unattached to the sculpture on the wall.

Stretching out his leg, he pushed his foot against it. With a soft click, the fireplace swung open and revealed a secret stairwell leading up. He wasn't sure where it went, but it was the only escape option in front of him; he couldn't afford to be picky.

He grabbed the Driftstone, tucked it back into his waistband, threw his satchel over his shoulder, and stepped behind the fireplace. The cool air of the passage brushed against his face. The door slid shut, leaving him in darkness.

Grazing his fingers along the damp, cold walls, the sound of his breath echoed around him, mixed with the unsettling noise of mice scurrying. He leaned against the wall and dropped to his knees for better tactile reassurance. His limbs trembled, urging a slow, steady crawl.

After enduring several minutes of relentless damage to his knees, his

head suddenly collided with an obstruction above him. Stretching his palms over his head, roots dripped dirt into his hair. Spiders scurried at his invasive touch.

Panic set in while he fumbled around, searching for a way out. *Please don't let this be a dead end.* His frantic groping finally guided his hands to a small crevice between two bricks. Clenching his fist, he pushed his hand into the hole. His fingers clawed through worms and other sticky residues he preferred not to think about. Finally, they found a wedged latch.

Pulling it as hard as he could, he heard another click. A sliver of moonlight pierced the darkness. Pushing through the opening, he emerged from a secret door and breathed in the fresh night air. He looked around and realized he was in the front gardens of the Palace of Order, exiting underneath the statue of Pan.

He glanced back at the palace. He assumed all guests and staff were gathered inside for the evening. The suns had already set, and the light from the fireplaces lit the windows. Assuming the dinner was underway, it wouldn't be long before they collected him for his performance; he didn't have much time.

He hurried through the manicured paths toward the ivory bridge until a familiar voice stopped him.

"Birk, is that you?" shouted Ravenshire, emerging from the shadows. "What are you doing out here in the gardens?"

Grabbing Ravenshire by the arm, Birk dragged him into the tall hedges. Placing his finger to his lips, he signaled to his friend to remain quiet. "You can't tell anyone you've seen me," he whispered. "Is Talbot with you?"

The soldier's tan face scrunched in confusion, "Talbot's the one who sent me."

"What?"

"He pulled me aside privately an hour ago. He said Pan was anticipating an incoming visitor, and she wanted him to be escorted discreetly to her palace. He instructed me to keep watch on the gardens. It was all bizarre. I thought our aunt had finally taken a lover and was trying to

hide it from Edi," he laughed. When he realized Birk wasn't joining in, he straightened his face. "Anyway, why are you hiding out here?"

"The escort is for me," Birk said, glancing furtively from side to side. "And shouting out my name, by the way, isn't the definition of discreet."

"Sorry," Ravenshire whispered loudly, leaning into Birk's ear. "But why do you need an escort? It's not like you don't know your way."

"It's a long story," Birk sighed. "I don't have time to share it with you now. I'm not sure why he sent you either, but I need you to trust me. I need to get to Pan's without anyone seeing me."

Ravenshire laughed, "Are you playing a joke on me?"

Birk gave him a dead-eyed look.

"Okay," Ravenshire's smile dissipated. "But c'mon, when has anyone in Balincia ever needed *real* protection, especially you? I'm pretty sure you could've handled this on your own. Did you do something to upset the aunties?"

Birk looked down, "something like that, but . . . *bigger*."

Ravenshire reevaluated and straightened.

The two were thick as brothers, the youngest on the Royal Isle. If Birk required help, Ravenshire wouldn't hesitate, even if he didn't understand; this is why Talbot trusted sending him.

Processing the situation, Ravenshire took a sharp inhale. "Alright, if we're going to do this, let's do it," he said, poking his head out from the bushes, "I think we're clear to move."

The two friends moved with stealth, barely discernible in the shadows. Sidestepping pools of light, they weaved through trees and across the bridge, concealing themselves from any staff wandering between the palaces and a group of Guardians playing cards near the front steps. They were only comfortable speaking once they crossed the threshold of the Palace of Chaos.

"Thank you. I know you're dying to ask me questions, and I'll share everything with you once things are sorted. I promise."

"Does this have something to do with everyone's odd behavior today?"

Upon hearing the question, Birk realized the guests would now be *sorted* if Edi stayed true to her promise. Talbot didn't send his friend just because Birk trusted him; *he was trying to protect Ravenshire.* He made sure he wasn't in the room.

Birk lowered his head, "Yes, but the less you know, the safer you are. I'll come find you when I can." He paused, "In the meantime, please stay close to Talbot."

Ravenshire read Birk's face, "Are you going to be okay?"

"Pan will make sure of it." Throwing his arms around Ravenshire, he hugged him tight.

Ravenshire hesitated to leave; his eyes searched Birk for answers. "Be safe," he finally whispered, and with a nod, he retreated to find Talbot.

FIFTEEN

A Chorus of Whispers

There were several places within the Palace of Chaos's walls to hide. Its architecture flouted every norm, with long hallways leading nowhere, ceilings towering impossibly high or sagging oppressively low, and rooms that switched positions of their own free will. Every surface was a clash of colors, patterns, and styles.

Chairs were upholstered in garish fabrics, tables were piled with bizarre trinkets, and an overstuffed couch threatened to swallow undiscerning guests. Plush rugs were strewn on cold stone, and large rocks were scattered on thin carpets. Heavy with incense, every room was pungent with rosewood and an acrid metal tang.

Pan refused attending staff, except for Feigh, who was currently serving guests at the Palace of Order. Birk relished the moment of freedom to roam and contemplate his next move. He'd rather be on his feet than tucked away in a forgotten corner. Besides, it was dark in the palace. If he positioned himself well, he'd be able to spot anyone crossing the bridge in the distance, without being noticed at the window.

While he crouched in a corner, peeking out, his frustration grew over his aunts' interruption of his search for the hallway of doors. Everything he'd risked had been for nothing, and given the circumstances, he was positive he wouldn't get a second chance. Even if Pan negated or temporarily quelled Edi's reaction to his absence, *which was doubtful,* he'd accepted that nothing would go back to the way it was before.

This thought led him back to the doors, and he was convinced the Driftstone intended for him to find it. In hindsight, he wished he'd double-checked the three entrances in the chamber after he woke from the enchantment. Reliving the moments from the chamber, he recalled when Pan took him by surprise, carrying a pile of books. She'd reshuffled them in an attempt to hide the titles from him. She wasn't quick enough; he read one of them: *The Gateways of Cyrus.*

Birk had no idea who Cyrus was, but the implication of gateways reminded him of portals *or doors.* Why would his aunt be reading a book on gateways? Was she searching for the same thing?

No, she wasn't searching for it; *she was researching it because she already knew where it was.* Maybe he was wrong. Perhaps the hallway was never in the library but in the Palace of Chaos.

The pantry!

The day he visited, there was an explosion in the pantry. *She wasn't out of sorts because of his questions; she was nervous he'd find what she was hiding there.*

Recognizing this was a considerable conjecture, there was still an effortless way to confirm his suspicions. Wasting no time, he found his way to the kitchen, threw open the pantry door, and leaped down the spiraling stairs. When he reached the bottom, his spirit withered.

Nothing but a pantry.

A dull, dusty pantry filled with jars of dried fruits and spices that lined the shelves on the back wall. Rust-covered iron cauldrons were piled in a corner.

He'd been so confident he'd find his answers here; it didn't make sense.

Exactly, *it didn't make sense.*

He was confident he'd heard an explosive sound here the day he visited. Pan explained it away as knocking over a shelf. Sure, she might have cleaned, but examining the shelves, he found them caked with dust, *as*

was the entire room. No signs of recent disturbance or evidence suggested the room was cleaned—something was off.

Clay-soiled walls surrounded the rest of the pantry. Upon inspecting the area, he found ample rubble and dirt at one of the partitions' bases. Learning from his recent experience in the library, he knew not to underestimate his aunts' craftiness to keep things hidden.

He leaned his ear against the clay-sealed barrier and knocked his fist against it, producing a faint echo. *That shouldn't be possible.* An open space where sound waves can travel without obstruction is essential for reflecting sound. A pantry carved into the ground should be surrounded by dense earth *unless* another open chamber was on the other side.

Listening intently, he knocked again, pressing his ear tight against the dirt surface. Something stirred on the other side of the clay. It sounded like a voice. *Or voices.*

He ran his fingertips against the hardened clay, a tingling sensation surged through him. Low murmurs of an unfamiliar language floated through his mind. Driven by fascination, he duplicated what he'd done at the witch's door. Placing both hands against the wall, he focused his intentions, commanding the wall to open. The underground pantry shook; dust trickled from the ceiling and into his hair. And with an ear-splitting rumble, the barrier collapsed at his feet, revealing a room bathed in a soft light.

Birk burst into laughter, his eyes alight. Driftstone's prophecy at the witch's door wasn't a fluke; he *was* Magic-Born—*this changed everything.*

Exhilarated, he took a moment to notice the grand hallway of doors, an exact replication of the one in his vision. Seven doors, each unique in its properties, promised entry to unknown destinations. Taking a cautious step into the center of the chamber, he was overcome with awe.

"Traveler," "He's here," "Storyteller," "Come in," "We've waited for you," "The Storyteller," "Do not be afraid."

A chorus of whispers inundated him, each voice a different octave and volume, creating a disorienting cacophony. He stepped back, suspicious he was no longer alone.

"H-hello? Is someone there?"

"Yes," "Storyteller," "Welcome," "We're here to help—" "Find your destiny—" "Traveler," "What do you seek?"

Birk spun; he couldn't escape the feeling someone else was with him. The voices came from over his shoulders and behind his back, yet there was no sign anyone else was in the room. *Were the doors talking to him?*

"Yes, we can speak," "Read your heart—" "Storyteller," "Your desires," "Do not be afraid," "You should turn back—" "Come closer!"

He jumped; he'd not spoken his thought aloud.

"Find your power—" "Claim your birthright," "—carry you to your legacy," "Choose your path," "Storyteller," "Choose your destiny," "Pick your door."

The doors invaded his mind, each vying for his attention. Seducing him with promises and temptations, they competed and pressed him. His eyes flitted from one door to the next, seeking to understand the choices offered. A crescendo of clashing calls sent him over the edge. Cupping his hands over his ears, he screamed, "STOP!"

The voices ceased.

"Please—stop. I can't hear myself think," Birk lowered his voice. "I'm not ready to make a decision. I don't even know if I *will* make a decision. I don't understand what you are or know where any of you lead."

"Driftstone" "You must choose—" "You are the Storyteller." "All doors lead to Driftstone." "Destiny awaits." "We will guide—" "Let us help you."

Reaching behind him, Birk removed the Driftstone from his waistband and reviewed the riddle for clues.

The first door, made of solid stone, drew his attention. It spoke of answers, destiny, and one's true fate—all things Birk was desperate to find. However, it also carried more troubling lines, alluding to nightmares and death.

He put his hand out to touch it; the rocks rattled. He quickly retracted when he heard the howl of the wind. A flash of dark mountain tops, wailing black creatures, and nightmares from his visions sent him stumbling back. He wasn't sure he was brave enough to face what was on the other side.

"Nightmares, yes," "—but all the answers you seek," "Bravery is required," "—path to fate," "—great love—" "Others are waiting for you—" "Destiny."

Birk digested the words and moved to the second; it emanated warmth and familiarity. This door's whispers swayed him with camaraderie, understanding, and even the potential of love. The magic growing inside him stirred. The roots and trees surrounding the door writhed and swayed, beckoning him closer.

The fourth door held no interest for him. It was cold, iron, and foreboding, locked in chains. Whatever was ticking and whizzing inside could stay there.

He was also wary of the door formed from swirling water. The shadows swimming behind it left him uneasy.

The third entrance, made of crystal, and the sixth, made of ice, were both enchanting in appearance, but neither offered the rewards he sought. The seventh, crafted from sand, appealed to him with the lure of prophetic visions. Insights into his future could be valuable.

"If I go through one of these doors, will a door on the other side lead me back?"

"We cannot say" "Always a risk to the traveler—" "Doors shouldn't open—" "—never return," "—find your way back—" "Choose your—" "Only you can decide."

Unhelpful.

He hadn't planned on walking through any of the doors when he first entered, but now he wondered if this was why he was led here. One of these doors may lead to answers.

However, the uncertainty of leaving the people he loved gnawed at his conscience. Should he trust the voices promising a new path? Or should he cling to the fragile hope of staying close to Pan, even if it meant facing uncertainty or more deceit?

The thought of abandoning his family to pursue his destiny twisted like a knife in his gut.

His decision had a broader impact than just his fate. The doors implied others needed him, lying outside Balincia's borders.

Was it the girl from his visions? Would any of these doors lead to her? And what about those he'd leave behind—Pan, Talbot, and Ravenshire? His aunt created the doors for a reason. *Why?* Maybe her goal was always to travel through them; perhaps she was also searching for answers. If he waited, maybe they could go together.

"Can more than one person go through a door? Am I able to bring someone with me?" he asked aloud.

"Magic-Born," "Only the Magic-Born—" "Destiny for you," "Cannot share your—" "—dangerous for others," "Magic-Born," "Do not wait."

So, only those born with magic could travel through the doors, eliminating Talbot and Ravenshire. Would Pan even go with him? No, she wouldn't leave her sister. Balincia and Edi would need her—the scales needed to remain balanced.

If he didn't leave, there was no guarantee he'd ever find the truth. Talbot would live in suspicion; other family members would be forced to live to Edi's will. Balincia would be a prison and a façade.

If he could defeat what Edi feared or prove her instincts wrong, he might have a chance of saving her from herself, freeing them all; a lot can change in ten thousand years.

"Others are waiting," "Lost souls," "Embrace your power," "Own your truth," "Storyteller," "Your true purpose lies ahead." "Make your choice," the doors urged.

If he left now, he could avoid Pan and Talbot, who would attempt to dissuade him. They'd be hurt and worried at first, but as surrogate guardians, he believed they'd understand. If they were working together, he trusted them to keep Balincia safe. And if he returned, *no, when he returned*, he'd bring home answers.

"Balincia needs you—" "Leave now," "Answers await at" "—fates intertwined," "Do not wait," "Trust your instincts," "Storyteller."

Birk struggled to make a decision. Each option was like a diverging path in a forest, each with its own consequences. He decided, if fate brought him here, it should also choose for him. He knelt on the floor and extended his arm to connect with the island, willing it to show him the way. The chamber shuddered, and the floor beneath him cracked,

creating fractures and fissures in the earth that traveled from his hand to the base of the stone door.

"You have chosen," "Storyteller," "True fate lies—" "Open the door," "Be brave," "Traveler," "Destiny awaits."

With a silent nod, he stood; the decision was made. His features softened, and a determination set in. Unprepared, he carried only the Driftstone with him. Every comfort, every relationship, everything he knew or held dear would be left behind.

He reflected on his stories and the heroes who ventured into the uncharted, with only their wits and faith as companions. He once read, *"One can only be considered brave if he is willing to lose everything."*

He reached for the door.

"I promise I'll return," he whispered into the room.

SIXTEEN

A TEARFUL GOODBYE

"Birk!" Edi's voice broke the spell of voices emanating from the door. Lowering his hand, Birk spun to find his aunts standing over the remains of the crumbled wall.

"Birk, what are you doing?" Edi asked, taking slow and cautious steps into the room.

"What is this place? Where do these doors lead?" Birk's voice shook; Edi's presence was a surprise.

"It doesn't matter," Edi's response was curt and urgent. "Even though I'd also appreciate an explanation," she added, under her breath to Pan. "You need to step away from that door this instant."

"Ignore the witch," "She deceives you," "Mind stealers," "Open the door, Storyteller," "She fears the truth," "Your power," "Open the door!"

The voices returned, hissing louder. The stones on the door knocked against one another, dislodging chunks of rock scattered across the dirt floor.

Pan's attention shifted between the door, Birk, and the book strapped to his waistband.

"Birk, I won't repeat myself." Edi gritted, attempting to take control of the situation. "Step away from the door now so we can discuss this calmly. This *isn't* a request."

"Or *what*? Will you attempt to erase my mind again? I promise I won't make it so convenient for you this time," Birk shouted, finding his voice again. "I remember *everything*. Do you think I'd ever trust you again? I'm only standing here because Pan protected me."

Edi glared at her twin, hit with a realization, "You . . . it's been *you* all day. How could I be so blind? The touch of your chaos magic was everywhere. Was this your intent? To lead the boy here? *What is all of this?*"

Pan entreated her sister, shaking her head, "I've nothing to do with Birk finding his way here. I'd never put him or Balincia in danger. Yes, I protected him from the enchantment because I can't bear what we do anymore, Edi. He's—" She paused, catching herself. "I couldn't infringe on his mind any more than I could yours."

"But you *were* responsible for today's events? The chaos at the docks? *The lunch?*" Edi's mind raced. "This explains everyone's odd behavior; you weakened the enchantment and sent me to face them alone. I can't believe you'd do this to me, *your twin*. Forgive me; you don't get to free yourself of accountability and frame me as the villain."

"Edi, I didn't tamper with or disable anyone's enchantment. I understand the consequences." She lowered her voice. "I've seen visions in my sleep—the fall of Balincia. They made me think of Cyrus's work. I've been trying to manufacture a way for us to leave if needed."

"What?" Edi gasped. "Why didn't you tell me? I thought you blocked yourself from the Dreamscape."

"I did; they were sent to me; I don't know by whom . . . an urgent feeling, a rush of images, a warning. We must connect with our siblings; we've been cut off from them for far too long." She took her sister's hands and confessed, "I did throw in a little chaos magic this morning to take advantage of your distractions; I needed more time to test my theories before sharing this with you." *Partially true—the entirety more complex, and now wasn't the time.*

"This needs to be shut down; you've invited danger to our home.

We're supposed to be in balance with each other; everyone's *lives depend on it*. Now, look at where we are," Edi gestured to Birk.

"What were you working on? Where do these doors lead?" Birk interrupted, drawing his aunts' attention back to him. "There is someone or something behind them. I can sense it—them—whatever it is. They're speaking to me, imploring me to travel through them."

"Don't listen to those voices!" Pan beseeched. Birk's disclosure frightened her; the doors never spoke to her. Portals exhibited their own form of sentience as conduits between different realms or dimensions. They could be cooperative or resistant, based on the will and intention of the traveler. In the past, her brother Cyrus was the only sibling who understood their language. If they were beckoning Birk, it meant they had an intention—it also indicated *he was manifesting powers beyond her capabilities.* "Tune them out if you can. I know we haven't earned your trust as of late, but you must believe us."

"*Liars,*" "*—since your birth,*" "*Deceivers,*" "*Imprisoned your potential,*" "*—taken advantage of your trust and abused you with—*" "*Deceived you,*" "*Deceived everyone,*" "*You are no longer safe here,*" the voices derided, a darker undercurrent emerging.

"*No longer protected,*" "*You must open the door,*" "*Balincia is in danger,*" "*—Fate's hand will guide you,*" "*—webs of deception,*" "*They fear your awakening,*" "*hinder your potential,*" they warned, continuing their vicious assault.

"The voices are telling me Balincia is in danger. I want to find the truth, and they're promising answers." Birk declared, staring at the stone threshold.

"Let us find them together," Pan begged.

"You've lied to me my entire life; how can I believe anything you'd share? You speak about the welfare of your people but treat them as cattle. What have you done to the other guests to be here now? What have you done to Talbot? Where is he?" he demanded.

"How dare you speak to us in this fashion?" Edi's voice rose, and her skin cracked with magic. "We love you. We have raised you as our own, but don't forget for a minute that we aren't only your aunts—we *are*

witches. *You* have no authority to question our decisions on our people's behalf. You won't hurl accusations at us within our own homes. You *will* respect us."

Birk scoffed, "You literally tried to alter my mind hours ago for the crime of curiosity. I think you've lost any moral high ground. Am I not allowed to have my own ideas and opinions?"

"Not when your ideas and opinions can potentially put lives at risk," Edi retorted.

"Are you listening to yourself? You justify your actions based on *potential* outcomes, thereby reinforcing there *are* possible alternatives. If something is endangering our lives, don't we get a say in how we want to face it?"

"Birk, what is the book in your waistband? You held it with you in the library. Where'd you get it?" Pan interjected, taking slow steps toward him.

"Book? What book?" Edi fumed.

Backing away from Pan, Birk kept his distance. "I received it from an old woman at the market; she's . . . not from Balincia . . . at least, I don't think she is. I've never seen her before." Taking the Driftstone from his waist, he held it, protecting it.

"What's in the book?" Pan pressed.

"It was blank when I received it, but it speaks to me through pictures and texts, communicating in visions. I think it's responsible for disabling your enchantment. It allows me to see things in ways I couldn't before. It led me to these doors."

"You took an *unauthorized* magic book from a *stranger*? Where is this woman? Your aunt and I would be alerted if someone outside Balincia entered; we have wards preventing such things." Edi exchanged a swift, worried look with her sister. "Give us the book, Birk."

"No. The book was gifted to me for a reason." Tightening his grip around the Driftstone, he took another step back. Eyeing the stone portal, he tried to determine if he was quick enough to run for it without his aunts intervening.

"I've had enough! Give *me* the book." Shooting her hand out, she summoned the book, yanking Birk along with it toward her.

"No!" he shouted, digging his feet into the ground. He strained against his aunt's magic. The underground chamber vibrated around them. His feet burrowed into the earth, halting his momentum. *Or was the earth rising to hold and aid him?* Given the astonished look on his aunts' faces, he wondered if it was the latter.

Edi's eyes flew open with alarm, prompting her to temper the situation quickly. His burgeoning magic was an unexpected escalation of events. His raw inexperience and emotions could spiral things out of control if she didn't end this now.

"Birk, you need to calm down. This book has awakened innate magic in you," Pan panicked. "Please give Edi the book. We can help you. We're only trying to protect you."

"Protect me? You keep using that word as if it nullifies everything you've done. *Protect me from what?* Who is protecting me from *her*?"

"Enough!" Lowering her arms, Edi was exhausted from the tug of war. This would require a different approach. "Something inside of you *is* awakening. I have no idea how these abilities reside in you, but you aren't familiar enough with them to control them, nor do we understand their origins. In your state, you could bring the whole palace down on our heads by accident."

"You employed your magic against me; what's the difference?"

"The difference is we have centuries of experience using our magic, and *you* were never in danger. I'm not going to stand here and argue. This ends now," she declared, lifting her face; her voice thundered across the underground tunnel. "You've left me no choice—there are still lessons for you to learn, Birk."

Casting her arms forward, streaks of white-hot magic flew from her fingertips, crashing into Birk's chest. The earth holding his feet exploded, flinging his body across the room and slamming him into the iron door. Clutching the Driftstone against his chest, he curled into a ball, yelling in agony; his body pulsed with fire.

Turning on her sister, Pan screamed. "Stop this! You're hurting him!"

"He is only hurting himself by resisting. I take no pleasure in this,

Pan, but you know as well as I do that if Birk goes through the door, everything we have built and protected could be lost. I'd never inflict anything he couldn't recover from."

While Pan distracted Edi's attention, Birk attempted to crawl back to the stone door. Thrusting his hand against the ground, it wrapped around his fingers, steadying him and dragging him closer to the gateway; his other arm clung to the Driftstone.

"Birk is right, Edi. Our way isn't working. This is why I built the doors. I understand they aren't tested or ready, but *maybe this is a sign.* If others are calling to him, maybe it's our siblings. What if the world has changed?"

Edi refused to look at Pan. She thought of Balincia and what came before Balincia. She remembered the deaths and the destruction. She remembered her vows to protect her sister and those in her care. "I'm sorry. We can't risk losing order."

When he reached for the door, Edi struck him again, doubling down; she held him, unflinching, tears descending her statuesque face.

Birk howled as the magic fire coursed through his body, making it impossible for him to move. Struggling to lift his head, he found Pan's eyes and pleaded with her.

"Auntie Pan, you once told me some rules were meant to be broken. You told me I could use *my* discernment."

The air in the room tugged and pulled around them. Debris of dirt, wood, and rock floated and whipped around the cavernous hall. Birk recognized this magic, Pan's—the atmosphere was changing with her emotions.

"If you walk through the door, Birk, there's no guarantee you'll find your way back. There are dangers out there you're not prepared to face. Are you willing to leave everything and everyone familiar to you behind? Are you willing to accept the risk and the consequences?" Keeping her eyes frozen to his, she waited for his words.

Continuing to pin Birk with her magic, Edi ignored Pan, taking slow and cautious strides toward him; there wasn't much time left.

"I'm ready to be the author of my own story. I accept the risks that come with it. You, out of everyone, should understand this."

Nodding, she closed her tear-filled eyes. Tilting her head slowly, she jerked it back, instigating the winds to smash her sister into the stone wall, knocking her out cold.

The roar of the gales stopped, and everything came crashing to the floor. Immediately crawling to her twin, she lay Edi's head on her lap. Caressing her face, she stroked Edi's hair and cried.

Exhausted, Birk slid his body across the ground and sat beside her, taking her hand. "Thank you. I'm sorry. I didn't want this to happen."

"I know you didn't. We should apologize to you." Pan paused, "We both love you more than you know." Birk glanced at Edi, doubtful. "Yes, *even* Edi. Our secrets, magic, and laws were never meant to hurt anyone. Everything was built to keep us safe."

"I still don't understand?" Birk confessed.

"Well, if you plan to still walk through the door, *which I suggest you do before Edi wakes up*, I have no doubt you'll find the answers you seek. I wish I had more time to tell you everything, but sometimes learning things ourselves is important. We all view life through the skewed lens of our experiences, no matter how true our intentions may be."

Pausing, Pan leaned into Birk. Placing her head on his shoulder, she squeezed his hand. "Birk, be aware; sometimes, the truth we seek isn't what we hope to find; it can raise more questions. When you find what you seek, I only ask that you remember us with grace as you reflect upon our choices. We must do our best with what we understand at the time."

"So, is it true? If I walk through the door, I may never be able to return?"

"In full transparency, I'm not sure, *but* I've taught you that unpredictability is when we accomplish some of our best work." Pan winked, trying to encourage a bit of levity. "I promise you, if there isn't a way, I'll build one."

"Thank you . . . for everything." Birk softened his voice. "I want you to know I'm doing this for us, for all of us; I'll make you proud."

"I'm already proud of you," Pan said, taking his wrist. "Before you

go, I have something for you." She pulled a bracelet from her pocket, braided with dyed emerald leather. Pulling out a few strands of her hair, she wrapped and bonded them with an incantation. "Keep this on your wrist, always. If there is a way back, it will help you to find me, and I to find you."

She threw her arms around him and clung to his neck. "Be brave, Birk. Be as strong as your namesake. I pray your destiny finds you," she whimpered in his ear. "Now go, quickly. Edi is stirring; you don't want to be around when she wakes."

Throwing his satchel onto his shoulder, he kissed his aunt's cheek goodbye one more time before making his way to the stone door. Reaching to open it, he paused, glancing back at his aunt one final time. "Auntie, I have one more question."

"FIINE!" she said, playfully rolling her eyes. "But make this your last."

"Do you still love me?"

Pan teared. "Oh, sweet boy, I love you even more."

Returning her smile, Birk reached out to the stone door. The rocks rolled away, revealing a dark passage. He wrapped one hand around his aunt's bracelet, closed his eyes, and stepped through.

"Pandi, what have you done?" Edi moaned, rousing to consciousness.

"I did the only thing I could."

PART
TWO

SEVENTEEN

Nightmares

Birk stood on a mountain path near snow-covered peaks. Disoriented, he remembered nothing about his arrival. After walking through the stone door, he found himself deposited here, with the gateway vanishing into the night as if it had never existed.

The twin moons lit the forest trail ahead. He wondered if he was close to reaching the top of the Cosimo Mountains. The wind's chill cut through him like knives, reminding him he was unprepared. He should've paid more attention to Talbot's concerns about his wardrobe, not to mention his lack of food, supplies, or defensive gear.

The Driftstone and his wits were going to have to suffice.

His breath hung in the cold air, and he pulled his cloak tighter. Basic needs pushed him forward; finding shelter and warmth were going to be essential to survive his first night. He didn't leave home to give in to discomfort. Many challenges awaited, and he wasn't about to fail his first test.

He headed down the path stretched out before him, searching for cover from the biting cold. If he found a cave or a hollowed-out trunk, he could burrow there for the night. With rest and the rising suns, his options were bound to look different in the morning. There was no point in stumbling blind.

The howling wind muffled his footsteps on the blanket of snow, breaking the evening's silence. Shadows flickered at the edges of his vision, gnawing at his unease. He jolted at every sinister snap of a branch. Nocturnal creatures scurried in the darkness, and leaves rustled in the cold storm, conjuring images of his nightmares.

He walked faster.

His heart pounded against his chest, and intrusive thoughts of being stalked and trailed by silent predators overwhelmed him. Descending the trail, he came upon a cluster of sequoias, their towering forms casting long shadows that obscured his view.

There was a fleeting glimpse of movement among them. *Did one of the trees step toward him?* He dismissed it, a trick of the mind brought on by his mounting paranoia and the falling snow. Still, he remained rooted to the spot, hesitant to move. Suspicious, he held his breath; the hairs on his arms stood on end.

In a moment of surreal horror, one of the colossal sentinels lurched onto the path ahead of him, separating from the grove.

The tree grew, doubling the size of the others in the forest, its dark form stretching toward the midnight sky. What once appeared as misshapen branches revealed themselves as a nightmarish array of twisted horns at the tree's top. Long appendages with razor-sharp claws sprouted from its body. Searing crimson eyes sprang open and stared at Birk, causing him to slip and fall on the ice. A gaping maw split open, completing the frightening face. It unleashed a primal howl, displaying a mouth full of foaming fangs. The redwood's feral roar reverberated through the woods, sending Birk into a frenzied scramble.

Finding his footing, he raced back up the trail from which he came. He panicked as the creature's monstrous strides devoured the distance between them. With each landing of its clawed feet, the force of the beast's weight sent rocks tumbling down the peaks to his left.

The monster's long arms plunged into the snow, attempting to snare Birk. He jumped—narrowly evading their crooked clutch, his agility proving his only defense. Dodging and weaving between the creature's colossal legs, he avoided its claws' manic attempts at contact.

Realizing he couldn't keep to the open path, he sought cover. Veering sharply into the thicket to his right, he hoped it would shield him from the beast's pursuit. Branches lashed out at his face, and the heavy snow impeded his flight. Tripping over roots, he had difficulty remaining upright.

Destruction echoed through the forest behind him. He heard the disturbing sounds of trees being uprooted and hurled aside. Enormous trunks soared over his head, crashing into rocks and splintering explosively around him.

The forest's inhabitants fled in terror with him while their homes were ravaged. Foxes and rabbits outpaced him; birds frantically took to the skies, and squirrels leapt across the high ceiling of the trees. Above him, a swarm of ravens descended upon the towering shadow beast. A storm of black feathers and piercing caws, diving and clawing at its face. Enraged, the creature swiped at the birds, their assault goading it into a frenzy.

Using the distraction to flee further into the woods, Birk hoped to lose his pursuer. Instinctively, he reached out to the nature around him, his untamed magic pleading for the forest's help, waking a connection between them. The trees responded, arching their branches above him, clearing a path for him to escape. With each step, the roots responded, obediently retracting into the ground, ensuring his route remained unhindered.

A new threat emerged—another dark beast, four-legged and wild. It bound through the forest toward him, closing their gap. Its dark fur was matted and unkempt. Black foam dripped from its mouth. Sensing the creature gaining proximity, Birk wheeled mid-stride. Extending his arm behind him, he projected his magic into the surrounding trees, begging them to protect him.

The boughs colluded and snapped back at the foul beast, the forest rising to its defense. The roots surged back up from the earth and wrapped around the creature's legs, prompting it to stumble and crash. Birk pushed forward, his sight fixed on a distant opening.

Snow crunching under his boots, he burst into a clearing and spotted

a river nearby. Quickly formulating a plan, his best chance was to reach the water and cross it. From there, he might be able to escape the creatures and hide in the ridge of the canyons, visible on the opposite side. Racing toward the river's edge, the beasts closed in behind him.

Adrenaline filled his body, pushing the limits of his endurance. To his not-too-distant left, a crinkle of movement in the tall grass signaled another presence. An indented wave in the brush rushed toward him.

You have to be kidding me!

Refusing to succumb, he took off at full speed toward the riverbank.

With the water feet away, he prepared to jump, only to have the creature hidden in the grass burst forth with vicious speed and crash into him. The force of the impact sent Birk smashing into the ground, knocking the air out of him.

Rolling to his side, he faced a grotesque hybrid of man and insect; its inky black body glistened with a sickly sheen. Twisting and undulating like a serpent, it hissed at him. Arms sprouted from its stretched belly, resembling a nightmarish centipede.

Terrified, he screamed, channeling his fear into the earth beneath them. The ground beneath the creature erupted outward, repelling the abomination. The hideous bug was hurled through the air, its inhuman form contorting into a wild arc, crashing to the ground some distance away.

Pulse drumming in his ears, Birk scrambled back to his feet, fixed on the river separating him from safety. Mustering every ounce of resolve, he plunged into the icy currents, sending a shock through his body. Needles of frozen water bit at his exposed flesh—his muscles contracted involuntarily, trying to conserve heat.

The current was fast, and the river was more robust than expected. The water swept him downstream, repeatedly pulling him under while he fought toward the distant shore. The rapids slapped against his face, draining his strength and giving him no time to think.

Using the water's momentum, he positioned his body to be pinned against a large, upcoming rock in the river's center.

Smack!

His head cracked against the surface when he slammed into the boulder. He started to bleed. Initial shock subsided; he glanced around him, only to find the four-legged beast now running alongside the riverbank, quickly gaining on his position. He prayed it couldn't swim.

Shifting his attention to the opposite bank, he splayed his hands across the giant rock. He pleaded with the stone to help him in the same way he did with the forest. Under his legs, the ground rose to meet him, slowly pushing him above the water. Larger stones emerged to the surface, creating a bridge to the other side. Clambering onto the rocks, he crawled across their slippery surface.

Collapsing on the other side, he rolled onto his back, eyeing the far bank. The fur-covered beast paced back and forth, growling at him. For a few seconds, Birk thought his plan worked. Propping onto his elbows, he monitored the creature's movements on the water's edge, noting its hesitation.

A tortured wail bellowed from the trees. He swiveled to watch the giant tree beast stomp into the clearing. The mammoth creature roared, extending its appendage, and pointed at Birk. The four-legged beast turned to face its companion, howling back at him, before directing its attention back to Birk.

It hunched and bared its teeth.

The lupine leaped forward, crossing half the distance of the river. Its legs skidded and steadied against the same giant boulder Birk used. Terrified, Birk pushed himself backward. Clenching his fists in the soil, he yelled into the cold night air.

The stones heeded his cry and answered, sliding back into the depths of the water. The beast ran, realizing the foundation was sinking; it jumped to cross the remaining divide. Fortunately for Birk, nature was on his side. The waters, dammed minutes ago, rushed forward in a wave of rapids, slamming into the beast, pulling it under the water and propelling it down the river.

The giant tree shadow raged. Leaning forward, it spat in Birk's direction.

Rotating onto his stomach, Birk ignored the creature and pulled his

body toward the canyon walls. Frozen, every muscle ached; his energy was depleted.

His aunts were right; he was unprepared to face these dangers. He was foolish to have doubted them. If this is what they were protecting Balinica from, Birk was beginning to understand their decisions. Despair outpaced his will. He inched across the ground, losing the fight within him.

From the corner of his eye, he saw the giant beast root up a sequoia and carry it over its shoulder to the riverbed. The slithering abomination had reappeared and was creeping along the sides of the water, testing it with his arms. It would only be a matter of time before they found their way across the river.

Unable to lift himself, Birk gave in, curling into a ball. His thoughts drifted to his family back home, regretting his decision to leave them behind. He was going to die out here alone. Closing his eyes, he allowed his head to hit the ground. In the distance, he heard the splash of wood hitting the water; the creatures were attempting to build a bridge. They'd descend upon him soon.

The only thing keeping him awake was the warm, heavy breath sweeping across his face, prodding him to stay alert.

Wait? What?

Birk's eyes flew open to find the furry muzzle of a giant grizzly bear licking his face. Too scared to move, he lay there, the bear's slobbery, warm saliva blanketing his wounded skin. When the bear's tongue barrage finally stopped, the grizzly pulled back and huffed at him, pleased to find his eyes open.

Before Birk could react, the bear grabbed the neck of his tunic with its massive jaws and dragged him toward the canyon walls. Birk's legs kicked in resistance, much to the bear's irritation, who yanked him harder. Having no experience with bears, Birk couldn't tell if the animal was helping him or if his situation had just worsened.

The bear's strength left no room for Birk to do anything but comply until he was dropped, unceremoniously, against the wall of the ridged

canyon. Leaning against the backdrop, he watched as the grizzly focused on the dark beasts hunting him. The slithering eel-like creature was nowhere to be seen, but the branched monstrosity was crossing its makeshift bridge, angered by the bear's presence.

The bear stood upright in front of Birk and roared at the horned nightmare. With a thud, the grizzly dropped to all fours and ran off, preparing to charge the beast. Another growl came from the distance to the right; the four-legged beast had survived the river and was now advancing toward him.

A howl above Birk answered it. An enormous white wolf stood on the ridge. Honing in on the approaching furred beast, the wolf jumped from the canyon wall, rushing to confront it. Their bodies merged in midair, colliding in a flurry of motion, contesting for dominance.

The white wolf, more prominent in stature, overpowered the darker one with sheer strength. With a mighty leap, the wolf pinned the howling beast to the ground, its jaws clamping onto the creature's neck to subdue it. Despite the wolf's initial advantage, the beast was too slippery, twisting and flipping; it eventually broke free from the wolf's teeth.

In a swift counterattack, the shadow creature seized the opportunity to reverse the battle. He threw the white wolf onto its back, causing it to let loose a pained yelp. The creature relentlessly battered the canine, unleashing a savage onslaught with its razor-sharp paws.

Renewed with adrenaline from the rescuing aid of the beasts, Birk ran forward to help the vulnerable wolf. Before he could reach the fray, a sudden, sharp tug at his ankle sent him hurtling face-first onto the unforgiving ice. With alarming speed, he was dragged off through the mud, snow, and rubble, which whipped at his face and body, leaving stinging welts and bruises in their wake. Glancing back, he realized the insect and snake hybrid was responsible for this assault; its tail was constricted around his leg.

Birk tried to anchor himself, but the creature moved too quickly, and he was mercilessly yanked away toward the valley. His fingers clawed at the ground, trying to seek purchase.

Then—they came to an abrupt stop, and the slimy figure flung Birk high into the air. The world spun around him before he crashed back down, sprawled and helpless on his back.

Meanwhile, the towering beast was trying to cross the bridge he constructed from one of the redwoods. The grizzly rammed the sequoia's base with his massive frame, splintering the wood and throwing the horned giant off balance. The oversized monster lost its footing, slipping into the river. The currents swallowed the beast, and it disappeared into the churning waters, leaving the bear to redirect his focus on the wolf.

The moment was fleeting; a long arm broke the surface of the river and buried its finger into the shoreline like roots. Slow but steady, the massive creature surfaced while the bear was distracted. Letting out a primal scream, the giant grabbed the discarded tree bridge and threw it at the bear, narrowly missing. Unfazed, the bear stood on its hind legs, fur bristling, and responded with another deafening roar.

Across the valley, Birk was in a life-and-death struggle.

The leviathan creature's mutated form slithered up his body with unnerving speed, trapping him in a ruthless vise. Its centipede legs punctured his flesh as it ascended. Twisted versions of human forearms popped out of its wormy core and wrapped around his neck, constricting his airways. The creature snapped hungrily at him, its jaws dripping with corrosive saliva, searing his skin.

Birk's fists slid off the slimy creature. Pushing his elbow in front of its face, he attempted to prevent the beast from consuming him. Tapping into the last of his reserves, Birk held the creature back with one arm, wrenched a large stone from the earth with his other and brought it crashing upon the beast's insectoid head. The monster hissed in response, releasing its suffocating hold on Birk's throat, and tumbled off him.

Birk used his momentum to roll with the creature, straddling it on the ground. Its many legs tore apart his tunic, slicing his chest as it fought back. Birk wrapped his hands around the creature's throat and mustered his remaining strength to push the beast into the ground.

The earth around him quaked. A ring of standing stones sprouted from the valley, pushing their way through the frozen dirt and surrounding

them. Their surfaces were covered in mud, and their faces were carved with runes. The beast thrashed, tortured by their presence.

Birk held firm; blood dripped from his head wound like sweat. The ground beneath him began to sink and swallow both of them. The creature panicked, feeling itself being pulled into the muddy depths; it fought harder. Birk clung to the shrinking form, elbow-deep in mud, refusing to let go until the earth claimed it.

Only when the last vestiges of the creature disappeared did Birk release his hold. His arms shook. With one final burst of energy, he yanked free from the earth's grip—the standing stones looking down on him in a silent vigil.

In the distance, he could hear the dying sounds of battle among the other beasts. He attempted to stand, but his legs buckled beneath him. Darkness clouded his vision, and as his mind faded to unconsciousness, it collected the last images of the approaching silhouettes of a bear, a wolf, and . . . a man.

DRIFTING

Floating in the shallow depth of semi-consciousness, a bone-deep cold gnawed at Birk, generating an uncontrollable shiver. Blood from his wounds congealed against the unforgiving ice. Strands of hair encrusted with rime stuck to his face, adding to the numbing sensation weighing him down. His vision darkened.

He barely registered the soft crunch of snow behind him. A voice floated in and out of his fading awareness. The unsettling presence of large animals sniffed around him. A warm breath enveloped his face, and a tongue explored his wounds. Gentle fingers brushed away the hair from his brow, and the lift of solid arms encircled him, carrying him away.

A voice broke through the emptiness, whispering promises of safety in his ear. Light blinked around him. He was immersed in a warm fluid. The tension and pain plaguing his body melted away, leaving him adrift.

He was wrapped in warmth, broken by brief moments of awareness. His cheek rested against soft, furry skin. The steady beat of a heart eased his mind. The scent of pine and musk filled his nostrils. Strong arms held him close, offering a sense of safety. He pressed into the hold and drifted into a more peaceful sleep.

His eyelids fluttered, catching a faint image of a crackling fire, an agile figure moving around the flames, tending it with purpose. The aroma of stew filled the air, and the quiet padding of paws shuffled behind him, casting shadows against a cavern wall. Feeling safe, he allowed his body to fall back to sleep.

NINETEEN

THE BEAR, THE MAN, AND THE WOLF

Birk's eyes squinted open, gradually adjusting to the fire's soft glow, illuminating the small cave. His head throbbed while he tried to piece together fragments of his memory. The fear, the nightmares hunting him, and others coming to his aid.

There had been a bear and a wolf?

He remembered he was dying from his wounds, lying on the ice.

Someone carried him to this cave.

He sat up quickly and assessed his current situation. Throwing back the animal skins covering him, he was shocked to find himself naked—his wounds dressed and healing. He placed his hand on the bandages and examined them. They were clean, and except for a bit of bruised tenderness, he couldn't feel the puncture wounds underneath them.

He shouldn't have been able to sit up so fast. How long had he been asleep? And where were his clothes?

He covered back up. His gaze fell on a slumbering bear in the corner. Panicked, he took a moment to breathe. *Was this the bear who saved him?*

Propping his back against a large piece of sanded-down timber, Birk took in his surroundings. The cave was a cozy alcove; animal skins and patterned, colorful textiles decorated the floor. An iron pot dangled above the flames of the fire. His stomach growled, catching the scent of stew.

A crude wooden table stood against one of the walls, laden with provisions. Wooden bowls, carrots, potatoes, and an array of leafy herbs and greens sat in a jumble. Alongside the table, an assortment of well-used axes and knives rested next to a pair of waterskins and worn leather boots.

Scattered parchments and recently used candles lay randomly around. Handmade pants and parkas made from animal skins and fur were piled in a corner; skinned rabbits and a pheasant hung from the ceiling. This cave was someone's home.

He decided to search the clothes for his belongings, but was interrupted by an approaching sound. Turning his head to the entrance, a man around Birk's age stepped in, naked and dripping wet, accompanied by a large white wolf. His chest and legs were covered with hair. "I'm glad to see you're awake. Winter and I were worried about you."

The man was tall, with a strong build highlighted by intimidatingly thick thighs and calves. Birk stammered for words; his face turned red. He focused on the fur modestly covering his body. "Confused, sore . . . grateful. Who . . . who are you? What happened?"

A smile played on the man's lips. "I'm Grey. With the assistance of Brunt, the big guy in the corner," motioning to the bear, "and Winter, we rescued you from the arcanivores. They were about to take your life. Although I must give you credit, you took one down alone."

"Arcanivores? Is that what they're called?" Birk's gaze once again involuntarily dropped, his cheeks on fire.

He was uncomfortable sitting on the ground, staring up at the man.

Crossing the cave, Grey pulled a cloth from the table and dried himself with his back positioned to Birk. "That's what people call them; I'm unaware of a formal name. I've been tracking them since they passed my village. They're new and foreign to this part of the world."

Self-conscious and still clad only in fur, Birk continued to fidget.

Turning around, Grey finally recognized Birk's underlying discomfort and explained, "The beasts tore apart your garments. I removed them to tend to your wounds. I've some spare clothes you can wear, although they might be a little loose."

To Birk's relief, Grey tossed him some clothes from the pile, which he gratefully scrambled into. "Thank you. I confess I'm a little embarrassed."

"I should apologize; I'm afraid I forget the social boundaries of modesty when I'm out here. You have to understand, a wolf and a bear raised me. I didn't learn to adapt to more *appropriate* norms until my foster mother, Shayvonne, took me in."

"How'd you survive without clothes? Don't you get cold in this weather?" Birk asked, feeling more at ease when Grey finally slipped into some trousers.

Grey laughed again, drying his dark, shoulder-length hair. His unabashed abandon was both off-putting and charming. He took Birk's hand and held it against his light brown chest. "Do you feel that?"

Birk drew a breath. He *did* feel something, in fact, several things at once.

Grey's heartbeat was the one he'd heard in his sleep. *Perfect. He'd slept with his face smashed against this man, probably drooling.* The hairs on Grey's chest must've been what he burrowed into when he was half-conscious. *This was becoming more humiliating by the second.*

But it was the warmth radiating from Grey's body that took him most by surprise; it was an unusually intense amount of heat.

"Your temperature is boiling!"

Grey laughed, prompting Birk to crack a smile. "I'm Magic-Born. My sister and I connect and communicate with wildlife. We tend to absorb some of their abilities, including the biology to adapt to different temperatures."

Birk removed his hand from Grey's chest, suddenly and painfully aware he was still touching him.

"When you were unconscious, I took you to the healing springs to tend to your wounds. Your temperature was still too low when I carried you out. I was worried we might lose you, so I did my best to keep you

warm. Skin-to-skin contact is the fastest way to raise your body temperature, especially when in direct contact with *my* skin. If I didn't keep you close all night, you might've become hypothermic." Upon seeing Birk's reaction, Grey immediately added, "There was a blanket between us to protect your modesty."

"Of course, I didn't think . . . uhm . . . what I'm trying to say is . . . thank you," a sliver of insecurity passed through him. "I'm Birk, by the way."

Grey smiled, looking relieved to be past that part of the conversation. "It's nice to meet you, Birk. I apologize if I've made you uncomfortable. It wasn't my intent."

"No, please . . . I'm just awkward and feeling a bit displaced. You've nothing to apologize for. I owe you my life."

For a moment, their eyes locked.

Grey, the first to break contact, distracted himself with the pot hanging above the fire. "I'm sure we both have questions, but let's get some food in you first, and then we can get to know each other."

Birk's stomach rumbled in response. "I'd like that."

Sitting in front of the fire with Winter curled at his feet, Birk watched Grey chop vegetables and listened to him tell his story. Running his fingers through Winter's alabaster fur, he scratched behind her ears and hung on Grey's every word.

He learned Grey's first encounter with an arcanivore was only a week ago, while he was out hunting. The creature resembled more of a man than a beast, with the same red irises and sharp talons on its fingers. When it attacked him, Grey quickly found that regular weapons were ineffective against it. No matter how often he stabbed or sliced it, the creature's body reformed and healed.

"How'd you kill it?" Birk asked.

"I didn't. I could only dismember it enough to retreat here until daylight."

"Weren't you afraid it'd follow you?"

"No. This is sacred land. It's where the blood of the Protector was spilled ages ago. No dark or evil thing can cross its boundaries."

"The Protector?"

"You don't know about the Protector?" Grey raised his eyebrows, intrigued. "He's one of the original Magic-Born, popular in this part of the world. History says he's responsible for protecting the lives of all sentient things. He was killed in the Witches' War."

Birk's aunts alluded to siblings and a war. The Protector must have been one of the brothers they lost. Opting not to share this information, he continued to probe Grey about the arcanivores.

"You mentioned you waited until daylight. Can they only travel at night?"

"As far as I know. I've never encountered them in the suns. To whom knows what foul place they disappear?" Grey walked to the iron pot, brushing in the vegetables he'd prepared while he reflected.

Joining Birk on the ground, letting the stew simmer, Grey continued his story.

"A few days after I was attacked on the mountain road, the same arcanivore, along with an antlered companion, crept into our village at night. The beasts broke into our homes, pulling screaming children from their beds and animals from their barns, sending the town into chaos.

At first, the creatures had no interest in the villagers. They were hunting someone or something in particular. They discarded them, flinging them to the floor or through windows as they ransacked a house. When the villagers defended themselves, the arcanivores' reactions became more aggressive and deadly: gutting our women, beheading our livestock, and leaving our elderly to bleed on the streets.

My home is near the mountains on the edge of town. Shayvonne and I woke to distant screams and smoke in the air. The village was burning.

I hurried into town to see if I could help, and one of those creatures stood in the middle of the street holding a small girl by her ankle. Unhinging its jaws, it swallowed the girl in one bite.

The girl was a water sprite, her powers still mostly dormant. The abom-

ination absorbed her essence after consuming her—gaining the ability to rep-licate her magic. Its form twisted and contorted, melting into a fluid puddle of black ooze, it launched at my feet.

I realized it was hunting those with magic. It had tracked me home—it was there for me.

I tried desperately to kick it off, but it coiled around my body. It was run-ning up my legs and torso faster than I could respond. I threw myself to the ground, rolling and spinning, trying to get it off. When it reached my neck, it squeezed my throat until Winter arrived with Shayvonne.

She knelt beside me, grabbed my hand, and pressed a rune from the Protec-tor in my palm. She prayed to him. The creature's response was immediate. It released me from its grip. Screaming in my ear, it untangled from me, repelled by the rune. Winter took advantage; she lunged forward, grabbed it with her teeth, ripped it from my body, and pinned it to the ground.

Rolling over with the rune, I slammed it against its chest while Winter held it down. The creature smoked and spasmed, dissolving underneath us.

Realizing the runes worked, we hunted its antlered companion and killed it."

Birk let the silence sit for a moment. At a loss for words substantial enough to respond, he settled for placing a tentative hand on Grey's knee, which was pressed against his own, for comfort.

His touch pulled Grey's mind back into the room. "In the days that fol-lowed, we installed runes outside our homes, hanging them on the street lanterns. Winter brought in a pack of wolves, who stand guard at our doors through the night. A traveler recently passed through, sharing news of sightings across the realms. They've grown in numbers in only days."

"They were hunting me because they sensed my magic?"

"They must have heightened senses, tuned to detect carriers, sniff-ing them out. From what we've been told, they'll feed on anything with magic, from tiny wizwarts or goblins to giants if they can catch one. That's why we call them arcanivores, consumers of magical beings."

Birk shuddered, "And the runes are the only thing that kills them?"

"It's the only thing *I know*. They look like they're born from dark magic; if that's the case, only light magic can hurt them. I've destroyed six since my first encounter, but it usually takes a combination of this," he handed Birk a large hunting knife, its handle carved with runes, "and the assistance of these two to bring them down." He paused and said, "The creatures are learning, getting stronger, and traveling in larger packs. The ones we encountered the other night with you were the most challenging yet."

"Is this how you killed the other two creatures attacking me?" He acknowledged the decorated knife in his hand.

"Yes, but Brunt took some damage from the big one," Grey motioned to the sleeping bear. "He'll be alright, though; he's tough."

"I don't know what I would've done if Brunt hadn't arrived when he did. He pulled me to safety and gave me the energy to get back into the fight."

"You did a surprisingly respectable job protecting yourself. Raising the ancient standing stones from the Protector's Valley was smart thinking. I didn't even realize they were there. They must've been buried since the war. You must be Magic-Born, too."

"I didn't know they were there, either. It wasn't my intent—my magic's new to me. I'm still learning about a lot of things," Birk confessed.

Grey decided this would be an excellent place to pause the conversation and scooped the stew into the bowls. "Why don't we take a break from talking about somber things? Instead, let's celebrate. Our paths crossing has been fortuitous."

Grey ladled out steaming bowls of rabbit stew, and the inviting aroma mixed with the woodsmoke from the fire. Seeing the hunger in Birk's eyes, he served him a generous portion first, before attending to his faithful animal companions. Rousing Brunt from his sleep, he poured a hefty amount into a bucket, scooping the remains of the rooted vegetables on top. Winter, not forgotten, was given one of the skinned rabbits. She chose to take it outside to enjoy alone.

Two days without eating left Birk's rumbling stomach ravenous. The

tender rabbit meat and savory herbs rivaled even Saffrona's finest dishes. When his hunger dissolved into contentment, he returned for seconds and thirds, infusing his fatigued body with new energy.

A smile crept into the corner of Grey's mouth while he watched Birk finish his third bowl. "Did you get enough?" he poked lightly.

Embarrassed, Birk greedily shoveled in his last bite. "Yes, thank you. I can't remember the last time I ate so much. It's possibly the best meal I've ever had," he said, wiping his mouth with his sleeve.

A loud belch came from Brunt in agreement, triggering laughter.

"Ha! I think it has more to do with your delirious state of hunger than my cooking. I could've given you one of Winter's rabbit bones to gnaw on, and you'd be just as pleased. You required the sustenance." Grey responded, collecting the bowls and placing them on the table. "I'll take the compliment, though."

Rejoining Birk on the floor, Grey sat cross-legged in front of him. "Tell me more about you. What brought you into the mountains last night? Not many travelers pass through here."

Birk hesitated to share too much, despite the hospitality. He was a stranger in this land and worried that if he shared too much, he'd put himself or his home in danger. After all, most of his aunts' and Talbot's warnings were already proving true, and it'd only been a few days.

He considered the man in front of him. He'd saved his life—dressed his wounds, provided shelter, and fed him. Who'd put so much effort into dragging someone back to their cave and nursing them to health, only to have nefarious intentions?

Maybe Birk was naïve, but as physically imposing as Grey was, he didn't give off disingenuous energy. There was a charitable mildness to his demeanor, similar to an oversized puppy.

He *was* in *his* home, and he owed him the truth; more than that, he wanted to be transparent with him. He left Balincia because of the lies and secrets. If he were to be true to what he believed, shouldn't he lead with honesty? Throwing caution aside, he decided to place his faith in the kindness of the stranger in front of him and hoped he wouldn't bite back.

"I'm not sure where to start."

"Why don't you begin by telling me where you're from?" he encouraged.

Thankful for the prompt, Birk began painting a picture of his home. Unsurprisingly, Grey had never heard of Balincia, so he leaned in as Birk regaled tales of his aunts, their palaces, and growing up on the Royal Isle. Defaulting to performance mode, he shared anecdotes about Talbot, Ravenshire, and the townships and found himself enjoying Grey as his audience.

The way he'd throw his head back to laugh or how his eyes lit at colorful descriptions encouraged Birk to draw out his stories. When Birk explained Balincia's laws, Grey wrinkled his nose, indicating he had an opinion but chose not to interrupt. His expressions were contagious.

When Birk neared the night of the festival in his story, dread suddenly prompted him to stand in a panic. *"The Driftstone!"*

"What? What is it?" Grey rose to his feet alarmingly fast.

"Uhm . . . this book. I carried it with me in my satchel. I lost it when I was running from the . . . I can't remember what you called them—*those things*. We have to go back. I have no way to—"

"It's ok," Grey interrupted, touching his arm. "I saved it. Winter found it after she searched the area for more beasts. I assumed it belonged to you." Walking over to the corner of the cave, he pulled out Birk's satchel and handed it to him. Birk's shoulders dropped in relief. "I also pulled this from your tunic when I removed your shredded garments."

Grey dropped Birk's silver pendant into his palm. "Thank you . . . I was about to share that these things mean a lot to me. They're the whole reason I'm here." Opening his leather bag, Birk pulled out the book, motioning for Grey to follow him.

Taking a seat in front of the fire, Grey sat slightly behind him, peeking over Birk's shoulder while he continued his story. Placing the book in his lap, Birk kept it closed while telling the story of his encounter with the old woman. He shared with Grey the questions she posed and how they instigated the unbinding of his enchantment, which led him here.

"And she gave you this book? You called it the Driftstone?" he probed.

"That's the book's name."

"You know you're in Driftstone, now? Don't you?" he inquired gently.

Birk's brow pushed together. "What?"

"Driftstone isn't a book. It's where we live. It's this world. Everything you see around you."

Birk was embarrassed. "I . . . here . . . let me show you. It will be easier."

Opening the book, he pointed to where the name came from and explained how the Driftstone communicates with him. He propped it against his knees and carefully turned each page, discussing their revelations. Grey scooted in and attentively listened as Birk told him about the hallways of doors, Talbot, and the betrayal of his aunts. Before either of them knew it, the minutes turned to hours, and neither noticed Birk's gradual lean against Grey.

Coming to the end of his story, Birk flipped to a blank page.

"Thank you for sharing all of this with me," Grey said, next to Birk's ear, making him suddenly aware of how close they were. "What's next? Where will you go from here?"

Birk fought the urge to create distance between them. He wasn't used to someone being so physically close to him.

"I don't know. I assumed the Driftstone—or fate—or some magical voice of destiny would guide me," he said, poking fun at himself.

Grey's body shook with another deep laugh. "It's a good thing I came across you, Birk the Storyteller. It sounds as if you require help and a plan. What are you hoping to find out here?"

It was a fair question; one Birk hadn't given enough thought to. "I'm on a quest to find the truth. I want to understand why my aunts have concealed Balincia from the rest of the world. If we're in danger, I want to remove the threat so my people can be released from their enchantments and my aunts freed from their fears." He paused. "Maybe, there's a piece of me hoping to find myself, too. It sounds foolish when I say it aloud."

"None of this sounds foolish." Grey paused, "It's also a lot to carry on your own."

Birk nodded in agreement, "I've no idea what to do now that I'm here. I almost got killed as soon as I arrived."

"The old woman wouldn't have gifted you this book unless she knew you could do something with it," Grey assured. "Trust there's a bigger picture; maybe this part of the story hasn't been revealed yet, because it's waiting for you to write it."

Birk had an idea. "Do you want to ask the book with me?"

"Will it respond with me here?"

"There's only one way to find out," Birk said, scooting back into him. "Place your right hand on the empty page," he instructed. Taking Grey's hand, he positioned it and placed his own hand on top; a spark passed between them and the book.

Grey smiled at the tickling sensation. "Now what?"

"Close your eyes and concentrate. Think about what you want the book to reveal to us."

Grey's chest rose, his body tense with focus.

"Open your eyes," Birk said, removing his hand. "The book is talking back to you."

Grey lowered his hand, letting it rest against Birk's side. Breaking into an astonished grin, he watched the ink on the page come to life. Holding their breath together, they waited for the Driftstone to complete its response.

Another map revealed itself, this time a dotted line marked a path within it.

"This is incredible," Grey reacted, awestruck. He pointed to the book and asked, "May I?"

"Of course!"

Grey traced his finger along the map. "This is where we currently are, right here, hidden inside the canyon's walls. And this village here is Everglenn. That's my home!"

"The book is showing us a route to your village? What did you ask it?"

"I concentrated on where we should go next."

"Where *we* go next?" Birk raised his brow in surprise. "You're coming with me?"

"Was that too presumptuous of me? I thought we might make a good team and—"

Birk interrupted, saving him, "I'd welcome your company on the road. I'm just surprised you'd want to join me."

"Why? Do others not enjoy your company?" Grey teased.

Birk cracked another smile, "You barely know me."

Grey raised his face. "Birk, you chose a door to lead you to your destiny—and it led you here. I'm not sure what role I'm supposed to play in all of this, but I was raised to believe when magic doors and books talk, we listen. Perhaps our fates lie together in this adventure, or perhaps our roads will diverge, but for now, I'm guided to stay with you. If for nothing else, we've a common foe in the arcanivores, and it'd be wise to stick together." He paused, elbowing Birk. "Besides, who will keep you from getting lost?"

"Together it shall be," Birk affirmed.

"The only thing I don't understand is why it's taking us on this route."

"What do you mean?" Birk asked, reviewing the map with him.

"If you look at the map *here*, this is the path I'd normally take. It's less than a day's journey. But this route—" Grey traced his finger to the far side of the page to demonstrate the distance "—is at least three days. It takes us up through the mountains before we descend."

"Hmm, strange. Do you think it's giving us a safer route? Maybe it's helping us to avoid the arcanivores?"

"The outlined route isn't easy either. It runs through giant territory. I usually try to avoid it."

"Giants?" Birk tried to contain his eagerness.

Clocking his reaction, Grey laughed, shaking his head. "I wouldn't get excited about giants. I doubt they're like the ones you've read about in your books. They can be dangerous, especially if there is more than one."

"I can't believe giants and fae and—all of this exists. I promise to be properly terrified when the time comes," he laughed.

"Alright, we'll trust the book, but *only* since you promised to be properly scared." Grey jested.

Walking back to the fire, Grey stoked it, adding more wood. "It's late; you still need rest." He reflected, "I want to take you back to the healing

springs tomorrow for one last soak before we travel. We can prepare to leave the day after tomorrow if that'll work for you. You'll also need provisions; you can't wander around with only a book and a bag."

"I'm in no rush," Birk confirmed. "I'm lucky you found me. After all, what good is a Storyteller in the forest?"

"I guess we're about to find out." Grey chuckled.

Piling up the animal skins for Birk's comfort, Grey circled the cavern, trying to make it snug. He provided Brunt a bucket of water, and the bear lapped it up before turning his back on them with a goodnight huff. Winter rejoined from outside, curling up next to Birk.

By the time Grey settled on his other side, Birk was reinvigorated about his mission. When Winter burrowed against him, forcing him closer to Grey, he didn't resist.

TWENTY

PAN'S CONFESSION

There are many misconceptions about the power of chaos. Most believe it is a disruptive and destructive force—unpredictable. The word's definition hints at confusion and disorder, an implied warning of where one might descend when rules and procedures are abandoned. Chaos is considered dangerous, altering the safe, the known, and the comfortable.

There is truth in all these understandings, particularly when considering chaos in relation to its results or impact on initial conditioning. None, however, takes a holistic account of its origin or the driving force behind it. Bestowed at birth with the powers of chaos, only Pan carried the lonely understanding of its origin—chaos magic is driven by love.

Just as minor changes can lead to dramatic shifts in chaotic systems, love can pivot the course of the world, *for better or worse*. The Witches' War didn't start with corruption or dark magic, nor did it initiate with greed, regardless of how these actions fueled or spiraled the conflict. No, it was a simple act of love that rotated Driftstone on its head, casting them all into fates unknown. An act Pan couldn't and wouldn't take back, forcing her to forever face the consequences.

Love, in its essence and manifestations, gives birth to life and creation, similar to the transformative energy and emergence of chaos in a universe. This power, gifted to Pan, spawned all living things, large and small, magic and mundane, and she considered all of them her children.

So, when her siblings abused their positions and hurt, cheated, and sought dominion over every breath she brought to life, it was the fierce love of a mother that started a war.

Years later, it was her twin's loyal love that rescued her from her rage and influenced her to submit to containment to avoid losing everything. And it was the love found in grief that pushed her to create something new and more substantial—forcing her to leave her first children behind.

But love never rests, and it never forgets.

For ten thousand years, her love simmered, held warm in its kettle, bits boiling over from time to time. Her twin was always there, ensuring it was tempered and cooled, keeping the steam from rising. Their morning tradition and chants, the laws, and the practiced regimen were all there to keep things in balance—*to keep her in balance.*

It worked for a time, but Edi couldn't comprehend a mother's deep ache and loss.

Pan was a creator; her connection to Driftstone was intimately personal, whereas Edi's gifts were catered to securing sustainability. Her sister worked with what was in front of her, and to her credit, she focused on the disciplines essential to survive each day. Pan's magic was instinctual, raw, and emotional, amalgamating past, present, and future.

It was foolish to attempt to bottle a storm; her magic couldn't be forced into routine forever.

Over the years, she allowed herself secret outlets, tooling and testing ways to return to her first home. She became obsessed with her brother Cyrus's work, *the Spell Forger*. Sneaking into her pantry late at night, she'd review his studies on portals. Unbeknownst to her, her magic slipped out while she experimented in the dark, seeping into the waters underneath her palace and spilling over the isle's edge.

Diluted, it traveled through the mist—barely registered drops blending into Crystaline Lake. Too weak to cause disturbance, it found its way into the bellies of fish and moist dew on the ground. The fish found their way into the mouths of men, and the crops absorbed the dew. Months turned into years, and the leaked magic culminated in small doses, providing an added nutrient to the diets of beasts, trees, and humans across Balincia.

The effects were subtle, starting with an itch in the back of the mind or the emergence of new ideas. Pan first became aware of the problem when an unfortunate incident happened in the farming township: two young lovers wandered into the mountains. Edi dismissed it as a hiccup, perhaps due to overdue maintenance needed in their spell work; however, Pan wasn't convinced.

When similar incidents occurred, it became apparent to her that these were symptoms of exposure to her magic. Instead of sharing this with her twin, she allowed her stalwart sister to continue believing cracks would occur if not managed diligently. Out of loyalty, she dutifully followed her directions, mending the ripped fabric of their enchantments and course-correcting the few who strayed.

However, she didn't go out of her way to report *all* infractions.

For instance, she knew Talbot had avoided their correction in the farmlands and went out of her way to ensure he was always absent during their rectification. Always faithful, he never confronted them with his questions or initiated trouble, stirring a longing in Pan for the way things used to be—before Balincia.

In her heart, she wanted the people to awaken; she wanted them to cause a little trouble, to disrupt the status quo. She wanted to be punished for her past and criticized for her present decisions. The problem was that she couldn't find it within her to betray her sister, to whom *everyone* owed their lives.

These were tough decisions every day, but to ease her pain and perhaps her guilt, she turned a blind eye to the minor disruptions. Allowing nature to take its course, she redirected her energy to the hallway of

doors, doubling her efforts. She needed to discover what became of her creations and her family, but she also agreed with Edi that Balincia had to be protected at all costs.

When the time came, she intended to travel through the doors alone, taking all the risk.

She just couldn't figure out how to return to Balincia if she traveled through the doors, and she refused to risk losing Edi forever.

One somber night, twenty-three cycles ago, under the eclipse of both moons, the grief of being torn from her first love, the children of Driftstone, caught up to her. In her garden, underneath her oak, her unbottled magic seeped from every pore while she mourned the choices before her. An emotional tempest brewed inside her, one she could no longer contain in the frail confines of a heart.

Her magic rebelled—weaving a cocoon of energy around her. Born of chaos, fed by her love and grief in equal measure—her wild magic pleaded to create. When she denied it, it retracted back into her, causing her belly to swell. The magic of Driftstone merged with her chaos magic and took shape inside her womb.

Flesh began to form, chaos sculpting a miracle: a heart, lungs, chubby fingers, and fat little toes. Never a physical mother, Pan was unprepared for the pain. The insulation muted her screams, while she beat the walls around her and prayed to Driftstone for relief.

A dam burst, and true magic occurred—a soft cry reached her ears.

When the cocoon faded away, Pan cradled a baby boy against her breast. A child conceived of magic. The first and only born from her flesh.

She named him Birk.

Birk changed everything. She abandoned her search for the outside world and sealed the hallway of doors. She dedicated her full attention to the child and committed every action to his safety and future.

With the eclipse's powers boosting her residual life-giving magic, she sealed the secrets of his origin shut. Summoning a wave of energy to pass over Balincia, she enchanted the citizens and her sister as they slept. Birk

would forever be remembered as an abandoned orphan left in their care when they awoke.

Given her twin's immunity to chaos magic, Pan relied on spell work. Birk became a hidden anomaly to avoid detection—wiped clean from every record, census, or second thought. Shamefully, Pan knew enchantments were more powerful against those who trusted the caster, and Edi would never doubt her sister.

But in her celebratory bliss, Pan overlooked the intensity of her magic and didn't realize it cracked through the protective barriers of Balincia and traveled through the veins of Driftstone. Her long-lost siblings couldn't escape its touch, and Birk was only the first in a new wave of creation.

The price to maintain balance.

Birk was granted full access to her heart and her life. When he grew into a young man, his potential for magic stirred, and she realized she couldn't conceal his true origins forever. So, she nurtured his relationship with Talbot, a guardian, to replicate a father untouched by Edi and Pan's enchantments. Her son would need someone to trust when he eventually learned the truth. Her deceptions would scar him, but she trusted those wounds would heal. Exposing his magical nature too soon, even to her sister, could endanger him and upset the balance of an already fragile Balincia.

Then came the visions: lurking enemies in the dark, floating islands plummeting from the sky, and citizens awakening and angry. Balincia was crumbling; Birk was unsafe.

Picking up where she left off, she returned to fixing the two-way travel issue with the doors. They would require adjustments for non-magical beings to pass through them, a necessary accommodation if Talbot were to accompany him.

She'd only needed a few days to work out all the kinks, but they were stolen from her.

When Edi became aware that Birk and several members of the township were breaking free from their enchantments, things became more

complicated. Struggling to adapt throughout the day, Pan conspired with Talbot to hide Birk in her palace. She had no other option but to send them on their way that evening; she'd devise a way to cloak Talbot so he could accompany her son; there was no time left to consider other options. It was unsafe for them to be in Balincia if her visions were coming true.

Fate, however, wasn't kind and karmically projected all the chaos back in her direction. When Birk found her hidden hallway, it set off a magical alarm, triggering her *and* Edi. Faster than she could react, her twin put everyone asleep in the palace, including Talbot, fearing an attack from a magical intruder. Forced to follow behind her, they hunted the magic stream to her pantry, horrified to find Birk standing at Cyrus's portals.

She was tempted to follow him in the end, but as she looked at her twin on the floor, her heart shattered. She couldn't abandon Edi or run from the problems she created *again*. It was better for Birk to leave without her. It was his time; she'd squandered hers.

Perhaps it was meant to be this way for both of them; after all, he was born to be the bridge between both worlds. The magic of the hearts of Driftstone resided inside him.

Now, moments after losing him, the only son from her flesh, she confessed all of this to her sister and wept.

Backing away, Edi propped against the wall. Her twin sat in silent disbelief while the palace's foundation creaked and stretched around them. Birk's departure upset the balance of Balincia, and when the island supporting the Palace of Chaos began to elevate—the Isle of Order descended.

After ten thousand years, the scales were now broken.

TWENTY-ONE

THE NIGHT BIRK LEFT

"Edi, please say something. We need to talk about this." Pan cried out, scurrying across her front lawn after her sister.

Edi marched furious and silent into the night on a mission to assess the exterior damage. If she faced her sister right now, she'd lose the remains of her composure, and once it was lost, she feared it could never be regained. So, she focused her energy on what she did best: cleaning the mess made by others.

When she approached the bridge, the damage was apparent. Summoning a torch from the gardens, Edi took a moment to mourn the once beautiful ivory bridge that now hung between the two islands. Cracked and broken, their symbol of unification clung to the wisteria vines, the only thing keeping its now sagging form from falling into the waters below.

An appropriate metaphor for her relationship with her sister.

Edi's eyes raged with tears when she realized she was now forced to look *down* at the roof of her palace.

The island still hovered above the water, but it was a visible statement to the land: *order was losing ground.* Bending, she touched the bridge's edges, transforming it into a grand, sweeping staircase, which now descended. *Appearances still mattered.*

Tailing her, Pan begged Edi to stop and speak with her, but onward she went.

Stepping onto her firmament, she veered to the front gardens, withdrew her wand from her cloak, and quickened her pace. *Edi rarely used her wand; it was unnecessary at her skill level, but helpful when speed and precision counted.* Pan's irritating pleas continued to follow her as she maneuvered through the hedges of the maze, zeroing in on her target.

Raising her wand when she rounded the corner, she channeled every negative thought and emotion at her disposal and flung them at the statue in homage to her sister. The giant likeness of Pan's feet broke from the marble's foundation and stepped with a colossal thud into the courtyard. Keeping her arm raised, Edi walked the monument across her beautiful gardens, destroying every immaculate aesthetic she and Toliver curated together.

Pan gasped at the sight of her marble image destroying everything her sister had built—a clear tribute to her betrayal. Edi walked the massive puppet to the island's edge and rotated the statue to face them, its back teetering on the brink.

Staring into the carved face of her twin, her one constant, Edi unleashed the anger boiling inside her. "THIS IS ALL YOUR FAULT!" she screamed, directing her ire into a bolt of magic. The hex blast hit the statue right between its eyes, obliterating it and dramatically sending it in pieces to the bottom of the lake.

Falling to her knees, she buried her face in her hands and cried.

Approaching her sister with caution, Pan sat in silence beside her.

After several minutes, she attempted to break the tension by elbowing her sister, "Did you have to aim for my face?"

"I wanted to wipe your smug smile off it," Edi muttered into her hands, her head still bowed.

"It was an effective way to get me to shut up," she jested back, inducing a small laugh from her older twin.

Edi sighed, raised her head, and stared into the horizon. The first sun was rising, and its trickles of pink and yellow faded the remaining stars in the sky.

"You've been lying to me for years," Edi's voice was slow and quiet. "You've been practicing dangerous magic and inviting our past into our home. You made plans to leave me. You used your magic *against* me." Edi turned her tear-streaked face to her sister. "*You bore a child*—a child who is my flesh and blood, nephew. You kept all this hidden from me."

"I'm sorry, I—" Pan lost her words. No excuse or apology was going to be sufficient to heal the damage she inflicted.

Edi shook her head. "And tonight, you were planning to abandon me. Leaving me to pick up your pieces—*again*? After all I've done for you." She met Pan's eyes, "I saved your life. I put you back together after everything you went through in the war. We built this land from *our* vision, with the consent and insistence of Balincia's first generation. *You* designed its laws and practices to protect them from *your* magic."

Pan couldn't face her sister; her words were true.

"I won't be the scapegoat for your conscience," Edi continued bitterly, "You hurt me, Pandi. All I've ever done, I've done for you."

"You're right; you didn't deserve this," Pan sniffed. "Forgive me, Edi. I projected everything onto you. You've always been there to protect me from myself and others, and now I've abused your love."

"Why?" Edi implored.

"In hindsight, I'm not sure. I was afraid that with all we've sacrificed to get here, *with all you sacrificed*, you wouldn't hear me out or understand. Our powers—the essence of our true natures—are so different and distinct."

"But we've worked through this before. I'm aware I can be resistant. I understand you might perceive my first instinct would be to dismiss you, but I'd like to think we would've come up with a solution together. I didn't deserve to be abandoned or become a monster in your narrative."

Pan grabbed her sister's hand. "No, you didn't; please forgive me. I should've tried harder. I let my emotions control me—I'm all heart most of the time. That's why I need you in my life."

Edi clenched her sister's hands and allowed herself to cry. "I suppose I'm all head—what a pair we make. I should've sensed your anguish, your loneliness, your doubts. I should've been a safe space for you. And now, look at this mess we've made together."

"What do we do?"

Edi stood, brushed off, and clasped her hands. "First things first. We must get Balincia back in balance, and it originates with us. We promised to protect these people. I believe Birk was telling the truth about this old woman. If someone has found their way into Balincia, carrying magical relics and concealing themselves from us, we can make no positive assumptions."

"And what of the township leaders and our staff sleeping in your palace?"

Edi reflected, "It's time to do things a different way. I've compromised myself."

Pan stood and linked her arms to her twins, resting her head on her shoulder. "*We've* compromised ourselves. So, we wake them and tell them the truth?"

"Yes—it's time. We'll need a plan in place. If we're to be accountable, they must understand what's at risk. If they genuinely love their home, they must share the burden of defending it." Edi turned to her sister. "I hope things have changed for the better, I do. But if the dangers we left behind are still out there, we'll need all the help we can get."

"Maybe Birk will prove us wrong, and our people will surprise us." Pan pulled her sister closer. "Do you think he'll be safe?"

"He's the best of both of us. If there is anyone who might lead us to a future where love can mend the rifts we've built, it will be him. Who knew chaos could birth the most beautiful order?"

Pan smiled at this reassuring thought. "I hope he's not alone. He deserves to find someone as protective and loving as you."

TWENTY-TWO

THE HEALING SPRINGS

Birk awoke to fish sizzling over the campfire. The cave, his make-shift sanctuary, was busy with activity. Grey was hunched over the fire, seasoning the fish with an assortment of salt and herbs drawn from a well-worn leather pouch. Winter lay at the entrance, engrossed with her breakfast: a rabbit, from the looks of it, painting fresh blood stains across her white muzzle. Noticeably absent was Brunt.

"Good morning," Birk said, trying to find his voice. Grey's gaze lifted to meet him, and a warm smile crossed his face.

"I was hoping a warm breakfast would stir you."

"It smells delicious. Can I help you?" Suddenly, acutely aware of his disheveled state, Birk attempted to tame his wild bed hair, a futile effort that only heightened his self-consciousness.

Grey pretended not to notice. "No, it's almost ready. Relax."

Clad in Grey's oversized tunic, still bearing his scent, Birk wrapped it tighter around him. "How long have you been awake?"

Plating the fish, Grey handed it to Birk before serving himself and joining him on the ground. "We woke at sunrise; I wanted to ensure we ate something fresh this morning."

"You should have woken me; I would've gone with you," Birk said with his mouth full.

"I didn't want to disturb your rest; besides, I was accompanied by two skilled hunters."

"Where is Brunt?"

"Oh, he's probably still at the river, filling himself with fish. Like you, he's required extra rest over the last couple of days and woke famished this morning. How are you feeling?"

"I feel fantastic. I don't think I've ever slept so well," *and oddly, it was true*. It was hard to believe he almost died two days ago. His body was energized and strong.

"That's the power of the healing springs," Grey confirmed. "Lift your shirt; let me look at your chest and stomach."

Birk hesitated, his cheeks pink.

Grey chuckled, "I want to see how your wounds are healing."

Birk lifted his tunic, slightly embarrassed; *no one but Pan had ever examined him*. He looked down, while Grey removed the bandages and was shocked to find the deep puncture wounds and scratches left by the arcanivore were barely visible. Grey traced his fingers across his faded scars, inspecting them.

Birk squirmed at his touch.

"How's that possible? The spring did this?".

"Yes, after one more dip today, your scars will disappear since they're still fresh. I want to take you there after breakfast to ensure you are well enough for tomorrow's journey. After we can hunt a few more provisions for the road."

"A soak in the springs sounds perfect. I'm in desperate need of a wash. I'm sure I'm ripe and offensive."

"You forget I spend most of my time with a bear and a wolf. I promise you smell the best out of the four of us."

The leftovers of their meal lay scattered on a table of flat rocks by the time the sunlight streamed in from the mouth of the cave. Stretching his arms overhead, Birk relished the sensation of his muscles waking after two days of stillness.

"I can't wait to feel the sun on my face again," Birk shared, anxious to explore.

"I think you'll love the surprises waiting outside. Let's gather what we need and head toward the healing springs."

A smile tugged at the corners of Birk's mouth.

When they left the cave's confines, a faint sound of rushing water tickled Birk's ears, growing louder when they descended toward the entrance. Rounding the corner, he stopped and stared at the back of a waterfall tumbling over the mouth of the cave with a thunderous downpour.

"You didn't tell me we were behind a waterfall?" Birk exclaimed, rushing over to extend his hand underneath it. I've only seen waterfalls from a distance. This is—beautiful." Birk leaned closer to the edge, allowing the mist from the downpour to kiss his face.

"If you appreciate the view from here, you should come to the front," Grey encouraged, gently guiding him.

When Birk stepped from behind the curtain of water, a lush green oasis straight from his storybooks stared back at him. Towering trees with expansive canopies draped in fairy moss spread across an enclosed valley. Oversized daisies freckled the area, attracting giant butterflies. Wiggling his toes in the soft emerald grass, he understood why Grey was often barefoot. In the distance, rabbits bobbed in the undergrowth. "Where are we?"

Grey soaked in the sun, enjoying Birk's reaction. "We aren't too far from where we found you. We're over the canyon walls from where you were headed. This is an extension of the Protector's Valley, where his blood was spilled and infused with the land. It's hidden and only allows his descendants and those they bring in good faith to enter."

"Hidden—I wonder if it's similar to the magic keeping Balincia guarded. What made you trust me enough to bring me here?"

"Brunt and Winter's intuition. They were his familiars, *the last of all the familiars*, and my sister and I are the last of his descendants."

"You must be proud. He left a beautiful legacy."

"I wish I'd known him and understood more about my history. It's

complicated." He paused, leaving his thoughts to hang in the air. Before Birk could follow with a question, Grey pointed to the valley's heart. "Those are the healing springs. It's where his magic is strongest. It can't bring someone back to life or make you younger," he joked, "but it can heal most wounds and illnesses over time."

Following Grey's direction, Birk focused on a series of clear springs. Water trickled over mossy stones, flowing from one pool to the next, each larger than the previous one. A mist of steam hung over the water.

"Do the springs keep the valley warm? On the other side of the canyon, there was snow and ice only a few days ago." Birk asked.

"I think it helps, but this valley has many secrets, including its climate," Grey motioned for Birk to follow him to the valley floor. "Come on, I can't wait for you to try them out."

Except for Ravenshire, Birk never spent much time around young men his age. Raised by his aunts in the palaces, he was often embarrassed for standing out among his peers during his travels. Talbot, the primary male influence in his life, was more of a mentor, and he always considered Ravenshire a kindred outcast.

He wasn't a stick in the mud, but he was more reserved than most. Talbot kept him athletic and agile due to his strict exercise regimen, but Birk was never competitive or rowdy. So, he was surprised when he found himself charmed by Grey's rambunctious energy.

Grey filled space with an ease Birk could never muster—he was boisterous, unafraid to throw his whole body into a joke or story. He carried a playfulness that always caught Birk off guard, teasing with a nudge of his shoulder or daring him with a grin. Jumping barefoot from rock to tree stump, he exuded a boyish energy trapped in the build of a warrior.

When they reached the water, Grey's trousers fell to his ankles. Kicking them to the side, he dove in and disappeared under the surface. Standing at the pool's edge, Birk stood rooted, with a modesty he couldn't shed. Grey surfaced in the water, staring back at him with a goofy grin, motioning for him to join him.

"The water is warm; you're going to love it," he encouraged.

Taking off his shirt, he neatly folded it, placing it on the ground next to him. Sensing Grey's eyes, his hands hovered when they reached the hem of his pants. To his relief, Grey politely spun around and pretended to swim in the opposite direction, allowing Birk the discretion to undress and slip into the water.

Thankful and more secure, Birk submerged himself, allowing his body to float underneath the surface. He could feel the heat sinking deep into his muscles and bones. The water tingled as it caressed his skin, melting away his wounds and scars.

When he broke the surface, he was revitalized, and any fatigue dissolved.

"I can't believe you can experience this anytime you want. We don't have anything like this in Balincia."

"It's great. I can't tell you how many times these pools have saved my life."

Birk wasn't sure if he should be alarmed or if Grey was having a laugh. "Are you in danger often?"

"Brynn, my sister, says I have a death wish." Grey rolled his eyes. "She doesn't remember how it was before—when we were alone. It's hard to shed my nature to protect my pack. I've experienced a few close encounters because of it."

"Why *were* you on your own? You mentioned Brunt and Winter raised you; what happened to your parents?"

Grey's mind wandered backward as he swept the wet hair from his face.

"I apologize; I shouldn't have probed. It's too personal." Birk quickly interjected, realizing the invasiveness of his question.

Grey gave Birk a reassuring squeeze on his arm and winked. "You need to stop apologizing and second-guessing yourself."

Grey swam over to a shallower part of the pool to lean against the edge. "Brynn was only a baby when my mother and father were killed, and I was barely fourteen years around the suns. We lived in a nomadic community, the remaining heirs of the Protector. We lived a simple life

connected to the land, all hunters, musicians, and artists—never carrying more than necessary."

"That sounds like a lovely way to live."

Grey gave a sad smile. "It was; you'd have liked my parents; my father was quite the storyteller himself." He paused, thinking of the best way to explain things to Birk. "Some wander in our realms, living as we did, never settling. There are the Sivaelin and Lorathil, two tribes of traveling elves, along with the Herdsmen, humans, who ride with the centaurs and lunar horses. All allies, except for a group called the Free Roamers."

"The Free Roamers?"

"A group of humans who hate anyone and anything Magic-Born, even those loosely associated with magic. They call themselves purists. They were initially disgruntled citizens who were sick of the ways of witches, elves and fae. They left their kingdoms to roam without the oversight of laws or biases toward magic. Over the years, their hate grew, as did their numbers—united under a mission to wipe all magic from the earth."

"Why?"

"They consider magic an abomination. In truth, their hatred stems from jealousy and fear of anything different or more powerful than themselves. They seek out and indoctrinate others who are desperate and searching for purpose. Latching onto them and feeding their insecurities, they convince them they are oppressed, and true freedom can only be achieved by destroying magic. Their armies have grown, and they are purging the lands of Magic-Born as they march across them."

"And by purge, you mean—"

"Torture . . . dismember . . . kill."

Birk was horrified. He had no words or experience with such deliberate cruelty. Grey crossed his arms over the edge of the pool, staring blankly into the canyon.

"We were a small group, only about sixty. We were caught off guard when they attacked us in the hundreds early in the morning," he continued. "I was still having breakfast. My mother handed me my sister and told me to run here without stopping, warning me not to look back or turn around," Grey swallowed. "I heard the sounds of the slaughter. I

listened to my family's screams as arrows whistled overhead. I wanted to run back and help them, but I made a promise to my mother: my sister's safety above all else."

Grey's shoulders sagged. "Brunt greeted us. Sensing my panic and desperation, he charged into the valley. Winter stopped me from following him, herding me and my sister into the cave. She didn't let me leave until Brunt returned three days later, his front paw broken, his snout covered in blood."

"And your parents?"

Grey shook his head in silence. "All of them—gone. My parents, grandparents, cousins—I buried every single body when I returned with Brunt days later. My sister and I are the only survivors."

Birk quietly leaned next to him. "Grey, I can't imagine losing so many people you love at such a young age. I understand why this place is important to you."

"This is where my powers manifested, albeit too late. Brunt and Winter taught me to hunt and live off the land, but my sister needed human connection. She needed a mother. Winter knew this and led us to Everglenn." He laughed, "When the village saw two children being escorted by a giant bear and a massive wolf, they had no choice but to take us in. Shayvonne became our second mother, raising us as her own."

"So, when the arcanivores attacked your village, you must've been terrified of reliving your past." Birk now understood why Grey was tracking them alone.

"I was attempting to use myself as bait, leading them away from the village." His face straightened when he looked Birk in the face. "I aim to hunt them proactively—I won't lose my remaining family."

"Let me help you as you've helped me. We're both trying to protect our people; let our quests be tied together." Birk offered his hand as a pact.

They shook on it.

Sitting in silence for a while, they reflected on the days ahead. Their arms and thighs pressed against each other as they soaked in the warm water, neither pulling away, both aware of the other leaning in.

"I don't want to be the first person to break away from our time here, but if we're to leave tomorrow, we still need to gather provisions." Grey nudged.

Knowing this was true, Birk returned a soft smile. "Lead the way; show me how I can help."

When Grey stood in the shallows to exit the pool, the steam barely covered the crest of his hips. Birk stared at his broad brown back; the only surface of his body not covered in hair. His eyes followed droplets rolling down the smooth exterior of his skin and into the small crevice of his lower back.

Distracted, he didn't expect Grey to spin around.

Grey grinned, catching Birk's quick redirection of his eyes and his face turning cherry red. Catching Birk by both arms, he rescued him from stumbling backward into the spring.

"I almost forgot," he chuckled. "I wanted to check your scars before we left."

Birk stepped back, allowing Grey to examine his chest and stomach. Unable to find his voice, he held his breath while Grey ran his hands over his torso. His touch was gentle and warm, his thumbs gliding over the empty spaces where his recent puncture wounds had been.

"They've disappeared. Not a single mark left on you."

Birk exhaled and looked down, inspecting his own body. He couldn't find a single bump, scratch, or scar.

"Your skin is so white in contrast with mine," Grey mused, "I'm glad to see it remains unscarred."

With a quick upward curve of the corner of his mouth, Grey led Birk back to land, where they dressed in quiet.

TWENTY-THREE

An Inconvenient Inquisition

It had been three days since Birk's departure, and Edi was waiting to be summoned—*inside her own home*. To the remaining council's credit, they were more civil than expected, given the circumstances. She'd played her part in return, contrite yet honest, out of respect.

She needed their support, even if she didn't want to admit it. However, she found it all a bit performative. She wasn't infallible, but she didn't appreciate the façade of accountability to their inquisition. They lacked the contextual experience and knowledge *collected over centuries* to judge her actions unbiasedly.

She course-corrected her thoughts; they were exactly what led them here.

If she wanted to be a good leader, *and she did want to be one*, lowering one's station was necessary occasionally, even if begrudgingly. It proved the value of the voices she governed, she supposed.

Granted, they had valid reasons to be upset about the mental intrusions. She admitted that she and her sister had gone a *little* overboard.

Her intentions were never to suppress free will; at least, that wasn't how it started. Today's citizens are unaware that their inaugural laws were created in consultation with the first generations of Balincians, and there's no one left to confirm this fact.

This foresight would've been useful when they decided that the history and knowledge of Driftstone were best kept hidden. During that time, they were all focused on survival, driven by a deep fear of being discovered. Building a society so quickly had been an enormous challenge. They couldn't overextend the space they were hiding in or ask for more resources than they could provide.

Not to mention the most daunting challenge was containing her sister's more *willful* magic.

In truth, Edi was proud and impressed with what she—*they*—had built. Born a natural leader and problem solver, Balincia, in many ways, was her child as much as Birk was Pan's. Yes, it wasn't perfect, but close—and it's not as if she was unaware of the morally grey issues in her decisions; she'd chosen to ignore them.

Gifted with structural vision, she always knew the most expedient path to bringing things to order. She confessed it wasn't always the ideal way—*or even the ethical way*—but she always yielded the quickest and most efficient results. If anything, in self-reflection, she surmised this was her greatest weakness—she lacked patience, waiting for others to come to her conclusions.

Okay, that sounded a bit narcissistic, but it was true, more often than not.

So—she made the hard calls. She wasn't heartless or cold; she just forgot to be thoughtful when applying logic. In reality, she "felt" things deeply; she was merely better at burying emotions—their tendency to obstruct decision-making was bothersome.

After all, her love for her sister and the first generation of Balincians built this place. They owed their lives to *her*. This is why she was struggling with the indignity of the current situation.

Sighing, she tapped her fingers on her lap, replaying her defense. She knew the township leaders were less moved by her arguments than by

Pan, but Edi wouldn't begin the practice of throwing herself on the floor, pleading for forgiveness from *anyone*. Much less, Porticia Prombey.

After her healthy release in the gardens, *Pan called it a tantrum, as if she were one to talk*; the sisters agreed on an approach to restore balance. To forge a new direction, which she'd taken a while to acknowledge they needed, the path forward required remorse, accountability, and reconciliation.

Waking the council and staff after a forced twelve-hour nap wasn't exactly the best way to start on the right foot.

It took an entire day, filled with breaks, to share *everything*.

If they were to build trust, the transparency of their history, actions, intentions, and even their most recent events needed to be shared as an act of good faith, a presentation of humility. The people deserved to know they may be in danger if they were to make their own decisions in supporting Balincia moving forward.

Edi added only one caveat: regardless of where the Balincians landed, it wouldn't detour her loyalty to protect them. Expecting a lot of questions, *which there were*, they also dealt with a copious number of emotional reactions. Doing their best to handle each with delicate care, they offered full, authentic explanations.

The most heartbreaking confession was to the staff upon learning *they did indeed have parents* who no longer remembered them. There was no escaping the guilt of this moral compromise. Despite all the privileges she offered to those she took into her home, she couldn't replace or give back the precious gift of the family she stole from them.

Her penitence, *and maybe a bit of shame*, kept her awake the first evening.

Wandering the palace in her nightdress, she wondered how she'd slipped so far from the idealistic young woman she used to be. The avoidant eyes of Feeona, or the quick shuffle around the corner by Saffrona as she walked the halls, added to her suffering.

Carrying the shame with her into the morning, she made a decision without consulting Pan.

The original plan was for everyone to assemble so they could have the opportunity to respond after sitting with Edi and Pan's confessions. Dawning on Edi, this request may be too soon or unfair to require presence and solutions; she encouraged anyone who wished to process this alone or be with family to take leave.

She promised that everything discussed would be shared over the following days with anyone who left, and she and Pan would be available for those who preferred to share their thoughts privately. Urgent matters of the realm requiring immediate attention would be handled by those who stayed behind. Still, no one was obligated to take responsibility.

Leaving the room with her twin, she gave them a few hours to discuss and decide the best course.

Hours later, Talbot was sent to deliver the news that several township leaders, including Samuel and Beatrix, decided to return home. Unsurprisingly, Edi's most invested critics intended to stay to adjudicate. Perhaps the most painful blow was his last announcement—most of her younger staff opted to leave their positions and wait on the Royal Isle until a consensus was determined.

Attempting to soften the news, Talbot advocated their extended family's need for time. He emphasized their preference to engage the sisters without an audience. The Royal Guardians and Saffrona were committed to staying on, as were more senior members of her staff, until a more permanent solution was in place.

Spending the day quarantined in Pan's palace allowed the remaining council to determine judgment and Balincia's next steps. While Edi was willing to hear their suggestive reparations and eager to partner with them on a path forward, her reluctance to trust still lingered. They were mistaken if they believed she'd hand over the reins quietly.

On their third morning, Edi's growing seeds of doubt were now spiraling. It took her every ounce of self-control not to barge into the council chamber and seize control of the situation. The only thing holding her back was her promise to her sister.

Luckily, Talbot's entrance was timely and welcomed.

"Your Royal Practitioners," Talbot greeted. Edi appreciated his deference to their titles. "Thank you for waiting so long. Everyone is ready for you."

Standing and linking arms, Pan gave Edi a reassuring squeeze. Her sister always had more faith in humans' unpredictability. Edi, preferring a sure thing, envied her come-what-may attitude.

"Before we go in, may I say something personal?" Talbot asked the sisters.

Edi nodded, "Always."

Standing straight, he adjusted his posture. "It has been an honor to be in your service. Regardless of what you may hear, you should be aware that there is great admiration and love for all you have done, including your admissions. It is the sign of great leaders to step aside and acknowledge when they've failed."

"Thank you, Talbot," Edi said, fighting the urge to tear.

"On a personal note," he continued, "I want you both to know I believe in you and love you. None of us is without fault. I'm not alone among our staff in appreciating the home you have provided for us."

Swallowing a lump in her throat, Pan threw her arms around his neck. "Forgive us, Talbot. We never meant to hurt any of you. We love our family more than any of you will ever know."

Edi offered a thin, sad smile. Perhaps Birk was right; she underestimated the best in people.

She changed her mind when she entered the room and saw Porticia sitting in her seat, Marina and Lars at her sides. With grim faces, the council members motioned for the witches to take a seat.

Ravenshire stood at attention against the wall. Saffrona and Xavier gazed at their laps; all the staff were avoiding eye contact. Talbot sat beside the sisters, demonstrating his allegiance and comforting them with a friendly face.

"It's been no small task to review with discernment everything you've shared with us." Porticia kicked off, clearly the self-appointed speaker for

the group. "The clarity one can achieve when your faculties aren't obstructed is remarkable."

Edi's eyes narrowed; of course, *she'd begin with a strike.* "I know you may find this difficult to believe, but I find no pleasure in the position this has put me in." Porticia continued. Edi resisted rolling her eyes. "Balincia has long been blessed with your gifts since its creation. The land's prosperity is due to you, as well as its safety—as we understand now. This is no small gift we take for granted."

Everyone at the table nodded, murmuring in agreement. Porticia paused, turning to Lars and Marina for silent support. "What we didn't know, however, was the price it cost us. Whatever agreements you made with our ancestors, regardless of the contextual justification at the time, you withheld from us. Sacrificing our rights and privileges to weigh in on their application today."

"If you'd educated us on our history and allowed us to work with you, we may have surprised you with our support," Lars added. "But we'll never know because you took those choices from us. You took away our voice to dissent."

"Additionally," Marina interjected, "you have taken away our basic living rights. The ability to have children when we want, live as long as our bodies allow us, and choose work that makes us happy."

"You stole the right to know our parents," Ravenshire shouted from his post against the wall.

Xavier rose, "And while I'm thankful I was taught to read and write in my position, you have taken away the gift of literacy and education from your people. Forcing them to remain stagnant in their development."

Pan's head hung, her tears hidden by the hair covering her face. She couldn't stomach it. In contrast, Edi was determined to look her victims in the eyes. It was vital they were heard—it was the least she could do.

"These aren't small grievances against your people," Porticia emphasized.

"No, they're not," Edi confessed; her actions overwhelmed her as she listened to them recounted aloud.

Porticia, surprised by Edi's countenance, softened her own. "How-

ever, as Talbot and you have reminded us, dire times call for dire measures." Porticia paused and met Edi's eyes. "I also personally believe intentions *do* matter. It is clear to us you thought what you were doing was for our best interest—for the most part."

"Your confessions and desire to change things moving forward also impacted us. We're aware you didn't have to subjugate yourselves to us." Lars added.

"I can't speak for the people of Balincia, but for those present in the room, after careful consideration—we want you to know we support you," Porticia informed, to Edi's surprise. "We disagree with your methods, but, as of now, we rely on your abilities and expertise. We aim to create a partnership and rebuild trust."

"There are, of course, a few caveats," Lars jumped in. "First, this council will serve as your advisors. We will require the same amount of transparency we provide to you. We must forge our future together to rebuild trust with the people."

Edi was speechless, "That's only fair."

"The laws will be rewritten in partnership with us, as you did with our ancestors. We acknowledge the needs of our past, but moving forward, everyone is granted the right to have children, live full lives, and receive education, allowing us to decide our own paths. This is non-negotiable," Marina informed.

"And it should go without saying all enchantments on Balincians should be lifted *immediately*," Porticia emphasized.

"We know you're protecting our borders, and we ask you to continue until we better understand what we're up against. We'll hold town halls in each of our townships and send out communications through the falconers, ensuring our citizens understand the dangers and safe holds in place." Lars continued.

"We can discuss many things in detail as we get Balincia back to its feet, but I think these are the priority issues. Am I missing anything?" Porticia surveyed the room.

Saffrona, who had remained silent, raised her eyes to meet the twins. She spoke softly. "I speak on behalf of our younger staff, who may have

parents who are still alive. If you can help reconnect them, healing their graces toward you will go a long way."

"May I ask why you did it?" Ravenshire interrupted with a bite. "I mean, I understand the intent behind a lot of your decisions, but stealing children from their parents is incomprehensibly selfish and cruel. *Did you need a staff that badly?*"

"We were never staff; we were family." Talbot reprimanded.

Edi placed her hand on Talbot's shoulder, letting him know she could take it from here. "If we are to be transparent, let us start now. Ravenshire, you deserve the truth, as does everyone." She paused, wringing her hands. "Divination is the magic of foresight. It's not always one hundred percent reliable, but it provides enough to predict certain things in someone's life."

She walked the room toward Ravenshire, taking his hands in hers. "A newborn is easier to read than an adult. Their path and potential lay before us, reminiscent of a string, enabling us to see the length of their lives and potential talents. The reason the divination required more time for each of you was because we had difficulty finding your string."

"What do you mean?" stuttered Ravenshire, confused.

"It means there was no lifeline," Pan answered for her sister.

Edi squeezed Ravenshire's hands. "Your precious lives would've been cut short days from your birth. Whatever else we've done, we believed every breath brought into Balincia deserved the chance to live. By bringing you here and taking away your parents' memories, we were able to alter your trajectory. Trick the fates, if you will, by hiding you in a new life."

"We can try to rebind you to your parents' memories, but once the deception is removed, your original fate may find you," Pan joined her sister.

"So, you saved us—all of us," Saffrona said, taking a moment to absorb the news.

"It doesn't justify us keeping this information from you. We didn't want any of you to carry this, nor for your parents to grieve the loss," Edi admitted.

The room was silent while the staff reacted to this news.

"I think this speaks to the heart of my defense," Talbot stood. "We can't imagine all the complex decisions these women have faced over the years. We may not agree with all their choices, but considering the circumstances, I'm not sure we can say we'd do any better. Edi and Pan attempted to do what was best and are demonstrating this even now."

"I agree, Talbot," Porticia said, standing to address the twins. "If we have your commitment to the proposed changes, you have our support moving forward. There is too much for all of us to lose by not heeding your warnings and coming together."

Walking to the back of Edi's chair, Porticia pulled it out, motioning for her to take her rightful place at the head of the table. "Edi, I believe it's time we get back to business. If you believe there is an intruder in Balincia, we may be compromised or in danger. How can we help?"

Edi met Porticia's eyes and bowed her head in deference. Placing her hand on hers, they met each other for the first time. Acknowledging her with a smile, Edi sat, clasped her hands, and said, "Let's get things back in order, shall we?"

TWENTY-FOUR

THE OLD WOMAN

As the days wore on, the old woman grew tired of staying confined in the Inn.

The weight of her deception was bothering her. Mind you, it wasn't the outcome she cared about, but the loose ends were piling up. How could she enjoy her freedom when the results had yet to be delivered?

On top of that, the remains of her wish magic were straining. She'd expended too much of it in creating the Driftstone and accessing Balincia. What little she had left went into protective wards for herself. She didn't want to dip into the reserves loaned to her; she'd need those when she faced the witches.

Spending her days in seclusion, she'd remained undetected so far. An illusion cloaked her proper form, allowing her to masquerade as a nondescript stable hand, affording her a semblance of normalcy. She knew this charade couldn't endure indefinitely. Her energy to maintain it was dwindling with each passing day, and the bonds of familiarity in Balincia were too tight.

She'd see the sisters soon anyway, to finish this. When the boy slipped beyond Balincia's borders, it released her from his spell. Then, she witnessed the Isle of Order descending, heralding a shift in the land's balance.

The twins, harboring histories of mistrust, would seek out the culprit who planted the new ideas in the boy's head and would blame her for driving him away. An inevitable confrontation was approaching; there was no choice but to continue playing the part she was cast in.

Her life depended on it.

TWENTY-FIVE

THE THIRTEEN FOXES

"You're wearing clothes?" Witnessing Grey slip into a tunic and some boots, Birk couldn't hold back the surprise in his voice. Grey threw his head back in laughter. "Do you prefer me out of them?" he teased suggestively.

"Yes . . . I mean, no . . . sorry, I've only seen you barefoot and in trousers and many times . . . in nothing," he stumbled over his words. Aware Grey was getting a kick out of this; he tried to straighten his composure. "What I mean to say is you look nice in clothes . . . and without . . . I'm making this worse . . . please stop me . . ."

"Ha! I *do* wear clothes when I'm not here. Were you worried I'd embarrass you in public? I'm not untrained," he winked. "I don't require the warmth, but I've learned to appreciate the boots when I travel." He continued to laugh and tied some blankets and provisions onto Brunt's back.

"I didn't mean to imply that," Birk handed him a bag of dried rabbit meat. "I'd never be embarrassed by you."

Grey scratched Brunt behind the ears, whispering something private to the beast before smacking him on his end, sending him to the cave exit. Tilting his head to Birk, he smiled with his eyes. "Relax; I enjoy giving you grief. I will, however, take on the personal challenge of testing you on this."

Walking past Birk, Grey goaded him, poking him in the side.

"I don't think we have to test it," Birk called out, scrambling to keep up.

"By the way, I'm flattered you appreciate me in my clothes," Grey yelled over his shoulder, *"and without them."* His laugh echoed in Birk's ears as he rounded the corner.

It didn't take long for Birk to realize he was hindering the group's progress. It was challenging to keep pace with a bear, a wolf, and a man with the agility and endurance of both. Always observant, Grey suggested Brunt carry them when they stopped to rest.

"We have several miles of ascent before we come back down again, and we'll want to be in a good position to camp for the night," Grey pointed to the map in the Driftstone. "If we can make it here, there's an ideal spot underneath this bluff."

"We won't be too much weight for him?" Birk was secretly relieved but felt it proper to offer a mild protest, even if Brunt was three times larger than the average grizzly bear.

"I assure you, Brunt won't even notice we're there. Isn't that right, buddy?" Grey scratched his back. The bear shook his head side to side, releasing a strangled groan. Birk couldn't tell if he was agreeing or groaning in protest; either way, Brunt lowered onto the ground, offering Birk the opportunity to climb on. Perhaps he, too, was tired of waiting for Birk to catch up.

When Grey joined, he was relieved; otherwise, he would've caused another scene trying to ride the bear properly. Saddling up behind him, Grey wrapped one arm around Birk's waist, while the other held the rope he'd used to tie their supplies. Unsure of what to do with his arms, Birk awkwardly tried to find a natural place for them. Playing it safe, he placed one arm across Grey's, which was wrapped around his waist, and the other across his companion's sturdy thigh.

"Are you all settled?" Grey leaned into his ear, tickled.

"Yes," Birk squeaked.

Leaning back against Grey, he unconsciously looped their fingers together at their waists as Brunt rose from the ground—*for steadying purposes.*

The suns bathed the terrain with a warm blanket, casting it in a new light. No longer dark and forbidding, the towering trees around the trail swayed in the breeze.

The soft thump of Grey's heartbeat against his back and the synchronized rhythm of their breaths enhanced the mood. Grey was stirring something unfamiliar inside Birk, a pull so new it made him almost shy about his own thoughts. It was strange, this restless pull toward him. Not loud, not sure—more like a whisper he could almost ignore if he tried hard enough. He didn't understand what it meant or why it mattered so much, only that he both liked and hated it at the same time.

Winter darted off the trail, resembling a playful pup, unwilling to slow her pace to Brunt's steady gait. The wolf allowed Birk to divert his attention. Leaping from rock to rock, she added a touch of entertainment for the young men by chasing grouse in the underbrush and diving into streams, giving them something to laugh and talk about. Now and then, Brunt did his part by slowing at the most scenic portions of the trail.

Enjoying himself, Birk pointed at every tree, bird, and flower alien to Balincia. With his affable charm, Grey taught him their names and chattered away about his adventures in the forest when he was younger. Sharing stories and teasing each other, they forgot all about the Driftstone and the arcanivores.

"I still can't believe you were raised by two of the Original Thirteen," Grey commented, pulling Birk away from the moment.

"The Original Thirteen?"

"*The Thirteen*—the original Magic-Born. They were Driftstone's creators and caretakers," Grey explained. "Did your aunts never share this with you?"

Birk's mind raced at the phrase, bringing him back to *The History of Driftstone* in his aunt's library. The book opened with a chapter titled

"The History of the Thirteen." *His* Driftstone was transcribing the chapter until Pan interrupted.

Birk sat straight. "Can you get Brunt to stop?"

With a quick pull of the rope by Grey, Brunt halted, huffing through his nose.

"Is everything ok?"

"Yes . . . I don't know."

"What is it?" Grey was concerned, unable to discern Birk's eyes.

"I think you handed me a clue as to why I was led here—why we're on this quest—or, maybe a part of it." Birk unhitched his satchel and retrieved the Driftstone.

"I did?"

"I'm foolish for not putting it together before, but I think wherever the Driftstone is leading us has something to do with the Thirteen."

Birk quickly caught Grey up on the night of the festivities when he performed a tale entitled "The Thirteen Foxes." *The night the old woman approached him.* "She'd mentioned she knew the story, but I'd never performed it publicly." Animated, he reminded Grey of the book he found in the library and Driftstone's attempt to transcribe the chapter on the Thirteen.

"You think they're related?"

"I think The Thirteen Foxes is about the Witches' War. My aunts requested I perform it during the festivities to remember our history."

"So . . . what does it mean? What are you searching for?"

"You cited we're in the lands of the Protector, correct?"

Grey nodded.

"What if all the doors, regardless of my choice, would've led me to the last location of one of the Thirteen?" Birk asked.

"Didn't you say there were only seven doors?"

"Yes, but if two of the Thirteen are my aunts, the total would be—"

"Nine—you're still missing four," Grey pointed out.

Birk was disappointed; he thought he was on to something. "I don't know; maybe it's not the doors."

Grey reflected, "Don't doubt your hunch, I think you're on the right track. The history of the Thirteen may hold clues to your quest."

Putting the book on the ground, Birk knelt beside it. "Should I ask to have it transcribe the pages it was attempting to show me before?"

Grey knelt beside him, "There's no harm in trying."

Opening the book, Birk swept his hand across its empty pages as he'd done before. Channeling his energy and intentions, he envisioned the transcription happening before it was interrupted. Focused and determined, he waited—not even a spark.

Frustrated, he faced Grey. "Will you do it with me? As we did in the cave?"

Honored, Grey leaned in, placing his hand on Birks. The energy sparked between them, their magic intertwining. Drawn to it, Brunt and Winter knelt with them, all eyes waiting for a revelation.

After several minutes, Birk lifted his head, disappointed. "Nothing. I was so sure it was important."

"Let's not give up; maybe we're asking the wrong question." Grey encouraged. "Instead of focusing on the book's transcription, why don't we ask about the Witches' War?"

It didn't work either. Nor did their focus on the history of Driftstone, the significance of the number thirteen, the original Magic-Born, or his aunt's history.

"Why is everything so complicated with magic?" Birk vented, trying to hide his agitation. Sitting back, he felt foolish, having wasted their time.

Grey, not as easily frustrated, stared at the book, trying to solve its puzzle. "Do you remember your story from the night of the festival? What was it called? The Thirteen Foxes?"

"I remember most of it, I think."

"If it were modeled after the Witches' War, *maybe* we don't need the history. What if you already have the information inside you?"

Birk considered this. "Possibly, but I remember the old woman saying my version held a happier ending. I guess it's better than nothing, but

I'd feel better if I saw it in writing. I'm not sure I'll be able to recall all the details."

"Let's try asking the Driftstone for the story of the Thirteen Foxes," Grey reflected. "Together?" he offered his hand to Birk.

"Together," Birk confirmed. Closing their eyes, they joined their magics, intentions, and hearts, pouring them into the Driftstone.

The page beneath them glowed between their fingers. Leaning in, all four watched as a story unfolded on the pages.

Birk skimmed the text as it was written until he pulled back, confused.

"This isn't the story," he commented.

"What do you mean? The title reads 'The Thirteen Foxes', is there more than one?"

"There are similarities, but it isn't the one I performed—it's much darker." Birk continued to read ahead.

"If the Driftstone is showing it to you, maybe it's the version *we need* to read."

Taking the Driftstone into his lap, Birk straightened his shoulders and read the passage aloud. "The Thirteen Foxes . . ." he began.

"At the beginning of time, a lonely enchanted forest gave birth to thirteen foxes. The forest offered them a home and provided each of them with a unique gift to shape the forest around them.

The eldest foxes were twins named Sister Chaos and Sister Order. Always together, tails entwined, they were gifted with the magic of creation and harmony. Able to breathe life into the world, they were also responsible for building and maintaining a system to sustain it.

Brother Protector and Sister Fate each held equally vital roles, blessed with magic devoted to serving all life. Brother Protector safeguarded the lives of every bird and beast, adding his varied creations to the mix. He taught his siblings how to communicate and connect with each animal so they could share the forest peacefully. Sister Fate read the

strings of destiny that guided them, providing every living creature with direction and purpose.

Brother Architect and Sister Innovation drove the forest's evolution. They possessed talents that enabled them to master the arts of music, weaponry, craft, and mechanics. They were the engineers of time and space, supporting development. Under their guidance, castles, kingdoms, and citadels were built in the forest, advancing the achievements of Non-Magic-Born, dwarves, elves, and fae alike.

Brother Dream was endowed with foresight and hope, while Brother Wisdom was gifted with knowledge and ambition. Together, they inspired the forest, enabling life to go beyond its original limits. Sisters, Body and Soul, served as teachers and healers of physical and spiritual balance. Together, they brought compassion and faith for oneself and others. The four contributed to the land with discipline, language, and medicine.

Brother Ocean, master of the waters, and Sister Earth, the steward of the land, were each blessed with the divine magic of the elements. Brother Ocean commanded the winds to help improve transportation and trade to the forest, connecting it to lakes, rivers, and oceans. Sister Earth used magic to multiply the fields and harvests so they'd never go hungry. She gifted the forest's citizens with the fires that fueled their hearths, homes, and forges so they'd never be cold.

Beloved and revered, each of the twelve foxes carefully cared for their creations and diligently managed their duties. All of them except one—the youngest—the Thirteenth Fox.

Unlike his elder siblings, he didn't care about discipline or routine. He held no loyalty to duty or gratitude for the gifts he was given. He was bored by their creations, whom they called children, bored by those who worshipped them, and generally just bored with the forest.

He didn't desire power, love, or riches, nor did he seek adoration or praise. What he craved was excitement—something, anything—that could rescue him from boredom and this endlessly slow life of peace. So, he decided to create a game for the foxes, a test to evaluate their resilience and integrity.

You see, persuasion and conscience were the young fox's gifts, earning him the name Brother Influence. However, he misused these gifts. Instead of sharing the truth, he persuaded others with lies. Instead of a disciplined conscience, he promoted indulgence.

He first whispered in Brother Wisdom's ear, tempting him with forbidden knowledge and sowing greed. Then he targeted Sister Body, eroding her insecurity and fueling vanity. Helping them pursue their selfish goals, they abandoned the pack and left the forest, ending up trapped, unwittingly, in prisons of their own making.

One by one, the young fox poisoned his family's minds, playing to their pride and egos.

He convinced Sister Fate destiny could be changed, introducing her to envy. Sister Chaos, he explained, was the key to unlocking her happiness. Urging her to lure her away from her twin, Fate could siphon Chaos's abilities as a creator and produce more powerful children loyal to her ambitions.

Pleased, the young little fox sat back and watched his siblings turn on each other. Lies became weapons, and Brother Influence turned into Brother Discord, his essence forever tainted.

The forest mourned, and the Chaos fox listened. She learned about fires that consumed the soil, stolen or hidden resources, and walls built to separate. She discovered her children were being enslaved and tortured behind her back; their essences twisted into darker forms.

One tragic day, she stormed through the trees, so furious that even Order couldn't contain her rage. No one remembered what happened next; all they could recall was the storm. The Scales of Magic shattered that day, and the youngest of the thirteen was found lying dead at his sister's feet.

The War of Foxes erupted.

Fate quickly formed alliances with Ocean and Wisdom to hunt members of their pack. The ocean threatened to submerge the forest, prompting Earth to build walls around it for protection. Innovation built weapons with magic to destroy her kin, but Wisdom stole her knowledge of how to use them. Stealing them, he hid them across the land so only he could find them.

Battle after battle, the foxes turned on each other. They destroyed the forest as they fought. Until one unfortunate day, in the Battle for the Valley, they lost their Protector.

The forest had lost its shield.

In fear for her sister, Order begged the Architect for help, who concealed them in a pocket and swore himself to silence. When the sisters disappeared, the pack mourned again, marking another turning point in the war.

Fearing for the lives in their realms, Dream and Earth retreated underground and deep into the forest, where no one could reach them. Brother Architect and his sisters, Innovation and Soul, were abandoned and left to fight alone. Taking advantage of Sister Earth's absence, Brother Ocean flooded the forest, drowning more than half of its inhabitants.

Sister Soul mourned. She cast her brother out to live in the waters he controlled, tearing herself apart in the process. The purest of the foxes was now broken.

This inspired the Architect and the Innovator to find a way to divide the forest into two parts. They named one the Over and the other the Under. Using their understanding of dimensions and space, they built an invisible barrier, the strongest of its kind. No bird or beast, man or magic, could pass through the walls, except for the purest light among them, leaving the broken Sister Soul its only key.

The engineers focused on new, experimental magic and built a hall of sentient portals. These doors, traveling through unknown spaces, led to the locations of each remaining fox. If they could lure Fate to walk through her door during battle, they could lock it and trap her forever in the Under, along with her treasonous brothers. Before the world split, they only needed time to bring Body and Dream back home.

But Body couldn't be found, and Dream declined the invitation. He knew the prison would need a guard.

Fate, as she does, predicted their plan. She attacked before the pair was ready and tore apart their glorious kingdom on the hill. Her armies and allies outnumbered them—her magic stronger than the two. In a final effort to save the forest, Brother Architect used his remaining strength

to drag Fate into the Under, taking a deadly bite to his neck. Another fox was lost to the forest.

Executing her brother's last request so his sacrifice wouldn't be in vain, Innovation destroyed the remaining gateways.

Innovation lived on—as innovation does—in the Over. Abandoned by Earth during their hour of greatest need, she never spoke to her sister again, leaving her to wither in her kingdom of trees.

Soul, her other sister, was shattered beyond repair. Unable to recognize herself, Soul fled to the fae, her children, to heal.

So, Innovation sat alone and bitter in the Over, building an army—always waiting for the Under to break through."

"Well, that's grim. I can't imagine you performing this for children." Grey commented when Birk finished.

"In the version I perform, the foxes have silly fights and play tricks on one another. Ultimately, they all learn important lessons about love and family . . . the living happily ever after stuff."

"Maybe your version is the outcome your aunts wished to be true. It's not such a dreadful thing, is it?" Grey said, attempting to spin a positive light on his aunts' motives.

A pang of sympathy stirred for his aunts. "I think it's dangerous to rewrite our history; how else are we to learn from it? We can't heal from our pasts if we don't accept them in their full truths."

"That's true, but remember, your aunts left during the war. They've no idea how it ended. All they have to hold onto is hope . . . or fear." Grey amended. "In many ways that's a choice we all make."

Birk hadn't considered it from this perspective, never experiencing loss comparable to Grey or his aunts. "Do you know the history of the war? Is this accurate?"

"No, I don't know the full history," Grey confessed. "Bits and pieces are similar to what Shayvonne has taught me. It happened so long ago. Most records were destroyed in the war and its aftermath. Many of the

stories we share now are myths and exaggerations, both of the witches themselves and their conflicts."

"It's still more than I know," Birk admitted, regretting he'd not smuggled *The History of Driftstone* from Edi's library when the opportunity was available.

"Many believe the Original Thirteen never existed at all, legends created by Lady Ironspire to scare the masses and keep them in order." Grey shared, continuing to muse on the subject.

"Lady Ironspire?" Birk never heard the name.

"The witch ruling Ironspire. Based on the story, I believe she's Sister Innovation. It'd make sense; she is lauded as one of the only survivors of the Original Thirteen. There are rumors of another who still resides in the Living Forest, but no one has breached its boundaries to confirm. Shayvonne refers to her as Faunwood; I assume she's Sister Earth."

"So, if we take the story as truth, does it mean we're in the Over?" Birk asked, trying to build some clarity.

Grey scratched his head and said, "Lady Ironspire claims it is, although it's the first reference I've seen of it aside from folklore. For centuries, she claimed Driftstone was split in two, and at any moment, we'd be under siege from the Under. For a while, the citizens of Driftstone believed her and lived in constant fear and panic. They sent out all their ships, and every single one of them found nothing. Every mountain was scoured, and every island explored, but they found no evidence to support her claims. There are no credible existing records, and the generations that were alive back then can't remember anything."

"It doesn't mean it's not true; Balincia has been concealed all these years."

"Yes, but no one knows that," Grey reminded him. "After a while, Lady Ironspire stopped talking about it. She's convinced someone has stolen the records and changed everyone's memories. This has only added to the belief she's a little mad, a genius, but prone to conspiratorial illusions. Most people believe there was a war and that she had siblings, as it's been confirmed by the dwarves, fae, and elves. However, they also

think the truth has been stretched and fabricated over time by the magical races to influence and control the human populace."

"But you believe in the Thirteen, don't you? You spoke of them when I mentioned my aunts, and you believe your family was descended from the Protector?"

"Yes, I was raised to believe the Protector died in the war, but we were taught that your aunts and several others did, too. Shayvonne is a bit of a historian; she'll have a lot more knowledge than I do. Maybe this is why the map is leading us to my home." He paused, "You have to understand, Birk, my background and village are not typical of Driftstone. We're in the minority in our beliefs."

This was a lot for Birk to digest. He flipped the page of the book absentmindedly, only to find more text. "Grey, there's more on the next page," Birk exclaimed, scanning its content. "It doesn't appear to be part of the story."

Grey leaned in to read where he was pointing. "It's another riddle or maybe a prophecy?"

For each life lost, a different path unfolds.
To change the fate of Driftstone from its current mold
Since its inception, magic has been embedded in.
Leaving destiny to be decided by the witches' kin.

Eliminating the remaining original Magic-Born
Is the smoothest path forward, but one should be forewarned.
Life may exist without magic, but the land will pay a cost.
For all the souls attached to it, forever will be lost.

One must weigh the gamble of unbalancing the twins.
The second path that lies ahead is allowing Fate to win.
Lives may be saved, but all must bend a knee,
To the whims of darkness, which brings us to path three.

Thirteen is the number—of the power which is known,
But a fourteenth fox exists with a quest of its own.
The power of seven—multiplied by two,
Unites the magics needed with its binding glue.

An offering must be made for the lost lives of the three,
Only through this sacrifice will Driftstone be set free.
If zero paths are taken and nothing new is gleaned,
The Over and the Under will be swallowed by the In-Between.

"It is in the style of a prophecy," Birk noted, reflecting on Edi's lessons. "But if it's a prophecy, who made it?"

"The old woman who gave this to you?" Grey considered.

"I wish I hadn't left so soon. I should've tried to find her; it would've been the smart thing. She may have the answers we're seeking." Birk said, irritated with himself.

Grey placed his hands on Birk's shoulders. "I'm not sure that's true. She could've shared this with you the evening you met. She disappeared for a reason. You did your best with the information provided. If you'd stayed, you may have provoked a different outcome. Your aunts may have bound you under a stronger enchantment or confiscated the book."

"You're right. There's no value in wishing I'd done something different." Birk sighed.

"I wouldn't want you to change anything," Grey admitted, lowering his voice. "Your decisions led you here."

Winter unwelcomingly nudged between them. She tilted her head to the sky. The first of the three suns was setting.

"We're losing sunlight," Grey informed. "I'd feel safer if we could get to the bluff before it sets for camp. Can we pick the conversation up tonight?"

"Yes, of course. I need time for it all to sink in anyway." Birk closed the Driftstone and allowed Grey to help him back onto Brunt.

The next few hours were quieter. Brunt and Winter were determined to make up some ground, resulting in Grey's hold on Birk growing firmer. Grey *was* adjusting instinctively to Brunt's pace, securing Birk, *but* subconsciously, he was holding him closer for a different reason.

Raised by the Protector's familiars, Grey inherited their intuition. He could read energies and sense things undetectable to others. When he found Birk lying broken on the ice that night, something about his aura drew Grey to him. It didn't help that when he carried, bathed, and nursed him back to health, his animal genetics imprinted on him, forming an attachment.

A side-effect he kept to himself.

When Birk awoke, Grey couldn't help but be fascinated by him. He wasn't polished or suave, nor a skilled outdoorsman; instead, he was clumsy and genuine. Every stumble in his speech and nervous glance made him real and relatable. Grey was drawn to the innocence in him.

The way his laughter echoed in Grey's mind and lingered long after he spoke sparked an attraction and a strange new desire, one he'd never felt before. He ached to be close to Birk, and he was struggling to discern if this was a biological response or . . . something more.

This scared him.

He'd carefully kept only his sister and Shayvonne in his heart over the years; he'd lost too many others for one lifetime. They were enough and all he believed he needed—or so he thought.

Yet this man, *this terribly awkward man*, was shifting something inside him without permission.

A new and embarrassing version of himself was emerging. He was more playful. Less closed off. Motivated by Birk's smile, he chattered nonstop, which made him cringe inside at his attempts to keep his attention.

He knew their time together had been brief, but rationality faded when he was with him. How can you ignore fate bringing someone to your door or a bond born from saving a life?

Grey wasn't like other men. He felt things differently. He had more in common with the beasts of the forests.

His gut was telling him Birk was in danger.

So, Grey did what he was born to do.

He held Birk close to protect him.

TWENTY-SIX

The Truth About Giants

Birk was tucked into Grey, who was likewise tucked into Brunt's side, while Winter nestled against their legs. They'd made it to the bluff by the third sunset, giving them enough time to build a fire, scramble up some dinner, and settle in for the night. When Grey suggested they huddle close, Birk didn't require convincing. The winds were howling through their little carved-out camp, and Grey was warmer than any flames.

Grey, the last to nod off, had been trying to keep Birk company in front of the fire. They'd chatted a bit more about the prophecy and the Thirteen but concluded that getting a good night's rest was best. They'd tackle it with fresh minds tomorrow.

Grey's breathing eventually became heavier and slower until his body became slack, except his arms, which found themselves tangled tight around Birk's waist, while he slept.

Birk welcomed them, even if Grey wasn't conscious of doing it. It made him feel safe while he watched the fire burn amid the backdrop.

His thoughts drifted to home, and he wondered again about the aftermath of his departure. Running his fingers across the bracelet Pan had gifted him, he hoped she could feel his love reaching out to her and sense that he was safe.

It was hard for Birk to imagine that only a week ago, he was in bed with troubles of a far different nature. He was still worried about Balincia, but the other dilemmas seemed small when you compared them to carnivorous monsters and dark prophecies. His guardians' actions were *still* a violation, but a part of his heart was more sympathetic to their motives.

He imagined Edi chiding him with an *"I told you so"* speech.

There was a vibration in the earth behind him. Half lucid, he assumed Brunt was shifting in his sleep, so he ignored it. When it happened a second time, his body tensed.

"Be careful; we don't want to wake them," hushed a deep and gravelly voice.

"What am I supposed to do? The bear is all up in my hunches; I can't stay in this position all night," another voice, a bit higher, called out.

Birk immediately sat up, instigating Winter to raise her head in alert.

Their surroundings fell silent again until Birk saw the walls of the bluff move. Winter jumped to her feet and growled.

"What's wrong?" Grey stirred awake. Winter was facing him, focused on something beyond his shoulders, her teeth bared. Birk sat straight, frozen, clinging to his arm.

"I think there's someone else here. I heard voices." Birk whispered, afraid of alerting whoever was there.

With the agility of a wolf, Grey jumped to his feet, yanking Birk up and positioning him to his back. Grabbing a lit log from the fire, he waved it like a torch, joining Winter in a defensive stance against the bluff's wall. Brunt, slower, backed away from the partition, joining the others.

"Show yourself!" Grey snarled, sending Birk's hairs on edge.

The walls of the bluff came alive, shifting and crumbling around them. The roof that had only minutes ago sheltered them collapsed in a shower of rocks and debris. Swiveling, Grey wrapped one arm around Birk's waist and pulled him back just before the cliffside exploded.

"We've got giants!" Grey yelled, urging Birk to run to the trail ahead of them and away from the side of the cliff.

Grabbing Grey's hand, Birk bolted with him to the path's clearing as the parting debris clouds revealed what was behind them. The walls of the bluff were unfolding into legs, the peaks uncurling into backs—until three enormous shadows loomed over them. Out of the corner of his eye, Birk saw his satchel sticking out from the debris.

"The Driftstone!" Birk yelled, pulling Grey to a halt and pointing to it in the rubble.

"Leave it," Grey urged.

Sliding out of Grey's grip, Birk lunged after the book. "I can't. We need it to guide us," he insisted, only to be intercepted by Brunt, who charged him and threw him onto his back.

"I'll get it for you," Grey said, patting Brunt as he darted past them. "Keep moving! We need to get distance," he yelled to his familiars.

Riding Brunt backward, Birk watched the unstable bluff break apart. Above, three mammoth figures, now fully erect in the dark, slowly backed away from the evolving avalanche caused by their weight. Winter, realizing her cub was in danger, flew past them, narrowly escaping the falling earth with each jump.

Brunt came to a standstill, throwing Birk to the ground. Spinning, they witnessed the ground they'd just crossed disappear and crumble down a dark slope. Birk crawled quickly to the edge, with Brunt on his back legs beside him, desperately searching for Grey and Winter in the chaos.

"I see them," Birk yelled, pointing at a narrow ledge underneath the giants. Grey and Winter were balancing on a narrow strip of the fading precipice.

This was his fault; Grey and Winter were inches away from falling to their deaths *or* being crushed by giants, because he couldn't leave the Driftstone behind.

He needed to do something.

Refusing to sit idly, he and Brunt made a new path, carefully skirting the edges of the new landscape, trying to make their way back to them.

Keeping his attention glued to Grey, he realized their ledge was getting smaller on both sides.

Brunt was closing the distance, but the bear was leaving trees and shaky ground in his wake, blocking Birk's path in the process.

Birk was nearly halfway there when he spied one of the giants bending to his knees and peering over the edge. Its extra weight was causing the foundation to crack underneath Grey; *he wasn't going to make it in time.*

Suddenly, the giant swiped his arm at the ledge where Grey and Winter stood trapped. Its two companions turned in response and ran in the opposite direction.

The ground beneath them all gave way.

The giant fell headfirst into the deep darkness of the ravine, bringing Grey, Winter, and the remains of the bluff with him.

Birk's ears rang. He was unable to hear his shouts over the sound of the avalanche. Further down, another explosion of dust filled the night air, clouding their visibility. Sinking to the ground, Birk pounded his fists into the earth, screaming into the bleak night.

When the air cleared, Birk's entire soul crashed in on him. Brunt returned to his side, nudging him with his nose. Birk pushed the bear's face away, not wanting or deserving his sympathy. Brunt nudged him again, huffing and grunting for his attention.

"What? *What is it?* I know this is my fault. Are you angry with me? Go ahead, push me over the edge, too. I deserve it."

Brunt shook his head, slamming his front paws on the ground, prodding him to turn around. Giving up, the bear walked past him and stared into the ravine. His ears wiggled at the sound of movement.

Birk finally grasped Brunt's intent. "Are you trying to show me something?"

Brunt snorted in response.

Scrambling to the bear's side, Birk almost lost his footing when the edge rumbled beneath them. An enormous arm made from rock and

stone flew up from the pitch black, grabbing the earth beside them and prompting them to back away.

The giant had returned to finish them off.

Large eyes peeked over the edge as the giant dragged himself up with one arm. "I caught them just in time," he grinned. He slowly pulled his other arm into view and opened his hand on the ground, revealing a gently cupped Grey and Winter.

"Were you worried?" Grey said, stepping nonchalantly from the giant's hand. Winter followed, running circles around Brunt. "I've got your book," Grey said with a soft, playful edge, walking toward a paralyzed Birk.

"That stupid book . . I'm so sorry. It wasn't worth your life. I thought—" Birk's knees were about to give out from underneath him. "I thought you were gone."

Grey tilted his head, his grin softer than usual. "Takes more than that to get rid of me."

It was such a Grey answer—light where Birk was heavy—and it undid him even more. His hands were shaking. He didn't know whether to shove Grey for scaring him or throw his arms around him.

Grey spared him the choice. He stepped forward, caught Birk's wrist, and steadied it.

Birk jumped at his touch. His breath stuttered, and their eyes locked.

His hand drifted up, his thumb brushing the line of Grey's jaw, and all the feelings he'd buried, all the fear, uncertainty, and desire, tumbled free.

Unable to hold back, he flung his arms around Grey's neck and kissed him.

The world narrowed to the heat of their kiss. Grey's arms cinched him close, and the Driftstone fell forgotten to the ground. For the first time in what felt like forever, Birk wasn't thinking about tomorrow. He was here, with Grey, and nothing else mattered.

"Ahem," the giant interrupted, "Pardon my intrusion on this embarrassing display of affection, but we haven't been properly introduced. It's

awkward watching the two of you stuck together without an acknowledgment that I'm still here."

Birk, *who had forgotten about the giant*, lifted his head and peeked at him from around Grey's shoulder. The giant was unlike anything he expected. His skin was camouflaged and rough, akin to the stones and earth around them; it was no wonder they had blended in with the bluff. Everything else, from his face to his fingers, was similar to humans, except the wild grass, which grew where his hair should be.

Facing the giant, Grey laughed, keeping his arm secured around Birk.

"I'm sorry, my friend; almost falling off the side of a mountain tends to make one forget their manners. I'm Grey, and this is Birk. The wolf you saved is Winter, and the bear is Brunt; they're my companions."

"An odd combination of companions you travel with," pondered the giant, still sitting after his climb. Bowing his enormous head to them, he smiled, revealing yellow, boulder-sized teeth. "Pleased to meet you. My name is Flynt."

"I believe the wolf and I are in your debt. You saved our lives." Grey bowed back.

"Yes, thank you," Birk squeezed Grey's hand. "It's I who is in your debt, though. They required rescue because of me. I owe you everything for returning them safe and unharmed."

"Seeing how much you appreciate him, is debt paid," answered Flynt. "More importantly, it is not your fault; it's ours. We should have announced ourselves to you. It wasn't our intention to scare you. It was the carelessness of our movement that upended the mountains. When you are our size, treading slowly and carefully is a necessity."

"It's not *all* our fault," a voice boomed behind them.

Shaking the already unstable ground on their approach, two more giants joined them: one female with long mossy hair and the other chubbier and bald. Birk assumed they were the two who ran away when the bluff collapsed.

"Petra, be nice. These two young men have been through an ordeal." Flynt directed to the female.

"I'm only saying, everyone knows this is Giant Country, so maybe

check and make sure you aren't setting camp in someone's backside," she complained.

"Well, if your backside weren't so big, maybe they wouldn't have confused it with a bluff," the bald giant laughed, shaking the trees around them. Grey repressed a snicker.

"I'm sorry for my friends; this is Petra and Boulder," Flynt motioned to the two standing giants. "Would both of you please sit? We've caused enough damage tonight."

Boulder leaned, offering his hand to the two men. "It's nice to meet you." Birk gave his hand in response. The giant shook his arm vigorously between two fingers before sitting with a large thump, almost knocking them off their feet.

Petra ignored the introduction, appearing displeased with staying and continuing the conversation. Finding a large tree that Brunt had knocked over, she plopped down on it with a resigned exhale.

"I wasn't aware giants slept in such close quarters," Grey commented. "Don't you usually prefer your space to avoid things like this?"

Flynt nodded and said, "We've been sleeping in groups at night since the arcanivores appeared. We do our best to blend into the land and keep stationary until morning."

"Have they made their way this far into the mountain?" Grey asked, concerned.

"We've been driven farther north over the last week to avoid them. We heard rumors from an Elven hunter and chose to ignore them at our peril. Anything rarely challenges us due to our size." Flynt frowned at Boulder. "We learned too late that whatever they consume adds to their mass. One grew strong enough to overtake Boulder's younger brother. Since then, we haven't taken any risks."

Boulder sniffed, wiping away a tear from his eye with a large pinky.

"I'm sorry for your loss," Grey said. "I, too, have lost people in my village to these monsters. We encountered one about a week ago, nearing your size. It was hunting Birk."

"Hunting you?" Petra interrupted, sounding surprised. "If it was hunting you—you must be Magic-Born. You don't look Magic-Born to

me. Why didn't you use your magic to help your friend? Or do you have a useless kind?"

Birk shrank.

"Petra, that's rude," Flynt came to his rescue. "You can't go around asking people about their magic."

"No, it's okay," assured Birk. "I only recently discovered I'm Magic-Born. I lack the skills and experience to be efficient with what I'm doing; I'm still learning. I was afraid I'd make the situation worse. I have a connection with the earth; I just haven't learned to control it."

"Sounds like elemental magic to me," Petra noted. "Most of your kind never leave the Living Forest to rub shoulders with the likes of us."

"He's not from the area," Grey jumped in, saving Birk from further questions. "He's a traveler on a quest; one we unfortunately can't talk about."

"One we unfortunately can't talk about," Petra repeated sarcastically, mocking Grey. She was becoming bored, so she opted to play with the long strands of moss growing from her head.

"Oh—I have an idea. Can you make breakfast, elemental?" Boulder asked.

"Breakfast?" Birk looked at Grey nervously.

"Oh yes," Petra squealed, regaining interest in the conversation. "I'm tired of eating limestone and dolomite. Maybe you could ask the earth to cough up some gemstones for us."

"Now let's not impose on the lad," Flynt chided. "*But* if you're still interested in paying a debt, a few gemstones would be a fair trade for a few lives."

"Wait—you eat rocks and gemstones?" Birk asked, astonished.

"Of course," Flynt mused, "what did you think we ate?"

"Well, I've never met a giant before," Birk confessed. "I assumed you ate us."

All three giants roared with laughter, a little too long and cruel for Birk's taste, triggering the ground to shake. Birk searched for Grey's hand.

"That would be disgusting," bellowed Boulder, contorting his face, "all the mess."

"And zero nutritional value," Petra added in agreement.

Flynt, a little kindlier, explained, "Those are old stories we used to spread to keep humans away from our land."

Birk shot Grey a glance, who turned sheepish and white, shrugging at his error in judgment.

"I'm a Storyteller where I live. I collect stories from books and perform them for people. Giants were always described as man-eaters and villains, and lived in kingdoms in the clouds." Birk explained.

The giants broke out in laughter again. "That's hilarious. Can you imagine us—living in the clouds? Prancing around with our big feet?" Petra howled, miming little tap steps with her big fingers.

Boulder rolled to his side, laughing, "There's no cloud strong enough to carry you, Petra!"

Not finding Boulder funny, Petra picked up a fallen tree and threw it at his head.

"Keep telling those tales, Storyteller. People should be afraid to come up here. It's safer for you and safer for us. We're friendly, but with arcanivores and Free Roamers traveling the land, we all should stick to our kind." Flynt advised.

"We don't bother anyone as long as they don't bother us," Boulder added.

"Unless they fall asleep against your crack," Petra scowled, sending Boulder into hysterical fits all over again.

"The world *is* scary, but if there are dangers out there, don't you think having friends is important?" Birk asked. "I understand you don't trust those different from you, but if you ignore everyone, who will come to help you if you're in need?"

Grey was both entertained and inspired, listening to Birk counsel a small court of giants. "Birk's right. It's important to have allies right now. You saved my life, which shows me your character. We have a common enemy, and it would be wise to have others we can call on for aid. I told you I owed you a debt, so if you find yourselves in trouble, send word through the wolves, and Winter and I will come."

"This is honorable of you, little man with the big legs," Flynt bowed.

"We will consider. It has been ages since the giants counted others as friends. We're learning our size alone doesn't count against our enemies."

"I'd still rather have gemstones for breakfast," Petra grumbled.

This time, Birk laughed, "Let me see if I can help conjure some. I make no promises."

Walking between Boulder and Petra, Birk made a big show of kneeling and placing his hands into the earth. Winking at Grey, he riled the giants and made the earth around his wrists dance in circles. Imagining diamonds, rubies, and sapphires in his head, he summoned them forth from their deep beds in the mountains.

The giants reacted like gleeful children when the stones popped their heads above the surface, resembling a blooming field of flowers.

While Flynt acknowledged the two young men, Boulder and Petra dove in greedily, filling their cheeks. "Thank you. This will fill our bellies for a week. It was exceedingly kind of you."

"It's the least I can do," Birk smiled, glancing at Grey.

"The path may be obscured due to our commotion last night, but if you detour around the grove of trees, there's a trail leading you to Everglenn." Flynt pointed into the distance. "I'm assuming that's where you're going based on the direction you were heading, right?"

"Yes, thank you," Grey affirmed.

"It's only a day's journey from here if you keep pace with your bear and wolf. Maybe more if you rely on your tiny legs alone." Flynt shared, helping himself to a few gemstones, signaling his readiness for them to move on.

With no provisions or belongings left, save the Driftstone, there was no need to saddle Brunt. Reliant on their legs and confident in their abilities to find what they needed throughout the day, they departed with goodbyes.

TWENTY-SEVEN

PRAYERS TO THE PROTECTOR

Shayvonne lived in the back corner of Everglenn, closest to the mountains and farthest from the village center. Never married, she treasured her space, preferring the company of her books, garden, and sheep. She'd had suitors when she was younger, and if she were to believe the compliments afforded her, she was attractive, even now, in her middle age; she just carried an independence she'd no desire to tame.

There was nothing a man *or anyone* could bring into her life that she wasn't already supplying herself. If no value were added, it would only subtract from the peace and joy she'd already obtained on her own.

This all changed when a huge bear and a giant wolf came to her doorstep, terrorizing her sheep and throwing her into a frenzy. Accompanying them was a feral young boy with untrimmed hair and nails. He stared defiantly at her, dirt covering every inch of his naked body. He carried an infant, wrapped in animal skins and shivering.

Her first instinct was to round up some of the villagers who were parents, to take them off her hands, but something about the boy made her hesitate. She wished she could say it was a desperate yearning in the young boy's eyes that changed the direction of her heart, but maternal sympathy wasn't her strong suit. If anything, she was irritated they were at *her* door, leaving her obligated to do *something*.

No, what changed her mind was the boy's eyes didn't yearn; instead, they reflected their own irritation from being forced to be there. He had a soul similar to hers.

Admittedly, the presence of the two enormous wild beasts also played a significant role in allowing them to come in. Through a series of grunts and posturing, the grizzly signaled that he and the wolf would stay on her front porch until everything was settled, *much to her chagrin*.

The boy didn't speak much at first, which was fine with her; mutual silence was preferable. He was also eager to prove that he was capable of taking care of both himself and his sister, *which was a relief*. The only conflict they had was the enforcement of hygienic routines: cutting their hair and nails, ensuring they bathed, and, most importantly, maintaining a sense of modesty around the home.

The boy jumped in with the labor and chores without being asked or needing much direction. He was naturally good with the sheep, and after disappearing for a couple of hours one afternoon, he came back with six wild pigs, a dozen chickens, and a long-haired cow, expanding her homestead and providing milk for the baby. *She didn't dare ask where the animals came from.* In exchange, she taught him how to cook, sew his clothes, and educated him with books.

She didn't prompt him for his story or ask how he ended up in the company of beasts, but it was clear he once had parents who loved him. He spoke eloquently, with manners and insight, and he had an affinity for music and an aptitude for craft and carpentry. Treating him like an adult, she respected his privacy and went out of her way to avoid the intrusions she hated at his age.

She figured if he wanted to share something, *he would*.

All in all, she was pleased to find she enjoyed his quiet addition to her life.

Brynn, the young girl, was a different story.

Brynn required more attention, which Shayvonne assumed was why the children were brought to her. The girl held no memory of her mother and was in obvious need of a replacement.

Shayvonne lacked considerable experience in that department; her only qualifications were her intelligence, ability to endure, and being born a woman. She surmised this was enough, confident in her competence to figure it out. The boy helped her bond with the child, demonstrating how she preferred to be held and what her different cries meant. It was obvious he was protective of her, and the way she giggled and cooed around him spoke to their mutual adoration.

After several months, they fell into a routine and worked as a family unit. Not long after, the bear and the wolf disappeared. She assumed she'd passed their test, and they were now officially passing on the responsibility of ownership.

A year later, after her nightly prayer to the Protector, the boy surprised her by sharing the history of what had brought them to her door. That was when Shayvonne realized why she was chosen.

In her more formidable years, she'd picked up the ideologies of a group of misfits who named themselves the Free Roamers. Together, they romanticized philosophy about liberating Non-Magic-Born. She'd come to detest the reliance on magic in larger cities and been insulted by the diminutive positioning Non-Magic Born citizens were granted. Gaining influence with her academic voice, she led protests against the magical elite in Ironspire, resulting in a banishment for her role in a small rebellion.

With her options limited, she joined the nomadic group and thrived among individuals she believed to be like-minded. It didn't take long for her to regret this choice when she saw their flames of sovereignty turn into hate, and the hate evolve into violence.

She wasn't aware or warned of the first raid—when a group of men

from her camp secretly plotted an evening ambush on the Lorathil tribe of Elves—until she awoke to the smell of burning flesh and children screaming. A bonfire built of Elven bodies, young and old, towered in the center of her camp. Horrified, she hid and watched while the faces of those she lived among danced in celebration and spat on the carcasses of the innocent. Twisting and using the words she taught them, they connected her to their wicked deeds.

Sick to her stomach, her conscience gave way to repulsion, leading her to flee on horseback during the macabre festivities. Riding for days, she never looked back, and no matter how fast she went, the horse couldn't outrun the guilt she carried for fueling their aversions.

Eventually, she arrived at Everglenn, her spirit ripped and depleted. Here, she found a refuge to hide in, far away from the nomads *and* the cities, in a village where no one knew her sins. After months of self-prostrating and punishing herself, she gathered her strength and went to the Church of the Protector to ask for forgiveness. Humbling herself before them, she repented of her past and found herself inspired by a stronger ideology. A life centered on love.

Her new faith and the warlock who inspired it led her to evolve into a local historian, a status achieved by collecting archives, stories and records from travelers and refugees about The Original Thirteen. Carving out a small, simple life on her sheep farm, she learned to view magic through an educational lens, developing a new relationship with it. She reasoned she owed the magic community; learning their history was her way of giving penance for any suffering she'd indirectly caused.

So, when Grey finished sharing his story, Shayvonne hung her head. The Protector was calling her to serve for the debt she owed. It didn't change anything when she found out the children were his kin; she would've dedicated her life to protecting them anyway. She'd already grown to love them as her own.

Grey grew larger than the other boys in the village, his athleticism and brown skin attracting many followers—if he'd cared to notice. However,

his interests, similar to hers, didn't wander to mates. Instead, he found solace in the company of beasts, hard work, and escapades in the forests.

When he got older, she worried his frame and affect would confuse others into thinking he was a grown man, when, as a mother, she knew his heart and mind were still naïve, innocent, and young. She knew there were evil hearts who'd take advantage of such things, so she hesitated to let him trek too far or too long from the village. He never argued, always obedient to his core.

Over time, due to the trust he'd built, she slackened the leash, allowing him to disappear into the forests in small increments and practice his burgeoning gifts. Proving he was capable, he always returned with treasures and tales for his sister and enough fresh meat to stock the entire village's market. Her son hadn't only become his family's sole provider but also one of the main suppliers of goods for all of Everglenn, and with all the responsibilities he'd taken on, Shayvonne struggled to continue limiting the risks he chose to take.

For her part, Brynn was a smaller version of her brother, with *none* of his gentle spirit. If he were the rain, she was the thunder—loud and opinionated, taking space in any room she occupied. Shayvonne had to remind herself that it was *she* who cultivated this force of nature and bore sole responsibility for nurturing Brynn's more willful attributes.

She held no desire to raise a daughter unable to forge her own path, as well as any man. Still, there were days when Brynn's youth, not yet embedded with the time imperative for maturity and wisdom, tested her limits. While Grey reflected her present introverted nature, Brynn channeled the rebellious spirit of Shayvonne's past.

When the arcanivores attacked, everything changed. The monsters were drawn here for her children—she held no misconceptions about that. The other deaths in the villages were tragic, but Shayvonne knew they were collateral damage in a hunt for a bigger prize. Brynn and Grey were descendants of the Protector. If these creatures were hunting those

touched by magic, her children's scent led them to the village. Yet another guilt added to her pile.

Grey insisted on leaving the village and pursuing them, and he was at an age and temperament where there was little she could do to sway him. His connection to the Protector—evident when he arrived—had only grown stronger over time, replacing the safeguards she had instilled in him. And while she didn't doubt his skill or capability, this wasn't a normal hunt. Her son wasn't trained for battle, much less against dark, magical beasts.

She knew, however, fighting against the Protector's nature or ambitions would be pointless, but it left her to worry about who'd protect her son in return.

Driven to shield the last of his family at all costs, her son was overzealous. His emotions were fueled by fear and loss, which opened the potential for hasty decisions—he'd risk his well-being without thought, when there might be an alternative course. Who'd help to temper his spirit? Who'd navigate him toward a rational pause?

Not the bear or wolf.

Yes, she trusted they'd put their lives ahead of his, but they were warriors in their own right. They were aligned with him in intention and goal, not substitutes for someone instilling caution or reason. They couldn't quell his martyr instincts with love.

Grey, her sacrificial son, would offer his life for many, but she longed for him to find someone to give him a reason to live.

She and his sister weren't enough.

Not because he didn't love them; he loved them in a way that only protected *their* future, not his own. He held no securities for himself, sans the bear and the wolf. He was still a lost boy in a man's body, trying to heal the guilt he carried for surviving, something she unfortunately had experience with.

Ruminating on these thoughts, Shayvonne herded the sheep in from the pasture as the second sun began to set. Every day since Grey's departure, she traveled this route, scanning the northern trail in hopes of seeing his

buoyant shadow descending the steep mountain path. It had been two weeks since he left, the longest he'd been gone. *She was worried.*

Setting herself to task, she listened to Brynn running and wrestling with the young cubs in the wolf pack. Brynn pretended she wasn't worried about her brother's absence, but a mother knew a lie when she heard one. She could sense her daughter's anxiety growing every day.

Last week, she caught Brynn chopping her hair with a hatchet from the barn and staring in the mirror. She was trying to look more like him. Every day, she hurried to do chores at the farthest edge of the property, closest to the trail where he'd probably return. And every night, she carved more runes onto arrowheads and spears with nervous energy, eager to show him the fresh supplies she'd made for him.

"Shayvonne!" Brynn screamed. "Come over here, now!"

Picking up her skirt, Shayvonne ran full speed toward the open field where she last left Brynn. She heard the wolves in the distance. *She ran faster.* The adult male wolf at her side raced off in the same direction, sensing her urgency. Grabbing one of the rune-carved spears she'd left in the field, she darted to the commotion, praying she wasn't too late.

When she arrived on the scene, she saw Brynn standing on the cobblestone fence, staring into the mountains. The wolf cubs yipped and circled her. Slowing her pace, she stood behind Brynn and attempted to identify what she was looking at in the distance. "What is it? Did you see an arcanivore?"

Shayvonne clambered onto the stone wall with Brynn's help, clutching the spear in one hand and her daughter's arm in the other. Peering out into the fading light, every hair on her arm stood alert.

"I don't know," Brynn confessed, her voice shaking. "I saw four dark figures coming down the mountain. The switchback hides them, but they should appear soon."

"Four?" Shayvonne reacted with alarm. "We shouldn't be standing here. We should head back to the house and ring the town alarm. Everyone needs to get inside."

Brynn grabbed Shayvonne's hand, "Let's wait until we get a better view of them. I'm not sure they were arcanivores."

Shayvonne was uncomfortable waiting.

The figures were still far enough away that she and Brynn could make it back home, but she didn't want to put anyone else at risk. There was still too much they didn't understand about the arcanivores, and while she was capable, she'd rather not tempt fate. However, Brynn's eyesight was better than hers, and she didn't want to set off a false alarm, sending the village into a panic.

"Fine, but as soon as they reappear around the corner, I need you to make a quick determination. We don't have time to second-guess ourselves."

The next few minutes stretched while they waited, silently holding their breath with the wolves. Every eye was aimed at the opening of the switchback, while every leg was ready to move at a moment's notice. Shayvonne prepared to usher them back when four dark forms appeared.

Brynn was right. They didn't move or act in the same manner as arcanivores. Two of them appeared to be humans.

"Can you tell?" Shayvonne asked Brynn, squinting.

"I think it's Grey!" Brynn squealed with delight.

Not wanting to get her hopes up, Shayvonne probed again. "*Are you sure? Why are there four of them? Can you tell if Brunt or Winter is with them?*"

"I think so—there's only one way to find out. Seraphine, call out to your mother!"

A young cub to the left of Brynn raised her head and howled into the distance. The four figures all appeared to stop. One replied with a long, loud howl, prompting all the wolves to leap from the walls and run toward them.

"It's them! It's Grey! He's back!" Brynn screamed with excitement. Leaping from the stone wall, she followed the wolves, running toward the trail entrance.

"Be careful!" Shayvonne cried after her, "Wait until he's down the mountain!"

Shayvonne smiled; she now recognized the familiar figure of her son. There was no mistaking his swaggering gait or the world's largest bear next to him. Putting her hand over her heart, she thanked the Protector for keeping Grey safe and returning him home.

Walking to join the others in greeting him on his descent, she kept her sights on the fourth unknown character. Appearing to be a man, he was shorter than Grey and far less broad. What drew her attention was how close they walked together.

Even from a distance, she could discern their bodies speaking to each other with familiarity and intimacy. Spying Grey's hand resting on the small of the other man's back, she could tell her son was gently helping him down the mountain, sparking hope within her.

Had two of her prayers been answered?

TWENTY-EIGHT

A Mother's Intuition

Birk was relieved and intimidated when Grey's home came into view. He was ready to sleep in a real bed tonight, but anxious about meeting Grey's family. The welcoming reception of a pack of wolves hurdling toward them did little to calm his nerves. Grey steadied him with a touch.

"You're going to love them," Grey assured. *Birk was more worried about their reaction to him.*

Stepping in front of Birk, Grey lowered to his knees and opened his arms for the first incoming wave of wolves. The pack of pups launched themselves at Grey in twos and threes, licking his face and pulling at the edge of his pants with their teeth. Winter, further down the trail, was already wrestling and pawing more prominent members of the pack, whining with excitement.

"Hey, Bear Butt! You're late!" A young girl's voice yelled.

A skinny adolescent girl with brown skin ran toward them, stopping to throw her spindly arms around the great bear's neck. Leaning into Brunt's ears as she scratched them, she teased, "I wasn't talking to you, handsome. You're always right on time. I was talking to the doltish, hairy ape behind you."

Birk choked on a laugh, "She's not wrong about your butt," he teased, baiting Grey out of the side of his mouth.

Grey gave him a quick fake frown, "Be nice to me," he mouthed, pivoting to catch Brynn in his arms. "Hey, wild one!"

Spinning her around in the air, she hung on his neck. "You stink," she complained.

"I missed you, too!" Grey nuzzled his nose against hers. "I like what you've done with your hair. Are you attempting to be as dashing as I am?"

"Don't flatter yourself; it was getting hot," she said, holding back a grin. She punched him in the arm.

Feigning hurt, Grey poked back, "Is the heat helping you get stronger, too? Or is it the goblin growing inside you?"

"I'm stronger because I'm overworked. Shayvonne has been brutal. She has me in the fields all day, and since you're not here, I have to pick up all *your* slack," Brynn dramatically rolled her eyes.

"Don't believe a word she says." A woman close to Talbot's age made her way to them. "The only things Brynn does are the things Brynn wants to do."

Grey laughed loudly, "Now THAT I believe!"

Touching Grey's arm, the woman leaned in to kiss his cheek. "Welcome home, son. We missed you." Peering around her son's massive frame, she waved at Birk with a warm smile. "And I see you've brought home . . . a friend?"

Birk didn't miss the subtle poke for information; it was a skill Edi mastered. Stepping forward, he offered his hand and returned her smile. "I'm Birk."

Shayvonne took his hand and pulled him closer, placing her other hand on top. "Birk, I'm Shayvonne. You'll have to forgive us our manners; we're excited to have Grey home."

Grey winked at Birk, "And this beast is my little sister, Brynn."

Brynn scowled at the introduction. Jumping from her brother's arms, she looked Birk over, settling on a skeptical nod and a "hi."

Shayvonne wrapped her arm around Birk's shoulders, guiding him

to walk with her. "Why don't we get you home before it's dark? I'm sure you're both exhausted, hungry, and needing a wash."

Grey glanced back at Birk, a silent check-in to ensure he was ok. With a quick nod, Grey smiled and walked ahead, catching up with his sister. Shayvonne linked her arms with Birk's, milking the opportunity to have him alone.

"Birk is a beautiful name. Your mother must've loved birch trees. They happen to be one of my favorites." She complimented, putting him at ease while they strolled.

"Thank you. I'm not sure, to be honest," Birk confessed. "I don't know my mother. My aunts raised me." Shayvonne smiled; it was an encouraging sign women raised him.

"How did you meet, Grey? Are you traveling between destinations?" she asked, prompting her son's ears to perk up.

"He saved my life."

Shayvonne stopped. "Grey? *What happened?* Please don't tell me—" She was interrupted by a firm look from Grey. Shaking his head, he nodded toward his sister. Holding Birk back for a moment, Shayvonne took his hands. "Thank the Protector, you're both okay. We'll talk more about this later, once Brynn is asleep."

Leaning against Birk, Shayvonne shared Everglenn's history while they descended the trail. The village, covered in stone-walled fences and cottages, was surrounded by pastures filled with sheep and long-haired cattle. An old stone church, complete with a bell tower and stained-glass windows, was erected in the town center.

Birk was intrigued by the church. Balincia had never adopted religion, only spiritual beliefs linked to the Scales of Magic, so it was interesting to learn they believed Everglenn was built on sacred land. According to Shayvonne, the Protector's vision for Everglenn was to be a sanctuary for travelers, refugees, and migrants seeking a peaceful or less nomadic life.

The town's core belief and practices were a commitment to live in harmony with nature, causing as little disturbance as possible. When the Protector died, the villagers built the first and only Church dedicated to

one of the Original Thirteen. She explained their faith was less about religious worship and more about honoring the principles of his life.

"According to history, when Farren died, *that's the Protector's real name*; he imbued this land with his magic, his last gift to Driftstone." Shayvonne shared. "By doing this, he ensured his magic would sustain and nourish what he loved most instead of it being siphoned by his siblings. Whether one believes this or not, the land here has always thrived."

"And the purpose of the runes? They were on the standing stones in his valley, and I noticed some carved into the trees when we traveled."

"Ah, yes, the runes demonstrate our respect for the land, a reminder of Farren's sacrifice. An extension of light magic, his followers believe they provide protection. To be honest, I think they've also evolved to serve as borders, signaling to other nomadic tribes this land is occupied."

She pointed to a few symbols carved on trees and painted on stables. "The runes center on the seven core principles created by the Church. This one means love," she said, motioning to a rune etched into a rock. "The one over there means loyalty, and then there is compassion, honesty, and courage—the remaining two are sacrifice and balance."

"You mentioned the Protector's followers; are you not one of them?"

"I wouldn't consider myself a follower, but I'm a respectful and interested party. The values they focus on are close to my heart, but I learned long ago even the best ideologies have the ability to turn dangerous." Shayvonne paused, reflecting on her past. "I'll admit, however, when Brynn and Grey entered my life, I adopted a few practices of faith. I find prayer a beautiful medium for introspection and giving gratitude."

"You listed balance as one of the Church's core principles. The concept of balance weighed heavily in my upbringing, too. It was written into our laws." Birk shared.

"Interesting. I suppose, as it is with many things, it's how you define it. Balance, contradictory to belief, doesn't *always* mean all things in equal measure."

"What do you believe it means?"

"I believe balance isn't supposed to be quantifiable. Sometimes there is a clear right answer, and sometimes there is a clear wrong answer, but many times, truth and love, life and death, any beliefs or ethics, are more complicated."

"Depending on circumstance or context?"

"Exactly. In addition to several other random factors on any given day. If we are defining it in the context of a principle of protection, balance is safeguarding space for life, love, and innovation to flourish in different ways. We shouldn't limit things to one path, choice, or way of thinking."

"Appreciate the unpredictable," Birk recited aloud, reflecting on Pan's lessons. He smiled at Shayvonne, "My aunt would like you."

"You've been chatting non-stop; should I be worried?" Grey interrupted, strolling back to them with a smile. Engrossed in his conversation with Shayvonne, Birk didn't realize they were now standing in front of Grey's home in the pasture.

Shayvonne pinched Grey's chin, passing him to open the door. "I don't know. Have you done something *you* should be worried about?"

Grey blushed.

It was amusing for Birk to see his interactions with his foster mother and sister, discarding the mask of the warrior he first met in the woods. "Your mom was sharing with me the history of Everglenn. No embarrassing stories of you *yet*."

"Oh, I have plenty of those!" Brynn yelled from somewhere inside the house, signaling she was listening. Grey rolled his eyes, closing the door behind him.

"Brynn, why don't you join me in the kitchen?" Shayvonne yelled back. "I could use your help with dinner. As for the two of you, I'm sure you'd appreciate the opportunity to clean before we eat. Birk, please make yourself at home; Grey will show you around."

Emerging from the washroom, Birk felt like a new man. Fresh clothes, clean skin, and a home filled with the savory fragrance of lamb pie restored his spirit.

"It's about time," Brynn complained, "how long does it take for two people to wash?"

Grey grabbed her by the sides, tickling her ribs, "Some of us have more areas to clean. We're not all as dainty and quick as you."

"Eww . . ." said Brynn, disgusted. "That's because you have too much hair. I hope he doesn't shed on you tonight, Birk."

Birk tried not to laugh. Shayvonne shot Brynn a rapid glance to behave. "Please, have a seat," she motioned. "I figured you both haven't eaten a home-cooked meal in a while, and Grey always comes home starving. Besides the pies, we've got some cheese, grapes, mint jelly, and freshly-baked bread."

"Don't forget the apple crisps for dessert." Brynn licked her lips.

"This all looks delicious. I can't thank you enough for your hospitality. I know you weren't expecting me." Birk sat beside Grey.

"It's my pleasure; it's not often we have guests." Shayvonne added, "In fact, I don't think we've ever entertained a guest."

"We're anti-people," said Brynn, shoving her mouth full of food.

"We're *not* anti-people. My mom and sister are trying to say we're glad you're here." Grey interrupted, wrapping his hand around Birk's thigh.

"I'm not saying that," Brynn mouthed again.

"It's been the three of us for a long time, Birk. You'll have to forgive our social graces. We're a little out of practice." Shayvonne admitted.

"There is nothing to forgive; you've made me feel right at home. My aunt Edi wouldn't know what to do if I showed up unexpectedly at the palace with someone, *and she has a full kitchen staff to help her.*" Birk laughed.

Brynn stared at him; mint jelly hung from her uncovered mouth.

Shayvonne sat back in her seat. "Did you say palace?"

"Are you a prince?" Brynn leaned forward on her elbows. Birk suddenly became remarkably interesting.

Realizing how he sounded, Birk peeked at Grey for help, only to have him laugh in return. "How about you start at the beginning, as you did with me, and tell them where you're from?"

Birk shifted in his seat. Taking a deep breath, he told his story again.

Brynn and Shayvonne, more interactive and inquisitive as an audience, constantly interrupted him. Like most children her age, Brynn was fascinated by the floating islands, the colorful characters, and the fact witches raised him. Shayvonne, intrigued by his aunt's history, was astounded they were alive and had remained hidden for so long.

Grey, in turn, reminded him to share details about being a Storyteller, the island full of chickens, and the mysterious hall of doors. Grey's face glowed, listening to Birk speak—which didn't go unnoticed by Shayvonne. For over an hour, Birk shared his story while they collectively emptied the table of food in front of them.

Leaving out some of the darker elements and the discovery of his magic, he stopped when he reached the part about his arrival in the mountains. Looking at Grey, he heeded his warning, hesitant to share more in front of Brynn's ears. Shayvonne, noticing this, stood and began to clear the dishes from the table.

"Thank you, Birk. Balincia sounds fascinating. I can't believe a whole civilization has been hidden from us all this time. The implications of this change everything we know about our past. I also imagine it's not easy adjusting to new surroundings for you. It's a good thing Grey found you; not many can survive those nights on the mountain alone." Shayvonne stacked the dishes in the sink.

Birk rose from the table, helping her to clear the plates. Reaching for Brynn's, she pressed him with curiosity. "Yeah, how did Grey find you? You mentioned he saved your life. You didn't tell us that part."

Grey intervened, kicking his sister under the table. "Why don't we let Birk take a break from talking? I think you've interrogated him enough for one night."

"Fine, *you* can tell us." She kicked him back. Grey and Shayvonne exchanged looks.

"Brynn, it's been a long day; why don't you prepare for bed? I'm sure the boys are exhausted and will follow soon." Shayvonne instructed, averting her gaze out the kitchen window.

"I saw the look you gave each other. I'm not a little girl anymore.

There's something you don't want me to hear." She rooted into the seat. "It's about the arcanivores, isn't it? I already know why you were out there. I'm not scared of them; you might as well tell me."

"You *should* be scared of them," Grey snapped (a little too harshly). "They came to this village for you and me."

"That's why I deserve to stay and listen. *It involves me.* Did you find more? Is that how you saved Birk's life?" Brynn demanded, angry for the way he scolded her in front of Birk.

Grey sighed, running his hand down his face. "Yes. Okay? Brunt, Winter, and I were hunting three of them."

"Three of them?" Shayvonne exclaimed.

"Bigger than the ones that attacked the village, stronger."

"Were they headed here?" Shayvonne peered out the window again.

"No, they were heading in the opposite direction, hunting Birk."

Brynn brightened with interest. "They were hunting you? That means you're—"

"Magic-Born." Birk nodded.

"You must have strong magic in you for them to prioritize you over Grey," Shayvonne said, concern rising.

"*And* I didn't save Birk; he's being generous. At least not from the arcanivores. He killed one with *his* magic, raising the standing stones in the valley." Grey shared.

Shayvonne placed her hand over her mouth.

"Impressive!" Brynn said, continuing to reassess her initial impression.

"Brunt sent one down the river, and Winter and I double-tagged the third. If Birk wasn't there, I'm not sure we would've been able to manage all three alone. He saved my life as much as I did his." Grey walked over to put his arm around Birk. "He was fatally wounded, so I carried him to the healing springs. It took a couple of days to get him sorted."

"Let's not forget the giants," Birk poked, stirring Grey's sister and receiving a sharp elbow to his ribs.

"You met giants, too?" Brynn asked. "That's not fair! You never take me that way! I miss out on all the fun."

"Wild one, none of this was fun. It was terrifying and dangerous, and we're lucky to be alive. Now listen to Mom and get ready for bed. We need to have an adult conversation about what we'll do next. I promise we'll share more stories with you tomorrow." Grey kissed her on top of the head. "I realize you're not a *small* child anymore, but you're *still a child*. It's my job as your older brother to protect you."

"Fine," she relented. Promise me you won't leave tomorrow or make any plans without me."

"I promise. We'll be here a few nights and catch you up on everything." Grey pulled her in for a hug.

"Birk, I hope you stick around if bear butt doesn't frighten you away," Brynn called out, peeking around her brother, wriggling out of his arms.

"That's high praise coming from her," Shayvonne teased, following her out of the room to ensure she stayed tucked in for the evening.

Grey and Birk lingered in the kitchen. The moonlight through the window painted the kitchen in soft lights, and a calm settled over the house. The sounds of dishes clinking, water simmering, and the fire crackling in the hearth lulled Birk into a daydream. He warmed to the sight of Grey in this domestic setting, lighting candles and attending to routine tasks.

Grateful to share a moment alone with Grey, he was taken watching him hum a tune under his breath. Through the kitchen window, the sight of Brunt, stationed at the front porch, and Winter curled up beside her pack under the stars added to the atmosphere. The prospect of uprooting Grey from this picturesque setting sank in, as did the repercussions it would have on his mother and sister.

Selfishly, he didn't want to consider being separated from him, either. Not when they were just beginning to explore this connection between them.

Birk grappled with the reality of the lurking dangers necessitating their departure. Their priority had to be eliminating the arcanivores if they hoped to return one day and explore something—more.

Feeling the need to convey his feelings, he approached Grey from

behind, who stood at the kitchen sink. Wrapping his arms around him, he rested his head against his sturdy shoulders. Grey stopped what he was doing, interlaced his fingers with Birk's, and leaned back into him. A silent acknowledgment passed amidst the candlelight.

Shayvonne stood in the doorway, fixed on the touching sight. For a fleeting moment, she remained frozen, her heart moved by her stoic son's tenderness. Her hand moved to her chest, an unconscious gesture of gratitude, witnessing Grey's vulnerability in Birk's arms.

Reluctant to intrude on their intimate moment, Shayvonne made her presence known by lifting the kettle off the flames. The light click as it was set on the table prompted Grey and Birk to slowly disengage, redirecting their attention to her. "Should we continue our conversation in the library?" she proposed.

Grey nodded, helping her to pull down the large clay mugs for tea and aiding her with the preparations. "There's something we wish to show you where the insights from your research would be valuable," Grey shared, signaling Birk to go and collect the Driftstone.

Entering the library, Grey set to work on building a fire. Birk joined them a few minutes later, the book in his hands. He laid it on the wooden table in front of Shayvonne.

"Is this the one you were telling me about?" She asked, running her hand across the cover.

Birk nodded, "Yes, but we didn't want to discuss its entries until we were alone with you."

Shayvonne's gaze shifted from the book to Birk to Grey while she listened to the Driftstone's significance and what lay revealed on its pages. The three drew closer, discussing Birk and Grey's theories and the questions plaguing them.

When the boys finished, Shayvonne scooted her chair back and reflected. "Before I begin, I want to remind you both that I don't have any experience with magic except from an educational point of view." Facing Birk, she directed her following statement to him. "I agree the

book seems prophetic in nature, but I *also* believe it's contingent on your choices."

"What do you mean?" asked Birk.

"For example, it didn't instruct you on what door to use; the choice was yours. The riddled language is coded for your benefit, *as frustrating as that might be.* When I've researched the magics of fate and destiny, it indicates you can't be pushed to do anything you don't want. This is good because it means your choices *matter*," she emphasized.

"But what about the last entry? The prophecy only gives three choices, all describing loss and sacrifice." Grey asked, concerned.

"I wouldn't get too caught up in the language of prophecies or get ahead of yourselves. The biggest error you can make is assuming they only mean one thing. Once you've decided *on this one thing*, you've destined it to be true. You've convinced yourself it's the only interpretation."

"It's similar to our discussion earlier today; there can be multiple versions of truth based on the context provided," Birk glanced at Shayvonne.

"Or, in this case, based on the reader's interpretation. Here's the thing: it's not the answer you want to hear, but since the Driftstone won't respond with full, detailed instructions on what it wants you to do, your best course is to take it one step at a time. Manage it like a puzzle; place each piece where it belongs until you see the bigger picture."

Birk and Grey looked at each other, disappointed. Shayvonne knelt before them, placing her hands on their knees, "If it brings you comfort, I believe you need to do this together."

She faced Grey first. "Birk's choices led him to you. When you took him in, you became a part of his story." Moving her attention to Birk, "And likewise, you became a part of *our* story. The arcanivores are hunting you both, and considering your nightmares—they may represent a larger danger to everyone in our lives. You'll be stronger if you face this together."

"So, what do we do next?" Grey asked. "Should we ask the Driftstone?"

Shayvonne paused, "Let's do it tomorrow. I want you to enjoy your rest tonight. You'll be taking my bed; it's larger." Before either of them

objected, she insisted. "You don't know the next time you'll have a few nights to share in comfort. Please do it for me and yourselves."

Grey kissed his foster mother's cheek, "Thank you."

"Birk, do you mind if I hold onto the Driftstone tonight? I want to study it a bit more. Maybe I'll have some fresh insights tomorrow." Shayvonne asked.

Birk hugged her, "Yes, of course. Thank you for your hospitality. I see where your son inherited his generous spirit."

By the time Birk made it to the bedroom, Grey was already lying on his back, shirtless, with the sheet pulled to his waist. Lying with his arms behind his head, his hair strewn across the pillow, he stared at the ceiling.

"Are you okay?" Birk slid into the bed from the other side.

"I'll be okay; it's a lot to process." Grey's mind was far away.

Birk understood, "I'm glad you're processing it with me."

"I am, too," he answered vacantly.

Birk fidgeted. "This feels strange."

Grey's attention returned to the room. "Why? Because we're in my mother's bed? She means well—"

"No," Birk cut him off. "I mean, it is a *little* weird being in your mother's bed. I was referring, though, to how much space we have between us. I've grown accustomed to leaning against you to stay warm."

Grey lifted his brow and said, "Only to stay warm, huh?"

"Mmmhmm," Birk played indifferent.

"Well, I can fix that," Grey said, sliding over. Propping on one elbow, he rested his calloused hand on Birk's chest. "Better?"

"Much. You were lost there for a moment."

Grey's hair fell to the side of his face when he leaned in, tickling Birk's nose.

"I'm here now," his lips grazed Birk's mouth. Sliding his hand off Birk's chest, he moved it under his back, drawing him in for a kiss.

Grey slid his thigh over Birk's waist, straddling him with a suggestive smile.

"Wait a minute—are you naked?" Birk's eyes flashed.

"Do you have to ask?" Grey growled in response.

"But—there's no blanket between us."

Grey raised his eyebrow, shameless, "Do you want one?"

"No," Birk wrapped his legs around Grey's thick trunk.

"You think I have a bear butt?" Grey teased between kisses.

"I mean, it *is* fuzzy and . . . big."

Grey pushed himself up on his arms, feigning hurt in his face, "Big?!"

Birk laughed, pulling him back. "I didn't say I didn't like it."

"So—you *like* my bear butt?" Grey enticed.

"I *love* your bear butt," Birk said, dragging him under the sheets.

TWENTY-NINE

THE VOYEUR

Birk stood on the arena floor of an enormous Colosseum. Beside him stood the bear and the princess; once again, she was dressed in warrior attire. The sky above them was filled with brooding dark clouds. Lightning flashed, illuminating the scene below.

The stadium surrounding them roared with panicked voices. The audience was jumping over each other in terror, pushing each other to the ground, trying to escape from the stands. Arcanivores oozed and crawled from the walls of the arcade and up from the earth beneath them. Soldiers with azure blue hair clashed with the beasts, their weapons flashing with light as they engaged in a desperate battle.

A voice—feminine, dark, and cruel—rang from the heavens, addressing Birk. "I see you, Storyteller. I seeeee you," she taunted. Her laughter echoed across the arena floor.

The princess faced the advancing shadows, holding twin swords of light. Swinging and slashing, she screamed into the night. Her skills, however, were still not enough to fend off the relentless horde bearing down on her. They swarmed her with their numbers, grabbing her beautiful form and dragging her into an Abyss.

They lunged at Birk, but the bear, his fearsome guardian, jumped in to *protect him. He ripped the evil entities to shreds with his claws and teeth. In response, the shadows multiplied by twos and fours, growing larger and stronger with each fall. The dark army descended on Birk's protector. Wave after wave, they stormed, overwhelming the bear, tearing apart his flesh and fur until he lay lifeless and still on the ground.*

Birk's cries were drowned in the clamor of the battle raging around him. He tried to reach his fallen friend, his screams hoarse with grief and rage. Kneeling beside the bear, he cracked the earth with his fists. Facing the encroaching evil, he challenged them with a defiant roar.

A single ray of light pierced through the sky directly above him. It burned and pushed back the approaching beasts, surrounding Birk with a protective radiance. A familiar voice called out from inside the light—the voice of someone who'd burn the world to save him.

The voice of Pan.

"This isn't real, Birk," she soothed, dispelling the fear ensnaring him. "You're safe," she reassured. "You're safe. Wake up, my love, you're safe."

His eyes snapped open. Beads of sweat covered his chest, his heart galloping. Grey gave a slight twitch beside him. He wrapped his fingers around the bracelet Pan had gifted him, and reached out to touch Grey—his chest's steady rise and fall offered him a sense of grounding. Carefully unlatching Grey's arms from his waist, he slipped out of bed. Throwing on his discarded pants, he went in search of fresh air.

When he passed the study, lit candles drew his attention. Peeking inside, he found Shayvonne still awake. Leaning over the Driftstone, she jumped upon Birk's entrance. "Birk! Is everything okay?"

Shaking his head, he collapsed into the chair in front of her. "The visions came back. I needed some air."

Grabbing a blanket, she wrapped it around his shoulders. He was pale and cold to the touch. "Let's warm you," she offered, rekindling the fire. "Do you want to talk about it?"

He wasn't sure he did, but it was a better alternative than letting

it wrestle inside him. Walking her through the nightmare, he choked, describing the arcanivores killing the bear. "I'm sure it represented *him*, Shayvonne," he agonized.

"Who?"

"*The bear is Grey*. I'm terrified if he remains with me, something bad will happen. You have to help me persuade him to stay behind with you."

"Oh, honey," Shayvonne shook her head, "I realize it felt real, but your aunt's voice was right. It was *only* a dream. It doesn't mean everything in them is going to happen."

"It doesn't matter. I almost lost him once; if there's a risk—"

"Shhh," she hushed, "you can't give energy to those thoughts. Besides, you and I know Grey will follow you wherever you go. He's already smitten—and stubborn." She leaned forward and hugged him, "Nothing is set in stone. Everyone has choices, and as far as I can tell, Grey has chosen *his* path. You can't take his choice away."

Birk knew she was right. Even if he tried to sneak away, he wouldn't get far before Grey found him.

"What *does worry me* is even if your visions aren't literal, they *have* warned you with metaphoric perspectives of things to come. I'm nervous about the voice you heard."

"She called me Storyteller; she *knew* me. She indicated she was watching me. How? Who is she? What do you think she means?" Birk cast a glance at the Driftstone. "*You don't think she can see me through the book, do you?*"

Shayvonne reflected on it. "I think it would be a good idea for you to take a break from using it for safe measure until we understand it better. I'm not saying it's connected, but we can't rely on its intent without knowing its origin. It wouldn't be the first time in history an item infused with magic could be used as a window for its creator."

"Do you think they can hear us now?" Birk lowered his voice, scanning for a hovering invisible entity.

"I don't think it works that way," she reasoned, tickled. "And I don't want to imply its origins are nefarious. I've been studying it, and I think it was created by someone who needs your help. Someone who needs your

powers awake, your mind aware. This book was created to communicate with *you*."

"When I met the old woman at the market, she told me she knew who I was. She implied she knew everything about me," he replied, still trying to solve the mystery of the haunting voice.

"And if she intended you harm, why not take advantage? You were alone, powerless, and without insight," she pointed out. "It wouldn't make sense for the voice to be hers, *but* I pulled out some of my records of the Thirteen, and I think I've come across a few helpful things. Would you care to hear?"

Birk nodded, happy to change the subject.

"According to folklore, including the story you shared of the Thirteen Foxes, each of the Thirteen was responsible for the creation, balance, and shaping of life as it exists today. To be effective, they had to work together; otherwise, too much of one thing and not enough of another might spoil the pot."

"Like my aunts, Chaos, and Order," Birk agreed. "*The scales must always remain balanced.*"

"Right, but they weren't the only pair to keep the other in check. You have the juxtaposition of the body and soul, intellect versus dream, and, of course, the polarizing elements of earth and water. The only two that gave me pause were the Protector and Fate, but if you think about it, their magics represent the cycles of life and death."

"That makes sense, but what about the foxes they call Innovation and Architect? Aren't they similar?"

Shayvonne pulled out another book, *The Ruler of Ironspire*, handing it to him. "I admit the names in your story are confusing. Innovation's real name is Sable, the most prominent member of the Thirteen," referencing the book. "She's led the most public life since the war, known widely as Lady Ironspire. Her brother, the Architect, was named Cyrus."

"His name is familiar," Birk reflected. "My aunt was studying his book when crafting the hallway of doors."

"It doesn't surprise me; his magic specializes in space. He helped engineer Driftstone as a planet, creating our systems and geographies to

operate harmoniously. Once finished, he focused on creating and discovering new spaces and realms, expediting travel between them. He was an expert in portal magic, rumored to break through dimensional thresholds." Sitting next to Birk, she leaned in, "I have the impression he's the one who helped your aunts to hide all those years ago."

"What about Lady Ironspire? What's the opposite of space?"

"Density. Sable was blessed with the ability to condense magic at an atomic level. She is called the Innovator because she condenses her magic into objects: machines, weapons, and even buildings. Her enchanted inventions fast-tracked progress for Non-Magic-Born, elves, dwarves, and fae alike. Ironspire is the most advanced city in Driftstone, using magic *and* science as its fuel to operate." Frowning, she added, "which has come at a cost to those who live there."

"That's only twelve—there's thirteen foxes. Why didn't Discord have an equitable counterpart, particularly since he caused all the trouble?"

She enthusiastically nodded and said, "That's what I thought too, *except* I reread the last entry in the Driftstone prophecy, which mentions—"

"A fourteenth fox!" Birk interrupted, sharing her excitement. "*A fourteenth fox on a quest of its own.* But why is this the first mention of a fourteenth? Where were they during the war?"

"Maybe they were always there, but removed from our records. *Or* maybe they weren't born yet. Keep in mind the youngest wasn't always referred to as Discord. He was born with persuasive magic," she refreshed him. "If used wisely, he could influence reason and inspiration, a power with the ability to balance his entire family."

"Instead, he used it to create division, pushing his siblings to their extreme natures, leaving them unchecked," Birk theorized. "*He* was intended to be the original glue holding them all in place, but abandoned his purpose."

"Both the history and the magic of the Thirteen are complicated, even more so when they involve the forces of fate and destiny," Shayvonne warned him. "I would caution us from making claims about their purpose, even *they* had choices."

"What if the fourteenth fox is the old woman I encountered?" Birk

contemplated. "Although it would be odd for her to send me on a quest if she were on her own. *Unless I was her quest? Or* what if it's the girl in my visions I keep seeing? She has to play a role in all of this."

"Possibly, an argument for either candidate is valid. One could even surmise it might be *you*, Birk," she posed. "But for tonight, I don't think that's the right question."

"What is the right question?"

"This book is potent magic; it alludes to earth-altering events impacting us all. I don't believe it's a coincidence you received the Driftstone around the same time the arcanivores were first sighted."

"You think they're connected?"

Her face was grim. "I don't want to scare you; I think it's more than a connection—I think it's a response. The formidability required to create this book may have alerted others. When you use it, you may send signals to others who can identify them. We know three of the Thirteen are deceased, but most are unaccounted for, meaning they are still on the board. One or more may want to prevent your quest."

Birk sat back. "What are they trying to prevent me from?"

"*That's the right question.* You don't have all the information you need. Putting the pieces you have together, I believe this is bigger than arcanivores. The book implies you play a critical role in restoring balance in Driftstone—bringing about a new age of peace among witches."

"Fate," Birk announced abruptly, staring into the candle flame. "I think the voice in my dream was the fox they call Fate. According to the prophecy, she's the only one who'd benefit from destroying the remaining Thirteen. *And it was a woman's voice.*"

"Her real name is Morvana. Logic does point to her, and the arcanivores are something her dark magic *could* conjure if historical records are true."

"The story referenced she was imprisoned in The Under."

"The only person with knowledge of the Under, existing today, is Lady Ironspire. This is why I am uncomfortable with prophecies; they could be metaphors, actual geographic locations, or if Cyrus's magic

were involved, maybe she's trapped in a hidden prison or dimension outside Driftstone—something similar to Balincia."

Birk shook his head. "I don't think Balincia is in a different space outside Driftstone. I think we're hidden from view on the other side of the mountains, where Grey and I came from."

"There are only oceans on the other side of those mountains," Shayvonne premised, "which, when you think about it, *would* be a perfect place to camouflage yourself. Your aunts hid themselves in plain sight. Smart witches."

"They were right to be scared. If someone were powerful enough to break through my aunt's defenses after ten thousand years, it's possible someone else could break free from this Under. *Wherever it may be.*" Birk stood.

Shayvonne rose with him, sensing it was a suitable time to pause. "I apologize if I've troubled you even more."

"No, this has been helpful." Birk took her hand. "Thank you. I want to understand what I'm up against."

She squeezed his hand for assurance, "Get all the rest you can tonight and clear your mind. We'll continue talking tomorrow."

When Birk started to leave, Shayvonne lightly touched his shoulder.

"Birk, one more thing, if I may be so bold. Grey has experienced a lot of loss in his life. If he loses someone, he—" She stopped herself from saying the word, realizing it wasn't hers to share or define, "someone special to him, again, I'm afraid he won't survive it. It's not fair to ask you to shoulder the responsibility of his life, but I'm asking you to please protect his heart."

"I'll protect it as if it's my own. I promise."

"Oh, sweet thing," Shayvonne kissed his cheek. "Don't you realize—I'm referring to you."

THIRTY

A Rude Awakening

Pan burst through the door of Edi's bed chamber in a disheveled patchwork nightgown, stumbling over her feet in panic. "Edi, wake up! Something is wrong," she screamed, crumpling to the floor.

Edi shot up in bed in one fluid motion and summoned her wand from across the room. Tearing the eye mask from her face, she scanned the room and found Pan on the floor in a frantic state.

"What is it? What's wrong? Are we under attack?" Edi demanded, her mind racing to assess the situation. Talbot, followed by Ravenshire, tumbled into the room, both drawn by Pan's urgent call. Still in uniform, they sprang into action, triggering Edi to become even more alarmed.

Ravenshire moved around the room, inspecting every corner for a sign of intrusion. Talbot knelt beside Pan, ensuring she was uninjured. Offering his support, he helped her to stand and wiped the tangled hair from her face.

Edi, her nerves frazzled, approached her twin with a steadying hand. Holding Pan's wrists firm, she sat beside her, "Talk to me, Pan. What is it? I'm here."

"It's Birk," she cried, "I had a vision. He's in danger!"

Edi's expression shifted.

"Ravenshire, I believe the room is secure. Would you be kind enough to step out momentarily and guard the door?" Talbot asked, noting the need to preserve the sister's privacy.

When the door closed behind the young Guardian, a sense of urgency settled on the trio. Through tears and a quivering voice, Pan recounted the dream. "He pulled me in, Edi. I don't think he was aware he was even doing it," she shared. "I was able to see everything he saw in the Dreamscape."

"If that's true," Edi mused aloud, "his magic is manifesting new abilities. Remember, he is your son—we have no idea what the limits of his potential are."

Pan shared the darker news, "I wasn't the only one there, Edi—so was Morvana. I heard her voice. She could see him, too. The creatures attacking him were creations of *her* black magic."

"Ok, let's think about this," she tempered. "This may be a good sign. Our experience with the Dreamscape is that it provides visions of things that *may* happen, and they're not *always* literal. It might be days, weeks, or even months before these projections come true."

"Which means Birk is alive *and* safe right now," Pan exclaimed, clutching her heart. "And giving us time to change the outcome."

Talbot interrupted, "It also sounds as if he's made some friends and allies who are fighting with him and protecting him."

Edi offered another insight. "That's right, *and* he found a way to communicate with you."

"This opens the possibility for me to communicate back."

"Our pressing concern is Morvana," Edi reminded. "Based on our intel, we believe she may be the old woman who interacted with Birk. We also believe she's still in Balincia. If we can stop her here, we can prevent Birk's nightmare from becoming a reality."

Pan's tenacity changed after her initial fears were chased away. Heeding her sister's words, she looked to Talbot, "Where are we on our strike plans?"

"We're ready to take action; we're only awaiting your orders."

"Good," Pan declared, "let us move under the cover of the moons tomorrow. We've no more time to waste. We *all* raised Birk; he is *our* child—he needs his family's help."

THIRTY-ONE

THE VALUE IN WAITING

"You sleep a lot," Brynn observed. "We ate breakfast hours ago." Birk blinked, surprised to find Grey's sister sitting at the edge of the bed. The third sun was already in the sky. "I had trouble falling asleep last night," he admitted.

"Yeah, Mom mentioned you were having nightmares and up late," she said, standing and scanning the room. "I told her it was Grey's snoring. He told me to leave you alone and let you sleep, but I'm bored, and we're all waiting on you before we go into town."

"Oh! I wasn't aware we made plans." He replied, looking around the room for his clothes. "I don't want to keep everyone waiting."

"It's okay; Grey hasn't been home for a few weeks, so he's been catching up on all the work on the farm. I told him there was nothing for him to do because I took care of everything, but he never believes me cuz he's a pig-head."

"I'm sure that's not the case; he probably feels guilty for not being here. He wants to feel he's doing his part," Birk offered.

"I guess—I think he thinks I'm younger, and I can't manage it," she retorted.

"I get frustrated, too, when people think I'm unable to manage something because of my age. My aunts were always overprotective or underestimating me," he admitted, attempting to validate her.

"What did you do?"

"Honestly? I did what they didn't want me to do anyway to prove them wrong," he smiled, inciting her to flash a grin. "*But* I also learned two significant things. Most of the time, *they were right*, which I hated. I usually *didn't* understand as much as I thought; I'm still learning that now. I also learned that's okay."

Brynn drew her brows together and said, "What do you mean?"

"Even if they were right and I failed, learning and making my own mistakes was important. Some lessons are more valuable when we experience them ourselves, even if we get hurt."

"Maybe try telling Grey that and get him to lighten up on me," she rebuffed, shuffling her dirty feet.

"People who love us don't want to see us get hurt. I'm positive Grey feels this way about you. I'll do my best *if* you promise to lighten up on him, too."

"Deal, but he's still a goat gobbler," Brynn said, jumping off the bed and walking toward the door. Spinning around, she cocked her head at him, "You're alright, Birk."

After a quick refresh in the washroom, Shayvonne filled Birk with leftover bread, jam, and honey, broaching the topic of their imminent journey while he ate. Joining them from the field, Grey carried in an earthy scent, giving Birk a quick peck on the cheek before he sat. Across from them, Brynn swung her legs in her chair, eager to hear the plans.

Under firm and gentle conviction, Shayvonne impressed upon them the necessity of a week-long preparation before embarking on their quest. Emphasizing the importance of proper provisions, she outlined a schedule, including visits to the tailor, a stop at the forge and bowsmith for equipment upgrades, and the need to arrange horses. Reading the agitation on Grey's face, she underscored the significance of his patience.

"We're not discussing a trip into the mountains for a few days or

weeks. There is no telling how long you'll be absent or . . . if you'll be back." Shayvonne held their gaze, stressing the importance of her words. "The challenges ahead will demand individual resilience and a cohesive unit forged between you."

"I think we're already working as a successful unit," Grey jested with too much bravado.

Reaching across the table, Shayvonne grabbed her son's hand. "When relationships are new, you may *feel* you can conquer anything together, but you *will* encounter stressful situations, unusual environments, and dangers you haven't faced before. You *will* be tested. Your communication and connection must be strong."

"I'm not trying to dismiss you. I don't see the difference between doing it here and on the road." Grey explained, "I don't want to sit here while the arcanivores are still hunting us. Birk and I, being here, place a target on our home."

"You're as safe here as anywhere else, if not more. This town is covered with runes and wolves, not to mention Brunt and Winter," she reminded. "The village wasn't prepared the first time; neither were you. We aren't the same people anymore."

Birk rubbed Grey's leg, trying to pacify him; he knew Grey's resistance came from his desire to protect his family.

Shayvonne continued, "I want you both to practice your magic daily with each other. Push your limits, admit your challenges, and strategize—learn how to use them together. Additionally, I want you to train your long-range and close-quarter combat skills *without powers*. You shouldn't become overly reliant on your magic."

Grey scoffed, his irritation growing. "With due respect, don't you think this is overkill?"

"No, I don't. My son will not go off into this world to face forces strong enough to reshape existence with only his brawn, beasts, and arrogance," she snapped. "You're lucky I'm not forcing you to stay here for months or years to prepare. *You can handle one week.*"

Grey lowered his head. "I'm sorry. You're right. A week it is."

Accepting his apology, Shayvonne recentered. "Finally, I don't want

to embarrass either of you, but I encourage you, *if you are inclined,* to carve out time for intimacy and physical . . . connection while you can, this week."

"Mother!" Grey shouted, reaching his limit. Birk's ears turned red. Brynn sank under the table.

"Stop being so modest, the lot of you," Shayvonne ordered, dismissing their reactions. "I didn't raise my children to be embarrassed or ashamed of discussing adult needs and topics. There *are* physical and emotional benefits attached to intercourse that'll serve you well." Rising from the table, unshaken by their response, she added one more jab, "You could both use the increase of vitality for the journey."

Spinning on her heels, pleased with herself, she ordered, "Let's not dawdle; we have a lot to do in town," leaving the children stunned and silent as a pixie in a jar. Refusing to be left alone with the two of them, Brynn shot out of her seat, hurrying after. Taking a moment to bury his face in his hands, Grey laughed uncontrollably.

"I now see where you get your incorrigibility from," Birk teased, pulling him to follow.

The town center was busy with street peddlers and crowds in the open market. Birk found it quaint. Its stone-masoned buildings framed against the mountain landscape reminded him of the charming markets from home.

Paired with Shayvonne, as they split tasks, her eyes assessed the fit of his clothes with a critical scan.

"You have a nice build, but Grey's clothes do nothing to flatter you," she assessed bluntly. "Anyone would swim in his clothes," she added, attempting to soften the remark. "You need something maneuverable so you aren't tripping over yourself."

Guiding him to a local tailor, they selected a set of outfits and sturdy boots more practical for the road ahead. During this visit, Birk learned about currency for goods and services, a concept foreign to Balincians. Shayvonne assured him they earned more than enough to cover him due to the success of their wool and dairy farm.

"It's a bit unfair to the rest of the village, based on Grey and Brynn's ability with animals, but we do more than our fair share of contributions and giving back." She apprised.

Grey and Brynn shopped the market stalls, their laughter drowning out the vendors. Falling back into the routine rhythm of a brother and sister, they picked and teased one another while gathering an assortment of dried meats, preserved cheeses, and freshly baked bread. Making their way through the aromatic stalls, Grey attempted to ignore the stares they were receiving.

"Do they ever bother you?" Grey inquired.

"Who? The Church lookie-loos?" Brynn scanned the market to identify who her brother was referencing. "Nah, they're harmless."

Brynn's indifference amazed Grey. "You don't mind the attention?"

"I like being related to the Protector. It makes me feel important."

"Brynn, your life carries value regardless of our relations. You'll make an impact in whatever you choose to do. I worry the Church romanticizes and pressures you with their vision instead of you seeking your own path."

Brynn stopped and stared at her brother. "I don't feel pressure. It's not like we attend their services, *and* they respect our privacy. They've never shared our history with strangers from outside the village. They protect and believe in us, which is nice. Are you afraid they'll ask you to perform miracles or something?"

Grey snorted, "Maybe; I don't know. I may be oversensitive."

"Or maybe you don't believe in yourself like they do, *like I do*," Brynn said, squeezing her brother's hand.

Grey paused, "When did you become so wise, wild one?"

"When my big brother started acting like a baboon," she quipped, "someone needs to lead this family."

After gathering their essential supplies, the duo met with their mother at the smithy. To everyone's surprise, Birk showcased his knowledge of swordsmanship, both in craft and skill, while they browsed the shop. As

he shared stories of Talbot's training and inspected blades, he became nostalgic and appreciative of the hours he spent training as a child.

"Will you teach me how to swordfight?" Brynn pressed, growing ever fascinated by Birk.

"I'll do my best," he chuckled.

Birk stood at the counter, searching for the right hilt to match the blade. The bladesmith asked if he wanted to embed any specific design. Grey placed his hand on Birk's waist, leaned forward, and set a pendant on the counter. "I was hoping you might fashion something in this style."

"My protection of truth pendant. I lost it in the shuffle with the giants," Birk exclaimed.

I grabbed it when I went back for the Driftstone. It was sitting on top of your satchel." Grey attached it to a thin leather strap he found at the market. Raising it above Birk's head, he hung it around his neck. "I figured this way; it'll always be with you and harder to lose."

"You were right, I'd be a mess without you." Birk turned to the bladesmith, remembering he might need the pendant to make a mold. "Do you need to hold onto this or make a sketch?"

"Not at all; I'm familiar with the design, although it's rare to find someone else who remembers it," he answered, to Birk's surprise. "I'll have to dig through some of my grandfather's old moldings, but the Protection of Truth was inspired by the Protector before the War. Legend says when Farren was at the height of his power, he transformed into a dragon."

The bladesmith leaned forward and lowered his voice, "Between us, the Church popularized the rune symbols, resulting in the emblems from our past being forgotten. The runes keep me in business, but it gets boring after a while. I'd be honored to take on this project for you."

"Can you make two?" Shayvonne interrupted, joining them, Brynn tagging behind her. "I'm a bit of a swordswoman, myself, Birk, from back in my day."

Grey looked confused. "Do you feel unsafe at the house?"

"Oh, this isn't for home defense. Didn't I mention Brynn and I will

be joining you?" Upon hearing this, Brynn threw her arms in the air to celebrate. "I want a sword too!"

"No, I think we'll pick you up something at the bowsmith. Given your size, a longer-range, lighter weapon will serve better." Shayvonne stated.

Grey shot Birk a cursory glance before grabbing his foster mother by the elbow and pulling her to the side. "Absolutely not!" he barked in hushed tones.

"Pardon me?"

"It is far too dangerous to have you and Brynn go with us while the arcanivores are at large. We'd be a moving target. Not to mention the Free Roamers, goblins, and trolls, and the Protector only knows what else we may find out there," he snapped.

"Well, isn't it a good thing we're traveling with two familiars of the Protector and two strapping young men with inherited magic from the Thirteen?" she dismissed. She set her pouch of coins on the counter. "Make the order for *two*, please."

Grey pushed in front of her, refusing to be ignored, "You'll be a liability to us. *I can't protect all of you.* I'll be distracted and worried all of the time."

"You need to learn to trust we can oversee ourselves," she scolded.

"Yeah," Brynn wedged between them. "I can last longer outdoors than Birk can."

Birk, slightly insulted, was about to object, but retracted, realizing this was probably true.

Grey passed his eyes between Birk and Shayvonne, breathing heavily through his nose. Turning to the bladesmith, he ordered, "Make it three hilts, not two, but the last one fashioned for a dagger." He faced Shayvonne, "If we're doing this, Brynn should have more than a bow."

Brynn wrapped her arms around Grey's waist. "You won't regret this, you'll see. Shayvonne and I can handle ourselves."

"The only reason I relinquished is because you'd both follow us anyway," he griped. "I'd rather keep you where I can see you."

"Funny, I referenced something similar to Birk about you," she winked at Birk. "We share a stubborn streak in this family."

"*There will be terms*," Grey underlined, attempting to assert some authority. "I make the calls. You can't question me if I ask you to hold back, run, or hide at any point. Brynn may not be a small child, but she is still too young to take the same risks as the rest of us."

"Agreed," Shayvonne encouraged Brynn to do the same with a nudge.

"I'm not too young," she defied, but *recognizing now wasn't the time to argue this case*, she begrudgingly agreed. "I will accept these *terms* as long as Birk agrees with you. Because sometimes you can be dragon snot just to be dragon snot."

Grey threw his head back in defeat.

THIRTY-TWO

WITCHES ON WATER

Edi was reminded why Talbot was the Captain of the Royal Guardians. Enlisting Marina, Lars, and their collective men, he quickly formed Balincia's first army. She'd hoped she wouldn't live to see the day when such defenses were necessary, but she supposed a ten-thousand-year reign of peace was nothing to be balked at.

Talbot's strategy was straightforward. The witches needed to regain the people's trust to build an army swiftly. *Healing would have to wait.* Balincians required preparation and education on the imposing threat at hand. This task, *she was instructed,* couldn't be delegated; it was essential for leaders to be visible, and pairing one of the sisters and a council member together demonstrated allegiance.

Much to Edi's relief, it was decided that Pan was better suited in demeanor to provide the contrite spirit and congeniality required to face the public. An extra gift to Edi was Pan's selection of Porticia to accompany her to the townships, thereby removing her as a distraction from the remaining council. Edi considered this a small gesture to mend the wounds between them.

Porticia, for her part, relished the visibility to be seen as a trusted advisor. Taking the role seriously, she alluded to herself as a stand-in for

Edi when addressing the crowds. To her credit, she was quick to wrangle questions, defend the sisters' actions, and keep the focus on uniting as a community. *Who knew there was a gift to herding squabbling chickens?*

Still, Pan drew a little pleasure from Porticia's discomfort as she traveled by throne. She never adjusted to the speed, so her heavy chest and bottom jostled in the seat, while recurring splashes of water smacked her in the face. The ride didn't have to be so bumpy or wet; it was Pan's way of reminding Porticia—a mother never forgets a slight.

In one week, they met with every township, excluding Capital City. If the intruder were still here, logic dictated, she'd be where Birk met her. Balincia's population made it difficult to travel on any ship without raising questions. Capital City was the most tactical place to blend in; Balincians from all over were in constant transit.

After a few exchanges, led by Xavier and his falcons with the Innkeeper, they gathered intel.

A young, stable hand, unrecognized by anyone, had become a permanent fixture at the market and Inn. Following a few more correspondences with other townships, they confirmed his description didn't match anyone on the census, nor was there any absence unaccounted for. As painful and cumbersome as Edi's record-keeping was, it saved the effort of an organized search.

The information on the stable hand confirmed three things. Since Edi and Pan couldn't detect the intruder's presence or entry into Balincia, the intruder was capable of puissant magic. Second, if the intruder was trying to conceal their identity, they were attempting to hide their activity. Finally, if the invader knew Birk, they knew about his aunts.

Given this information, they passed around several theories—including the old woman's intent to destabilize Balincia by pitting the sisters against each other. Aware of Birk's potential, the visitor may have devised a plan to remove their nephew from the picture *or* exploit his talents. All possibilities considered, Edi prepared for the worst. Balincia wasn't in a position to afford an appeal to someone's better nature.

Unaware of what happened to most of their siblings after the war, the witches narrowed their list of suspects. They believed only Calder,

Goetfeather, and Morvana might have retaliatory motives. It was hard for them to believe anyone else would come after them without revealing themselves.

It was feasible; with his proficiency over the waters, Calder may have found an entry point into Balincia through Crystaline Lake. The approach, however, didn't lend to his style. He was arrogant and direct, more apt to flood the lands with his armies than resort to subterfuge and deception.

Goetfeather thrived on manipulation; it was conceivable for him to craft a plot with his intellect, where he pulled the strings from the shadows. The wisest among them, he was a master of deception and could mask his identity. An enchanted tome would be an appealing device for his trickery.

Morvana, however, was the most probable candidate. Her recent presence in Birk's dreams amplified these suspicions. Of all their siblings, they feared a conflict with her the most. Her jealousy and hatred of the twins initiated the war. Her powerful ascent, under dark magic's aid, is why they fled.

Isolating Morvana before the confrontation was a priority.

Their last encounter with their sister showed she had no hesitation about using innocents as shields and weaponizing them in battle. The citizens needed to be evacuated to the farthest reaches of the realm. If the witches were defeated, the enchantments surrounding Balincia would also fall, giving their people a chance to escape.

During the day, in quiet shifts, Marina's sailors harbored the tenants and visitors of Capital City in small groups away from the island. Only a handful were left to avoid suspicion. Marina would escort the remaining stand-ins to safety once the witches attacked.

The remaining islands were vacated, and the border townships migrated east. Lars's group, being best equipped, would lead the citizens over the mountains if the need for flight arose.

A small group of volunteers, including Talbot, Ravenshire, and Xavier, along with some of Marina's most capable ships, would be anchored off the shores of Capital City. If the witches required aid, they

were a last resort to help provide the others a head start to escape. If they were called on, it would signal Balincia's final stand.

Edi banished the thought—even if she appreciated the contingency. Too much was at stake to ruminate about the possibility of failure. If there was one thing she was confident in, it was her ability to establish order.

Talbot and his men departed shortly after Pan's alarming night vision. Leaving in the middle of the night, they required a day to reach the rendezvous point. The sisters had the day to themselves alone in their palaces.

"I never thought I'd be the one to say this, but I miss the noise," Edi confessed to her sister at the small table in Pan's kitchen.

"Odd, isn't it? You were always more reserved and introverted, yet you kept yourself surrounded by people." Pan reflected, sipping her tea.

"And you, the people's favorite, were most comfortable living alone."

"Maybe there is a bit of both of us stirring around in each other. We've been inseparable our entire lives; it'd be hard to imagine we haven't rubbed off." Pan mused, placing her hand on Edi's.

"Or maybe I enjoyed a staff catering to my every whim," Edi smirked.

"Are we okay? Before we do this, I must ensure our hearts are right with each other."

Edi sighed, "Pan, we will *always* be okay. You're my twin. We may bend, but we'll never break."

"Do you remember our dream of building the perfect paradise when we arrived here?"

Edi reflected, "We were naïve, thankful to be alive—we wanted to build a utopia our way. You *insisted* on these floating islands."

"*And* I was right; they accentuated the whole landscape," she declared.

"We've made some mistakes along the way—forgotten some of our intentions, but I'm proud of what we've built here. Not everyone gets a second chance to start over."

"And now we're pushing for a third," Pan sighed.

"I'll start over as many times as we need in this lifetime, as long as it's with you."

"Edi, I'm not sure I ever found the words, over the years, to thank you for back then, much less for now. We have all of this because of you. I want you to understand; I see that."

"I know, Pandi." Edi stood and walked to the window, hiding her face. "Please, let's not speak as if these are the last words we shall say to each other. I won't be able to stomach it."

"How'd you like to spend our last few hours before dark?" Pan asked.

Interlacing her fingers into her sister's hand, Edi raised her chin and said, "Let's sit in the garden and watch the suns set. Let's remember who we are and what we're fighting for tonight."

Perched on the edge of the island, the witches resembled little girls, holding hands as they gazed upon Balincia. They reminisced about the birth of every creation they crafted together—each memory a precious gem. Finding themselves transported back in time, they relived their joys and sorrows, the triumphs and challenges shaping their journey.

The nostalgia was bittersweet, memories unfurling like petals in the wind, filling their hearts. As the third sun set, they retraced their morning steps to the docks below.

"Our differences are our greatest gift," Edi said.

"When we are in harmony, the land is in balance," Pan continued.

"Balance is essential to the land's survival."

"Balance is essential to *our* survival."

"One of us can't survive without the other."

"As it was written."

"As it was pledged."

"Our Magic."

"Our Lives."

"Forever connected."

"May the scales always remain balanced," they repeated together.

They didn't reach out to embrace one another or feel the need to speak. They'd shared everything already in their hearts. Climbing into

their thrones, they stared across the dark glass of the lake with fire in their veins.

The night air was warm, whipping past them, the swashes of water invigorating. Speeding past the shadowed boats of their citizens, who were heading to the shores, the Balincians cheered, watching the sisters of Chaos and Order, legendary warriors, fly into battle on their behalf. Pan's hair billowed behind her, a banner of power. Edi's wand sent streams of white lights under the waters, pulling the ships to their destinations faster.

Edi's voice cut through the wind. "If it is Morvana, we can take no chances. We have to put her down quickly."

Pan nodded, "Whoever it is, they've made a mistake breaking into our home—endangering my son. We will remind the world today of how powerful we are together."

With a silent exchange, Edi lifted her wand high into the air. Pan intoned an incantation. Slowly, the waters beneath them stirred with a life of their own. Two heads attached to serpentine necks emerged from the lake, jaws snapping in the air. The body of a dragon sculpted from the lake's waters followed, reflecting the twinkling stars above.

With a flick of her wrist, Edi bound the thrones to the massive aquatic dragon, securing their seats. It spread its gigantic wings, and with each powerful beat, it left enormous swells in its trail. Breaking free from the lake, the duo launched into the sky, the dragon's translucent form camouflaging their approach.

Edi shouted to her sister above the pounding of the dragon's wings. "I've missed this!" Pan squeezed her sister's hand.

Pan leaned forward and spotted their destination. She pointed to the surrounding ships, where Talbot and his crew were waiting for their signal.

"It's time to make our entrance," Edi yelled. "C'mon, girls, let's give

our visitor a welcome they won't forget." She tapped her wand on the dragon, and both heads reared back and roared.

"That's the signal," Talbot shouted. "Fire the cannons!"

Cannons and flares invaded the sky surrounding the island. Edi lowered their descent. Waving her arms, Pan summoned a walled circle of fire to surround the beaches. The enchanted flames illuminated the island, preventing an escape. The cannons and flares created a storm of confusion to keep their invader guessing the direction of their approach.

"Let's circle first; I still don't see anyone," Pan directed.

Lowering the dragon, Edi flew around the perimeter. The flames' smoke obscured their vision. "We need to fly over the market, down its center. We can't see anything from here," she coughed.

The water dragon's shadow covered the isle. Edi slowed their pace. Flying first over the Inn, they began to glide toward the marketplace. Straight in front of them, a quick flash of light—a bolt of blue lightning aimed at their heads came zipping toward them.

With seconds to react, Edi swerved the dragon too quickly, rotating it on its side as they spun. The beast's tail crashed into the Inn, sweeping across its exterior and sending wooden planks and glass flying. The building collapsed, and a cloud of debris burst outward.

Pan pointed down the cobblestone street, past the open market: "The blast came from there, near the amphitheater!"

"Let's fire back!" Edi ordered through her teeth. Pulling the handlebar reins, the dragon launched toward the outdoor theater with the speed of an arrow. The mythic creature reared its heads back like a striking snake, leaning their necks forward, and spewing a forceful jet of water.

Moving her hands with rapid speed, Pan hardened the water when it hit the air, transforming it into a flurry of razor-sharp, crystallized swords. The sheer volume created a weaponized wave of destruction that pierced the ground, market stands, and structures with alarming force. The projectiles exploded into melting shards upon impact, showering Capital City with a dangerous storm of shrapnel.

The cloaked stranger caught in its crossfire sprinted for cover. The

dragon closed in on her. Leaping into the nearby descending amphitheater, she took cover behind its wall as the dragon flew over her head. The beast launched itself upward into the night sky, turned, and hurtled toward its intended victim.

Another deluge of water and deadly hardened quills sprang from its mouth, aiming to obliterate the stranger. The dark figure raised her hands, prepared this time, and drew a circle in the air; a portal formed above her. When the full force of the dragon's attack was about to make an impact, it was sucked into her conjured blue gateway.

Another portal materialized behind the witches, and the dragon's blast spilled through, slamming back into its origin point. The hardened water spikes sliced through the dragon's form, generating a violent explosion and sending daggers of crystallized energy flying in every direction. The twins were caught off guard and thrown into the sky. The dragon dissipated into steam and heavy rain.

Stunned, the twins plummeted towards the earth, accelerated by the impact of their unleashed powers. Pan summoned an upstream wind to soften their imminent impact with the earth. The winds surrounded them in a cyclone of currents, cushioning their descent and guiding them toward a safer landing amidst the wreckage.

Edi grabbed her wand and quickly regained her bearings. She swiftly traced a geometric shape in the air. A white hexagon formed underneath the stranger, expanding to create a walled barrier, enclosing her within a glowing prism. Their opponent, now trapped inside the confines of the prison, stood stock still, studying the surrounding walls.

Edi reviewed her handiwork, confident in the precision of her magic. Her gloat was brief. Unfazed by her predicament, the hooded figure approached one of the prism walls and tapped it gently. To Edi's astonishment, the wall folded on itself. Repeating the process with two more walls, their enemy stepped out effortlessly into the open.

Twirling her wrist, Pan moved forward, spinning the amphitheater. The stone benches retreated into the ground. The robed assailant lost her balance and slid to the center. The ground became quicksand, pulling her flailing body into the earth.

Edi and Pan stood in silence. The flames from the lake exposed the devastation around them. Inching forward, they peeked down where the stranger was swallowed, hesitant to believe the battle was over.

The ground shook aggressively, providing only seconds of warning.

A blue sphere exploded from the earth, blinding them with its blast. The twins were hurled across the town square. Lying on the ground, covered in bruises, they struggled to get on their feet.

A woman's commanding voice halted them. "Enough!" The cloaked figure stepped out from the haze, drawing back her hood. An elderly black woman with long white hair stood before them—*not* Morvana.

"Edict and Pandora," she intoned. "Is that any way to greet your mother?"

THIRTY-THREE

HERE AND THERE

I t had been ages since anyone new entered the Dreamscape, so when three visitors appeared within a week, news spread quickly. Two were dreamwalkers, from what Slygoth could gather. While intriguing, it also made them less susceptible to his persuasions.

The female was already being tampered with by Morvana. Despite the witch's popularity among the minor minions in the realm, he preferred to keep his distance from her. He noticed new abominations walking the halls, poisonous cocktails crafted by her. It wasn't uncommon for her to use his home as her canvas, turning it into an oil painting of macabre and ugly things.

The other dreamwalker was a boy who resembled their old warden, Nazeem, whom Morvana had kicked out. The old man created the Dreamscape to house oddities and curiosities born from the imagination of dreamers. He appreciated their whimsy and set laws for the land. He kept things clean and on board. Nocturnians knew what to expect from him.

Before he was banished, Slygoth had an amicable, if not mutually beneficial, relationship with Nazeem, but the reports on his younger version were disconcerting. The boy was intent on disinfecting the forgotten realm, and his technique was ruthless and concrete. He wiped anything troubling him from existence.

Considering the boy lacked fluency in their dimension's abstract and conceptual language, it became clear *everything* troubled him.

So, as a result, everyone stayed clear of him, *including Morvana.*

It was the third visitor who *wasn't* a dreamwalker, who tantalized him. A young warlock related to the great witches of old, a delicious temptation. He was clueless about his whereabouts.

His dream chamber was locked, signaling to Slygoth the boy was a Magic-Born. This meant none of the other nocturnians would harbor more than a passing interest in him. Only shadebinders could slip in under the locked doors of witches, and Slygoth was the last in the realm.

This, however, is also the reason he hesitated.

His prior brethren had been notoriously impatient. Greedy to satiate their desire to exist among the living, they were indiscriminate in their selections. They gobbled up every plate of opportunity the dark witch offered them during the war. Their choices enslaved them to her service.

What good was a life without freedom?

This boy's world was cut off from the rest of Driftstone. Hidden from the bickering witches and wars. His eidetic dreams painted a picture of a utopia filled with floating islands, crème-filled treats, and music in the streets. Slygoth envisioned sitting beside the crystal-clear waters, enjoying his remaining years in scenic hedonist bliss.

There were concerns, however. The boy exhibited prophetic powers; whether he knew this was questionable. Those same idyllic images could take a darker turn on occasion. The floating palaces, Slygoth loved, would burn and fall from the sky, the crystal lake would be filled with ash, and the music would be replaced with lamenting in the streets.

Slygoth knew the dark dreams were not fixed certainties. They were, however, a call to action—and he was confident the boy would answer. The boy would do anything to prevent the decimation of his home.

The question was whether or not he would succeed. Maybe a deal with the boy would benefit them both. What if Slygoth's intervention pushed the boy onto his path to save his home?

Their home.
He hoped.

Picking a sleepworm out of his drooping right ear, he caught the scent of nightshade approaching behind him. "What do you want, witch? I have no desire to entertain one of your propositions."

Morvana stood by his side, peeking through the window of the dream chamber. "Well, that's a relief—since I carry no proposals."

Slygoth glanced at her with bulbous eyes, "Then what are you doing here? Besides irritating me."

Her lips twisted, "It is my favorite pastime."

"Hrmpfh," Slygoth grunted. Sniffing the worm, he licked the wax off it before popping it into his mouth. "You can't claim this boy—you can't reach him."

The raven-haired witch sighed, "Not yet. Am I not allowed to watch?"

"Why?" Slygoth poked, "Are you bored with your other plaything already? Or have your attempts failed with her? I've seen your experiments roaming our halls—they can't find their legs here, can they?"

She turned sharply, lowering the hood of her cloak. "My plans with the princess aren't your concern. As for the boy—let's say you and I have mutual interests."

"Doubtful," he said, returning to the warlock. "Do you know him?"

She raised her brow and said, "Ah, if I did, it would be helpful to you, wouldn't it?"

It would be helpful. The more he understood about the boy, the easier it would be for him to land his greeting. The introduction was the most important.

He didn't, however, trust the witch's aim. There was a reason she slithered her way through the Dreamscape to find him. "I don't need your help."

"You're getting old, Slygoth. How many more opportunities will come your way before you wither away?"

She was right, but he didn't want her to know.

She tapped her singed fingers on the window, "You must be careful

with this one. His mind is guarded. If you aren't discerning with your form, he'll repel you. I could help you. Or are you willing to gamble your last play for life beyond this realm?"

"Why do you care?"

She scoffed, "I don't—not about you. In this particular instance, however, it is worthwhile for me for you to succeed."

Slygoth turned to her, straining to look up. "Why? Don't play games with me. I'm not one of my foolish siblings."

She knelt to look him in the eyes and said, "And I'm not a witch who wastes her time. I need the boy separated from the twins who raised him. I have use of him—and if the boy leaves his home, your fear of revelation is removed. If he stays where he is, he'll attract your treasure's destruction." She stroked his fuzzy chin with her hand, "Don't you want to enjoy your last days uninterrupted in your new home? Not to mention, you can relish the idea its location is hidden from *me*."

Slygoth considered the witch's words. This was a bad idea. It was evident she was vested in this boy's future. On the other hand, if she only wanted the warlock, it would serve his interests to lure the boy away from his beautiful retirement oasis. She never stops pursuing what she wants. What did he care about their fates if his piece of happiness was spared?

"Even if I agree with a form you suggest for an introduction, I can't guarantee his actions. Once the exchange occurs, I will be forced to play the role given until our contract expires."

She laughed, "You have a limited imagination—it's a good thing I have a plan."

The old woman fidgeted with her dress while waiting on the banks of the lake. A collection of books strewn haphazardly around her. Slygoth consented to the form suggested, understanding it was temporary. It wasn't his first choice, but he was ancient anyway. What did he care? He couldn't afford to be picky now. Not with the stakes so high.

Waving his weathered fingers across his lap, he summoned a beaten leathered tome with his wish magic. Playing with the wax insignia and the bindings, he fashioned it to look cryptic and divine. Details mattered.

It only needed to give the *illusion* of power; if the boy accepted the exchange, *he* would add its real magic.

Pleased, Slygoth sat back and admired his work. He double-checked his figure. Everything was in order: toes, ears, fingers, face, and all the other grandmotherly parts. Satisfied, he pursed his lips like the old woman and blew into the air.

Sweet-sounding notes drifted into the boy's subconscious, drawing him closer with their enchanted melody, alerting him to her presence.

A voice suddenly appeared to the old woman's right. "What are you reading?" the boy seated beside her asked. Slygoth grinned.

The old woman pretended to be surprised, "You startled me. I wasn't expecting to find anyone else here."

"I didn't mean to upset you; I rarely run into strangers *here.*"

The boy's face was kind and apologetic. Puzzled, he turned his head from side to side.

"I always get turned around here," he said. "One moment I'm home, the next with Auntie Pan in her palace, and sometimes I find myself wandering into places I've never been. It's odd."

"Do you know where you are now?" the old woman asked. Slygoth was curious to find out how perceptive the warlock was.

"I know I'm not in Balincia," he answered, studying each object around him. His lips parted slightly, tilting his head; he turned to Slygoth and asked, "Am I in a dream?"

The woman winced a little. The witch was right; he had to be careful with this one. "How insightful of you," Slygoth answered, impressed.

"Which means—this isn't real," he pondered aloud, turning back to the woman, "and you're not real."

Slygoth needed to rein him back; he didn't want to lose him. "I guess it depends on the angle you view it." Extending her arm, she offered him a piece of her cloak, "Can you feel my sleeve?"

The boy ran his fingers along the intricate embroidery, adorning the edges, feeling the delicate threads and smooth fabric. A faint frown creased his forehead.

"Now touch the ground around you," she instructed. The soft blades

tickled his palms and bent under his weight. The texture of the earth beneath him was alive. He was back. "I assure you, it's all real," she comforted.

Slygoth studied the boy's face. A shadow descended over his features. His once bright and lively eyes dulled with a hint of sorrow. The lines in his brow deepened.

For a moment, he sympathized with the boy with beautiful dreams. "This unsettles you. Doesn't it? Why?"

"I've seen unsettling things here," he answered honestly. "If you're real and the grass is real, everything in my dreams is real."

"Yes. And no. It depends."

"I'm confused."

Confusion was perfect. It was time to lead him to the well-laid snare.

"You asked what I was reading; what if I told you it was a book holding the answers to all your questions? One that could help you decipher what's real and what isn't. Would you be interested in reading such a book?"

The warlock leaned in, his eyes wide. "Yes," he paused. "But where did you get your hands on such a book?"

"You gave it to me," the old woman answered without hesitation.

He shook his head, "I've never seen that book before."

"This is your dream, isn't it?"

"Yes . . ."

"Then it's your book," she smiled. "I'd be glad to give it back to you."

She began to hand the book to him, but then retracted the gift before he could touch it. He raised his head, flustered.

"There is one thing I forgot to mention: if you read the book *here*, you won't remember it *there*."

"*There?*"

"Where you wake up," she nodded. "When you revisit *here* after traveling *there*, it will be as if you never read it all."

He twisted his mouth, "That's unhelpful. I need to remember *there* what I read *here* because I think what I see *here* explains what is happening *there*." He cocked his head, "All of this is very unclear."

"Is it? I understood you perfectly. It's a conundrum, yes, but the solution is easy. You need someone from *here* to give you the book *there*."

The boy was growing on Slygoth. A typical tactic was to use language to confound the dreamer, but the unbothered warlock easily transitioned into it.

"But how?" he asked, "If you're *here* and I'm *there*?"

Slygoth waited for him to figure it out. Dreamers were always more prone to trusting *their* solutions.

"Could I bring you *there*?" he asked.

The old woman patted his hand. "Now, you understand."

"How do I do that?"

"It's a simple exchange. A transaction between friends. You need something from me, and I need something from you."

The boy leaned back, skeptical. "What do you need from me?"

The woman tapped her fingers on the book, pretending to ponder. "Well . . . I'm leaving my home *here* to bring you something *there*. Once I'm *there*, I can never return *here*."

"Oh . . .," the boy retreated as if he'd offended her. "I couldn't ask you to leave your home."

Drat! Slygoth hadn't counted on him being so compassionate; he needed to correct course quickly. "While it's a great sacrifice," he feigned, "I am getting old and a change of scenery would be good for my health." He checked for the boy's reaction. He was pulling him back in. It was now or never. "However, to survive *there*, I'll need a fraction of your magic *here* and, of course, access to your memories."

He sped through the last part, hoping the boy didn't catch the clause.

The old woman waited, gritting her teeth. The boy mulled it over.

"I don't have any magic to exchange," he replied, disappointed.

This time, Slygoth didn't fake his alarm. He had guessed he was ignorant about the extent of his power, but he didn't count on him being completely unaware. This was more complicated than he expected, and it may cause issues. Did the witch dupe him?

"Why, of course, you do; that's why you're *here*. Didn't you know?" A

shadebinder could withhold the truth, but they couldn't lie. In this case, the truth benefited Slygoth. He required the boy's magic.

The boy shook his head. "Although it does explain my dreams. Maybe I don't require a book after all. My aunts are experts on magic."

NO. No, no, no, no, no. Blast his stupid mouth. He was foolish for trusting the witch. It was too late now; Slygoth would have to roll with it *if he could still salvage the situation.*

Grabbing the boy's arm when he rose, the old woman panicked. "I . . . I wouldn't be so certain." She cringed inside; that sounded awful. She needed something to tug at his heart. "Wouldn't you prefer to have a book to help you explain everything? Can you trust your aunts to be honest with you? What if they're frightened by your dreams? Or *jealous* of your new magic?"

The boy sat.

Slygoth was back in the game.

"Why do you need access to my memories?" He was cautious. Circling.

Slygoth needed to choose the woman's words carefully. "To exist out *there*, I need to reflect what's in *here*," the old woman said, placing her hand on his heart, "and *there*," and the other on his head.

He was resisting. "How will I know you'll keep your end of the bargain? What if you're only using me to get *there*?"

She sighed, "I can't be free out *there* until I've completed what we have agreed upon *here*," she answered, sealing her words to law.

The boy measured her, "There will be complications out *there*. My aunts are powerful witches. They can't find out you gave me the book until I've had time to digest and understand it."

The old woman bowed, "As you say it, so mote it be."

"And we'll need a story for you. If and when they find out."

"You have experience as a Storyteller, don't you?"

The boy nodded, enthusiastic about the idea of writing a story.

Slygoth had nothing left to offer. It wasn't the exchange he planned, but it'd still be worth it if the results were the same. "Do we have a deal?"

The warlock smiled and offered his hand, "We have a deal."

Before the old woman took his hand, she played her last card: "One more thing, think of it as a protection provision for both of us."

"Okay?"

"You'll have to agree to erase the memory of this dream."

"Why?" he asked, pulling back his hand.

"The moment you reveal me out *there*, even if by accident, I'll disappear, and I won't be able to fulfill our contract. It's better for us both if you don't recognize me."

The boy considered her one last time. "Deal," he said with finality, binding their agreement.

The shadebinder and the warlock shook on it, unaware of the little white fox with feathered wings watching them—who was from *there*, and *here*, and also *nowhere*.

THIRTY-FOUR

ONE MOTHER

"Mother?" Edi, incredulous, brushed off. "We have no mother."

"Of course, you have a mother. *Everyone* has a mother. How do you think Driftstone birthed you?" The old woman smiled, returning Edi's displaced wand to her as a peace offering. "Even if you don't remember her." She faced Pan, who was still on all fours from the blast. She offered her hand, assisting her up. "Some of you sensed my presence stronger than others."

When Pan took the old woman's hand, a memory flashed in her mind. Both younger, the woman stood behind her, teaching her the incantations of creation. "One Mother," she whispered.

The woman's eyes glinted at the recognition. "Yes, my love. I was always there, existing in the background. My role was not meant to be out front, like my children. Each of you is a piece of me, just as you are your father, Driftstone."

"I assumed you were a figment of my imaginings, or perhaps . . . a dream," Pan softened, holding the woman's arms in her own. There was a familiarity to her touch—also something troubling. Pan had often wondered about her creation with Edi; Driftstone had always remained silent. The woman might have been telling the truth; Pan recognized her energy.

"Do you take us as fools? If you're our mother—why would you attack us?" Edi retorted, pulling Pan away. Something didn't feel right.

"I would never take you for a fool, Edi. You're among my brightest," One Mother objected, "and it was *you* who attacked me. If you will note, I only acted defensively."

"You fired first!" Edi argued.

"*Only* after your grandiose display of charging me with a dragon. I fired a warning shot. If I wanted to hit you, I would have," she raised her eyebrow. "I knew you were coming tonight. Did you not think I would notice the island's evacuation all day? I didn't expect you to come in magic blazing."

"You'll have to forgive us; we were expecting someone else," Pan apologized. Still, she wasn't sure of the woman, either. She couldn't place her finger on it, but there was something One Mother wasn't sharing— something odd below the exterior.

"I know who you were expecting. I don't take it personally. It's my fault for not coming to you," she admitted.

"Why *didn't* you come to us?" Edi pushed, "Why, after all these years, when we have no memory of you or evidence of your claims, should we believe anything you're saying?" Edi did a quick, discreet twirl of her finger to summon her gift of sight. There were no traces of illusory magic, but it didn't rule out transformative properties; her biology would mirror the form.

"I respect your caution, Edict, and your forthrightness. But perhaps we might discuss this somewhere more comfortable. You have exhausted what little magic and energy I have left, and we've much to confer."

Edi laughed, "Do you think us simpletons? I won't bring you anywhere near our homes."

"Bind me if you don't trust me. I give you my permission," the old woman said, extending her wrists.

Edi paused. If a witch offered herself for binding of her own free will,

she couldn't break its release. Perhaps they were misguided. Still, she wasn't ready to take any chances, and it would give her peace of mind.

"With threads of light and woven spell,
I bind thee now, thy powers quell;
No harm, no hex, no sorcery,
Thy will entwined, forever be."

As Edi's lip completed the spell, a light materialized around her arms and shot forth from her wand. The magic surged toward the old woman, wrapping around her wrists. Ribbons, inscribed with luminescent script.

Edi curved her lips into a smile.

"Feel better?" One Mother asked.

"Yes, I do, but it doesn't resolve my suspicions," Edi declared.

"Can we find a comfortable place to sit? I wasn't lying when I said I was old and tired, and the two of you have left our current surroundings inhospitable for a visit."

Edi scoured the scene around them; the old woman was right. Wielding her wand with reluctance, she cast a flare into the night sky. Talbot, positioned high above on the lookout, caught the signal and swiftly descended the rugged cliffs to join them. With their mode of transportation destroyed, their only option was to travel by Marina's ship.

Waiting on the shoreline, Edi still couldn't shake her doubts of suspicion. She perceived little reassurance from Pan, who remained silent since the old woman's disclosure—standing frozen on the beach behind them.

Edi turned to check her sister's well-being, whose eyes opened wide. "Belay that order!" Pan shouted to Talbot, who was arriving on the scene. Thrusting her hand out to the waters, she pushed the ship back, keeping it a safe distance from the shore.

"When you took my hands after the battle, I detected an exchange

of magic between us. A memory was sparked," she spoke softly, marching toward the One Mother, "leaving me to wonder if it was real or implanted. I recognize you. Not because of the memory—it wasn't mine. I recognize your magic; *it's chaos magic.*"

"What?" Edi exclaimed, moving from her sister's path.

A long smile grew across the old woman's face. "Of course... where do you think your magic came from?" Her mouth twitched.

"You aren't our mother. You aren't even real. You're a leech, a *shadebinder* from the Dreamscape. Created from a dream—my son's dreams. Reveal yourself," Pan commanded, grabbing the thing by its wrists.

The woman's face contorted; her wrists burned under Pan's touch. Chunks of silver hair fell to the ground—replaced by dark ebony locks. Her skin turned milky, and the sinister familiar face of Morvana appeared. A devilish laugh spewed from her mouth. Their sister's face melted, contouring into a misshapen head with bugged eyes and long, hairy ears. "Let go of me," it retched, clawing at Pan.

When she released it, the hideous deformity fell on its backside, choking to spit words out. "I . . . am . . . your . . . mother!" Grasping at Pan's cloak, it grabbed her hem. "I only wanted freedom . . . I meant no harm. You must know she is coming for the boy."

Talbot drew his sword. "What is this thing?" Repulsed, he winced when the creature's face attempted to copy his own. The shadebinder's body shrank, twisting like clay, unable to hold its form. Its ears, eyes, and limbs melted grotesquely into the sand.

"It can't harm you; it's nothing but a sentient construct, an idea—a dream," Pan said, feeling pity for the unfortunate thing convulsing in the sand. "Any power it held was removed when I called it by its name. A dream can't hold form when faced with reality."

"Birk created this?" Edi's mind spun, "He wouldn't—"

"I agree; this isn't Birk," Talbot defended, stepping back when the remaining pieces of the shadebinder popped with finality at his feet. He kicked at the black puffs of smoke until the breeze stole them.

"No, it isn't," Pan explained, "not willingly. But the shadebinder used *his* magic; I recognized his essence and needed a minute to assemble it. Birk's powers have been manifesting far longer than we realized, *longer than he realized.* Pulling me into the Dreamscape the other night should have alerted me to how powerful he's become."

"Pan, what are you saying?" Edi probed.

"I believe Birk has been visiting the Dreamscape for a while; it may have been the first manifestation of his awakening powers. I don't think he was aware he was doing it or remembered, leaving him susceptible to those who might take advantage. Shadebinders read our unconscious thoughts, desires, and even memories we've locked away," she explained. "I believe it could see the potential of Birk's power, the truth of his origin, and disguised itself to him."

"For what purpose?" Talbot asked.

"Shadebinders want to escape the Dreamscape. They want to live in our world. This can only be accomplished if they can trick the dreamer into helping them take a physical form." Edi inserted. "Once here, they can live forever, *as long as they go unnoticed.* The only caveat is they must sacrifice their own identity in the process. They're forced to take the form the host agrees upon in their dream."

"Birk is a child born from chaos. At some point, his latent magic unconsciously broke our enchantment—the exposure of our betrayal conflicted with a reality he didn't want to accept. Chaos is driven by emotion; he was attempting to create his own order to cope with our deceptions." Pan took Edi's hands, "He didn't want to believe we'd lie to him—the shadebinder took advantage of this. It took the shape of someone removed from Balincia, but still a form connected to us—someone credible to help him accept the truth."

"Birk created his *own* story?" Talbot asked.

Pan nodded and said, "A Shadebinder is forced to play out his narrative in exchange for life in our realm—they require some of the dreamer's magic and memories to aid in their role. We weren't battling this creature; we were fighting my son's magic in more experienced hands."

"What about Morvana?" pressed Edi. "We saw a glimpse of her in the shadebinder, which means her influence is behind this. She's always held power in that realm, and based on your shared vision, we know she *is* actively watching him."

"The creature's last words were—she is coming for the boy," Talbot reminded.

"We have to assume he's in danger," Pan affirmed.

"We need to figure out a way to communicate with him and warn him," Talbot urged.

Pan shook her head in disagreement, "She wants him separated—we need to figure out a way to bring him home."

THIRTY-FIVE

THE POWER OF ONE

Everyone felt the weight of the impending quest. Under Shayvonne's guidance, they decided not to enlist the Driftstone's help until they trusted its source. Considering this, they agreed the best course of action was to seek counsel from a member of the Thirteen.

Since Birk was unable to reach Pan and Edi, the only available alternatives were Lady Ironspire, *whom Shayvonne held reservations about,* and Faunwood, otherwise known as Sister Earth. The only challenge was Faunwood dwelled in the Living Forest, where neither man nor beast had entered uninvited for millennia.

Reflecting on the hallway of doors, Birk shared his predilection for one resembling the Living Forest's description. He recalled being drawn to it, a favored second choice. Agreed, this was their best chance; they mapped out a route. If their entry was denied, they could travel around the forest to Ironspire.

Their mornings began on the far edges of town in front of the mountains. This spot served as their training ground for honing their magical abilities. Grey, having more experience, mentored Birk and Brynn.

"If you want control over your abilities, you first have to understand the source of your power," he explained. "You want to achieve a singular mind; instead of commanding it, you must become one."

"How do I do that?" Birk asked.

"Think about it as a two-way conversation. Instead of ordering it out of fear or pulling from it with emotion, respect it as its own entity. When I connect with animals, I embody their spirit, their life force. They share their gifts willingly because of my intent to honor them, not harm them. Let me demonstrate."

Walking to Brunt, he placed his hands around the Grizzly's ears and lowered his head to the animal's brow. He closed his eyes, emptied his mind, and reached out to the bear's spirit. His eyes transformed, taking on Brunt's round and dark features. Muscles expanded in his chest, arms, and legs. Rising to his feet, he was sharper, stronger, and more connected to the earth.

Charging into the thicket of trees at the edge of the clearing, he swatted enormous trunks to the side, plowing through them at massive speed. With the agility of a bear, Grey ascended a towering tree, swift and fluid; his fingers gripped the core like claws. Reaching the tree's apex, Grey unleashed a deep, rumbling roar through the forest, more beast than man. Brunt answered his call.

"My turn!" Brynn shouted, eager to display her abilities.

Kneeling to her pack of wolves, she welcomed their lapping tongues on her face. In an instant, a similar transformation unfolded—a blur of motion—before she leaped onto all fours. Dashing, she ran the length of the terrain with a litheness, bounding from boulder to boulder. The wolves moved with her in synchronicity, following their pack leader to the white river's edge.

Crouching on a rock beside the rapids, Brynn spotted a wave of salmon jumping. Growing gills on her neck, she plunged into the frigid waters and effortlessly cut through the rough currents upstream. Leaping out of the river, she landed on the bank, a half mile up, with the poise of a prowling wolf.

"I'm officially impressed and intimidated," Birk said when Grey rejoined him. "Also, a little jealous, if I'm being honest."

"We've been using our powers since birth; give yourself time. The more you engage, the faster you'll learn to connect with your source."

"Can you channel the abilities of any animal?" Birk asked.

"There are limitations to the skills we can mimic," he said, pointing to an eagle circling them. "For instance, I can't adapt my body to fly, but I can do this . . ."

Placing his hands at his mouth, he let loose a high-pitched whistling sound from his throat, drawing the predatory bird's attention. Responding, the bird emitted piping notes back to him before diving talon-first into the river and snatching one of the salmon. Fish in its grip, it flew straight to Grey, dropping it at his feet and landing on his outstretched arm.

"We can communicate with any beast, bird, or insect, but we can't replicate every ability." Grey shared.

"Not right now," Shayvonne called from behind them, arriving to monitor their training session.

Grey made a face at Birk. "Shayvonne believes the Protector was able to transform into any beast, not only replicate their abilities."

"The man at the smithy referenced his transformation to a dragon," Birk remembered.

"She thinks Brynn and I will inherit this ability, too."

"But you don't believe this?"

"I believe it's a myth. There's no evidence of anyone being able to execute this kind of magic."

"Truths can hide in myths, too," Shayvonne side-eyed.

Brynn rejoined them, "I heard you talking, you know—*super wolf ears.* I think Shayvonne's right; one day, we'll be able to transform. I already grow gills when swimming; even Grey can't do that," she said, smugly.

"She's proud of that," Grey rolled his eyes. "Some skills we adapt temporarily when connected with an animal, but others are permanent absorptions, depending on the time spent with them and the bond developed."

"I'm faster than Grey; I spend more time with the wolves, but Grey is stronger because he's spent his whole life with Brunt and Winter. We both have enhanced sight and auditory skills—we can even see in the dark." Brynn bragged.

"Why don't we allow Birk to show us what he can do?" Shayvonne suggested. "I haven't been able to witness your powers in action."

"Me either!" Brynn agreed, excited.

Birk gave Grey a nervous look. "There's no pressure," he assured him. "Start slow; speak with the earth as you have in the past."

Resolved to put Grey's teaching into practice, he put distance between himself and the others. Kneeling to the ground, he pushed his fingers against the soil, taking a moment to connect with intent. The atmosphere thrummed around him. A dormant voice was straining to commune.

Attempting to listen, Birk became frustrated, unable to comprehend the language. Aware of Grey and his family behind him, his desire to impress them prevailed over his patience. He imposed his will on the ground—a tremor shook beneath the family's feet. Boulders tumbled down the mountains. The ground split underneath them—fighting and resisting Birk's command.

"I'm sorry," Birk yelled, crouched on the ground, his arms covering his head. Embarrassed for creating the calamitous environment around them, he attempted to explain: "I tried communicating with the earth—I didn't know how to interpret or translate the language. I grew impatient—pushed too hard."

Grey headed over to console him. Shayvonne tapped his shoulder, indicating she wanted to step in.

Sitting beside Birk on the ground, she took his hands. "It's a lot of pressure to perform when everyone is watching. Let's try a different approach. I want you to close your eyes and sit still with me for a minute. Clear your mind and be in the present. Focus only on the sounds of the forest."

Following her instructions, he concentrated. The chill of the mountain air brushed his face, the trees swayed, and the rivers babbled. He

heard every bird chirping, felt the sun's rays against his neck, and inhaled the sweet aroma of pine and evergreen.

"Everything you touch. Everything you see. Everything you hear, smell, or taste out here is the source of your magic," she instructed. "Now, put your hands on the ground without saying anything. Listen."

Birk sunk his hands into the soil, tuning everything else out. He could feel the earth's depth, layer after layer of life, moving underneath. He heard an ancient voice, used to being ignored, sad and tired, desperate to make a connection.

"Now, I want you to think about everything that makes you happy, including everyone you love. Share your most treasured memories. Let it see who you are," Shayvonne encouraged.

Birk thought of his childhood: gardening with Pan, curling up on the couch with Edi, sailing with Talbot, and playing with Ravenshire. He shared his joy of performing stories and reading books. Finally, he opened up about his quest—the excitement and the trepidation—his growing affection for Grey. The earth rose to meet Birk's hands, wrapping around his fingers. They exchanged energy, connecting over their love of the forest, the world, and the balance they wanted to create.

Opening his eyes, he stood calmer.

Extending his arms, he concentrated, endeavoring to mend the fractured earth and reclaim the order he disrupted. Lovingly, he poured his magic back into the ground, and the fissures and wounds he inflicted sealed themselves.

Walking to the side of the mountain, he raised his head and carefully rolled the boulders from the avalanche back into place. Touching the trees, he healed their fractured trunks and branches. Taking longer strides, he waved his hands across the land's surface, creating new growth—patches of grass, flowers, and emerald moss rose from the earth and surrounded them.

He exhaled deeply when the last stones were set in their rightful place and the ground beneath them was restored.

Shayvonne wrapped her arms around his shoulder. "It's easier to

command destruction than to coax something to heal or grow. When the root of your connection is love, you won't have to work so hard."

Since the mornings were reserved for practicing their magic, the afternoons were dedicated to refining their defensive combat skills. Finally, having a place to shine, Birk showed off the knowledge he'd gained from hours of diligent practice in his childhood. Guided by Birk's patient instruction, Shayvonne learned the art of ripostes and feints, anticipating and countering an opponent's moves.

Grey, in turn, impressed them with his adept use of his spear. His strikes were as swift as they were powerful, able to disarm both Birk and Shayvonne in one swing. His added strength and enhanced sight didn't hurt, allowing him to hit targets from a long-range distance with unerring accuracy.

He took his sister under his wing, hoping to impart the finesse and precision required to use a dagger. Emphasizing fluid wrist movements and timed strikes, he attempted to instill in her the discipline to control her impulses. After stealing her dagger and throwing her to the ground for the fifty-third time, Brynn kicked him in the shins.

"It's not fair; you'll always win. You're bigger and stronger," she pouted.

"Brynn, out here, you have relied on your natural gifts; when in combat without powers, you will have to rely on your wits. There will always be opponents bigger and stronger; you can't expect to overpower them all." He paused, sitting next to her on the ground. "Out of the two of us, you have always been the fire—your spirit is your strength *and* your liability. You will always be bested until you curb your urge to react."

Brynn snapped the branches in front of her. Stewing, she watched the wolves play in the distance. "When is the best time to strike a larger opponent?"

"When their guard is down, and they least expect it. You don't want

to allow them to—" Grey was stopped short by the cold press of a blade against his throat.

Brynn grinned, "Like this?"

He laughed, "You're learning."

The cottage's hearth stayed perpetually lit under Birk's growing control of his powers. Practicing daily, he restored their crops, created new wells, and strengthened the structures of their home and stables—an act of appreciation for their hospitality.

"You've made everything so beautiful. It's going to be hard to leave now," Shayvonne thanked him.

"It's the minimum I can do for your family's support. Everyone deserves a home they're excited to return to."

"Enough sap!" Brynn interrupted, breaking the mood. "We leave tomorrow, and Mom promised she has one last challenge for us tonight."

"The challenge is to see if you can last a full night without talking," Grey quipped, throwing a dinner roll at her.

"How about if the two of you can last a full evening without sucking each other's face off?" she mouthed back.

"The challenge," Shayvonne declared, speaking above them, "is to evaluate how much you've learned about your powers and each other. We'll make it a game—one last night of fun."

Revealing her plan, Shayvonne described a competition requiring strategy and cunning. Each of them would be required to navigate the forest at night while pitting their powers against each other in a battle of wits and skill. In thirty-minute intervals, one would be released to hide, their objective to outlast and outmaneuver their opponents through a combination of magic, combat skills, and tactical acumen.

"This will be a cinch," Brynn taunted, "the two of you are too big and loud."

"We'll see, wild one," Grey narrowed his eyes.

As dusk descended upon the forest clearing, the participants lined up in the moonlight. Birk was excited to put everything he learned into action, but equally terrified of being hunted by Grey and his sister. There was no mistake—*he was the prey on the menu tonight.*

Signaling the beginning of the game with a nod, Birk ran into the dark. Since the siblings already had predatory advantages at night and familiarity with their home, they all agreed he should go first.

He was also aware—he was the slowest.

Lacking the innate animal instincts of his counterparts, he knew his victory lay in his connection to the earth beneath him. Birk's mind raced with choices while he made his way through the tangled undergrowth on the side of the river. With a full hour to prepare for Grey's arrival, he understood his best chance was to eliminate Brynn first and focus his current efforts on tricking her heightened senses.

Drawing upon his powers, he requested the wind, weeds and pine needles to mask his footsteps while he walked. He'd use the rushing water to mask the sound of his movements and make it difficult for her to catch his scent. He explored the area and found the perfect hiding place inside a hollowed-out tree near the riverbed. Slipping into the trunk, he concealed himself, summoning the branches to cover the entry while he waited.

Acting instinctually, he dug his hands into the soil, seeking subtle vibrations to alert him of Brynn's approach. Grey, he knew, was an expert in stealth. On the other hand, Brynn was reckless. She'd be determined to prove herself; her moves would be spontaneous and susceptible to distraction. He counted on her boldness and impatience to give him an upper hand.

The minutes ticked by before he sensed a vibration beneath his fingertips—signaling an approach. His muscles tensed. He readied to spring into action, hoping to ambush Brynn before she knew he was there.

The cadence of the footsteps changed. They now relayed multiple sets of footfalls, confusing him. *It was too early for Grey to be with her. Was someone or something else lurking in the woods?*

The cloud-covered sky stole what small light remained from the

stars, plunging his hiding place into pitch-black darkness. His visibility stolen, he was caught off guard when a furry muzzle intruded into the trunk's recess. *She brought the wolves with her*, a tactical move he failed to anticipate. The wolf howled, alerting its mistress, betraying his location.

Refusing to be cornered, Birk crawled out from his concealed hideaway. The wolf snarled, seeking to keep him in place with its menacing growl. Birk flicked his wrist, and the vines of the forest answered him, trapping the canine and binding its jaws shut. The wolf released a muted whimper.

With the stakes high, Birk had to adapt to the evolving situation.

Locking onto the approaching figures running toward him, he made a split-second decision and hopped into the bank of the river. The icy water stole his breath. Birk summoned the riverbed to anchor his feet against the rapids. Brynn's yellow eyes glowed in the dark, closing in on him.

Holding his ground, Birk bid his time, waiting for the perfect moment to strike. When she jumped into the air to attack, he unleashed a solid wall of water to collide with her in mid-flight.

The water knocked Brynn backward until she collided with a sturdy tree. Birk wasted no time. Calling upon the vines and roots of the forest once again, he bound her and her lupine companions to the trees.

He hurried to her side to ensure she was unharmed. "You're rotten, but that was BLOODY BRILLIANT!" Relieved, he bent forward to catch his breath. "You better run, though," she warned, struggling against her leafy constraints, "big brother's coming."

With a grin tugging at his lips, Birk raced back into the forest, Brynn's voice ringing in his ears, *"Grey will avenge me!"* she yelled.

Birk believed her.

Unlike Brynn, Grey was seasoned. He'd been raised to hone his skills in unforgiving environments. Directly confronting or outpacing Grey was out of the question. Once he found Brynn by the river, he'd be cautious and stay away from the water, refusing to allow Birk to use the same trick twice. Birk required a more cunning strategy.

The darkness played to Grey's strength, and Birk's knowledge of the terrain wasn't comparable. To stand a chance against him, Birk needed to lure Grey into a situation where he controlled the dynamics. With a plan taking shape in his mind, Birk scouted out a small cave among the roots of some old trees. Its single entrance offered both a strategic advantage and a potential trap.

Setting a fire at the cave's center, he removed Grey's ability to hide, bathing every corner of the enclosed space in light. With his back against the cool stone wall, Birk faced the entrance. Lines of sweat trickled down his crown while he waited.

A long, sinuous shadow materialized at the cave's entrance, announcing Grey's arrival. He sauntered into the cave, deceptively casual. He smiled, more of a baring of teeth than an expression of warmth.

His eyebrows lifted in a mocking gesture, emphasizing the mischief in his eyes. Channeling the movements of a feline, he reminded Birk of a panther stalking its prey. It was clear Grey knew its potential to unnerve him.

"It was smart of you to bring me here." Grey's voice cut through the silence. "You took away my cover of darkness." He grinned again; this time, Birk saw a glimpse of the playful man he knew, reminding him this was only a game.

Grey was shirtless and barefoot, leaving Birk to wonder if his clothes hindered him in this state. *Or was this another method to distract him?* The hairs covering his chest were damp, casting an intimidating sheen in the light of the fire. Taking in the cavern, Grey calculated every space and angle to move with his eyes.

"I think you forgot by bringing me here; you're also trapped in here *with me.*" He inched closer with every word.

Faster than Birk could blink, Grey pounced.

Surprised by the sudden jump, Birk threw his arms out in front of him to block Grey's incoming. Birk's magic came to his defense, conjuring a powerful gale; he forced Grey to the cave's ceiling and held him there. *Well, that was a complete surprise.* His magic was moving faster than his mind.

Birk redirected his focus to Grey, who was trying to fight against the invisible force, pinning him against the cavern's canopy. Thrashing his arms and kicking his legs against the air, his defiance soon melted. Ceasing his struggle, he let his limbs dangle, and they both laughed. His eyes returned to the beautiful brown pools they were meant to be and curved with amusement.

"You tricky, sexy warlock," Grey flirted. "You always manage to surprise me."

Birk lost his concentration, allowing him to slip a few inches before he could regain his hold. The lapse gave Grey an idea: if he broke Birk's focus, he might be able to flip the scenario in his favor.

Shifting his approach, he teased Birk, "What will your next move be? You can't hold me here forever. I have to come down, and when I do, you're in trouble."

For a moment, Birk thought about using the air to throw Grey across the chamber, trusting his animal instincts would ensure he landed safely. If luck was on his side, he might be able to move fast enough to make it to the entrance and collapse it behind him. This would trap Grey, providing him with the win.

But when assessing his options, he had a change of heart. He no longer wanted to do this—it unsettled him to be at odds with Grey. Birk knew his capabilities now. There was no value in prolonging the game.

He lowered Grey until his feet were sturdy on the ground. "My next move is to surrender."

Grey wrapped his arms around Birk's waist.

"Why'd you give up?" he asked, tickled. "You held the upper hand. I wouldn't have hurt you."

"I know," Birk's heart thundered against Grey's chest, "I didn't give up; I gave in. You won two weeks ago. You captured me the day I woke up in a cave similar to this."

Grey leaned in, his eyes reflecting Birk's vulnerability; their lips pressed into a tantalizing lock. Closing any distance between them, Grey pulled Birk into him until their shadows, shaped by the fire, merged into one form on the cave wall.

PART
THREE

THIRTY-SIX

THE PRINCESS OF IRONSPIRE

When she heard the knock at the door, she'd been expecting Indigo. Otherwise, she wouldn't have opened it. She was preparing for the disappearing tavern next week, followed by the Azure Trials. The last thing she had time for was a summons from her mother's lapdog, Vincent.

"Lady Ironspire requests the princess's attendance at the Royal Citadel Tower upon the hour." Ugh! She hated his pompous insistence on formality. Why not say, *Zara, your mom demands to see you right now*? She held no misconceptions; this wasn't a request, and she was expecting another lecture about her neglect of royal duties.

She ensured she filled her scowl with double the disdain when Vincent called her *princess*. She'd already asked him a thousand times to call her Zara. He continued the practice to spite her, knowing she hated the title. *He was such a prick of a needle.*

Vincent, the Royal Advisor, was always cozied up to her mother, whispering in her ear and dressing Zara down with his eyes. Yes, *she knew* she made a horrible princess. *You try being the only child born to the ruler of the largest, most advanced city in Driftstone*; she rued in her head. *No pressure.*

Her mother had taken hundreds of lovers over the years; why was Zara the only unfortunate offspring to stick around in her womb? Since the moment of her conception, all the attention of Driftstone has been on her, adding fuel to her mother's conspiracies. Trapped in a prison of her mother's making, she lived under constant surveillance.

Sable's political popularity was waning, which didn't help matters. Granted, her mother was one of the few surviving members of the *Original Thirteen* after the most significant war in Driftstone's history, but that was *ten thousand years ago*. Living in the past, her mother still feared attacks from unknown assailants, utilizing all her magic and energy to build the world's largest army. The famed evolutionary city of Ironspire was a giant fortress, unlike the city of innovation it claimed to be.

Not to mention, there was a growing contingent of humans denying the war ever happened. Her mother's ravings about *the Under* and hypothetical maniacal siblings seeking revenge didn't boost their confidence. While Zara did believe *most* of her mother's history, she also thought it was best to leave the ancient past where it belonged.

When Zara arrived in the world, it only amplified Sable's insecurities, resulting in her mother distrusting anyone's magic but hers. Under royal decree, anyone born with or by magic was exiled from the city unless they were a pledged member of the Azure or one of her licensed engineers. Even then, the only magic lawful to use was her mother's, condensed into the weapons they fought with or the inventions they created.

Once passed, the law banished half of Ironspire's citizens, leaving families tossed into massive encampments outside the city's walls. With the expansion of the Free Roamer tribes (and arcanivores now added to the mix), hunting them left the magic community defenseless. Zara listened to riots and protests over the walls every night, accusing her mother of betraying her own kind.

What would Sable do if she knew her daughter was one of them? Nothing good. She didn't hide her relief when Zara was born *without* magical

abilities. Sable wouldn't admit it, but her daughter threatened her. Zara's conception was miraculous, sans father, and unexpected.

Due to her inability to conceive, Lady Ironspire was convinced dark magic was at play. *How many other mothers believed their newborn was the literal spawn of a demon? Try carrying that knowledge with you.* In her early years, she avoided Zara. She handed her off to nursemaids and Vincent, who dutifully reported every diaper, tumble, and word from her mouth. Over time, once she was convinced Zara was only an innocent babe, she settled into a relationship with her. Growing to love her, albeit in her own restrained way.

These experiences *and lack of experiences* made Zara feel unsafe to reveal her late onset of magical puberty—*or whatever you wanted to call waking up with magical powers one night.*

How would the conversation even go? *Hey, Mom, I've been having weird dreams about boys. No, not those kinds of dreams, but bizarre ones where I roam this magical realm and can peek in on other people's dreams like a creep. Don't worry; they're always clothed, but everyone is having nightmares about those hideous, magic-consuming monsters. Oh yeah, and the other day while training with Indigo—which I know you forbade me to do... Poof! I summoned magic light swords! Crazy, right? Please don't kick me out!*

Yeah, she wished that were the relationship she held with her mother. If gross Vincent weren't *always* there, eavesdropping and adding his less-than-valuable insights, maybe they'd have a chance to connect meaningfully.

Zara couldn't remember the last time they were alone in a room.

This conversation required a more nuanced approach, which Indigo *was supposed to be here* to help her work on. Indigo, a few years her elder, was Zara's role model. The first daughter in a long lineage of men, born into the Azure, they were destined to be one of the Great Captains of the Royal Guard. Assigned to be Zara's escort because they were born a girl, the two became fast friends.

Outgrowing the role, they proved to be one of Ironspire's fiercest and ruthless champions in the tournaments. Chopping off their long locks of blue hair, Indigo declared they'd no longer be held back by the

titles or biases of men. Transcending gender, they'd forever be known as a warrior.

Zara aspired to be this type of leader. Indigo was the reason she wanted to be an Azure, *not* a princess. Only the Azure held influence with her mother. The title was imperative if she ever hoped to persuade her mother's thinking and break Vincent's hold on her.

Ironspire's army of warriors would be better served in dealing with the real threats surrounding the lands instead of preparing for the *inevitable* return of Sable's absent or dead siblings. It'd also regain the trust of those exiled, or provide them with the safety to migrate and build something of their own.

Indigo, too, shared this ideology. So, when Zara shared her plan, they were more than obliging and carved out their afternoons to help Zara train. Together, they devised a strategy for Zara to enter the Azure Trials in disguise. If she won, her mother wouldn't be able to oppose her candidacy, and as the first Azure princess, she was guaranteed the audience required to make a change.

All was going to plan until a few weeks ago, when Zara pulled two swords made of white light out of thin air in the middle of a combat session. Shortly after, she summoned other light-based weapons, including shields, spears, and knives. Upon reading Zara's face, Indigo knew this was a new, *if not an unwelcome,* revelation.

Indigo was also aware keeping these gifts a secret was critical to keeping Zara around. So, without word or judgment, they took the initiative to focus their sessions on helping Zara conceal her magic. *It was easier said than done.*

All Indigo could decipher was that the magic acted as an automatic defense mechanism. The only way to overcome it was through meditative practice. Zara would need to control her breathing and heart rate, deceiving her body into believing it wasn't under attack. *How was one supposed to be centered in a battle with swords and fists flying?* Zara had no idea.

Then the dreams came.

Zara realized instantly these weren't ordinary dreams. Her mother had thoroughly educated her about the abilities and magic of her twelve

siblings. She understood she was walking in Uncle Nazeem's Dreamscape realm. Initially, she thought he, too, had survived and was trying to reach her, but every vision centered around a young man her age.

It took her a while to figure out she was walking among *their* dreams, not hers. The first was a dark-haired boy in the desert, kneeling in the sand over an aging old man. His dreams were literal and minimal, hyper-focused on irrelevant details, straining her interest.

The second was a striking golden-haired young man who dreamed of love and escape. She enjoyed his dreams, but he reacted, alarmed and angry, at her intrusion when he noticed her lurking. When she attempted to talk to him, he rudely shoved her, prompting her to wake.

It was the boy with hair the color of autumn, *often accompanied by a bear*, who captivated her. His dreams were colorful and magnificent, full of fascinating and frightening stories. She kept returning to his dreams, feeling a serendipitous tug between them. Eventually, she revealed herself to him, and they connected, but he disappeared when she attempted to get him to follow her to an area where they could talk.

Lately, the two of them have been sharing the same nightmares *or walking in them together*; she's not exactly sure how it works. The most recent was a week ago, when she, the boy, and the bear were at the Ironspire Colosseum, fighting an invasion of arcanivores.

Oh yeah, and she died in it.

Her mother had taught her visions weren't literal or set in stone, but some *were* warnings—she'd never been trained to tell the difference. At first, she assumed the arcanivores in her dreams were conjured by the stories she'd heard from the kingdoms or metaphoric images representing her internal struggles, so she shrugged them off as part of her subconscious.

However, her, *or their*, latest nightmare hit too close to home. When she confided all this to Indigo, they suggested she seek a soothsayer. Zara knew most of the self-proclaimed psychics were frauds, but a few outside the city walls were capable of low-level clairvoyance.

If the nightmare *were* a vision of things to come, she feared it would happen during the upcoming Azure trials, Ironspire's next big event at

the Colosseum. She didn't share this with Indigo because she wanted confirmation before sending the city into a frenzied false alarm, losing any chance of influence in the future. So, both in disguise, Indigo snuck Zara through one of the Azure's hidden passageways into the encampments after dark.

While they weren't able to find any soothsayers, they were able to gain some intel.

Under double full moons, a tavern appears by the river for one night, a quick hike outside the city's borders. It can only be seen by Magic-Born or magical races, and only those seeking answers can enter. Rumors say it was an enchantment created by her Uncle Cyrus, used as a safe house to exchange information during the Witches' War.

Whether it was a myth or a wild fox hunt, Zara was out of other options. The next double full moon was two nights before the trials. If there *was* any truth to her dreams, she owed it to her people to do anything to prevent them.

Chewing on all this, she became increasingly irritated, following Vincent to the Royal Citadel Tower. Throwing the doors open in a performative display, he bowed with his head low to the ground. "Your Royal Highness, the princess of Ironspire," he announced with a booming voice. *A bit over the top, given only her mother was in the room.*

"That was unnecessary," she uttered under her breath, passing him. "Does she pay you double for groveling flamboyantly, or was that only to annoy me?"

"Everything is for *you*, my dear," he grinned, flashing his yellow teeth.

"You know, you're the first elf I've ever seen with a triple chin. Lowering yourself isn't the best angle for you." *She could do this all day.*

"Enough," Sable groaned, walking over to greet her daughter. Outside of the same dark black skin, high cheekbones, and violet eyes, Zara couldn't place herself in her mother—except, maybe their shared iron wills. Quick kisses in the air were exchanged. "I'm happy to see you. You've been avoiding me."

Zara sighed. "I've not been avoiding you; I've been busy."

"Vincent tells me you've been spending a lot of time with Indigo," she dropped, letting it hang in the air. "I'm glad you've been rekindling your friendship—I'm surprised both of you have the time—you with your royal duties, and they with the Azure."

"Well, you can tell *Vincent*," Zara quipped, curling her lip. "Indigo and I are working together on a special presentation for the upcoming Azure trials. I wanted to keep it a surprise." Shooting Vincent a glare, she added, "And we're not *rekindling* a friendship; it never stopped."

"That's nice to hear, darling. Don't be surprised when Indigo's time commitments change. They will surpass their father as the Captain of the Royal Azure, which I suspect won't be too far out." Sable informed, motioning for her to take a seat. "I'm glad you mentioned the Azure Trials; they're the reason I want to speak to you."

"Okay . . ."

"We're attempting to do something different this year. In addition to the candidates from the Azure Academy, we'll be opening the trials to twenty of the young exiled Magic-Born. The encampments will also be allowed to view the tournament in the Colosseum and cheer their children on." She announced.

"What? Why?" Zara immediately recalled her vision. They'd be herding all the Magic-Born into one confined place, a smorgasbord for arcanivores. However, if she shared this, she would have to reveal why she suspected it. "Mother, you're aware they hate you, right? Asking them to compete to pledge loyalty to you *after kicking them out* is a bit of a slap in the face, isn't it?" She dissuaded, deploying a different tactic.

"Don't be absurd; they don't hate me. I continue to supply food to their markets and provide aid to those who are ill. Why do you think they stay outside the city? You act as if I've abandoned them," she dismissed.

"I think the arrangement works well for everyone," Vincent interrupted, pretending to polish a nearby vase. "Your mother stationed Azure at the walls to provide security; what more could they need? It's more than most kingdoms provide lower-class troublemakers."

"They aren't *lower-class troublemakers* because they're born with or

by magic. Aren't elves an indigenous magical race created by Faunwood? Or have you come to believe your adjacency to my mother purified your blood?" Zara shot back, disgusted.

"Similar to the Azure, I have forsaken my magical ancestry in pledge to Lady Ironspire, our Witch of Innovation, the source of the *only* true and sacred magic leading us to our future." He bowed deeply, holding his hand to his heart, signifying his reverence and deference.

Zara felt the bile rise in her throat.

Zara continued to press her point by redirecting to her mother, who wouldn't intervene. "They aren't camped on your doorstep because you support them; they're there because they have nowhere else to go."

It was an error to believe Sable was vapid or witless like Vincent, but she *was* arrogant and out of touch. An unintelligent woman wouldn't be capable of building a city operating with the brilliance Ironspire does. However, Lady Ironspire carried the baggage of perceived betrayal and abandonment by her family during the war. Living alone too long, with only the voices of her genius and slimy elf-servant in her ear, she'd become blind and jaded.

"Don't speak to me as if I'm a child, Zara. I'm aware of prejudices against those with magic, hence why they were removed from the inner quarters of the city. It's for their safety *and ours*," she lectured. "They grew reckless and irresponsible with their charlatan tricks and inbreeding. Their laziness and disrespect for their gifts drew ire, creating the Free Roamers. They made us a target for our enemies whilst they remained in the city."

"How can you say that? You built this entire city *with* magic. Your DNA is coded *into* the Azure. Your magic is condensed into our walls. You're one of the Original Thirteen *Magic-Born*. Don't you feel any empathy or responsibility?"

Sable leaned forward in her chair. "You're correct. *My* magic built this city and still protects it, standing the test of time. I won't let you dilute what real magic is; it's *not* a breed or parlor trick."

"So, what am I?" Zara demanded.

"*You?* You're my daughter, and I'm thankful every day you weren't born with the curse of magic. It isn't for the weak. What I'm building here, I'm trying to build for you, for our future."

"I don't want what you're building. Give it to Vincent!" She was over the vileness of the conversation. If it weren't for the people in the city, a part of Zara wanted to watch her mother's creations burn.

"Stop!" Sable grabbed Zara's hand and rose from her seat. "I don't want to argue. Let's get back to the topic; believe it or not, I'm trying to quell the protests with the changes I have made for the trials. Whether you think it's a promising idea or not, we already have twenty volunteers who've shown interest in competing, with more piling in. All they've got to do is prove they're worthy by not using their magic in the event."

"The exiles aren't trained in the academy, which will disadvantage them. The trials could mean death for them if they can't use the skills they're born with." Zara argued.

"Then they'll die, which is the same risk everyone takes. If they succeed, there is a path forward for citizenship for them and their families." Vincent dismissed, placing his pudgy hand with his ugly ring on Sable's shoulder. His touch of familiarity was repugnant.

"Since you're a champion of the people, Zara, I want you to nominate a candidate. Members of our council, myself included, will all nominate someone from the volunteer pool," Sable explained.

"Why would I want to be a part of this?"

Vincent stepped closer, exposing his foul breath. "I'm surprised your bleeding heart will pass on the opportunity to endorse their best interest."

She paused. Maybe he had a point. She *could* use this to her advantage *and* their best interest.

"What's my responsibility?"

"As much or as little as you want." Sable offered. "You'll be allotted a day with your nominee and full access to the training facilities, preparing them as best as possible for the event. You may work with Indigo if you choose, or pass them off to the Academy soldiers. As a bonus, if your

candidate completes the trials, I will allow them to serve as your escort if you wish."

A plan formulated. It'd be easy to disguise herself as one of the exiled volunteers. If Indigo nominated her, her place on the arena floor would be secured. If the arcanivores were going to attack, she'd be in a better position to defend. If they didn't, her plans to compete and win the trials became easier.

"Fine, I accept the responsibility." She consented.

"Good. I confess I was prepared to do more convincing," Sable admitted with some skepticism.

"Perhaps I'm finally embracing my royal duties," Zara smiled.

THIRTY-SEVEN

GRIFFIN'S GORGE

The addition of Brynn and Shayvonne changed the dynamic of the traveling party. Birk missed leaning against Grey—the small touches passed between them when the hours became long. Now, Brynn's consistent chatter was the only thing filling the voids of silence.

Birk and Shayvonne rode on horseback, lagging behind the pace of the siblings. Acting as their scout, Grey kept them off the main roads and would run ahead to determine their safest route. To avoid Free Roamers, arcanivores, and other travelers, Grey constantly communicated with the birds and beasts, who aided their navigation. Brynn called it traveling *'the way of the wild.'*

From Everglenn, they followed the path of the water into the White River Valley, an expansion from the Great Protector's land. It was two days of travel over hill after hill of green slopes rolling into the distance. A patchwork of fields lay between them, filled with waist-tall grass and red sunflowers. Giant crickets, not much smaller than Brynn, sporadically jumped over them, scaring Birk each time.

Birk lay curled in Grey's arms at their small camp on their second evening. He was awoken by a stampede of hooves echoing through the ground. Grey's arms restrained him when he tried to sit up, putting a finger to his mouth, he signaled to stay silent. Shayvonne held Brynn and kept her eyes on Grey, who motioned for them to follow.

Keeping low to the ground, under the cover of tall grass, they crawled to the top of a hill, where Grey pointed to the valley's base. Squinting, Birk tried to figure out what they were staring at while they lay on their bellies. "Centaurs . . ." Brynn unmasked the mystery.

The centaurs raced aside a herd of wild lunar horses, their coats radiating under the luminant light of the moons. Grey wrapped his arm around Birk's waist while they watched the equine transform into living constellations racing across the shadowed land. "The red, yellow, and orange ones are the males. The silver, light blue, and lavender pelts are the females—honoring the suns and the moons."

"Legend says the Protector created the lunar horses as a gift to the centaurs, his sister Faunwood's children," Shayvonne explained. "This gift became a symbol of their friendship; the bond passed from the siblings to their creations—an unbreakable bond that still exists today."

"Seeing them together is a sign of good fortune, especially as we travel to see Faunwood," Grey assured, pulling Birk closer.

"May the Protector's gift bind his descendants and hers once again," Shayvonne prayed.

When they climbed their last hill the following day, the river led them to the Girantheam Fields. Towering creatures with long hair, the faces of water buffalo, and six legs roamed the landscape. Grey explained the girantheam were gentle creatures, considered sacred due to their size and impenetrable bodies. Grazing on apricot trees and mimosa flowers, they dotted the valley as the travel party descended toward them.

When they passed the giant beasts, their massive underbellies created curtains of shadow and light. Birk reached up and ran his fingers through the soft brush of their fur, inciting them to emit an echoing purr-like rumble. Brynn and Winter darted and dashed between their legs, making a game out of it—distracting them from the monotonous journey.

On their fifth night, around the campfire, Grey pulled them together. "Tomorrow, we'll pass through the Griffin's Gorge; we must release the horses in the morning. I've spoken with them, and they know their way home," he advised.

"Is the terrain too difficult?" asked Birk.

"It *is* steep and narrow, but I'm letting them go because they'll be too tempting to the griffins. Horses are a delicacy to their palate as are humans," he warned. "At first light, I'll enter and attempt to speak with them. No one should leave camp or go near the gorge until I've returned for you."

"Grey, you've never communed with a beast comparable to a griffin before; this is too dangerous. Magical predators aren't bears or wolves." Shayvonne voiced her concern.

"The gorge is the only clear path to the Living Forest from this direction. Otherwise, it'll take us another week to walk around."

"Then it'll take us another week," Birk answered firmly to Shayvonne's approval. "It's not worth putting your life at risk. We've talked about this."

Grey looked at him, pleading for Birk to drop it.

"What aren't you sharing?" Shayvonne asked, noticing the exchange.

Brynn spotted a hare close to the campfire. Walking over, she scooped it up and held it close to her ear. Walking back with the rabbit in her arms, she sat beside her brother, placing her hand on his leg.

A solemn moment passed between them.

"The arcanivores are closing in on us. That's what he isn't saying. The animals are migrating this way. The arcanivores will be here in a day if we don't move." Brynn announced.

Everyone stared at Grey, reflecting in silence. Birk didn't want to add to the pressure. They knew there would be tough choices; they'd been fortunate to make it this far without incident.

"All right, Grey," Birk said, breaking the camp's silence. "We'll follow your lead. I believe in you, and I trust you."

Grey met Birk's gaze across the fire with gratitude. "I do, too," Brynn added softly, hugging her brother's leg.

Shayvonne stood, presenting her back to the group to hide her face. "I don't care for this."

"You promised when we were out here, you and Brynn would take my direction. This is my call." Facing Brynn, he lifted her chin and said, "Listen to me, wild one. There will be no heroics or impulsive moves tomorrow. If something happens, you'll listen to Birk, and all of you will follow Brunt and Winter. They'll do their best to lead you on the safest path. Do you understand?"

Lying her head on his knee, she promised.

Later in the evening, Birk found Grey standing under a mimosa tree, staring into the stars. For a long moment, he didn't say anything, afraid of making the weight in Grey's chest heavier. Finally, he blurted, "Can't I go with you?"

Grey shook his head, a half-smile pulling at his lips. "I need you here. Protect my family. That's how you can help me."

The answer stung, even if Birk understood.

"Are you sure you can do this?"

"I honestly have no idea. I've never attempted communing with something so old and so powerful."

A knot sat stubborn in Birk's stomach; he didn't want Grey's last night before the gorge spent drowning in worry. He reached out, took his hand, and tugged him onto the grass beside him.

They fell back, the night sky wide above them. Neither of them spoke of tomorrow. They whispered half-formed jokes, fingers tangling. Their lips found each other in the quiet, a kiss carrying more than words could hold. It wasn't wild or hurried; it was a promise pressed into the night.

Birk whispered, "Return to me."

Grey stealthily slipped into his discarded clothes before the first sun rose. Covering Birk with a fur blanket, he waited for Brunt and Winter. Kneeling before them, he bowed his head between theirs, and the three exchanged a mute understanding. Rising, with one last look at Birk, he

marched toward the gorge alone, leaving Winter to head back to camp and Brunt to lie beside his sleeping heart.

When the first rays of sun broke across the ridged roof of the gorge, Grey first noticed the stillness. Despite the roar of the wild rapids carving their way through or the whistling high winds against the walls, the place was void of the usual chatter of life. There were neither morning songs from birds nor the pitter-patter of little rodents and lizards scattered across the arid brush, not even the hum of an insect.

The only path was a narrow, winding trail against the canyon's high wall. The rocky cliffs were filled with caves and holes, perfect for a predator's nest. Grey spied bones from men and beasts scattered across sharp rocks and dying trees along the sloping river's edge.

Grey stood at the entrance and spread his arms, allowing the wind to carry his scent into the gorge. He wanted the griffins to be aware of his presence; he held no intention of surprising them. Mimicking the language of eagles, he called out across the canyon, hoping his loose translation was similar enough to relay his message. Sharing his connection to the Protector, he requested commune and safe passage.

Satisfied he'd done all he could for the moment, he climbed with caution, entering the depths of the gorge. Keeping his back to the wall and his eyes to the skies, it wasn't until the second sun started to rise that he spied movement. Hearing a cry from below him, he looked down and identified a flash of a tail underneath a rock on the declining banks.

Getting on all fours, he peered over the ridge and called out again. The creature returned his cry, sounding desperate and in pain. Leaning closer, about to release a third call, Grey spied the shadow of two giant wings attached to a lion's body grow larger, rapidly descending toward him. Rotating onto his back with the agility of a cat, he narrowly missed the giant talons crashing onto the ledge where he was perched, sending it crashing into the river.

Rolling back onto his feet, Grey sprinted across the ledge, trying to distance himself from the beast. The griffin flew over the river to spin

around in Grey's direction. Its talons, the size of a man, opened, preparing for a second attack.

The griffin screeched, hurling itself at Grey, who was no match for its speed in the air and was forced to jump forward at the last second. A narrow miss. Gripping the wall with its front talons, the griffin whipped around, connecting with Grey from the back while he attempted to retreat, pushing him to the ground with a powerful kick from its hind legs. Grey's face smashed into the harsh stone rubble. His body slid to the edge, giving him a glimpse of the deadly drop beneath him.

He pushed up and spun around, unable to avoid the beast's talon. Making contact, the creature's nails sliced his chest—sending him reeling backward over the edge. The griffin dove after him. Flipping in midair, he spotted the branch of a dragonbrush tree growing from the canyon wall.

Latching onto it, he flung himself against the canyon's ridge, bearing into the wall with his fingers. The griffin, unable to adapt so quickly, plunged past him. Grey slid down the stone wall. Bleeding and bruised, he swiftly took cover under the resting boulders near the river's edge.

He could see the griffin circling, scanning the area for her prey. If he retreated from the boulder, his only option was to dive into the rapids. If he swam deep enough, he might avoid detection and be able to catch the current downstream to his camp.

Accepting defeat, Grey prepared to make a run for the river. Then he heard the call again. An anguished cry, not far from him. Crawling in the opposite direction, he found the origin under the rocks. A tiny baby griffin, pinned at the wing by a large piece of granite, most likely from an avalanche.

The tiny creature pawed and scratched the ground, pleading for help. With an open space between them, Grey would need to cover twelve wolf strides to reach the infant.

Peeking out, he was relieved to find the adult griffin lost interest in their chase. It frantically circled the area above her trapped cub. Throwing itself against the large piece of granite, it attempted to dislodge the rock, lacking the strength required.

Grey saw the issue; the rock was wedged between two other boulders

and required lifting from below *if there was any chance of moving it*. Making a fast decision, Grey made a run for it, grabbing the adult's attention, and slid on his back to reach the injured cub underneath.

Furious, the adult screeched and slashed, pushing its beak into the entrance. The babe, scared and panicked, backed away. "It's okay, little one," Grey calmed. "I'm here to help. Your mother is only trying to protect you."

With little room to move, Grey was forced to crouch. The edge of the rock was slanted, the sharp side piercing the cub's wing. If he got underneath it on all fours, he *might* be able to push it up with the strength of his back and legs.

If he failed, the boulders could cave in on both of them. If he succeeded, the opening would leave him susceptible to the infant's mother. *Birk's power would've been beneficial at this moment.*

All out of choices, he did something he'd never done before: he prayed. Placing his hands on the ground, he prayed to the Protector. He prayed for Brunt's strength, Winter's cunning, Birk and his family, the cub and its mother—and that this wouldn't be the end.

Clenching his eyes, he braced his back against the rock and pushed with his legs. His thighs shook when he forced himself onto his knees. Sweat flooded his face and shoulders. The great boulders scraped against each other, inching and cracking. From his knees, he centered his hands underneath the great stone and positioned it onto his shoulders, demanding his legs to stand.

The rock moved as his body continued to push. With the weight off his back, Grey used his thick arms and shoulders to make the final push. Eventually, the protruding rock became top-heavy, toppling from the wedged crack and tumbling toward the river with a crash. The cub, wing bent but alive, crawled to him, affectionately rubbing its beak against Grey's calves.

The mother leaned in from the rock above them, wings spread. Her fierce yellow eyes darted between Grey and the cub. Drained and exhausted, he cradled the babe, lifting it to its mother. She took it with care by the scruff of its neck and flew to her nest.

Collapsing onto the flat surface of the boulder, Grey lay wounded, baking in the sun.

The griffin returned and landed next to him. With no fight left, Grey rotated onto his belly. Pushing to his knees, he positioned into a reverent bow before the beast. Nudging him with its beak, the griffin hopped and squawked around him. Sensing no threat, it finally knelt and settled before Grey, resting its head against his.

In the light of the rise of the third sun, the griffin and the man communed, and the spirit of the Protector united them.

THIRTY-EIGHT

THE LIVING FOREST

When they woke, no one knew what to do with themselves—Grey had left without saying a word. At the rise of the first sun, they made breakfast and ate in silence. At the second, they packed their gear and saddled it to Brunt, waiting—not a syllable passed between them. By the time the third sun was high in the sky, Birk and Shayvonne shared a worried look.

He'll be here. Birk kept repeating in his head. *He'll be here.*

Brynn ran to the edge of the Girantheam Fields, searching the distance for a sign of his return. If anyone could spot him from a long way off, she could. Protected under Winter's watchful eye, her distance allowed Shayvonne to confide her concerns to Birk.

"He implied the arcanivores would be here as early as nightfall. We've only got an hour before we need to move." She shared without tone. Standing next to Birk, they fixed their eyes toward the gorge.

"I know," Birk replied vacantly. *He'll be here.*

"We'll be exposed out here in the open field if we stay."

"I know." *He'll be here.*

"We have no idea how many are traveling toward us. Even with you, Winter, and Brunt, we may be outnumbered," she voiced.

He'll be here.

"If it were only us, I'd take our chances. Give him every hour of daylight to return. I'm worried about Brynn. She's overconfident and impulsive; if Grey isn't here, she'll overcompensate." Shayvonne's voice cracked. She lowered her head toward the ground.

Walking behind her, Birk placed his hands on her shoulders. "I understand, Shayvonne. I won't let anything happen to Brynn. I promised Grey I'd protect his family. We'll leave in an hour if—" Birk stopped. Brynn was racing toward them, her hands waving excitedly. Winter galloped enthusiastically beside her.

"He's coming! He's coming!" Brynn screamed with delight.

Shayvonne fell to her knees, clutching her heart. As it approached, a shadowed dot in the sky took shape. Covering his eyes to block out the sun, Birk made out the flying figure of a lion with an eagle's head—Grey saddled on its back.

He's here! Birk stumbled back a step, with a shaky laugh.

Brynn grabbed his hand when she reached him. Turning to watch her brother's approach, she looked on in admiration. "Typical Grey, showing off!" she said with a toothy grin. "He's so valorous."

"He's valorous, indeed," Birk shared her sentiment.

The griffin landed in front of the family. A single flap of its wings sent dust swirling around them. Grey cut a gallant figure atop its back—hair billowing in the wind, shirtless.

A pronounced gash streaked across his chest, his face and skin marred with bruises and grime. Flashing a roguish smile to his loved ones, he affectionately ruffled the feathers of the griffin, eliciting a melodic piping response. Dismounting the beast, Grey bowed to it, a silent moment of respect. Acknowledging its rider with a regal tilt, the griffin took flight back to the gorge.

Breaking free from Birk, Brynn raced toward Grey, throwing herself into his arms. "Everyone was scared, but I knew you'd be back. You always come back."

Birk gave the family some space.

"I want to hear everything," she said, sliding from his arms. "Do you think the griffin will let me ride it too?"

"In a bit, wild one," he welcomed Shayvonne in for a hug.

"You're hurt," she said, touching his chest.

"I'll heal," he said, taking her hand and kissing her fingers. "Don't worry."

Making eye contact with Birk, he lowered his head. "Are you angry with me?" he asked, offering an apologetic smile.

The corner of Birk's mouth curled upwards. "For not saying goodbye or almost getting yourself killed, *again?*"

"I returned to you," Grey ignored the question. Looping his fingers into Birk's waistband, he pulled him close.

"You did," Birk said, touching his forehead against Grey's. "How is it possible your arms are even bigger now?"

Grey chuckled, "The aftermath of the Protector's magic." Wrapping one arm around Birk's waist, he pulled him closer, demonstrating his new strength and kissing him. "Thank you," he shared.

"For what? I didn't do anything."

"You let me go because you believed I'd come back."

"Don't ever prove me wrong," Birk allowed Grey to break his hold and shift his focus to his family.

"We have safe passage. We should go now if we hope to pass during the daylight hours," he instructed. "I'll tell you about my morning as we walk, wild one," he said, ushering Brynn to follow him. Shayvonne took Birk's hand, passing him a smile of relief, and the party of six made their way back to the gorge.

Motivated by Grey's return and spurned on by the prediction of incoming arcanivores, they crossed the gorge quickly. Despite its length and treacherous path, they neared its end by the setting of the first sun. When the trail opened to the valley below, Shayvonne pointed to the largest expanse of trees Birk had ever seen, "The Living Forest," she informed.

From the top of the gorge, the canopy of treetops rolled on as far

as the eye could see in every direction. The river swept underneath it, disappearing into the blanket of green. Even from a distance, the trees towered above the land, creating an impenetrable wall.

Making their way down the ridge, they arrived at the forest's entrance in time for the setting of the second sun. Pink rays of sunlight dusted the white oaks, thick branches curled and wrapped from tree to tree, resembling locked arms. The group stood in awe.

The trees groaned at their arrival.

A golden-winged hawk flew past them, hunting prey at the edges of the forest. When it dived toward a hare, an invisible barrier knocked it back, and the aerial predator spiraled to the ground. Confused but unhurt, the bird shook its head and flew back in the opposite direction. "An invisible enchantment," Birk observed aloud.

"It's your turn, Birk," Brynn teased, wiggling her fingers, "Talk to the Trees."

Grey joined Birk until they were a few feet away from where the hawk collided with the wall. "These trees are ancient; pay them the respect they deserve," Grey advised, squeezing his hand. "Remember, you're communing, not commanding. Be gentle and patient."

Birk knelt on one knee before the forest. He buried his hands into the earth and introduced himself, asking for an audience. The heart of the Driftstone beat closer here, pulsing in his fingertips. Roots from the ground rose to meet him, wrapping around his forearms and entangling his feet.

Old voices—a chorus of them—chanted in his ears. They shared stories in a poetic language and recited ballads from their sapling youths. They spoke of the lives dwelling among them—a vast network dedicated to preserving Driftstone—in turn, they sought the protection from the trees.

In response, Birk also shared his desire to protect and save Driftstone. His quest: to seek truth and restore balance. Opening his spirit to their arboreal heart, he showed them the door that beckoned him to come. The roots around him untangled and descended back into the ground.

Coming up behind him, Grey helped him to his feet. "Did it work?"

"I'm not sure," Birk shrugged. "We communed—I received no answers. I guess there's only one way to find out."

Stretching his arm into the air, Birk opened his palm in front of him. Taking careful strides, he walked forward. Anticipating a wall at any time, he was surprised to find he was suddenly inside the trees. Taking a quick step back, he was on the outside again, Grey behind him.

"It worked!" he grinned, motioning for them to join him.

Birk's party stood in a cathedral-sized clearing and marveled at their new surroundings. The trees' towering canopy far surpassed their appearance from the outside, as did the illusion of density they provoked. Alternatively, the trees twisted and curled, forming natural hallways and spacious tunnels reminiscent of a hidden city.

The thick canopy overhead should have shadowed the forest floor. Instead, moon flowers bloomed, casting a soft, enchanting glow. Floating orbs of sentient warm light hovered around them, whizzing away when approached. Rays from the fading sun dripped through the trees across the clearing.

On his right, oversized red and purple phosphorescent mushrooms lit an adjacent path, housing white salamanders and gnomes. The white river could be heard further down the trail—the sounds of children playing in its waters. A brazen Faunerbil with big doe eyes and little antlers attached to its furry face squeaked at them from behind the stem of a mushroom. Kicking a twig at Birk, it turned tail into the shadows.

"Be still," Grey hushed the group. "We're being watched. They're all around us."

"Who?" Brynn stepped closer to her brother.

Birk sensed them, too. Elusive glimpses of figures cloaked in bark. A sudden movement of vines. The rustle of leaves. Whispers. Giggles. A flash of hooves, paws, and feet. More significant life hiding in the distance.

A white mist rolled up from the ground beneath them, snaking around their ankles and feet. Brunt huffed, shifting his legs, agitated at its arrival. It swept in, caressing the moss-covered ground until their feet disappeared. Gradually, it thickened, rising until it reached their waists. Winter, almost neck high, howled into the air, her ears pointed and alert. Grey picked Brynn up and held her above the rising fog. "Everyone hold onto each other," he ordered. The mist ascended above their heads, blinding them.

Birk stumbled forward, his vision constricted. He reached out blindly, calling out for Grey, his voice muffled by the eerie vacuum of the fog. With his hand outstretched, he grasped at empty air.

He was on the verge of panic.

He thought of Edi, always measured and in control, so he took a deep breath. He could feel the energy in the air, different than the earth, more fleeting. Channeling the disciplined energies of his aunt, he followed his instincts and moved his hands in precise and deliberate motions.

The mists drew back, pushed by the winds of his magic, until they had dispersed—revealing the forest—devoid of Grey and his family.

Only Brunt and Winter remained by his side, unfazed by the stranger before them.

A woman with sage green skin and elven features faced Birk. Her hair, the color of soil, poured over her naked breasts. A white fox with the wings of a hawk attached to its side curled around her bare feet. Familiar, Birk couldn't recall where he'd seen it before.

The woman grabbed him by the chin and examined him. "You're not of me, but you're *with* me. Otherwise, the Chamber of Roots wouldn't have let you in."

Birk, uncomfortable, gently removed her hand from his face. "Who are you? Where are my friends?"

Ignoring his questions, she circled him, studying him, the fox following her every move. "At first, I thought you might be a wayward child, returning home after being lost in the world. It appears, however, you are something more." Pausing, she took his forearm and traced her fingers across it. "Yes, the same source of magic courses through your veins."

"You're Faunwood," Birk stated, suddenly realizing who the elven woman was.

"Don't worry, you've nothing to fear here or from me." She reminded him of Pan. "Your friends are safe and unharmed. They'll be returned to you once we've been allowed to speak." Shifting her attention to Brunt and Winter, she knelt and hugged them as old friends. "And I see you travel in good company, escorted by my brother's familiars. It's been too long, my friends." She cooed in their ears, "It is good to see you."

"I'm Birk," he interrupted. "I'm the nephew of your sisters, Edi and Pan."

"Oh . . . I see," she straightened and gave him a curious look. "You've bestowed me two gifts today: a young warlock, bringing memories of my brother's spirit and news my sisters breathe. What can I do for you in exchange? Are you seeking refuge?"

"No, well, maybe for the night. I only wish to speak with you. I seek your counsel."

"You shall have it. We are family, after all. If the Chamber of Roots and the Protector's familiars trust you, your intentions are pure." She bent over and picked up the white fox and whispered in its ears; with a quick nod, it spread its wings and flew off down one of the many corridors, glancing back at Birk. "Now, where were we? Oh yes, follow me. My children are curious, and one can never be sure who's watching in these forests. Let's go somewhere a bit more private, shall we?"

THIRTY-NINE

THE HEARTS OF DRIFTSTONE

"Don't worry," Faunwood promised Brunt and Winter, "I'll take care of him. All those in your keep will be back with you soon." She stood with Birk at the base of a large oak tree.

A pang of concern hit Birk, glancing back at the familiars, the last of his companions. Reading his hesitation, Winter inserted herself between Birk and Faunwood, nudging the elven witch's legs with her muzzle. Brunt, in return, walked over and huffed, sitting stubbornly at the base of the tree.

"Winter insists on joining us while Brunt will wait outside," she conceded, "you have gained steadfast protectors, indeed."

Faunwood traced a pattern with her toes along the thick and gnarly white oak roots, which curled back, revealing a hidden staircase. At the foot of the descending stairs, under the tree, a witch's door guarded the entrance, granting them access when she knocked three times.

Winter entered first and scouted out the spacious underground burrow. Roots of the oak hung from the ceiling—a living chandelier surrounded by the floating orbs from outside. A small spring gurgled and glowed in the room's center. A solitary flower floated atop its surface, its petals large and cupped like a tulip, cradling something refulgent and palpitating.

Inviting him to sit, Faunwood moved to the opposite side of the spring. The cerulean blue of the water reflected on her face. "This is one of the hearts of Driftstone," she motioned toward the flower, stirring her fingers in the water. "I built the Living Forest around it to protect it. I'm its only remaining steward."

"How many hearts does it have?" Birk asked, hypnotized by the flower.

"Seven—one was destroyed in the Witches' War, a second corrupted. I left the battle to protect this one, even if history has recorded my absence differently. This and the one Farren has hidden in his valley are the strongest. As long as they remain, Driftstone will survive."

"It's so fragile."

"It's stronger than it appears. It's no easy feat to destroy a heart."

"I've only recently learned of Driftstone; I'm surprised by its sentience. I had no idea magic allowed us to talk to the earth, trees, or even, apparently, doors."

Faunwood raised her brow in alarm. "My sisters have neglected your education, doing you a disservice. Magic doesn't afford you the gift of talking to Driftstone; it simply elevates your fluency in the language. Let me demonstrate."

Pursing her lips, she blew a melody into the air, inviting the floating orbs to gather around her. She dipped her fingers into the enchanted spring, and the lights followed, submerging themselves. The burrow twinkled—the walls bathed in liquid blue.

"In Driftstone, all energy is imbued with sentience, granting consciousness and awareness to the earth, space, and even time itself. Everything in our world, from the smallest particle to the stars in our sky, possesses thoughts, feelings, and language," she shared.

Swirling the waters with her hand, spirits of woodland creatures emerged from the springs. Tiny pixies zipped through the air, leaving

trails of golden dust. Foxes darted and frolicked, tugging at Winter to chase them. Elves cavorted around them in a merry dance.

"These are the souls of those who departed in the Living Forest. Here, they are protected from crossing into the Nether, allowing them to shed light and guide their ancestors for eternity. We call them Gleamers," Faunwood explained, delighted by their revelry. "Energy never dissipates; it only transforms. Each is unique in personality and purpose."

With another lilting whistle, the spirits coalesced and gathered around her, taking graceful bows or stealing cheeky kisses. They dove and flew back into the enchanted waters. Dissolving back into warm orbs of light, they surfaced like miniature suns, spiraling back to the vaulted ceiling.

"Energy is attuned to its environment. It conveys emotions, intention, and knowledge through vibrations, frequencies, and patterns. Witches and Magic-Born are more sensitive to these subtle communications with our heightened intuition. Although rare, humans and non-magic beings can also learn to communicate *if* they dedicate the time to listen. Magic doesn't create sentience; it cooperates with it. Do you understand the difference?"

"I think so, thank you for being patient with me. I'm honored you shared this," Birk said, overwhelmed by the demonstration.

"You *are* honored. The decision, however, wasn't mine. It'd be best if you thanked Driftstone. You're the first in ten thousand years that I've been asked to share our commune. It's chosen you as a new steward."

"Steward?"

"To serve and protect it. As Farren and I have, before you."

"I don't know what to say . . ."

"You don't need to say anything. You and I are connected to the divine source. Share what has brought you here through our commune. I shall attempt to counsel you from what you share." Faunwood's thoughts were announced. She spoke in his mind, her lips unmoving.

"I haven't learned how to do that," Birk confessed aloud. "I've only begun training on communing. I wasn't aware we were able to connect this way with other people."

"Driftstone has its own life force and energy; it can commune like any living being. When you become one with Driftstone, you can commune with anyone or anything else connected to its source, similar to the Chamber of Roots, which let you in—and with me," her words echoed in his consciousness. "We can use more than words here; we can use our thoughts, memories, and emotions. It is the purest form of communication, eliminating the confusion over intentions created by physical sound."

"How do I start?" Birk scrambled to collect and organize his scattered thoughts. His experiences with his aunts made him nervous about letting someone else sift through his mind.

"Let's begin small. Focus on one question," she instructed.

"Are you my mother?" Birk blurted out. This question had been at the forefront of his mind since meeting her; their powers and connection to the source reinforced his curiosity.

"No, I'm not your mother, nor are any of my children, although, with your gifts, I understand why you'd ask." Faunwood's eyes smiled. She chose her following words with care: "Birk, if I may, I believe you already have the answer to who your mother is hidden in your heart. I suspected it upon meeting you. Open yourself. Listen to the voices inside you."

A deluge of memories and images flooded Birk's mind—a touch of her hand, the warmth of her embrace. Moments from his past unfolded before him, things he'd never seen and memories stolen: cradled in her arms as a newborn, taking his first wobbly steps under her watchful gaze. Laughter in the garden—tears shed on her comforting shoulder.

A close-up of her face. Her familiar smile matched his own. A tender gesture, a wink. Her acceptance, love, and unconditional faith in him.

"Pan," he whispered aloud, touching the bracelet she gave him.

"Yes, and it's obvious her love for you is tremendous," Faunwood smiled. "You're the first of your kind, a new generation, a child of Chaos, born out of love *and* magic from the womb of your mother, a creator."

"I have no father?"

She paused, "What is your knowledge of Magic-Born?"

"Based on your question, I'm assuming it's not adequate. I understood it simply as a definition of those born with magic."

"Over time, we often lose the origin of words; in doing so, we can miss the important contextual nuances. My siblings and I aren't siblings by blood. We don't share *one* mother or genetic energy, with the exception of the twins. We were born *from* magic, *with* magic in our blood, the only of our kind. Some are born *with* magic, but it's not something they're created from. The descendants of Farren you travel with are examples of this. They were born from men and women, with magic in their lineage—only shades of our power."

"I don't understand the difference between possessing and being conceived by magic. Isn't it all the same in the end?" Her statement rubbed him. He was insulted on behalf of Grey and Brynn. They were as powerful, *if not more powerful*, than he was. Why did it matter where magic came from?

"No, it's not all the same. The Thirteen were born from the magic of Driftstone, the divine source. We are magic incarnate," she explained. "Others who may achieve great power are still diluted by their humanity. Additionally, you have races and creatures created *by* the Thirteen who possess not innate magic but adjacent gifts assigned by us."

"Like elves and fae?"

Faunwood affirmed, "Yes, centaurs, sprites, or any of the magical beasts Farren created. Most of my children in the Living Forest identify as such. But, Birk, you're the *first* of your kind. Your mother conceived you through magic, but you were born from her body. A first—even among us. You possess within yourself the embodiment of all the magic of the Thirteen—if you can learn to use them."

"I'm the only one?"

"First, not the *only*," she corrected. "Your mother was always the most powerful of us, save her twin. Not only does she wield the power of chaos, but she's also a gifted creator. When your mother conceived you out of love and grief, she unknowingly set off a chain reaction—passed to other siblings on the eve of your birth—creating a new generation, stronger than the last."

"How do you know this?"

"When we commune, we are both connected to Driftstone. I see

all of you, your past, present, and potential for the future, including your creation. You possess the ability to do the same if you focus," she encouraged.

Reaching into Faunwood's mind, Birk bridged the gap between them, witnessing flashes of her memories and emotions.

"You also gave birth to a son. Conceived through magic as I was, but not your own. It was my mother's magic."

"Yes, although I was unaware of the connection until now. I assumed my son's conception was a gift from Driftstone for my stewardship. I confess I feel humbled by learning it wasn't." She paused, lost in thought. "I suspect I'm not the only sibling your mother's magic impacted."

"You think there are others similar to myself and your son?"

"If my other siblings are still out there, I do. Two miraculous conceptions in the same night can't be a coincidence, not for Magic-Born, *and not in this manner*." Faunwood stared at the beating flower in the spring. "The question is, why did Driftstone hide this from me? The creation of a new Magic-Born would need its cooperation and consent. Even your mother doesn't wield creation magic that powerful. Unless . . ."

Birk leaned forward, "Unless what?"

Faunwood raised her eyes to meet Birk's, "Unless she didn't know."

"Are you saying I'm an accident?"

Faunwood stood and walked over to Birk, kneeling beside him. "No, you weren't an accident. You were born from your mother's love; her magic answered her heart's request." She lifted his chin, "It isn't only her magic that resides in you, though; like us, you were also born from the magic of Driftstone."

Confused, Birk asked, "My father is the earth?"

"Driftstone is more complex than that, but if it helps it make sense, yes, all Magic-Born are its children. The Original Thirteen were born with an intended purpose, so I suspect you are, too."

"And what's that purpose?"

Faunwood ignored the question and spoke to herself out loud instead, "Driftstone added your mother's chaos magic to its own. I assume to strengthen its reach, which means my son, and most likely any other

children born that night from my siblings, were also not an accident." She turned to Birk, "What must always follow chaos to restore balance?"

"Order," he answered, trying to follow her thoughts.

"Driftstone has been out of balance ever since the war. Its aim may be to restore what we have broken," her eyes dimmed, "and it didn't share this with me because I helped break it."

Birk felt sorry for Faunwood; he could see the same shame in her eyes that reflected in his mother's. *He needed to learn what happened in this war.* He spoke his next words softly, "If that's true, why wasn't Aunt Edi affected? And what about your brothers?"

"Your aunt is the living embodiment of order; she is immune to chaos magic. She is only susceptible to its results. Your mother and her sister are two sides of the same coin. One can only gain an advantage if one turns to secondary magic. As for my brothers, there are more ways than a womb to conceive children when you are a witch." She gave Birk a sly smile and winked at him.

Birk squirmed inside; he didn't want to imagine what those *ways* were.

"All of this leads me to believe you've been guided here for a reason. Now that we understand each other, let us explore what brought you here."

Birk and Faunwood communed, transcending language with the speed of thought. Birk caught her up on every action, concern, and question he held inside. Sweeping through his memories of Balincia, he shared what his aunts had been doing since the war and asked her about the prophecies, the Driftstone and his quest. What usually took hours took minutes, creating a special link between them.

"You've opened yourself to me, hiding nothing," she revered.

"I know no other way to be. I've experienced living under lies; I aim to do better."

"I shared earlier that you have nothing to fear from me, but a word of caution: not everyone will treat your truths with such care. I'd advise you to guard your access; some will take advantage. When you entered my mind, I only allowed access to what I wanted you to see. You'll need

to work on this," she warned. "*Still*, I'm moved; you've offered me much to meditate on."

"What is your counsel?"

"Give me until tomorrow," she said, standing and taking his hands. "Until then, eat, rest, and let us show you the beauty of the Living Forest. We haven't entertained guests since the war."

The sounds of lutes and wind chimes filled the air as Faunwood led Birk and the familiars closer to the forest's heart. Stepping through an arched gateway of trees, they arrived at a hidden village deep within the woods. The white river crossed the town's bed, where stone bridges and huts filled with fires surrounded its banks, similar to a small market.

Above them, an elaborate system of roped bridges connected spiraling staircases and homes swung from the branches of the trees. Lanterns hung from vines—combined with lunar moths, orbs, and foxfire beetles—casting an illusion of a star-filled sky. Satyrs danced along cobblestone paths near the lit village center, playing their instruments for elves and sprites strolling along the riverbank.

"Birk!" Brynn yelled, grabbing his attention as she ran toward him. "Where have you been? Grey's been worried." Throwing herself at him at full speed, she hugged him so tightly he almost lost his balance. Winter and Brunt piled in, licking her face, happy to be reunited.

"Where, *indeed*, have you been? Only one of us is allowed to disappear each day." Grey's familiar voice echoed, approaching with Shayvonne.

Grey appeared healthier; the wounds on his chest and back were covered in dried clay, and the bruises on his face were disappearing. "I thought it only fair for you to experience what I felt this morning," Birk tenderly quipped, leaning forward to kiss him.

"I didn't like it," Grey held his forehead against Birks.

"How about neither of you disappears for a while?" Shayvonne came in for a hug. "I'm glad we're all back together."

"I'm afraid I'm to blame for whisking you away," Faunwood inter-

rupted. "My mists are a twist on my brother Cyrus's portal magic. They allow for expedited travel inside the forest. We've never had outside visitors, and although I trust the Chamber of Roots, I needed to understand with whom I was dealing."

Noticing Faunwood for the first time, shock washed over the family's faces. Growing up with Edi and Pan, Birk didn't share the same fascination as others. Shayvonne's cheek flushed with color—an awestruck grin pasted across Brynn's face. Grey, always a gentleman, kneeled before her.

"It's an honor to meet you," he bowed. "We thank you for your hospitality."

Faunwood took his hands and pulled him up. "There's no need for formality in the Living Forest. You must be Grey, the descendant of Farren, and this must be your sister, Brynn. I can see him in both of you." Birk smiled when they beamed at her words. She directed her attention to Shayvonne and said, "And you're the mother who has taken them all in, one of the most precious responsibilities of all. Farren and Pan would be comforted by your presence."

Shayvonne composed herself, shaken by her words. "Thank you, although I can't take credit for their characters or hearts; the children forged each."

"I can understand Birk's love for all of you; he's found something special," she said, touching Grey's face. "I hope my family has been hospitable and cared for you while you waited."

"Yes, thank you," Grey answered, "They've been more than generous, and the river sprite's mud has worked wonders on my wounds."

"Good, I'm glad to hear it. Please enjoy the rest of your evening and get some rest; I believe you've been shown your lodging. I hate leaving your company so soon, but Birk has presented me with a lot to think about. I'll send word for you in the morning to spend more time together." Offering a smile, she said her goodbyes and disappeared into the mists.

"I can't believe *the* Faunwood wanted to meet *you*!" Brynn exclaimed as soon as she was out of earshot. Elbowing Grey, she side-mouthed, "I told you Birk was a prince."

"I'm not a prince," Birk laughed. "She only wanted to meet me because I was the one who spoke with the trees. She didn't have any idea who I was until we communed."

Grey raised his eyebrows. "You communed with one of the Thirteen?"

"Yes . . . but . . . it's a long story; she and I share a connection with Driftstone." He tried to explain. "She was the one who knew what she was doing."

"That's still impressive, Birk," Shayvonne commented. "Were you able to glean any advice from her?"

"Why don't we give Birk some space? He just got back," Grey suggested. "Have you eaten? Are you hungry?"

"I'm starving."

"Let's get you some food, and you can catch us up while you eat," Grey urged the group to follow him.

"I'm warning you, even after you eat, you're still going to be hungry," Brynn complained.

"Brynn doesn't like the fact they don't have meat on the menu here," he shared, letting Birk in on the joke.

"I'm not a squirrel; I can't survive on nuts, berries, and leaves," Brynn grimaced.

"Yes, you can," Shayvonne corrected. "It's incredibly healthy for you. They have tarts at the market filled with honey, almonds, and stardust berries, which I think Birk will enjoy. They're filling."

"For a rabbit," Brynn ribbed Birk.

Finding a seat along the riverbank, the family settled in for an evening picnic of forest treats. While they ate, Birk shared the details of his conversation, including the revelation of Pan being his mother and Faunwood's theory surrounding the night of his conception.

He spared the details surrounding her definition of Magic-Born; it was minimizing to Brynn and Grey. The Thirteen were allowed to think what they wanted about themselves, but Birk refused to adhere to a hierarchical belief placing value on someone's origin.

"How do you feel?" Grey asked when Birk was finished. "That's a lot to process."

"I don't know," Birk admitted. "I'm anxious to hear Faunwood's advice in the morning. Deep down, I think I always knew Pan was my mother. I feel guilty for the way we left things. I miss her, and I'm worried about her."

"If Faunwood's insights on your conception are true, maybe the prophecy in the Driftstone is leading you to find the children of the other Thirteen—born of your mother's magic," Shayvonne suggested.

"I think so too; a line references the Thirteen's kin. Perhaps this is how the balance will be reinstated." Birk reflected. "But this also makes me nervous; why should the fate of Driftstone be left to such a small group? If the original Thirteen were divided so easily, how are their children, with a lot less experience, going to fare?"

"Don't underestimate the power of new perspectives. You're not your parents, nor do you need to be." Shayvonne advised.

"When we met, you were searching for the truth; that's what drew me to you," Grey added, placing his hand on top of Birks. "You started this mission to protect others, build a better life, and remove the threats against your people. Forget the prophecies; forget the Thirteen; focus on finding the truth you seek, not what others want you to find."

"Grey's right," Shayvonne agreed. "This is the only mission before us—to eliminate the arcanivores and the threat against our homes and the people we love. Keep this in the forefront as you receive all counsel."

"Birk," Brynn interrupted. "Can I ask you something?"

"Of course," he leaned in.

"Are you still hungry?" she grinned.

Laughter erupted amongst them, breaking the sober mood. "You know—I am," he laughed.

"I told you."

Birk walked with his arm through Grey's across a swinging bridge, leaning close against him. After ensuring the women were settled, Grey suggested some alone time. Strolling through the treetops, the breeze warm

against their skin, the lanterns provided a romantic ambiance to the tranquil village beneath them.

"It was quite a day for both of us," Grey commented. "I've grown accustomed to watching over you; I'm uncomfortable when things are out of my control."

"Perhaps you'll keep it in mind the next time you rush into danger, yourself."

"Fair," Grey chuckled, "I realize you're still processing everything. Are you sure you're okay?"

Pausing on the bridge, they stopped to appreciate the view. "I'm ok, I promise. I do believe this is about more than arcanivores, Grey. What if protecting those we love means being involved in something bigger?"

"If that's where the truth leads you, I'll be there every step of the way," he said, holding Birk's face. "You are becoming *my* something bigger."

The bridge bounced. Someone was approaching from behind. Turning, Grey was shouldered out of the way by a young man passing them. "Go home, mongrel! You don't belong here," the blonde-haired stranger hissed.

Birk's adrenaline spiked. Clenching his fists and tightening his jaw, he moved to confront the man. Grey threw his arm around Birk's waist, holding him back. "Let him go; it's not worth it."

"Who was that? What was that about?" Birk tensed, scouring the treetops for the assailant.

"I don't know. Remember, people here have never been exposed to anyone from outside the Living Forest. There are bound to be those who don't trust strangers." Turning Birk's face to meet his, Grey couldn't resist being charmed. "You're cute when you're coming to my defense."

"I could've easily blown him off this bridge with a gust of wind. No one would've been the wiser." Birk cracked a smile.

"My gallant prince."

Shaking his head, Birk laughed and kissed him.

FORTY

The Bog Witch

Before the war, the Boglands were a center of power for the witches. Temples, citadels, and sacred sites—hubs of spiritual worship and arcane knowledge. Renowned for its natural beauty, with lush jungles, pristine lakes, and fertile plains, the Boglands (known as the Sacred Grove then) attracted settlers, traders, and travelers from Driftstone, drawn by the promise of a bountiful oasis touched by magic.

Loved and worshipped, the Thirteen were at the height of their popularity, and no temple drew more crowds than Fate. There was a lure to knowing one's destiny—the desire to peek at the forbidden knowledge of one's future—to validate hopes or confirm one's fears. It mattered not if the outlook was good or bad; the knowledge fulfilled them, and Morvana satiated their needs.

Humans were simple to understand—they proudly exhibited their greed for lust, abundance, and immortality. The witch witnessed their dark side long before Discord whispered in her ear; the truth is, she enjoyed it. She drew pleasure from their hedonistic revelries and the adoration they heaped when she directed them to where to find it.

Now, *centuries upon centuries later*, only perpetual twilight exists—an all-encompassing realm of gray. Spoiled lands with rotten fruit and lakes turned to marsh. There were no more visitors; it now crawled with goblins, trolls, and the armies of hollow shadebinders—fashioned and enslaved by her during the war.

The Bog Witch, *they called her*. A demotion. Queen of the rotten in the Under. Her rage poisoned the land. Her bitterness spread decay. Her followers were lost to time.

She'd long since stopped caring about the state of her surroundings, knowing they were only temporary. It didn't matter if she was stuck here another ten thousand years; she'd escape—it was destined. She refused to give up her anger; it empowered her. Her lust for revenge fueled her dark magic. Let the walls of her home crumble; she had a new one in sight.

Besides, she barely spent time here anymore; she only returned to make preparations. A few thousand years in, she lost interest in conquering the Under. Goetfeather and Selene were sealed off in their own space on the islands; *they could keep their haunted and frozen forests*. They were no freer than she was. Calder cut her off with the oceans to her south, keeping her bound to the land, retribution for abandoning him during the war.

To the north, Nazeem—her only real threat—battled her on two fronts. She conceded the fight on land, losing the drive to gain inches forward from her wasteland, and won their war by stealing the Dreamscape from underneath him. When she wasn't working on her *other* project, she bided her time experimenting in the Dream Realm.

After all, it was important to keep one's options open when pursuing destiny; she'd counseled this many times.

Her powers didn't corrupt the Dream Realm like the physical world. Darker designs weren't only normalized, but the more twisted and absurd a construct was, the more celebrated it became. The nocturnians, the sentient beings of the realm, aligned with her machinations to escape, making it easy to overthrow and banish Nazeem.

Her remaining siblings no longer visited the topsy-turvy terrain; cautious of her mastery over it, they avoided her reach. Irritating—yes. However, she took it as validation; they still feared her. *They should.* While her

physical presence may be locked away in the Under, it doesn't mean she is incapable of releasing havoc in other ways to aid her pursuits.

Her sisters, Faunwood and Feyluna, may have shielded their realms against her dark influence in the Dreamscape, but Sable, *oh, sweet Sable*, was vulnerable. In the Over, where the citizens lived their humdrum lives, Morvana found fertile ground to hatch her insidious seeds. Whispervines, once used in dreams to bring comfort and inspiration, now planted seeds of discontent and fear in the unsuspecting populace. Sorrowkindlers evoked tears and heartache.

For millennia, she reveled in the discord she stoked in their minds. Fanning the flames of Free Roamers and rousing rebellious spirits, she chipped away at Sable's already fragile hold on Ironspire. Pan and Edi, her cagey twins, may have escaped her vengeance. But Sable, the inferior fool, lay susceptible to attacks from all fronts.

Unbeknownst to the ruler of Ironspire, Morvana uncovered a gift: a royal advisor within Sable's court—a man whose ambitions and thirst for power burned in the Dreamscape. Hibernating darkness lay within him, waiting to be activated. She summoned the shadowmires, her favorite pets, to feed on him. Shadowy figures with glowing red eyes—they lurked in the dark corners of a subconscious mind, preying on the insecurities and anxieties of the weak.

When the elf was softened and ready to eat, Morvana seasoned him with illusions of grandeur and influence. Under her invisible guidance, she led him down a path of subtle, treasonous touches. Due to his nudges, Sable's decisions and judgments were now clouded in doubt and conspiracy.

By the time Morvana finds her way to her sister, the once-witch warrior will be a mere shadow of her former self—ready to be crushed under a merciless heel. In the meantime, she wants to prolong her suffering.

Delighted in her plans' progression, she was surprised when echoflights delivered news of a dreamwalker's arrival a month ago. Her first thought: *Who dared tread into her domain?* She recalled laughing, thinking Nazeem had grown the courage to face her again. She prepared to remind him of why she reigned as Queen.

Making her way through the hidden channels she crafted in his absence, she expected to find the familiar face of her brother. Instead, she encountered a younger version with the same face, cloaked in the robes of his predecessor. This new dreamwalker, more boy than man, sharply contrasted the weakened, fragile husk she drained.

Intrigued and wary, she observed the boy from the shadows until a realization dawned on her—he wasn't merely an echo of Nazeem, he was his son.

His offspring exuded irritation and impatience, a stubborn determination to impose order and logic upon the pandemonium the realm excelled in. Unlike his father, he displayed no signs of compassion or curiosity. His powers were wielded with the intent to dismantle, reshape, and establish rigid structures, eliminating the land's versatility.

Granted, under other circumstances, she might be impressed with his ruthless approach, but not when it was directed toward her. He destroyed some of her most talented work with a mere wave. He extinguished and suffocated every aberration offensive to his sense of sequence. She blenched at the sight of her carefully curated monsters torn apart by his light.

The boy was a dilemma. He was a threat to her existence in the realm.

A confrontation would've been risky at this point, so she retreated into her corridors, biding her time to evaluate her next steps and study him. While a part of her relished the challenge the young dreamwalker presented, another part recognized the need for strategic patience. She was on the cusp of breaking Sable, *the* Lady Ironspire; she rolled her eyes. This task required her undivided focus.

The realm was big enough for her and the boy, *for now*. She knew where to stay hidden. She preferred to maintain the upper hand and operate from the shadows. When the timing was right, the boy would be humbled like his father before him.

Within days of the young dreamwalker's appearance, a second Magic-Born arrived. His close timing was suspect. Assessing the threat, she hid outside the dream chamber of a ginger-haired boy. Another familiar

face—reminiscent of one she despised above all else—one rumored to be dead—*this was the son of Pan.*

She might be able to exact her revenge after all.

A dark smile played upon her lips. It pleased her to see him unaware of the reservoir of power he carried. His ignorance of his potential made him all the more dangerous, a weapon waiting for a skilled hand. She skimmed through his dreams; he was becoming aware of well-crafted enchantments laid by the twins.

She learned of a hidden kingdom carved out by her sisters, whose whereabouts she couldn't discern. Their citizens were shielded from prying eyes, their minds blocked from the Dreamscape—*no doubt Edi's cleverness.* But the boy—he was different, a crack in their armor.

A wild card she could play to her advantage.

Just when she thought it couldn't get any better, a day later, a third child appeared—another dreamwalker, *Sable's spawn.*

This discovery unsettled her. It had been ages since fortune had been so kind. It was too calculated, too orchestrated to be mere chance. Were her siblings setting a trap?

She hesitated. The timing of their appearances gnawed at her. *Why now?* What precipitated the conception and arrival of her nephews and niece? Why were they all roughly the same age? *Were there more of them coming?* Or was she missing something larger?

Like the son of Chaos, the daughter of Innovation was naïve. Fumbling through the Dreamscape with abandon, she unlocked doors that shouldn't have been opened and left exits to the free world ajar. *Damn Nazeem's laws of the realm, which kept her from escaping through them.*

No, these children weren't deployed here under ambitions; they had no idea what they were doing, making them perfect vessels to infest.

For a brief moment, she considered possessing the girl, but after closer examination, she realized this princess possessed a different kind of magic—spirit magic—magic Morvana believed extinct—shattered with Feyluna. This would be a problem; she'd be repelled at the touch, revealing herself in the process.

No matter; there was more than one spell to boil a cauldron. Even light casts shadows.

Sitting atop her deteriorating balcony in the Castle of Fate, she reflected on the last several weeks since the intrusion of the brats.

Slygoth had prevailed in separating Chaos's son from his protected paradise and the twins' cover. In turn, the boy revealed a prophecy shedding light on the children's convergence in the Dreamscape and outlining a path to her victory.

The princess unknowingly helped Morvana release the shadowmires into the Over, and with a few minor tweaks, Morvana repurposed their appetites. Her beasts—growing in numbers and strength—were instilling fear and panic in their hunts, while eliminating the creations of her siblings along the way.

Oh, and she almost forgot another unearthed treasure—the descendants of Farren were along for the ride. *A bonus.* This saved her the trouble of rounding them up later.

In truth, she couldn't take credit for the boy's visions or prophecies; she counted them as victories since they played to her hand. It did, however, unnerve her that he was seeing things she could no longer predict. *Was her connection to the magic of Fate waning? Or had she been too distracted with her other schemes?*

She made a mental note to reconcentrate her efforts.

Still, she couldn't resist taunting the boy in his latest vision. It added to her elation when he accidentally pulled Pan in to witness it. Childish, she knew, but intimidating her sister's progeny in front of her was part of the fun. She may have been denied access to his chamber, but it didn't hurt to let them know she could still watch. Maybe it would draw his mother out of the nook where she cowered.

All in all, the scales were finally tipping in her favor.

FORTY-ONE

THALON

Thistle, a tall female wood sprite, knocked at Birk's door while the second moon was still in the sky. Wrapping a sheet around his waist, his hair matted to one side of his face, he stumbled over to greet her. Opening the door, only a crack, Birk stuck his head out.

"Pardon, Mr. Birk. Faunwood invites you and your party to join her at the Forest Palace for breakfast this morning."

Rubbing his eyes, Birk glanced back at Grey, sprawled naked, face down on the bed, snoring. "Uhm, and when would that be exactly?"

"I'm ready to escort you when you're ready," she smiled.

"Oh, uhm . . . of course. You see, we weren't expecting to be summoned so early. I think it will take a moment for us to get ready," he explained.

"Of course, Mr. Birk. I was told to expect humans to be late risers. I'll go and collect the females in your party and circle back," she offered with a quick bow.

"Late risers?" Birk muttered, closing the door. "It's still dark outside." He kicked Grey's foot to rouse him, "Get up! We're being summoned to the Forest Palace." Grey groaned into his pillow and covered his head, pretending not to hear.

Watching Grey slowly shuffle about reminded Birk of a drowsy bear coming out of hibernation. He felt guilty, knowing the powers Grey channeled yesterday had left him exhausted. He'd have let him sleep all day if they weren't guests at Faunwood's leisure.

Grey gave him an affectionate and lazy nuzzle. "Who eats breakfast this early?" He yawned. "If you think I'm moving slowly, wait until you see my sister."

On cue, Birk opened the door to find Shayvonne trying to tame the tangles from the nest on top of Brynn's head. Grey muffled a laugh with his hand, instigating a warning shot glance from his mother.

"Don't say a word," Brynn scowled, blinking in response to the first rays of sunlight.

"How lovely, everyone is ready," Thistle beamed behind them. "Let's see if we can't quicken our tempo even more on our way to the palace. Please follow me."

"Yes, let's quicken our *tempo* to go eat a bunch of mushy cold nuts," Brynn mouthed under her breath, resulting in a slap on the back of her head from her mother. Burying his face in the back of Birk's shoulder, Grey stifled another laugh.

The humans were on parade as Thistle marched them through the heart of the village. Every step was torture—catching the ogling eyes of centaurs and elves gossiping about the baggy-eyed bunch being herded by an overzealous walking twig. Grey smiled and waved dramatically as if in on the joke, being as incorrigible as possible, sending Brynn into hysterics.

"This way, we're almost there," Thistle clacked her tongue, hurrying them along a stone bridge leading to an extravagant treehouse. Situated atop a small hill, a gentle waterfall flowed from the river beneath the wooden palace, like liquid gold as it caught the first sun's golden light.

A centaur with a shiny black pelt greeted them at the door, looking unamused by their punctuality. Exchanging quick words and several looks of displeasure with Thistle, he sighed and invited the party to follow him inside. Escorting them upstairs, he led them into what Birk guessed was an open banquet room.

The river, which ran under the house, also crossed through the side of the banquet hall before plunging to the entrance from which they came. Open walls provided grand forest views. An ornate oak table was set to the river's left, where six seatings were set.

"I was about to send out a search party for you," Faunwood joked, entering the room to greet them. A handsome young blonde man followed her, wearing an open white vest that trailed to his feet. He looked familiar.

"Forgive us for keeping you waiting," Birk said, straightening and channeling his Aunt Edi's manners. "If we'd been aware of your plans to meet this morning, we would've been better prepared."

"I should've been more thoughtful. The forest rises early. It's easy to forget the customs of those living outside our walls," she apologized and motioned to the young man behind her. "I'd like to introduce you to my son, Thalon. I believe you will find you have much in common."

"We've already had the pleasure of running into each other," Thalon announced, haughtily shaking his hand. When his upper lip curled, Birk recognized the bastard who shoved Grey on the bridge.

"You ran off before we were properly introduced," Birk replied, gripping his hand tight.

"It would've been a shame to interrupt your night," Thalon sneered.

Grey sensed Birk tensing and rested his hand against his back to calm him. "I didn't get the opportunity to introduce my companion, Grey," Birk replied, "and this is his family, Brynn and Shayvonne."

Grey stepped forward, offering his hand. Thalon returned a dismissive look from the corner of his eye, ignoring him. "I'm sure we'll all get better acquainted over breakfast."

Faunwood, either choosing to ignore the tension or oblivious to it, walked her guests over to the table. Seating herself by Birk, Thalon sat to her opposite side, providing the perfect position to aim his smug stares across the table.

What was his issue?

Brynn sat next to Thalon, her face matching his disdain when the food was served. They resembled a grumpy pair of children forced to be

on their best behavior. She'd been correct again—a bowl of cold wheat porridge and honey was plated before them. Turning her nose, she opted for some fruit to gnaw on from the center of the table.

"Birk, it would be easier to commune with you, not to lose intention, but what I have to share is beneficial for everyone at this table to hear," Faunwood began. "I assume your companions have already been filled in on our conversation from yesterday and all of the details you shared with me?"

"Yes, there's nothing I've kept from them. I trust them."

"Good, this will make things easier. Let's start with this book, the Driftstone; I don't think you should fear using it," she stated. "*I also don't believe you need it anymore.* It's my opinion the book was only a tool for your awakening prophetic powers. Similar to how a witch uses a wand for focus, the book was a way for you to channel yours. Helpful, but inconsequential in the end."

"You're saying I exhibit prophetic magic?" Birk clarified. "But I didn't create the book; it was gifted to me by an old woman."

"Yesterday, during our commune, I shared your potential to encompass the magic of all of the Thirteen. You have already demonstrated proficiency with the elements—the gifts of my brother, Calder, and me. These are more visible forms of magic; it makes sense you'd identified them first," she explained. "The magic of Chaos, Order, Dream, and Fate are a bit more complex, but after communing, I believe you've channeled each of them, whether you were aware of it or not."

"You're saying I've been talking to myself?"

"Essentially, yes."

"And my dreams? Are they also a result of this?" he asked.

Thalon released a belittling guffaw.

"No. Dreams, visions, and prophecies may overlap, but they represent different forms of magic," she informed. "Whereas I'm *not* concerned about the book, I am concerned about your nightmares. I'm not an expert in these magics. My siblings, Nazeem and Morvana, practiced them."

"I, however, do have experience with them," Thalon postured.

"Similar to you, Thalon possesses the potential to tap into the magic of *all* the Thirteen, but his proclivities and abilities have leaned toward these specialties. I've requested he share his expertise with us." Faunwood explained, motioning to her son.

"Prophecy is a prediction or statement about something that *will* happen, but not how it will happen. My understanding is everything the book has shown you has been true. Your predictions have either occurred *or* revealed knowledge you found to be accurate. Correct?"

"Yes, except for the last prophecy," Birk agreed.

"Which we can assume will also come true, based on the accuracy of the others," he informed, softening the air of superiority on his face. "Dreams, on the other hand, for *normal* people are things we pick up from our subconscious. Charlatans and soothsayers often attach symbolic meanings to them, which they use to play on the gullible for interpretation."

"Some of my dreams *have* come true, or partially true." Birk contested.

"You're not normal, Birk. *We're* special; we're true Magic-Born," he emphasized. "When we dream, we can enter *or* be pulled into the Dreamscape—if we don't take steps to prevent it."

"What is the Dreamscape?" Brynn interrupted, much to Thalon's annoyance.

"The Dreamscape is an entirely different realm, a sacred realm, like the Nether. Living, sentient creatures and spirits exist there. They prey on dreams, with the power to mold them into reality," he forewarned. "If you're skilled, like our Uncle Nazeem, you can channel the magics of the Dreamscape into visions, not as accurate as prophecies but less riddled."

"If you enter the Dreamscape by accident, you're unguarded, as you were with me in communing. Your power could attract the attention of those in this realm," added Faunwood.

"Is that what happened?" Birk asked.

"You . . . attracted a shadebinder." Thalon hesitated; he lowered his tone. "They're creepers who bring your dreams to life in exchange for an escape from the realm. One disguised himself and tempted you with the Driftstone to help you understand your powers."

"I don't remember encountering a creature of this description. I'd never willingly agree to such an exchange," Birk insisted.

Thalon shifted in his seat. "You did," he said, firm, but surprisingly gentle. "You were struggling to face the reality of your mother's deception. You made a deal to hide this knowledge from yourself so you could process it in your own time, in your own way." Thalon's tone continued to crack into something more sincere, the way a parent might talk to a child about something difficult, catching Birk off guard. "You also . . . attracted the attention of Morvana."

"How can you be sure of all this?"

"I was in the Dreamscape with you. You may not recognize me, but I witnessed all your visions. You inadvertently exposed your mother and put those you love in danger."

"Don't blame yourself," Faunwood consoled. "Even I don't enter the Dreamscape with my years of experience. You're young and emotional; your honesty is a weakness your enemies will latch onto."

"It's also a strength," Shayvonne inserted, jumping to Birk's defense, "a weapon against lies and manipulations. Birk doesn't need judgment; he needs answers. How can he prevent himself from entering this Dreamscape?"

"Only time and practice will achieve that," Faunwood said. "I can assist by putting some temporary blocks in place to keep him and all of you from entering, as I do with the citizens in the Living Forest, but his power is unpredictable. I can't guarantee he won't inadvertently find his way around them."

"How come I didn't see you?" Birk circled back to Thalon, curious and skeptical. "How were you able to hide in my visions?"

Thalon smiled, "Like this."

White wings sprouted and popped from his shoulders, alarming everyone except his mother. Ivory whiskers and fur grew from his face and arms; a tail burst behind him. His form shrank, and when every inch of his body transformed, he stood before them—a snowy fox with feathered wings.

Leaping onto the table, he flew around the room, flipping and

spinning until he landed beside his mother, transforming back into a man.

"You change into a flying fox?" Brynn asked, unimpressed.

"I'm *not* a fox any more than you and your brother are the wolves you think you are," Thalon derided. Birk noticed his patience was thinner with Brynn and Grey.

"Thalon is gifted with the ability to transform into an Ashendrake, a sacred creature. He is able to enter any of the sacred realms, including the Dreamscape and the Nether. He stays concealed and protected in this form unless he reveals himself." Faunwood explained before addressing Birk, "Thalon is the most qualified to train you on the Dreamscape."

Thalon straightened, making a face difficult for Birk to read.

"I recognize you in that form; I remember glimpses of you," Birk confessed, searching his memories.

"If it makes you feel any better, you weren't the only careless and inexperienced Magic-Born in the Dreamscape," he joked, attempting to warm back up to Birk. *His words, however, didn't make him feel any better.* "Lady Ironspire's daughter has been drawing all the wrong kinds of attention, too, endangering everyone in Driftstone."

"Is she the young woman in my dreams?" Birk sat up.

"Yes, her name is Zara. She's a dreamwalker, although I don't think she realizes it. She's received no more training than you have—*no offense*. She's invading *everyone's* dreams. She even tried to traipse into *mine*; I forced her out. We can't afford to attract unwanted eyes."

Aware they were getting off track, Faunwood interrupted, "When we communed, I was unaware of my son's travels. I've discouraged him from entering the Dreamscape or any of the realms."

"She means forbidden," Thalon snarked.

Faunwood sighed, "Despite Thalon's gifts and abilities, I've been wary of risking our exposure since the war," she explained. "I assume your mother and Edi are taking a similar approach. Your visit only confirms what I've suspected: darkness is rising again."

"You believe the prophecy is true?" Birk asked.

"I believe, based on what you've shared with me, the destiny of Drift-

stone is entwined with the children of the Thirteen. Specifically, those conceived by your mother's magic. Chaos magic, though wild, often restores harmony." Faunwood paused, taking Birk's hand before she continued, "Your mother, a prime creator, inadvertently set in motion a quiet fuse by bringing new life into existence through you and a new generation of Magic-Born—to mend our missteps and heal the wounds inflicted by our magic."

Birk scrunched his face, "Excuse me if I'm being daft; I'm still learning. I'm unfamiliar with your terminology. What's a prime creator?"

"Every witch and warlock is born with certain abilities; they also possess the potential to expand them. Depending on our affinities and skills, we define magic as primary, secondary, or innate. Primary magic is the ability to extract power from pure energy, while secondary magic, still strong, requires building upon something tangible or that already exists," she explained.

"And innate magic?" Shayvonne asked, the scholar within her intrigued.

"Innate magic is the abilities you're born with, which require no thought or study. Although they can be refined and strengthened, they draw the least amount of energy from us." She turned to Birk and said, "You've shown proficiency in multiple forms of magic, as Thalon has, indicating your generation may have more than one innate ability. This prophecy suggests our descendants are key to our restoration, and I believe you were chosen to find them and guide them."

"My quest is to search for the other children," Birk clarified. "But, then what?"

"Fate has a way of finding us at our door. Each step will reveal itself at the right time." She paused with concern. "I'd advise you to seek them out quickly. If you don't, one of you, inexperienced and vulnerable, might fall prey to darkness or bring danger upon us all, as *you* almost did in the Dreamscape," she warned.

Shayvonne was unsettled. "The remaining Thirteen are obligated here; this is your mess. You can't recuse yourself and put this all on Birk. We came to you for help. We can't assume every child was raised with the

same privileges as your son and has the knowledge to tackle something so large. Don't make the same mistake you did in the war by retreating to your own."

Faunwood stood, "I'm the steward and protector of *the* strongest remaining heart in Driftstone. If the Living Forest falls, so too does Birk's quest. I'm not abandoning or forgetting my responsibility. You've misunderstood if you think I'm withdrawing. Our interests are aligned if you desire a future. While I can't leave the heart unattended, I *will* send my son with Birk to represent us." Faunwood reproached.

"You mean with us," Grey corrected, leaning into the conversation. "You'll be sending your son with *us.*" Grey's hand tensed around Birk's leg, pulling him closer.

The hair on Thalon's arm rose. He scoffed, "No, she *means . . .* with . . . Birk. *You* aren't essential. This quest is too important to have a twelfth-generation leftover and his brat cub of a sister tag along. We're discussing the fate of our world, not a romantic side trip for a simpering puppy-eyed boyfriend. This requires *real* magic."

Grey threw his chair back and growled. "And you believe you're the only one capable of *real* magic?"

"Aww, did I upset the dog?" Thalon jeered through his teeth. "Maybe we should put it down?" Swiping his finger across the air, he swept Grey's feet out from under him, sending him crashing to the ground.

Birk jumped to his feet in a protective stance. His anger flared, provoking the entire room into chaos. An explosion of magic erupted from his fingers, cracking the table and splintering the wooden beams supporting the room. Shaking the ground underneath them, he directed his attention to Thalon. "You pompous, arrogant ass! How dare you touch him? He's worth more than an army of men like you."

"Temper . . . temper . . . that's how your mother started a war!" Thalon taunted. "How unsurprising the child of chaos can't control his emotions. I told you this was a bad idea, Mother; you can't housetrain wild animals."

"Oh, shut up, you stupid fox!" Brynn shouted, launching herself at his throat.

In a blink and a puff of smoke, Thalon transformed into the Ashen-drake, zipping out of the way just in time to send Brynn tumbling across the room. Birk twirled his hand in response, slamming the feathered fox into the wall with a gust of wind. Changing back into human form to land on his ass, Thalon released a whelp.

"Enough!" Shayvonne yelled, rising from the table and grabbing everyone's attention. "You're *all* acting like children. If this is how you solve your differences, we've already lost."

Hanging his head, Grey lowered his shoulders. "I apologize; this is my fault."

"No, *it isn't*; it's his fault," Birk corrected, glaring at Thalon, sitting on the floor with his bruised ego.

"Grey, this isn't what you want to hear, but despite my son's crude and cruel delivery, *for which there is no exception*, he was right," Faunwood reasoned. "You and your family would be a distraction. If this is a sign of what happens under the slightest provocations, you could put the entire quest at risk due to Birk's emotional attachment to you."

With a sigh, Birk crossed the room to Faunwood, taking her hands. He was tired of the sanctimony of witches.

"Grey *is* tied to my emotions, but you're wrong about it being a distraction. He's a driving force. As you protect the heart of Driftstone, I protect the hearts of those I love and care about. While I appreciate your counsel and hospitality, this is *my* quest and prophecy. I'll make the calls on how we move forward."

"Birk, the prophecy concerns us all; you're only its messenger. You will *need* Thalon," she pressed. "Be careful of the decisions you make under the influence of love."

"We should be more careful of the decisions we make *without* the influence of love. A wise woman once told me prophecies are only true when we decide what makes them true," sharing a glance at Shayvonne, Birk smiled. "We both seek to protect Driftstone. In respecting our communion, I won't refuse your son's admission to our party. *But* I've already decided my fate, wherever it leads, lies with this family. Brynn and Grey may not share some magical conception, but they're the last of the

Protector's descendants. I ask you to honor your brother, and your son to respect them if he's to join us."

"Well said," Shayvonne nodded.

"I concede. Let us not break the long-standing bond with my brother over ill-chosen words," Faunwood bowed her head to him. "The Living Forest stands with you."

"Let's all agree we got off on the wrong foot this morning and put this behind us," Shayvonne echoed.

Offering his hand to Thalon, Birk pulled him to his feet. "If we can put our differences and egos aside, I've no doubt we'll learn from each other. Let's be the example of taking a different path than our parents." Pulling him in close by his wrist, he whispered in his ear, "But if you ever insult Grey or his family again, I promise you, I won't just slam you into a wall."

"Promises, promises." Thalon smiled back.

FORTY-TWO

TALBOT'S RESIGNATION

The witches worked without reprieve, day and night, studying Cyrus's portal magic. It wasn't as simple as picking a door and retrieving him. Birk traveled through the door before Pan figured out how to build its twin at its destination.

To make things more complicated, Pan used notes from Cyrus's work based on the last known locations of the siblings she trusted when they left the war. She had no idea whether these locations were still accurate or safe or if those siblings still deserved her trust. Additionally, it had been weeks since Birk left, making the chances of him being near his drop-off unlikely.

Growing impatient and panicked, Pan's spirit was stifled. Sitting with Edi and Talbot in the library, her restraint was slipping. "We're no closer than we started. Every day without action is another day Birk is in danger," her words spilled out, prompting Edi and Talbot to lift their heads from their books. "He's been quiet ever since the nightmare, and I fear the worst. We're already at risk; how much more damage can it do if I try to enter the Dreamscape on my own?"

Edi cast a concerned glance at Talbot before closing the book in front of her. "Pandi," she soothed, "you know you can't do that. We are as concerned as you are, but we can't afford to put Balincia in further danger. If you expose yourself to Morvana, she'll have the upper hand. Not only could you give our location, but you'd risk possession. If Fate steals your powers, everyone, including Birk, is doomed."

"Well, I have to do something," Pan cried, exasperated. The dam of emotions inside her was begging to burst. "I think we should take our chances. I can travel through the door Birk exited. He might be ahead of me, but I'm more familiar with Driftstone than he is. I'm confident I'd be able to catch up with him. We can figure out how to return once he's safe."

"That's not a wise option, either," Edi pushed back. "I understand he's your son, but Balincia can't lose you right now. The balance of our magic holds together its enchantments. We can't abandon our people."

"Instead, you're asking me to abandon my son?"

"We're not abandoning, Birk," Talbot assured her. "Edi and I have been discussing an alternative solution. Since you both can't leave Balincia, let me take a small party to go and retrieve him."

"You?" Pan shook her head and said, "Talbot, while I appreciate your offer, only witches can travel through those doors."

"I think I may've found a way around that," Edi informed. "If you recall, Cyrus created a portal we used to transport the original Balincian citizens during the war. It doesn't have to be limited to our travel; if I can deconstruct your original spell work, I can reset them."

"Even if you could, we still don't have a solution to bring them back. Nor does Talbot have any experience dealing with magic beyond our borders; he'll be more helpless than Birk." Pan glanced at Talbot, patting his hand, "I'm sorry to be blunt, but I'd rather spare your life than your feelings."

"If I may, reaching and aiding Birk is the critical piece of the mission. Bringing us back is secondary," Talbot stressed. "I trust you and your sister to find a way for our return. What Birk needs now are reinforcements. If you want to take action, this is how we do it."

"And you and I are more than capable of enhancing their weaponry,

giving them better odds," Edi added, pressing the point. "I believe this to be the best option in front of us. Talbot would give his life for Birk."

Pan softened, taking Talbot's hands. "I recognize you love him as if he were your own. If I can't be there, it should be you; I had planned it to be so. I'm just not convinced it will be enough, now."

"I have an idea that may ease your mind and will assist with pinpointing his location," Edi said, attempting to prevent her sister from spiraling. "Talbot, would you mind helping me remove the mirror from above the fireplace?"

Talbot lowered the reflecting glass on the ground, and Edi stood behind her sister, staring into its reflection. "You want me to try scrying?" asked Pan. "Neither of us is skilled in this art."

"If you can create portals, you can scry. There is nothing we haven't been able to accomplish together," Edi rubbed her sister's arms. "I can't believe I didn't think of it before because you, my dear sister, have already supplied us with an advantage."

"I have?"

"Yes, not only is Birk connected to your magic, but you also provided him a talisman, which connects to its twin here: the pendant," Edi informed.

"The Protection of Truth," Talbot said, proudly presenting his copy to her.

Edi, pleased and excited with her ingenuity, took Pan's hand. "If Birk is wearing it, I'm confident this will work." Handing her a piece of paper, she smiled. "I've prepared an incantation."

Pan threw her arms around her sister's neck, "Thank you. I'd be lost without you." Reading the parchment, Pan quickly memorized the spell and nodded reassuringly at her sister. "Let's find my son."

Clasping hands, their voices raised, Pan held the pendant.

"Reflecting glass, clear and bright," Edi led.

"Reveal to us, my son's lost light," Pan continued.

"Through every realm and beyond the veil,"

"Guide us true to find Birk's trail."

A faint image began to form and solidify, transitioning the glass into

a living painting. The twins' reflections blurred and faded until the mirror transitioned into a window. A figure appeared, familiar yet surreal, standing solid and alive.

A gasp escaped Pan's lips. Recognizing her son's smiling face, tears welled in her eyes. Reaching toward his reflection with her hand, she tried to touch her son once more. A tremulous smile formed on her lips when she whispered his name, "Birk."

The sight of him, safe, lifted the spirits of everyone. Edi tapped the glass with her wand, expanding their view to Birk's surroundings and capturing the image of a well-built young man beside him. The man's arm wrapped Birk's waist, protective and intimate. Birk leaned into him, whispering in his ear, triggering him to laugh.

"It appears someone is watching over him," Talbot's scruffy face broke into a grin. All three leaned in.

To her surprise, Edi choked with sentiment. "He resembles Farren, Pan."

Placing a hand to her mouth, Pan stifled a happy sob at the idea of her son finding a meaningful connection. "He has our brother's eyes, gentle and kind. Look at the way they make each other smile."

Wiping a tear from her eye, Edi forced them to move along, "Can you tell where he is? I'm not sure how long we'll be able to keep this open."

Edi tapped the mirror again, and the moving picture revealed Birk standing in a forest clearing surrounded by a small party.

"Faunwood!" Edi exclaimed, pointing at her sister. "She's aged well . . . they must be in the Living Forest . . . this is good news, Pan. Oh, aren't those Farren's familiars? What were their names?"

"Brunt and Winter," Pan mouthed, clutching her heart. "Oh, this comforts me. He has found a family to take care of him."

"Will they still be there by the time we're ready?" Talbot pointed to the bags saddled on the bear. "It appears they're setting out, saying goodbyes."

They watched as Faunwood hugged each of them and bestowed them with gifts. "You're right," said Edi. "Where would Faunwood be sending them?"

"Ironspire," Pan declared. "Birk's vision reminded me of the buildings in Ironspire. It's a day's journey, if not less, from the far side of the forest. He's heading into danger."

"We can't be confident in the accuracy of his dreams or when events may happen," Edi reminded her. "The good news is we have assurances he's safe right now, he has someone watching out for him, and we have a good idea of where he's headed."

Pan pressed her hand against the glass; her sister was right. "We stay up all night preparing the doorway. Talbot, can you and your men be ready by morning?"

"I'll leave now, so everything will be in order." Talbot gave a quick bow, hurrying up the stairs to rally the other men.

Pan looked back at the glass as Birk's image faded. "We're coming, my dear. We're coming."

Edi placed her hand on her sister's shoulder. "We can do this, Pandi."

Camping inside the Palace of Chaos's pantry, Edi and Pan toiled through the night. Edi, engrossed amid a scattering of tomes and scrolls on the floor, skimmed through them, her determination evident with each page turn. Pan shuttled back and forth to the kitchen, brewing steaming cups of tea to sustain their focus and agility through the night.

It'd been a long time since they'd worked so closely together to solve a problem, and their commitment to Birk united them. There was an unspoken rekindling of a bond defining their younger years, reminding them of the unshakeable strength they held as a duo.

"And we're positive there isn't a way to simply enchant Talbot and the others, tricking the portal's failsafe to make them believe they're Magic-Born?" Pan asked for the third time.

"No, these doors are sentient. Even if we were able to deceive them into opening for us, there is no way to be sure they wouldn't be detected passing through," Edi explained.

"Wouldn't it be too late?"

"No, the door could spit them back out here or, worse, change the destination and drop them off in a volcano. I wish I'd paid better

attention to Cyrus when he was around; he was always prattling, and it became so tiresome." Edi complained, picking up another book.

"He *was* odd, but he was a genius." Pan laughed, reflecting on her brother, "I do miss him; out of everyone, I would've thought he'd have come back for us. He was the only one who knew we were here."

Edi gave Pan a discerning look. "I think he would've if he'd been able." She lowered her head. "This is what concerns me about all of this, and it always has; it's been ten thousand years, Pan. Farren was killed because of us, and Cyrus never returned. Except for Faunwood and Fey-luna, we can't be confident in the allies we have out there. I don't trust the others as closely as we did our brothers."

Edi walked her sister upstairs to take a break at the kitchen table. "You've sparked an idea, Pan," she said, attempting to redirect her focus. "The witch's door guarding our library won't let *any* witch in. Its magic is also driven by intention."

Pan saw the gears of her sister's intellect churning, charging her memory to stir. "When Cyrus helped us to escape, he held his hands on the gateway the entire time. Maybe we're thinking about this the wrong way; it's not the portal needing adjustment; it's the operator's intention."

"Exactly," Edi was relieved to make a breakthrough. "What if we open the door with our intentions, focused on their safe passage with *our* magic?"

"We've no way of testing this theory."

"You're lucky the person you're sending has full faith in your abilities," Talbot's voice boomed, joining them. "There's no one I trust more with my life."

"Talbot, is it already morning?" Edi exclaimed, peering out the window.

"About an hour away from it. I couldn't sleep," he placed his uniform on the table. "And I wanted to bring you this."

"What?" Edi noticed Talbot was dressed in traveler's gear. It had been years since she'd seen him out of uniform. "I'm not taking this, Talbot. It's yours."

"You're going to need to find a new Captain for your Royal Guardians," he said gently. "You'll require one in my absence. I'd encourage you to consider Marina; she's done well in training and can lead the army you need to build. Hawthorne will still be here and can help liaise the adjustment in working with the palace."

Edi stood, placing her hand on his sleeve. "I'm without words, Talbot. I'm not sure we can do this without you."

"You can and you will, as you always have. You don't need to say anything; this isn't a time for goodbyes," Talbot affirmed, squeezing her hand. "It's been my honor to wear this uniform and be in your service. I will always be your Captain in my heart."

"You're more than our Captain; you're our family," Edi gushed. "I will accept your resignation only so when you return, you make no mistake; you aren't reclaiming your post, but you're coming home to those who love you."

"Agreed," Pan said, rising to hug him. "We'll never be able to adequately share our gratitude for your loyalty and love, or express the hold you will always have on us. We're so proud of you; no one will wear the uniform as you have."

Talbot clenched his jaw; he'd not mark the occasion by losing his composure. "Thank you."

"Who will you be bringing with you?"

"Ravenshire and Xavier both volunteered. I aimed to keep the travel party light. We'll be less conspicuous and able to move faster. They'll arrive within the hour. I thought it was best to arrive early to give us time to discuss our plans."

During the ensuing hour, the trio deliberated over extensive strategies concerning Birk's rescue. The witches intended to facilitate the men's approach as close to Ironspire as feasible; once on the ground, they'd operate solo. Edi cautioned Talbot about Ironspire's reputation for ingenious defenses and the meticulous design of its city layout.

"Our sister Sable was close to Cyrus. She *should* be an ally, but too much time has passed for us to assess her current state." Edi warned, "I'd

caution against involving her until you have a better read on her loyalties *and* the political environment. She was always ambitious; a step ahead in her city's evolution."

"And that was ten thousand years ago," Pan added. "Balincia will seem like an outpost in comparison."

"Understood. The art of subtlety will be in our best interests," Talbot noted.

Their primary objective centered on Birk, keeping him hidden until they devised a plan for his retrieval. "If he resists, which, *knowing my son's will when compromised by love or duty*, is a strong possibility, your mission is to shield him," Pan instructed. "Ensure he carries his talisman so we can ascertain your whereabouts."

"Speaking of enchanted objects, we've prepared a few to assist you," Edi announced, pulling out an assortment of items from the corner cupboard. "This bow will never miss its target, regardless of the arrows it shoots. The waterskin will never go empty, the pouch will always be filled with the currency you need, and the shield will protect you against direct magical attacks. I wish there were time to prepare more for you."

"If you give me your sword, Talbot, I have an additional gift," Pan declared. Placing her hands on his sword, she cast a spell. "Birk's vision included creatures born from dark magic. While I don't recognize their origins, I know dark is disrupted by light. I've enchanted the blade with it."

"This should be sufficient and cover all of our essentials." While Talbot spoke, Ravenshire and Xavier walked into the room carrying their uniforms.

"Gentlemen, I can't thank you enough for volunteering for this assignment. Your loyalty and bravery won't be forgotten," Edi shared, receiving them.

Stepping forward, Ravenshire addressed Edi. "I'm aware I had a strong reaction to your deception. In hindsight, I'm also cognizant of your act of love on our behalf. I volunteered for this mission to discover if there is more for me. I need to see the world existing beyond our walls."

Edi swept her fingers through the dark curls falling across Ravenshire's forehead. "I was wrong to limit any of you. We think of all of you

on the Royal Isle as our family, and I regret you were ever made to feel different. You deserve the opportunity to find your path, not adhere to the one we delegated." Standing on her toes, she kissed his forehead with care, "Find what you need, but be safe and return to us."

Wrapping her arm around Xavier, Pan escorted the party downstairs. "Xavier, I was surprised to hear you volunteered for this mission. Won't your falcons miss you?"

"Birk reminded me that none of us should be grounded. We all deserve a chance to test our wings. What am I, if not Balincia's falcon, with a mission to bring good news back to you?" he teased. "We all love Birk. Our family won't be whole again until we are all safe and reunited."

Touched by the selfless generosity of the men they nurtured and raised, the twins felt guilty for the responsibility they were asked to take on. Their readiness to confront unknown perils and risk their lives showcased a loyalty they perhaps didn't merit. Accepting the past couldn't be altered, they shifted their focus toward ensuring a future untainted by the same missteps.

With the resolve to part ways without sorrowful farewells, the men were sent with encouraging blessings and protective charms. Acknowledging Xavier's marksmanship, Talbot passed Edi's bow to him. To Ravenshire, he entrusted the shield to keep their youngest member from harm. With their belongings packed for the journey ahead, the trio stood united at the threshold of the menacing Iron Door.

"I feel I should be sending you off with a rallying speech," Edi confessed, wringing her hands, "but I lack the skills of my enthusiastic nephew. Instead, I will keep this brief—we are indebted to you—Balincia's finest."

Thrusting his fist into the air, Talbot rallied the men, "For Birk and Balincia," he shouted.

"For Birk and Balincia," they echoed back.

Pan and Edi, seeking the Iron Door's audience, placed their hands upon it. Together, they implored the gate for safe passage for the men who stood before it. Infusing their plea with the inherent nobility of the men's mission, they sought to sway the door's judgment.

The door, once silent, now whirred and clacked. One by one, the bolted latches securing the entrance disengaged. With a final mechanical shudder, the door creaked ajar.

A billowing cloud rolled out from the yawning darkness, triggering the men to jump back. Undeterred, Talbot rallied his small troop with another fervent cry, bolstering them with renewed courage. Steeled by his words, Xavier took a tentative step forward, disappearing into the dark, followed by a hesitant Ravenshire.

Holding back a moment longer, Talbot cast one more meaningful glance at the sisters, giving a silent promise of return before joining his comrades beyond Balincia's walls.

FORTY-THREE

THE DISAPPEARING TAVERN

"I don't like this," Indigo repeated. "You won't have an escort. If something happens to you in there, I can't reach you."

"If something happens, I'll pull out my magic light swords and slice the threat in half." Zara teased. Indigo wasn't amused. "Seriously, I've been training with the best warrior in the Azure for the trials. I'll be fine in a magical tavern for ten minutes."

"Ten minutes, no longer. If you don't get the answers you need, we're out of here," Indigo reinforced. Placing their face in their palm, they grumbled, "What am I going to do if your mother finds out?"

"She *won't* find out. She's too preoccupied with the trials," Zara marched down the wooden trail by the river. According to her intel, they were to follow the path beside the river for a mile once they descended. When both moons were in the sky, the disappearing tavern would appear to any Magic-Born searching for it.

"Which you should be, too! The nominations are tomorrow, and it's the last day we can train. You still haven't mastered the ability to conceal your weapons," Indigo pointed out.

"If we're going to be attacked by arcanivores, there'll be *no* trials,"

Zara stressed. "I can't get the creepy things out of my dreams, and I have a bad feeling about all of this."

Indigo pulled Zara's arm, yanking her back. "You told me the dreams stopped."

"No, I told you the dreams with the boys stopped," Zara insisted, pulling her arm free. Keeping her eyes on the last sunset across the river, she avoided Indigo's stare. Lowering her voice, she confessed, "I keep dreaming about the arcanivores every night, ok? And every night, it's the same. I die. End of story."

"Zara, *why are we out here*? Those things hunt people with magic, and we're out here alone, as night falls, in search of a tavern full of others similar to you. Are you out of your mind?" Indigo snapped, "I shouldn't have agreed to this."

"You're an Azure," Zara reminded them, "your entire job is protecting our people. Don't you think we have to determine if my visions are real?"

"Yes, but you're also my friend and, in many ways, the people's leader. You're too important to die out here in the woods."

"Don't let me die," Zara marched forward, chin in the air.

"How will we know when we get there? I feel like we've already walked a—" Stopping in their tracks, the answer appeared before Indigo in a clearing. A handful of elves leaned against a giant oak, two kobolds warmed their hands around a fire, and a scattering of others, disguised in heavy cloaks, were all restless, waiting for the sun to set. Placing their hand on the hilt of their sword, Indigo navigated Zara over to a group of flat stones to sit. "I *really* don't like this," they repeated.

Scanning the tree lines, Indigo saw more dark figures approaching from every direction.

"Relax; they aren't dangerous because they're born with magic. They're here to find answers, just like me." Indigo acknowledged her but didn't ease their stance. "And keep your hair covered. We don't want to attract attention. You'll have them assuming the Azure are staking out the place."

When the last sun disappeared across the horizon and both full moons were in the sky, the crowd in the clearing stirred. People stood

and raised their voices in anticipation. Everyone's eyes converged on the river. An emerging tavern spanning the river's breadth took form.

The tavern was constructed from weathered stone and carved cedar, covered in vines and wildflowers that grew from the thatched roof. Carvings of dragons, unicorns, and other magical beasts decorated the supporting beams surrounding the structure. From both sides of the river, wide wooden bridges lit with lanterns welcomed the incoming travelers.

"It's beautiful," Zara gasped. She'd expected a small, dark hovel where everyone operated from the shadows. This was warm, welcoming, and enchanting. Any fears or second guesses she held evaporated, and an elated eagerness took their place.

"What do you see?" Indigo scoured the river's edge, trying to discern the crowd's commotion and where they were moving. All she saw was the raging white river under the light of the stars.

"It's the tavern; it's grander than I imagined. I wish you could see it," she exclaimed. Filled with excitement, she shared the details with Indigo, helping to de-escalate some of their concerns.

"I do like that it isn't visible to others," Indigo consented.

"The magic for this enchantment is extraordinary; the magic to protect it has to be equally powerful. Please, may I go in now?" she pleaded.

Giving one last assessment, the once foreboding glade of questionable characters now held the atmosphere of an encampment of friends. While some made their way to the river, others broke out mead and music. Relaxing their shoulders, Indigo sighed, "Fine . . . go!" They released Zara. "Remember TEN minutes!"

Keeping a close eye on Zara, Indigo watched until she reached the river's edge and disappeared. Their stomach twisted. They trusted their friend's instincts, but her affinity for brash decisions troubled her. There was a fine line between being headstrong and brave; Zara was still finessing the difference.

Distracted by their focus on the river's edge, Indigo didn't notice the approach of the woman with her daughter. "Do you mind if we join you? I'd be more comfortable waiting in the company of an Azure."

"How did you recognize me as an Azure?" Indigo evaluated the

middle-aged woman. She held a kind smile but was armed with a sword; her hands were callused from either action or hard work. She appeared athletic, as did her daughter, although she didn't have the look of a soldier. The girl, brown-skinned, unlike her mother, looked wild and irritated. She carried a bow and a quiver of arrows.

The woman raised her eyes to Indigo's hairline, indicating their cloak slipped. Cursing, they pulled the hood back over their head, hoping no one else noticed.

"We won't reveal you. We're not seeking to draw attention either," the woman offered a smile. "My name is Shayvonne, and this is my daughter Brynn."

Indigo nodded but didn't offer their name.

"Normally, we care for ourselves and stay on the outskirts." Shayvonne explained, "But, observing the magic gathered here and the knowledge the arcanivores hunt at night, I believe there is safety in numbers. I trust the company of a warrior over a group of strange men."

Indigo respected this and invited them to join. At first, they sat in uncomfortable silence. The warrior could feel the girl's eyes inspecting them. "You're a soldier?" she asked.

"They're an Azure," the woman named Shayvonne informed. "A royal line of soldiers, dating back centuries, who have pledged their loyalty to Lady Ironspire. They are known to be the largest army in the world. Their fighting techniques are unique and guarded, handed down from each generation. Their weapons are embedded with the magic of Lady Ironspire."

"Where did you gain your knowledge about the Azure?" Indigo probed, "Are you from Ironspire?"

"Long ago, I used to be a citizen," Shayvonne divulged, choosing not to expand. Indigo didn't press.

"Do all the Azure have blue hair?" inquired Brynn.

Indigo cracked a smile at her curiosity. "Yes. When we pledge our loyalty to Lady Ironspire, we have a ceremony. Part of the initiation process includes a blessing, performed by magic, which transforms our hair to match the shade of hers. It symbolizes allegiance and carries a weight of respect."

"I like it," Brynn grinned.

"I assume you're also waiting on someone in the tavern." Shayvonne probed.

While their curiosity seemed innocent, Indigo was uneasy with the questions pivoting to Zara. "I'm observing, ensuring safe passage for our people."

"We heard Ironspire exiled its Magic-Born? It's curious an Azure is still invested in their safety."

Indigo attempted to read her intent. "We've not abandoned them," they answered with a defensive edge.

"My mistake," Shayvonne pushed her experiences with Ironspire to the back of her mind. "It's noble of you to be concerned with the safety of all your subjects."

"Are you waiting on someone?" Indigo redirected the conversation.

"My brother and his boyfriend," Brynn responded, "and a jerk traveling with us."

"Brynn!" Shayvonne reprimanded. Indigo grinned; they liked the girl.

"Well, it's true," Brynn retorted. "They told me I wasn't old enough to join them."

"You're Magic-Born as well?" Indigo probed, intrigued.

"Yup, you see the bear and wolf in the background; they're the Protector's familiars," Brynn pointed to the edge of the light. Indigo was barely able to discern them. "We didn't want to scare anyone, so I instructed them to fall back."

"A little girl with the ability to command and tame wild beasts. Where did you obtain such skills?" Indigo asked, impressed.

"I'm not little; my brother and I are the last descendants of Farren," she boasted.

Indigo glanced at Shayvonne and at the bear and wolf again. "I apologize. I didn't realize I was in the presence of a royal line," they scrambled to take a knee in front of Brynn. "Forgive me for my disrespect."

Brynn giggled, enjoying the gesture, "No one's ever done *that* before."

Shayvonne shook her head, "Please don't bow. The Protector never considered his blood royal. We do our best to lead a humble life under the radar."

"We assumed Farren's line ended," Indigo declared. "This child and her brother are sacred, as are his familiars." She stared in astonishment at Brynn, clocking the expression of concern across Shayvonne's face. "I understand why you'd want to protect them from others. Your secret is safe with me. I, too, am here guarding someone from a sacred lineage."

"Wait until you meet my brother's boyfriend, Birk. He's the real prince. He's the child of the Witch of Chaos." Brynn blurted out.

"Pan?" The girl grabbed Indigo's attention, "She's alive?"

"Please," Shayvonne interrupted, "my daughter speaks with no discerning filter. We can't let this get out until we speak with Lady Ironspire. There is much at stake here you don't understand."

"Of course, you have my word." Indigo rose to their feet. "I think our paths were meant to cross tonight. You've shared your secret, so I'll be forthright with mine, so you may be settled, and we can build trust between us. I'm here with Lady Ironspire's daughter, Zara. We were led here by her visions. I believe these dreams may be connected with your companion. What was his name . . . Birk?"

"Excuse me?" interrupted a voice coming from the dark. "Did you say, *Birk?*"

Grabbing their swords, Indigo and Shayvonne took a protective stance in front of Brynn as three men dressed as rangers walked toward them. Winter, leaping from her hiding place in the shadows, jumped in front of them, snarling at the strangers; Brunt growled behind them. They were surrounded.

The middle-aged man, with salt-and-pepper hair, held a soldier's face. He appeared to be their leader. Holding his sword, he slowly set it on the ground. The men behind him followed his lead, disarming themselves.

"I didn't mean to intrude; we mean you no harm. I heard you mention the name of a friend of ours . . . Birk. We've come a long way to find him," he said, raising his hands in peace.

"Who's asking?" Brynn shouted.

"My name is Talbot."

FORTY-FOUR

DREAMWALKERS

"This is incredible," Birk grinned, reaching for Grey's hand as they crossed the bridge to the tavern. "And your mother mentioned it only appears under the double moons?"

Thalon rolled his eyes, watching Grey interlace his fingers with Birk. They were acting as if they were on a moonlit stroll instead of a mission. "Yes," he replied, trying to scrub the irritation from his voice. "She believes we'll find answers here."

"I'm uncomfortable leaving Shayvonne and my sister behind," Grey shared, preoccupied with sizing up the parties coming and going into the tavern.

"From what I've seen, your family can manage themselves," Thalon muttered, still bitter from their last confrontation. Sighing, he added, "If it makes you feel better, I can sense the protection spells surrounding this space. It goes beyond the tavern and into the surrounding forest. I'm confident they'll be safe; Cyrus's work has never been breached."

Grey glanced back at Thalon, acknowledging the reassurance. "Thank you. It does make me feel better." They were both trying.

Entering the tavern, the fragrance of exotic spices and roasted meat greeted them. Thalon curled his nose, affronted by the smell. The interior spread into cozy alcoves, many with curtains drawn for privacy. A large man with the head of a bull and four arms worked behind the bar. A goblin slid two pints of dwarven stout to the kobolds.

Across the establishment, Birk identified a girl lowering the hood from her cloak. She appeared lost, trying to figure out where to sit or whom to speak with. Turning, the girl locked eyes with Birk, recognizing him.

"It's her," Birk nudged Grey with his elbow.

"Who?" Grey asked before spotting the young woman making their way over to them.

"Zara," Thalon answered, "Lady Ironspire's daughter. The one mucking up the Dreamscape."

"Shhh, don't be rude." Birk hushed Thalon on Zara's approach.

"I recognize you," she said, staring at Birk. She was more beautiful in person. Her violet eyes assessed him, a smile forming on her face. "I knew it wasn't only a dream." Taking in Grey, she touched his hair. "And you-you're the bear, aren't you? Always beside him."

"Erm . . . hi? I'm Grey," he introduced, smiling uncomfortably.

"I forgot my manners. I'm Zara," she smiled back, offering her hand. "I can't believe you're here," she mumbled, more to herself than them. "Do you recognize me?"

"Of course, I've been searching for you since we first met in the Dreamscape. I'm Birk, by the way."

"And I'm Thalon, son of Faunwood." Squeezing between Grey and Birk, Thalon pushed in front, kissing her hand.

After placing his face, Zara pulled back her hand. "You're the boy who shoved me."

Grey choked on a laugh, "Sounds accurate. His first impressions need work."

Ignoring Grey, Thalon shot Zara a defensive glare, "Because *you* shouldn't have been there. You can't roam all over the Dreamscape, spying on other people's dreams without permission or repercussions."

Zara's mouth fell open; she was unaware one *could* trespass in the Dreamscape. There was a lot she didn't know. "I'm sorry . . . I didn't . . . I

haven't been able to talk to anyone who knew what I was going through," she admitted, not wanting to upset them. "I'm here tonight seeking answers. I was *hoping* you might help me find them."

Thalon cooled at the apology, allowing Birk to jump in with a response. "You don't need to apologize; I'm also learning. I've made many mistakes myself."

She knew she'd like the redhead. Appreciating his save, she took him by the arm, sensitive to a connection between them. "Why don't we all grab a booth in the corner for more privacy? I've got so many questions."

Once seated, the four tripped over each other in conversation, excited to learn how much they shared in common. Swapping stories of their parents, magical awakenings, and families, they formed a kinship.

On one side of the table, Birk leaned against Grey, whose arm wrapped around him. Zara leaned across, expressive and uninhibited. Even Thalon enjoyed himself and kept the group laughing with dramatized stories of the beasts dwelling in the Living Forest.

Finding their way back to what brought them to the tavern, they shared their experiences over the last several weeks. The tone, taking a more somber turn, led them to discuss the prophecy, Faunwood's advice, and, finally—the topic of Birk and Zara's recent nightmare. After reaching a consensus upon hearing Zara's recurring dreams of the arcanivores, they believed the vision's warning shouldn't be dismissed.

"I've explained to Birk that dreams can be altered." Thalon shared with Zara, "Which *means* we have the opportunity to change the outcome."

"Can your mother cancel the trials?" Grey asked the obvious. "If there are no trials at the Colosseum, there can't be an attack."

Zara shook her head. "I wish it were so simple, but there's no way my mother would cancel them on your word. She's skeptical and untrusting of anyone with magic."

"Even if we're related to her siblings?" Birk pressed.

"*Especially* because you are related to her siblings. Upon hearing your story, she'd view you either as impostors or as a threat, showing up unannounced after all these years. She'd lock you up . . . or worse." Sitting

back in the booth, Zara reflected. "We need to prove to her you have Ironspire's best interests at heart."

Birk had an idea: "You mentioned the need to nominate one of Ironspire's exiled citizens. Would you be able to sponsor *two* of us? If both Grey and I entered under cover and passed the trials, we'd gain her respect and an audience," Birk suggested. "I realize you intended to enter the tournament, but if you're struggling to conceal your magic, it may be beneficial for us to replace you, which would change the variables."

Zara's lips thinned, insulted. "Let me be clear: I'm a princess, a warrior, and a daughter of Driftstone's most renowned ruler. I didn't come to this tavern to have *boys* convince me they were the solution and push me to the side."

Birk's face paled. "I didn't mean to imply—"

"While I appreciate your concern for Ironspire's welfare, don't forget they are *my* people. I may have difficulty concealing my magic, but you minimize *your* inexperience. I'm seeking partners, not saviors," Zara scolded.

Birk shrank in his seat.

Zara took a breath, her aim sharper than she intended. "I've just wanted to be an Azure for so long," she confessed. "I hate being a princess; it makes me feel powerless despite the title. I'm surrounded by people who flatter and pacify me to drive their interests but discard my ideas and opinions the first chance they get."

"I know the feeling," Birk nodded. "We can think of another option."

Grey leaned forward, "I didn't care for the idea, anyway; it placed us in the epicenter of your vision."

"In light of avoiding a placating approach," Thalon interrupted, facing Zara, "I'll be blunt. I have a theory you'll hate more than Birk's idea."

Zara sat straight and crossed her arms. "Okay . . . I'm listening."

"The arcanivores appeared not long after you and Birk's powers awoke. They hunt those with magic—the stronger it is—the more it draws their attention. They were first sighted in the farthest reaches of the realm, *near* Birk and Grey. This indicates they're targeting bigger game instead of areas with higher volume."

"Are you suggesting they're hunting those related to the Thirteen?" Grey asked.

Thalon nodded, "I think they've proven they'll eat anything along the way, but we're their primary target. According to my mother, there's no one Morvana hates more than Pan and Sable. What better revenge than going after their children?"

"If Morvana *is* trapped in the Under, *which we still don't understand or know anything about*, how are the arcanivores being created and entering into the Over?" Birk asked, "If we don't know how they're entering, how can we stop them from sending more?"

"I think I know how they're entering," Thalon said. "The collective dreams of every conscious being fuel the Dreamscape. Created by Nazeem, it was used in service to the witches to inspire and influence their creations. Morvana recognized its potential and learned to utilize the Dreamscape to manipulate the broader possibilities of fate."

He paused, alert to a group of elves passing them before he continued.

"When her ambitions and darker predilections grew, she manipulated and forced unconscious thoughts into reality, disrupting a delicate ecosystem. Awakening and birthing sentient beings in the Dreamscape, these new lifeforms craved access to our realm. Morvana used this to her advantage during the war, liberating them to build her armies."

"Why didn't Nazeem interfere? He controlled the Dreamscape," Zara asked. Birk was still trying to keep up with everyone's names.

"Under Morvana's influence, the realm outgrew its creator's ability to maintain control. Nazeem is a dreamwalker who was forced to become a warden in a prison too large to contain. He encouraged our parents not to enter the realm to keep them hidden and safe from corruption or possession."

"This is why your mother forbade you from entering," Birk reflected.

Thalon nodded, "We're the first generation to walk there since the war. When witches enter the realm, our vibrations are so strong they alert every sentient nocturnian. This is why I travel in the form of an Ashendrake—to avoid detection."

"I had no trouble seeing you," Zara said, a little on the defensive.

"I'm curious about that too," Thalon replied, sitting back. "I wasn't in my Ashendrake form when you found me, nor was I traveling *inside* the Dreamscape. I was in my dream chamber, which should have been locked and hidden. No one's ever detected it before."

"Well, it lit up in bright banners for me," Zara shrugged.

Thalon's mouth fell open. It was the first time Birk witnessed him speechless. Before he could respond, the four-armed bull approached the table. "Can I get you another round of elven mead?" Thalon nodded, looking in need of one. Grey indicated he wanted three.

Checking to ensure he was out of earshot, Thalon leaned into Zara. *"What do you mean it lit up for you?"*

Zara hesitated, fearing she was about to reveal another mistake. "When I'm in the Dreamscape, I manifest a key of light that grants me access to every door. I don't know how I do it, and I never know what lies beyond the door." She paused and hesitated briefly. "It's true; yours was hidden. When I walked past an ordinary wall, it flickered—casting a light. I was curious. I placed my hand on it, and it turned transparent, allowing me to see right through—like a window."

Thalon sat back, shaking his head in disbelief. "And this key you created allowed you to enter?"

She shook her head, "No. There wasn't a keyhole for me to use, nor on Birk's. I didn't enter your chamber on purpose, I promise. I just touched the glass and my dream self or my spirit... I think... I don't know how it works... projected me into your dreams." She turned to Birk, "Your chamber wasn't even hidden; it was open for everyone to look in, like a giant glass box. This is why I tried to get you to follow me outside your chamber when we first met. I couldn't speak to you inside your dream, but I knew you were important since everyone could see you."

Birk's memory sparked, "I remember; I tried to follow you—"

"You have spirit magic!" Thalon interrupted, disrupting the thought, scratching at the surface of Birk's mind, "These are the gifts of Feyluna, and a form of light magic. Only the fae can reveal what a witch has hidden or see inside their chamber in the Dreamscape."

"What?" Zara asked, confused.

"It's rare; none of the Original Thirteen could duplicate it." He turned to Birk and added, "Not even your mother."

Bartholemew returned with the mead, and the table went silent. Grey grabbed one—downing it in one gulp. Leaning in to snatch a second, he addressed the table with a hiccup, "I don't mean to change topics, but we're losing time. As interesting as all this is, I'm concerned about tomorrow."

Birk nodded in agreement, "Thalon, you were speaking about a theory surrounding how the arcanivores entered Driftstone. Did I attract these creatures like I did the shadebinder?"

His chest caved in, afraid to hear his answer.

Thalon shook his head, "No—she did."

Zara reeled back. "Me . . . but how?"

"When Birk entered the Dreamscape, he was limited to the space he created in his dream—a private room—locked and secured. Lacking the abilities of a dreamwalker, he can't access or open other doors. This is why Morvana required a shadebinder to reach him."

"But I do," Zara said aloud, piecing it together.

"You possess the key to *every* door in the Dreamscape. When you visited, you left doors open and unguarded, including those leading to Driftstone. The arcanivores recur in your dreams because they follow you and use these doors to escape, probably under Morvana's direction."

"Birk . . . I never . . ."

Birk shook his head, "No one's at fault; we're all still figuring this out. Thalon already scolded me for my own mistakes in the Dreamscape."

"If I opened the doors, why aren't there arcanivores in Ironspire? Why haven't I been attacked?" Zara asked.

"My guess . . . the doors you left open were adjacent to locations with whom you shared dreams," Thalon answered, motioning toward Birk. "Remember, the Dreamscape constantly shifts, shaping to our thoughts and actions. It would make sense the exits shifted to where you were dreamwalking."

"The arcanivores attacked Everglenn *before* Birk arrived," Grey reminded him, coming to Zara's defense. "I didn't appear in his dreams until he was here; even then, I was in the form of a bear."

"Yes, but Birk dreamed of the mountains dividing Everglenn and Balincia before he met *you*. The arcanivores couldn't reach him as long as Balincia remained protected by the twins' enchantments. It's the same reason they aren't able to breach the Living Forest. You and Brynn were the closest source of magic by default. I don't think you were on their initial radar."

"How do we stop them?" Birk interjected.

"I'm not sure. I can't prevent Zara from unconsciously entering the Dreamscape. My mother isn't here to put temporary blocks on her, like she did with you. I can train her, but there isn't enough time before the trials," Thalon informed. Turning his attention to Zara, he added, "If you find yourself back there, try to find an exit immediately—shut and lock all the doors behind you. It's the best advice I can offer."

Zara swallowed and nodded.

"Our initial priority is to prevent Birk's vision. The more variables we change and can control, the less probable it is to come to fruition," said Grey.

Zara sighed. "I'll remove myself from the trials so I won't be on the arena floor." It wasn't the call she wanted to make, but after learning of her culpability, she didn't want to add to the mess. Her people's safety had to come first; this is why she was here. "I'll nominate you and Birk for the trials. It might be beneficial for me to be near my mother, anyway. *But* I intend to intervene if lives are at risk. Fair?"

"Fair," Birk affirmed.

Grey stiffened, "No—I don't like this."

"Well, neither do I," Zara quipped. "Do you have any better suggestions?"

Thalon addressed Grey, "What if I entered the trials, too? It would increase our odds and blend the variables further. I wasn't in the arena in the vision." Grey bit his tongue. Birk nodded, open to anything. "Zara, would you be able to secure three nominations?"

"I know someone who might be able to help," Zara confirmed before jumping up. "*If they don't kill me first!* I forgot they're waiting outside. We've been in here for *hours*. We'll be lucky if the entire Royal Guard isn't stationed outside."

Zara rushed toward the exit, leaving the men to follow.

"Please don't be upset," Zara yelled, entering the clearing and spotting Indigo sitting amongst a group by a fire.

Indigo stood, crossing their arms, "Let me guess, you ran into three handsome young men who happened to be the guys you were dreaming about."

Zara froze, confused, but relieved Indigo wasn't furious. The boys walked up behind her. "Yes . . . but . . . how did you know?"

"You're lucky I ran into their families," Indigo gave a stern tilt of their head.

"Go easy on her. I'm sure I can figure out who's to blame," a familiar voice echoed from behind. "He's always been a chatterbox and has issues with punctuality."

Stepping into the light of the fire, Birk recognized Talbot's grinning face, followed by the laughs of his old friends, Ravenshire and Xavier. The air left his chest in a rush. For a moment, he couldn't move, couldn't believe it was real. His legs carried him forward before his mind could catch up.

He crashed into Talbot's arms, burying his face against his chest, as though he could fold back into the safety of his childhood. Talbot staggered under the force but tightened his hold instantly, one broad hand cradling the back of Birk's head, the other locked firm across his shoulders.

Holding him close, Talbot kissed his head. "I've missed you, too, Birk."

FORTY-FIVE

Mirror Images

Zara sat at her vanity, brushing her long ebony locks, the silver bristles sliding through her hair. She gazed at her reflection in the mirror—a strange sense of unease washed over her, creeping insidiously through her veins. A chill prickled her skin. She paused.

Something was amiss, out of place. Turning to the room, she scrutinized it. The paintings hanging on the walls rippled. Their colors caught in an unseen breeze. The candles' flames cast shadows, defying the logic of the room's layout. The scent of jasmine, her favorite fragrance, carried an exotic undertone she couldn't place.

Standing, her pulse quickened. This wasn't real.

"I shouldn't be here," she said aloud, stifling her words as if others were listening.

"What was that? Speak up! I can't hear you if your back is turned and you're mumbling."

Zara jumped at the voice, scanning the room; she confirmed she was alone. "Okay, now, I'm hearing things."

"You aren't hearing things, you idiot. You're talking to me," the voice snapped. "Or rather, you're talking to yourself."

She spun around. Her reflection stood with her hand on her hip, staring back at her with a salty look.

Zara's eyes widened.

"Okay, this is a first," she said slowly, reminding herself she was in a Dream.

"Talking to yourself? I hate to break it to you, but you've been doing it for years."

"Not. Like. This." She didn't have time for this. She needed to leave. It was not safe for her to be here, not now, not the night before the nominations and a day before the trials.

"It's nothing to be ashamed of; everyone does it. How else is one supposed to sort things out? Who else would filter out what you should say or do if you didn't have me to talk to? We both know subtlety, and let's be honest, any form of etiquette, manners, or spatial awareness isn't exactly your gift. Do you remember the time . . ." Zara tuned out her twin's gibber. Looking under her bed and behind the tapestries, she tore the room apart, searching for an exit. The door to her bed chamber had been removed. "Hey . . . are you listening to me? What are you doing over there?"

"Losing my mind?" she asked, growing irritated. "I'm looking for a way out."

"Out of your bedroom?"

"No, out of the Dreamscape," Zara plopped onto the bed, exasperated.

"Oh, right. The preening pixie prince warned you from coming here, didn't he?" Her reflection quickly searched her memories from tonight, attempting to decipher the images Zara flashed before her conscience woke to her surroundings. "What was his name, Thumblin?"

Zara cracked a smile; she was funny. "Thalon," she answered, correcting herself.

"And why did Thalpin say you . . . I mean, *we* were supposed to stay away?"

Zara sighed, trying to remember the details, "Apparently, I'm a dreamwalker, and when I visit other people's dreams, I'm leaving doors

open." She scrunched her face, "*And* the arcanivores are escaping into our world through them. *I didn't know!* No one explained the rules to me. I don't even know how I ended up here tonight, and I don't know how to leave either."

Throwing a pillow against the wall, Zara released a frustrated scream. Her reflection raised her eyebrow. Setting the brush down, she tapped on the glass. "Let's take a breath, shall we? There is nothing we haven't been able to figure out before. How can Thalgor be so sure you're the problem?"

Zara faced her reflection. "It's Thalon!" The joke was wearing thin. "He knows because he's also a dreamwalker—an experienced one, however," she added bitterly. "Unlike me, he can conceal himself, plus it didn't help that he's witnessed me leave the doors ajar."

Her reflection sat straight and suppressed a smile. "Interesting," she voiced to herself, not to Zara. "And why didn't he close the doors if he held the power to do so?"

"I don't know," Zara pondered. "I didn't think to ask. I assumed he couldn't; otherwise, he would have. *Maybe it would've revealed him?* He turns into this fox thing—I haven't seen him do it."

The reflection mused, "An Ashendrake! How clever." She wondered where the creature had hopped to when it left Nazeem; she'd been searching for it. The reflection straightened and returned her attention to Zara, who'd resumed her fruitless search for an exit.

"The point is," Zara continued, "I need to get out of here before I botch anything else up. The nominations are tomorrow; if Birk's visions are true, my presence here could endanger our mission."

"How are you supposed to stop from dreaming?" The reflection quizzed her, amused.

"I don't know!" She yelled.

The princess was agitated and desperate, right where her reflection wanted her. "Let's slow down, didn't Thalfong say . . ."

"It's THALON."

"Fine, Thalogen."

"You aren't even trying," Zara said.

"I'm not. We don't care for him." A little humor didn't hurt, and she couldn't appear too anxious. "Didn't he mention you left the doors open when you traveled to other people's dreams?"

"Yes, why?"

"Problem solved. Don't walk into anyone else's dreams."

Zara stopped her frantic search. "You're right. This is my dream. If I stay here, nothing can escape."

"See, I knew we didn't need anyone else's help. Now, would you like to change the topic? I've . . . I mean, *we've* been working on something. An idea is brewing in your subconscious for tomorrow's nominations. Would you like to see it?"

A soft rumble underneath Zara's feet caused her to step back. A crack in the stone floor released a faint breeze. The stones split open, revealing a descending staircase into a hidden chamber.

"B-but this is the entrance to the Dreamscape," Zara stammered. "I can't go down there."

"It's also where you keep your brilliant ideas," her reflection cajoled. "You won't want to ignore your plans for tomorrow's nominations. Vincent's head is going to spin."

"No," Zara said, "This is wrong."

"When have I ever steered you wrong?" Her reflection asked, only to be met with a disturbing glance back at her. "Fine, but this time, *we're* not wrong. No one is forcing you to walk through any doors. Just a quick trip down the stairs to collect your thoughts. We're not breaking any rules."

Zara hesitated. A part of her didn't want to set foot there. There was also a part of her yearning to be taken seriously. What role was left for her if the boys took her place in the trials?

Her reflection was right. She needn't be concerned if she didn't open any doors. She was strong enough to resist the urge to wander. She'd collect what she needed and come back up again.

"Fine, but *no doors*," she reiterated.

"Yes, your Royal Highness," the reflection demurred. She tapped on the glass to grab Zara's attention. "Ahem . . . I need a little help here . . . reflection glass and all."

Anxious about her plans for tomorrow, Zara didn't even think twice when she turned to find her reflection had crawled onto the vanity on the other side. Reaching out, she plunged her hands through the glass and helped her crawl through the mirror like it was the most natural thing in the world.

Her reflection led her down the stairs, holding back a smile.

Whenever Zara entered the Dreamscape, she lost her breath. Stretching out endlessly in every direction, the Dreamscape was filled with an infinity of doors in different shapes and sizes. Some were large and square, others circular and small. Red ones. Purple ones. Wood ones. And ones made of gemstones.

Music often drifted through the air, carrying forgotten melodies or ballads not yet written. Some doors cast light, while others remained hidden in the shadows. The halls sometimes resembled a maze and, other times, a wooded forest; on occasion, Zara could even walk on clouds. Today, the hallway resembled the Azure tunnels under Ironspire.

Is it any wonder she was tempted to wander?

Shaking, she turned to her reflection, refusing to get lost. "Alright, I'm here. Where is this idea of ours?"

Her reflection pointed to a corridor, where a box sat amidst a grove of golden trees. The box was carved from a single piece of midnight-hued wood and bound with a crystal lock.

"Why have I never seen this before?" Zara asked aloud.

"The Dreamscape is fluid; so are your ideas and your potential," her reflection answered. "It's important they're kept safe and guarded."

Zara picked up the box, mystified. *She loved magic.* "How do I open it?"

The reflection shrugged, "Perhaps, with a key?" it prompted.

"I don't have a key," Zara frowned.

"Yet you conjure swords or shields from nothing when you need them," her reflection reminded.

A twinkle flashed across Zara's eyes. Grinning, she placed her hand at her heart and pulled out a glowing white key. "This is the key I use to open the doors; perhaps it will work on the box, too."

She stopped.

"What's wrong?" Her reflection asked.

"I'm nervous to use the key. I don't want to open anything I shouldn't."

"This is a box, *your box,* not a door."

Her reflection was right. Why should she be afraid of her own ideas?

She inserted the key into the box and rotated it until it clicked. The magic container sprang open, and a dazzling light spilled out, bathing her and the trees. When she peeked inside the box, it was filled with colorful grains of sand. Each speck represented an idea, a vision, a creative spark pulled from her imagination. Distracted by its beauty, she handed the key to her reflection to free her hands.

She reached in and felt her emotions and memories tickling her mind. Each idea moved and came to life within her fingers. Absorbed with her thoughts, she missed her reflection, slipping the key behind her back and quickly unlocking several adjacent doors. Her reflection slipped back behind her and peeked over her shoulder.

Zara pulled away and hugged herself. "Thank you," she said, her eyes glassy. "This is the most valuable gift you could have given me. Now, it won't matter if I am in the trials. I know exactly what to do."

The reflection pulled her closer to speak in her ear, "You don't need to thank me; I'm you. Remember? *You did this all on your own.*"

Zara smiled. Closing the box, she placed it back on the ground, locked it, and headed back up the stairs, never noticing the five open doors.

"Don't forget this," her reflection said, placing the key back into her palm, "you wouldn't want to leave it here. You might get another lecture from Thalveron."

Zara snickered, "It's not funny anymore."

"Why are you still laughing?" her reflection smiled.

Zara held the key against her heart and reabsorbed it for safekeeping. Feeling its warmth seep into her, she remained oblivious to the subtle, dark, tiny forms wriggling within it.

FORTY-SIX

THE NOMINATIONS

"We didn't come all this way to ensure your safety, only to be sidelined and unable to reach you if trouble arises," Talbot barked with a stern face. "I'll only agree to this plan if Ravenshire is included in the trials and nearby."

Indigo was amenable; if for nothing else, it removed Zara from the crossfire.

Given the time it took to reach this consensus, Birk didn't want to risk spoiling it by arguing. He wasn't sure how valuable Ravenshire would be and didn't like the idea of yet another person he loved being placed in danger. Perhaps he underestimated his friend, but even he was feeling ill-prepared to meet the standards of an Azure. Balincia, this was not, and although no one was saying it out loud, they were all placing their bets on Grey to win this for them.

Talbot and Xavier would accompany Grey's family to the stands. Taking the high view, they'd have the best vantage point over the crowd and the arena. They'd serve as an early alarm if arcanivores breached the tournament.

Zara, who would now *not be* participating and *still a little sore about it,* would be positioned in the Royal Box with her mother, providing another angle.

In anticipation of tomorrow, they gathered their collective knowledge and discussed proven methods to destroy the creatures. Brynn would help Xavier carve runes into his arrows, while Shayvonne would escort Talbot to the smithy to do the same with Ravenshire's sword. All considered, it was the best they could do.

Now, they needed their plans for the nominations to succeed.

The size of Ironspire surpassed Birk's expectations, even from a distance. At first glance, the imposing city appeared to sit on a hill; however, as Birk drew near, he realized Ironspire *formed* the mountain.

The city was composed of eight concentric walled rings stacked upon one another and diminishing in size toward the top. Each level served distinct functions and housed different sectors of the community. The upper six levels revolved around a central core tower. Attached to large, foldable metal beams, they could extend themselves outward or fold back into the main tower.

Zara explained that the rotational design enabled each section of the city to leverage the natural cycles of the suns and moons, similar to the ones circling Driftstone's orbit. If the city were threatened, each level retracted to its original position, and the tower extended to pull them back in. When assembled, it resembled a stack of impenetrable plates. In addition, the walls, ceilings, and concealed staircases at every level were also retractable and mobile, forming a magic maze of steel and stone.

On the city's north side, a mammoth Colosseum straddled a deep ravine near the White River's origin point. Walkways and tunnels ran underneath the giant arena, bridging the canyon walls. On the opposite side of the river, a small military fortress faced the mountain paths. Travelers approaching from this direction went through search protocols before taking the bridge's underpass into the city.

On the south fringe of Ironspire, thousands of exiles had constructed a large settlement. When Zara first spoke of the encampments, Birk

envisioned a small cluster of tents and a few angry mobs. Instead, the population outside the city appeared to be three times the size of Balincia. Their markets and pop-up storefronts extended for miles in every direction, with no end in sight.

According to Zara, the principal populace in the tented communities consisted of elves, dwarves, and individuals of mixed magical ancestry. While they were born from magical races, most lacked magical *abilities*. There were some low-level healers and those with enhanced biology, but Birk didn't think anyone exhibited powers worthy of being deemed a threat to such a large nation.

Why was Lady Ironspire, the mind behind this remarkable city of innovation, so afraid of her citizens?

A growing assembly formed for the nominations, and a group of Azure were positioned around a stage-sized platform. Blue banners fluttered amidst the gusts of wind, and court musicians readied their instruments.

Spotting their party, Indigo raised the ropes and ushered them to join the other candidates in a tent adjacent to the stage. After a quick exchange of hugs, temporary farewells, and last-minute advice from their families, the four young men followed the warrior to join the others. The tent was packed with about forty candidates whose attention was drawn to a dark-haired elf with three chins clearing his throat.

"Congratulations on being a candidate for the Azure trials," he grinned, wobbling between them. "Only twenty of you will receive sponsorship after today's nomination and go on to compete. Today is a demonstration of health and presentation alone. You won't speak unless you're asked a question."

Stopping in front of a short young dwarf with a chubby little belly, he provided a quick appraisal with a disapproving tsk of his tongue.

"If you're selected today, you will join the other Azure applicants from the academy and be afforded the day to train and prepare for the trials. You and your family will be awarded Azure citizenship if you succeed at the trials. *After* you pledge your loyalties to Lady Ironspire, of course."

Pausing in front of a tall, black elf with arms comparable to Grey, the heavy elf offered an approving nod.

"By agreeing to compete in the trials, you acknowledge the risks of danger. Every year, the competitors face a chance of injury, whether temporary or permanent. If you're unwilling to risk your lives, this is your last opportunity to leave," he said, opening the tent's back flap.

A timid red-haired female elf and a gentleman who, while in decent shape, was much older than the rest of the candidates lowered their faces to the ground and slipped out.

The elf in charge clucked his tongue when they passed him, closing the flap in a condescending huff. "For the rest of you—don't say you weren't warned." Making his way back to the front of the tent, he spied the four new additions.

Grabbing Ravenshire by his chin, he moved his face from side to side. "I don't recognize you; I don't recognize any of you," the elf declared, waving his hand at the four of them.

Everyone in the tent turned to stare; Indigo was nowhere in sight. After a brief pause, Thalon stepped forward.

"We received a personal escort by the Azure warrior, Indigo, under the orders of your Royal Highness, Zara, the Princess of Ironspire," Thalon responded on their behalf, matching the elf's pretentious inflection. "*You* didn't travel to the back of the encampment, overlooking several candidates. We arrived late because your warrior was forced to do *your* job for you."

The elf clutched his chest and curled back his lip. "Zara, of course." He pinched his mouth, embarrassed by Thalon's derogation. "Fine. My apologies." Shuffling away, he shouted, "Get yourselves ready; our Lady Ironspire will be here soon."

A female elf with long chestnut hair standing beside Thalon elbowed him. "Quick thinking on your part; how were you sure he'd fall for the lie?"

Thalon eyed the girl suspiciously, "Why do you think I'm lying?"

"Don't you think we know our own? We've all grown up together; you aren't from here."

"Don't worry," said the young dwarf, inserting himself, "we all hate Vincent. No one is going to out you. We assumed if Indigo snuck you in, there was a good reason."

Thalon eyed them and nodded. "I've dealt with royal asses; they only respond to bigger asses," Thalon smirked. "Throw in a couple of important names to intimidate them, and you can usually call their bluff. He looked too lazy to walk around the city."

"It appears your self-entitlement does have its benefits," Grey poked.

Thalon didn't appreciate the shot taken.

"You'll want to follow their lead if you don't want to stand out," the elf informed them, pointing to the men removing their tunics and shirts and the women rubbing their arms in oil. "They'll be examining our physiques."

"What's your name?" Thalon asked, slipping his shirt off.

"Hyacinth," the elf answered.

"I'm Biddy," the stout dwarf introduced. "And this is our mate, Packington," he motioned toward the tall black elf.

Thalon quickly introduced the rest of his party.

"We'd be interested in allying to help each other reach the end," Grey said, rubbing the oil on his chest. Everyone except Packington eyed his physique out of envy or interest. "We have no desire to steal your slots on the Azure; we only wish to gain an audience with Lady Ironspire."

A few inches taller than Grey, Packington stared down at him and said, "Who says we need your help to win?"

Hyacinth put her hand on Packington's chest, pushing him back, "It'd be foolish not to consider an alliance, especially if they are in partnership with Indigo. How about we rein in the competitive masculinity and ego?"

"Let's see how everyone fares during the nominations before we consider alliances," Packington replied, turning his back on them.

Ravenshire pulled Birk to the side, "I've always considered us in fighting shape, but we don't compare to the size of most of the men in this room. I'm worried we're unevenly matched."

Birk agreed.

Overhearing their conversation, Grey leaned in, "Size doesn't equal

strength or agility in a competition. Talbot was wise to keep you lean, fast, and flexible."

An Azure with bronzed skin poked his head into the tent. "Alright, everyone, line up," he ordered. He pointed at Packington and Grey, "You two, follow me."

Positioning the strongest-looking candidates at the front of the stage, Birk was grateful to hide in the back with Ravenshire and the dwarf. To the stage's right, Lady Ironspire and Zara sat in thrones, flanked by Vincent, Indigo, and Kodalt, Captain of the Royal Azure.

Zara gave them a quick, discreet smile.

Stepping to the front, Kodalt addressed the audience first. Explaining the history of the Azure and the trials, he gushed over the honor of opening them to the people. After presenting the nomination rules, he introduced Lady Ironspire, who initiated the selection process.

Birk watched Sable take the stage and couldn't believe the uncanny resemblance between her and Zara. Her posture held an identical commanding composure. Her brilliant blue hair, the only difference between them, fell on the dark skin of her shoulders when she stood. Her sleeveless plum gown showcased her sculpted arms, highlighting her eyes. Silver wrist cuffs coordinated with her braided belt and boots, presenting the figure of a fighter.

Edi would've approved of her fashion choices.

Smiling broadly, she appeared indifferent to the forced smiles and strained claps—encouraged more out of obligation than admiration. Paying platitudes to the Azure and the candidates' families, she painted a portrait of herself as a forward-thinking leader who was generous to the future welfare of her subjects.

"Without further ado, I'm honored to have the privilege of nominating the first candidate for the trials. While the selection will be mine, my royal advisor, *Vincent*, will execute all sponsorship duties with my full endorsement. We wouldn't want anyone to think my nominee would have an advantage under my tutelage."

The announcement produced a wave of disgruntled and disappointed

reactions from the candidates—silenced by a quick tap of Kodalt's spear on the stage. Feigning surprise, Vincent bowed. Suppressing a smile, the tips of his ears burned red.

Zara, mortified, exchanged a quick, worrying glance with Birk.

Weaving through the candidates, Lady Ironspire touched and appraised the nominees as if she were picking out a prized, long-haired boar for a feast. The candidates lowered their eyes and shuffled their feet to avoid her attention. The idea of Vincent being a sponsor tarnished the notion of being the ruler's first choice.

She didn't bother to walk to the back or pretend her interest leaned toward anyone except a favored contender.

Pacing between Packington and Grey, she circled them. Letting her fingers trace their shoulders and arms, she scrutinized their potential—ordering them to puff their chests and jut their jawlines. Flexing and squatting, they turned and jumped, all to the crowd's amusement.

Positioning behind them, Sable faced the audience for her final reveal. Raising her hand over Packington, she teased them and shifted it—at the last moment—above Grey's head. "My champion!" She announced to the soft applause of the crowd.

Grey's shoulders dropped.

Scurrying over in delight, Vincent flashed his yellow smile to Grey. "And what is your name, champion?"

"Grey," he answered, standing at attention.

"Well, Grey, would you share how it feels to be personally selected by the Ruler of Ironspire?" Vincent asked, nudging him forward.

Grey stood silent, uncomfortable with the crowd's attention. With his tongue tied, and not knowing what else to do, he kneeled before Lady Ironspire, bowing and hiding his head from the audience.

Vincent laughed, "Your selection humbles him."

"There's no shame in being strong and silent; more should follow his example," Sable praised, lifting Grey's chin. "You'll need no words to make me proud in the arena." The audience was forced to cheer again when Vincent paraded Grey to the front before escorting him off the stage. Everyone felt sorry for him.

Grey's eyes found Birk, sending him a message not to worry.

Birk reminded himself that getting them all into the trials was the objective. It mattered little who sponsored them; Grey was the most capable among them, regardless of the training they received. Gaining Sable's vote of support and interest could play to their advantage.

Kodalt selected next and induced an entirely different atmosphere among the candidates and crowd.

Posturing and posing when he walked by, everyone except Birk and Ravenshire competed for his attention. Biddy, much to the delight of the onlookers, flipped and stood on his fingers, firing up both the audience and the Azure in laughter. To no one's surprise, Kodalt eventually picked Packington, who threw his arm into the air, sending a roar through the assembly.

The mood remained spirited. The ranking Azure and a few prominent members of the Royal Council made their selections one by one. The nominees, vying for consideration, created an enthusiastic show. Indigo picked Thalon, *as promised*, and a tall female Azure, who stood out prominently, selected Hyacinth.

The candidates dwindled to twenty-three, leaving only an Azure squadron leader named Alezander and the princess to make their choices. Biddy, who had taken to his knees, followed the squadron leader around the stage, his hands in a begging pose. When Alezander gave in to him, he received the most considerable applause of the day.

Now, only Zara's selection remained.

"Finally, your Royal Highness, the Princess of Ironspire, will pick our final competing champion," Vincent announced.

When Zara took the stage, the audience and the leftover nominees stood, whistled, and stomped their feet.

Vincent seethed with jealousy. The admiration she garnered shadowed the reaction granted to her mother. If Sable noticed the difference, she didn't let it show.

"I agreed to sponsor these trials because I believe all the citizens of Ironspire deserve to play a role in our future. I view this trial *only* as a first step in rebuilding your trust in us. I speak for my mother when I

say we will find a road back from your *temporary* displacement. And we will ensure reparations will be granted." Zara declared to the boisterous cheers of the market.

"You can't speak for your mother," Vincent hissed under his breath.

"I just did," Zara replied with a plastered smile. She'd been preparing for this moment since the idea occurred to her last night.

Sable's hand clenched the arm of the throne. Keeping a tight smile, she narrowed her eyes. Indigo lowered their head, shaking it—not read into this part of her plan.

Zara, well aware of the impact of her words, no longer deemed it necessary to participate in the trials to grab her mother's attention. Granted a platform, she intended to utilize it to her benefit. If her mother envisioned her as the heart of the people, she'd play the role and beat loudly for them.

She possessed a voice, too. It was time to be brave enough to assert it. If she couldn't engage in the tournament as a combatant, her tongue and wits would serve as her weapons.

Exchanging a glance with Birk, she silently urged him to trust her. She understood the deviation wasn't part of the original strategy, but she believed the improvisation might lead to a win on both fronts. If the offspring of witches were destined to bring about change, there were multiple paths to restoring balance.

"I've also decided to sponsor two candidates for the tournament instead of one," Zara continued, embracing the cheers from the crowd.

"You can't do that," Vincent squeaked.

"Uh-oh, it sounds as if the Royal Advisor is saying the *princess* can't gift the people an extra spot." She played to the jeering and booing crowd. "Has the Royal Advisor forgotten his place?"

"I'd never . . . no . . . I mean the rules state . . ." Distressed, Vincent turned to Lady Ironspire, who dismissed his objections with a wave of her hand, refusing to be pulled into it. "Fine . . . of course, as your Royal Highness wishes," he mumbled, stepping quickly out of the way.

Zara strolled among the remaining candidates on the stage. Taking her time, she smiled and thanked them for being part of the process.

"I'd choose all of you if I could," she flattered. "My predecessors today, respectfully, chose their candidates on optics and aesthetics, assuming all strengths are visible. I, however, believe an Azure is more than strength or speed; a good soldier must also have the humility to weigh their battles with careful measure."

Circling behind Birk and Ravenshire, she rested her hands on their shoulders. "Never underestimate the will and discipline of those who are often disregarded. My experience is they are often your most focused and fierce competitors."

Navigating them forward, she raised her hands above them. "I give you, my champions!"

FORTY-SEVEN

THE ACADEMY

Having a whole day to train for the trials was misleading. By the time the nominations ended and Zara escorted them to the Academy on the sixth level, it was almost midday. On top of that, she broke the news that she'd been summoned in response to her surprise declaration this morning.

"Will you be okay?" Birk asked.

Zara shrugged, "I'll be fine. What's she going to do? She can't retract anything I said publicly without a fallout. At this point, I've got nothing to lose. If we're going to rebalance things, we have to start dismantling *all* injustices."

"I think it's admirable," Ravenshire complimented.

Birk was still hesitant. It'd be hypocritical to fault Zara, but he was worried about the timing. "Let's not get ahead of ourselves. We still need your mother's help to get past tomorrow."

"I realize today is not what we expected, but we lucked out. Who would've thought my mother would end up picking Grey?" Zara said, reading his concern.

"Well, he was the biggest guy there," Ravenshire joked. Birk hid his smile. He wished Grey were with them.

A clanging of swords disrupted them, commanding Birk to pay attention. The courtyard where they stood divided into two sections. To the left of the entrance was a designated training ground, and to the right, a meditative area.

The training complex was already filled with young warriors around Birk's age diligently honing their skills. Wooden and metal dummies stood in neat rows, used as targets for archery and long-range defenses. A towering maze of balance beams stood beside sand pits and climbing cargo nets. Shouting commands—instructors guided their charges through elaborate drills and sparring sessions.

Opposite them was the oasis: a garden full of bubbling fountains and reflective pools. Stone benches were tucked away under cherry blossoms, offering a peaceful retreat. Students stretched, meditated, and lounged by the water's edge.

In the center, a prominent glass structure stood, its transparent walls giving visitors a glimpse of the activity inside. Reinforced steel beams crisscrossed around its surface, providing an artistic aesthetic to the Academy. Through the glass, Birk caught a glimpse of the open banquet hall, where residents dined. Zara explained the corridors on the side led to private bedchambers and classrooms for study. Large steaming pools and bathing stations were housed in the back.

Two distinct groups of competitors were clashing around the courtyard. The academy's aspiring athletes, clad in fitted royal blue gambesons and leggings, moved with confidence across the campus, trying to intimidate the outsiders when they passed. In contrast, the nominees from the morning, clad in worn white tunics, dusty boots, and tattered cloaks, bore the mark of struggle.

Under the Azure's watch, tension simmered beneath the surface. One group was resented for their privilege. The other—perceived unworthy. Remaining aloof, the academy athletes cast derisive stares, sharing laughs over cruel jokes and pointed piercing fingers. Their current target was Biddy, who was attempting to scramble up a cargo net.

"I don't see Grey anywhere," Birk said, completing his scan of the area.

Zara glanced around. "Who knows, maybe Vincent is still giving him a tour?" Realizing her dismissive statement did little to ease his concern, she reached out and touched his arm. "I recognize you're worried, but as much as I hate Vincent, he'll *always* want to see my mother win, especially if his name is attached. If I had to guess, Grey is probably receiving the royal treatment right now, quarantined from the other candidates."

Zara's reassurance helped a little, but Birk had become reliant on Grey's support over the last several weeks.

"Think of it this way: only one of you has to pass the trials. Grey was our best shot in the competition, and now Vincent will ensure he gets to the end," Zara offered.

Ravenshire flinched, "Uhm, while I appreciate the vote of confidence in Grey, aren't these trials supposed to be dangerous? We don't need to place well, but I want to *survive* them."

Birk nodded; he was more anxious than in the tent this morning. "I agree, without the ability to use my magic and little time to train, we're feeling a little unprepared."

Zara realized she may have been insensitive. Taking for granted her confidence in the arena and familiarity with the trials, she forgot this was new to them. "First, you're more prepared than you give yourself credit. Even though the rules state you'll get eliminated if you use magic, *that's only if they can detect it.* As long as you aren't projecting visible bolts of lightning or flying through the air, don't hesitate to use your magic *if you can use it unnoticed.*"

"Okay . . .," Birk wavered, not sure he'd mastered any subtlety with his magic.

"Second, work together because the academy trainees will. This isn't every man for himself; it's about teamwork. Some of the challenges will require it," Zara explained. "You'll have Grey and Thalon on your side, but the more allies you can make, the better."

Ravenshire sighed with relief. "That takes away a lot of the pressure."

"Finally, there's no shame in forfeiting a challenge. If Grey or Thalon are placing well, walk away; keep yourselves safe first," Zara underlined. "I mean it, don't be heroes."

"What can you share about the challenges?"

Zara motioned for them to sit on the ground. "Here's where it gets tricky; my mother changes it every year based on her whims and the talent of the engineers. They usually involve a combination of combat exercises and battling mechanical inventions fueled by her magic."

Pausing, she drew a line in the sand with her finger, giving them something to visualize. "The first trial is always a gauntlet, created to eliminate half of the contenders. You'll need to defeat several obstacles to make it to the other side of the Colosseum. Speed counts, but accuracy is better."

"Why do half of the contenders get eliminated?" Ravenshire asked, "It doesn't sound too difficult."

"Overconfidence. Don't take anything at face value. Every hurdle is a puzzle with multiple solutions; take the time to figure them out."

"So, there isn't much we can do to prepare for this one until we are on the arena floor," Birk reflected, growing uneasy. "Okay, what's next?"

"The team event. Only two teams can be left standing at the end," Zara noted, drawing four squares in each corner. "It's a game of endurance, where you'll need to defend a fort against attacks from sentinel soldiers, both on the ground and in the air. If all teams eliminate the threats before falling, your goal will be to eliminate the other teams by destroying their fortress and taking their flag."

Zara explained the game's rules and discussed strategy. She emphasized that wit and gameplay were more important than physical prowess. It also didn't hurt knowing Grey would give them an advantage over any other team.

Birk discovered the third trial would be a battle between the elements and nature. This test would play to his strengths. If he kept his alliance near him, he could attempt to use discretion and influence the outcome.

The final trial involved facing off against an Azure soldier one-on-one. To win, they'd need to disarm their opponent. Birk and Ravenshire exchanged confident grins—Talbot's training specialized in mastering this maneuver.

Relieved at their comfort, Zara smiled. "The trials are about strategy; everyone training today is performing to intimidate you. Let them. They'll strain or exhaust themselves before tomorrow's competition. You don't need to be the strongest or even the smartest; to succeed, you must be able to adapt."

"The strength training will come after the trials," Indigo teased, approaching with Thalon and Hyacinth in tow. "Zara's right, though. It would be best if you don't overexert yourself today. However, we need you to stretch and get limber. I also want to assess your capabilities to determine how you best complement each other."

"Do you mind if we join you?" interrupted the squadron leader, who nominated Biddy. The young dwarf stood behind him, appearing defeated.

"Of course, Alezander," Indigo stepped to the side. "The more, the better."

Alezander leaned forward in Indigo's ear, glancing toward Biddy, who stared at his feet.

"What happened? Where's Packington?" Hyacinth probed, "I thought he was watching out for you."

Biddy's bearded cheeks reddened, "He's acting as if he doesn't know me. The jerk joined with the academy asses within minutes of arriving. They're calling him Kodalt's *chosen one*."

Thalon glanced at the elf, eating the attention of his new admirers. "You don't need him, Biddy. No one needs friends like that." He placed his hand on Biddy's shoulders, surprising Birk with the gesture.

"Alright, let's get to it." Indigo declared, ending their conversation with Alezander. "All of you are with me for the remaining part of the afternoon. Zara has some royal duties, and Alezander is being called to the arena. Let's see what the five of you can do."

Running through drills, the team learned they were more versatile than perceived.

Hyacinth proved to be an expert sharpshooter with her bow and arrow. Biddy impressed them with his long-distance axe-throwing. Thalon, to no one's surprise, was the quickest and most agile on the balance

beams, but Hyacinth wasn't far behind. Birk and Ravenshire dominated the swordsmanship, while no one beat the combination of Biddy and Thalon in the wrestling pits.

After an exhausting afternoon, Indigo provided them with water and invited the group to sit by the reflecting pool.

"This team has a lot of grit. I'd take that over routine and polish any day. Your greatest strength tomorrow will be each other; don't leave anyone behind. Thalon is your strongest lead offense, scout, and hand-to-hand combatant, while Hyacinth should be your long-range shooter. Biddy, you should remain at the fortress during the team event; you're a strong wall, and coupled with your ax-throwing skills, you're perfect as a last line of defense."

Biddy radiated with an infectious smile—needing the boost. Indigo's leadership skills shined, making everyone feel like a valued asset. Turning to Birk and Ravenshire, Indigo continued, "You both are the most advanced swordsmen, but where you excel is your teamwork. You've been trained to identify, adapt to, and adjust your approach to your teammate's strengths. I want you both to lead; Birk makes the calls; Ravenshire, your second in command."

"What about Grey?" Birk asked, triggering a groan from Thalon. "He'll be joining us tomorrow."

"I haven't been able to assess Grey. From what I've seen, I assume he'd be on par with Thalon. Keep him out front. Do you have any other questions?"

"What about weapons?" Biddy asked.

"When the competition begins, you can take in one weapon of your choice. If you wish, you may select one from Ironspire's armament; each is engineered with Lady Ironspire's magic." Indigo cautioned them, noticing their eager faces, "My advice, however, is to stick with what you use and are familiar with. If you aren't trained on a weapon, it will prove useless against someone comfortable with theirs on the battlefield. Biddy, I wouldn't give up your axe, and Birk, I wouldn't replace your sword."

Answering questions until the third sun sank in the sky, Indigo ordered them to wash, eat, and get a good night's sleep. Hyacinth headed toward the baths while Biddy and Ravenshire continued to discuss strategy.

Thalon circled behind Birk, "Would you be up for one more duel? We didn't have a chance to spar, and I could use the practice," he asked.

Agreeing to his offer, Birk followed him to the courtyard.

"Are you nervous about tomorrow?" Thalon asked.

"Less than I was at the beginning of the day."

Thalon shifted his feet. "If anything, it allows us to practice working as a unit." Pausing, he turned to Birk and said, "I do want us to be a successful team, Birk. It's important to me. Not just in the arena, but on this quest."

Birk studied Thalon. A sincerity was poking out from behind his edgy demeanor—it wasn't the first time today. He was right; they hadn't spent much time together, and it was important for them to work cohesively. They needed to clear the air over their first interactions.

"It's important to me, too," Birk acknowledged, offering his hand, "Can we start over?"

Thalon nodded, relieved, and shook his hand. Offering a small smile, he jumped into a jesting stance and motioned to Birk. "Alright, show me your best moves, master swordsman," he teased.

Drawing their swords, they circled each other, waiting for the other to make the first move. Thalon lunged forward with a swift strike, aiming for Birk's chest. Birk deftly parried the blow with a crisp lateral movement, the clash of steel ringing out into the courtyard. Countering with a series of quick thrusts and cuts, Birk aimed at Thalon's exposed flank.

Thalon, undeterred, blocked and dodged with the footwork of a fox, fending off the assault. With a sudden twist of his wrist, he spun around and delivered a powerful overhead blow, aiming to bring Birk to his knees. Birk, his reflexes honed through years of training with Talbot, anticipated the move and sidestepped at the last moment.

Seeing a brief lapse in Thalon's defense, Birk seized the opening. With a swift twist, he disarmed Thalon with a quick flick of his wrist, sending the sword flying across the courtyard. Thalon stood stunned.

With Birk's blade to his throat, he flashed a suggestive smile, "I'll admit, you're better than I expected, but the fight isn't over." Using his bare hands, he deflected Birk's blade away from his throat. Surprised, Birk stepped back and reassessed the situation.

Thalon pressed forward, closing the distance between them. Launching a series of strikes and blocks, he utilized his fists and forearms to deflect and control Birk's sword. Impressed with his tenacity, Birk adapted his fighting style, using his blade not to strike but to parry and bind Thalon's limbs.

As the duel continued, Thalon saw his opportunity. Twisting his body lightning-fast, he disarmed Birk, sending his sword spinning into the air. They both stood facing each other, unarmed.

Transitioning into hand-to-hand combat, they grappled, trying to force the other to submit. Sweating, they circled each other again, seeking an advantage. Thalon, utilizing his brute strength, managed to gain the upper hand, throwing Birk to the ground with a mighty sweep of his legs. Straddling him, he immobilized Birk's arms, pressing his wrists firmly into the ground, preventing any retaliatory strikes.

Solidifying his dominance, Thalon locked eyes with Birk, who breathed heavily under his exerted weight. Hearts hammering—their faces inches apart—a physical friction rubbed between them. The applied pressure of their bodies, their adrenaline high, and a seducing whiff of musk stimulated a sudden arousal from Thalon against Birk's inner thigh.

Birk's body betrayed him with a mirrored, motivated reaction.

Thalon's face drained of its color. Birk's flushed pink.

In a quick and fluid movement, both men untangled themselves and sat with their backs against each other. Neither spoke, acutely aware of the other's heat pressed against them. After several excruciating minutes, Thalon stood and awkwardly walked away—leaving Birk's head to spin in silence.

FORTY-EIGHT

Muscles and Magic

"Are we interrupting?" Ravenshire asked, crossing the courtyard with Biddy.

Birk remained glued to the spot Thalon left him, replaying their interaction over and over again in his head. Relieved by the distraction, Birk quickly straightened and rose to meet them. "No, not all; we finished. Where did everyone else go?" he asked, noticing the cleared courtyard.

"Feeding time," Biddy informed, rubbing his belly.

"We were coming to see if you wanted to join us. We tried asking Thalon, but he rushed past us with his sour face on," Ravenshire commented.

"He didn't even make eye contact with us. He's a bit of a loner, isn't he?" Biddy asked.

"I wouldn't take it personally," Birk said, *taking it personally*. "I think the pressure is getting to all of us. Let's go grab something to eat."

The Banquet Hall was filled with noise and food. Ten long oak tables were scattered throughout, each with bountiful settings of fruits, rooted vegetables, cheeses, and roast boar. The academy attendees continued to set themselves apart, as evidenced by the predominance of blue leggings on one side of the room.

Scanning the area, Birk was disappointed that Grey was still absent. Despite Zara's reassurances of his safety, a pit inhabited his stomach. He knew he should eat, but his appetite was lacking.

Spying Thalon across the room, Birk walked cautiously over to him. He was alone, ignoring his plate of food.

"Hey, you left before we had a chance to talk," he said, sitting across from him.

"I wasn't aware we needed to talk," Thalon poked a potato with his fork.

Birk hesitated, "I don't want things to be awkward between us; I think we just—"

"Birk," Thalon interrupted, cutting him off. "I don't need a speech. We're fine. Not everything needs to be talked to death."

"Right," Birk lowered his head.

Thalon sighed, placing his fork down. "I enjoyed sparring with you," Thalon offered, attempting to change the subject. "Talbot trained you well. Who knew your little backwater town of Balincia produced worthy opponents?"

Birk chuckled at the jest, inviting the return of Thalon's cocky smile.

"Did you mention Balincia?" Ravenshire said, sitting, followed by Biddy and Hyacinth. "There is so much I need to catch you up on since you've been gone." He was right; there'd been no time to connect with his friend; it'd all been action and strategy since they arrived.

"Balinthia?" Biddy questioned with a mouth full of food. "What's Balinthia?"

Birk and Ravenshire grinned and leaned into the table, sharing stories about their home. Seeing his friend shine and talk about their youth helped Birk's nerves relax and his appetite come back. Thalon's attitude also shifted; enjoying the change in conversation, he allowed himself to eat and connect with his companions.

When the day became night, Hyacinth and Biddy took their leave, and the Balincian's conversation carried into the private bed chamber arranged

by Zara for the three of them. Ravenshire, distracted by catching Birk up on all the news he couldn't share earlier, threw himself across one of the two beds.

This left Birk and Thalon to sit uncomfortably on the edges of the only other mattress.

"When the enchantment broke, so did the chains limiting our belief in ourselves. You sparked a movement; even Edi and Pan have changed." Ravenshire rattled on. "I wanted to follow your example, so when the opportunity came up to volunteer for this mission to find you, I jumped at the chance."

"I'm glad you did; I've missed you." Birk paused and reflected. "Ravenshire, you know I think of you as my brother, right? We grew up together, raised by the same witches. I hope when I left that night, you didn't feel abandoned. I wanted to share what was happening with you in the gardens, but I was worried about your safety—everything happened so fast."

Ravenshire shook his head, "You don't have to explain; I knew I'd see you again. Although I didn't imagine it under these circumstances." His smile dimmed, softening the lines of his face. "It does feel a bit different now, you know?"

"What do you mean?"

"Us. You aren't the same. You're facing literal giants and wielding storms connected to something greater. I feel a bit in your shadow," he admitted.

Birk's throat tightened. "I hope you don't think your path has to follow mine," he said, hunching forward. "You have your own gifts to share. I want you to feel as supported as I have. You deserve an opportunity to explore beyond our borders, too."

"That's the thing. As exciting as all of this has been, I'm not sure I'm meant for a life beyond Balincia after today. I feel more lost here than back home."

"Why?" Birk crossed the room, using the chance to push his legs aside and sit next to him.

"I was part of our royal family in Balincia. Out here, I'm surrounded

by people with magic or warriors far better than our humble troops," he motioned to Thalon. "I'm just ordinary—an orphaned, non-magic human chasing my friend because . . . I have no idea what else to do."

"Okay, I'm going to interrupt before Birk answers with something trite like you don't need magic to be special," Thalon cut in.

"*Thalon*," Birk warned.

"The truth is you're *not* special. Neither is Birk, *and neither am I.*" Thalon raised his eyebrow toward Birk. "Bet you didn't think I was going to say that."

"You're right—given your elitist views in the Living Forest," Birk replied, irritated and wary of his intentions. "Where are you going with this?"

"*Elitist?*" Thalon's face contorted, and a look of hurt washed over him. "There's a lot you don't know about me or life in the Living Forest, Birk," he snapped, wounded. "Do you really believe I'm a supremacist?"

Ravenshire shifted uncomfortably.

"What else am I supposed to believe?" Birk shot back, his tone escalating in defense, "Have you forgotten how you dressed Grey and his family down?"

Thalon reeled back, creasing his brow, "That is *not* what that was. Of course—you'd make this about Grey."

"Birk, maybe we should give Thalon a chance to finish what he was trying to say," Ravenshire inserted, attempting to lower the room's temperature.

Ignoring Ravenshire, Birk jutted his chin at Thalon, "Please, enlighten me; what was it?"

The veins throbbed in Thalon's neck. Refusing to take the bait, he dismissed Birk's question. "What they're doing here in Ironspire is disgusting, *especially* to me. No one should have to compete for the privilege of safety and acceptance. Using a tournament to string along elves and dwarves, at the risk of their own lives, *for entertainment* is sickening."

Birk was taken aback. "While I agree with you, what makes your beliefs toward Grey any different than Lady Ironspire's?"

"My *beliefs*? What do you know of my beliefs?" Thalon rounded on

Birk, thrusting his finger into his chest. "As much as I don't like your boyfriend, I'd never treat him like cattle and leave him to rot outside my city. Yes, I'm a condescending jerk, and I didn't want him on this quest, but if you didn't notice, we don't abandon anyone in our city," he yelled.

"No, you lock out strangers," Birk retorted, standing to meet him face-to-face. "Would you be this upset if the situation were reversed? And the Non-Magic-Born were banished? Or is your hatred only directed toward Grey?"

Thalon screamed into his palms. Sliding his fingers into his hair, he pulled them, attempting to settle his face. Exasperated, he pleaded, "Can we please not do this right now? This . . . *tug of war* . . . between you and me. I was trying to be helpful and share some advice with your friend. *Can I do that?* I promise you can return to hating me and defending Grey after."

"I . . . fine . . . go ahead," Birk said, crossing his arms and sitting back on the bed.

Thalon took a deep breath and directed his attention back to Ravenshire. "I was *going to say* that none of us are born special. But you—you woke up and decided you wanted something different. You chose to leave every comfort behind. You're fighting uphill in a world where you feel small and intimidated. That takes more courage than any muscle or magic in this room. Don't underestimate yourself."

"Thank you, Thalon," Ravenshire straightened, "I appreciate that." He shot Birk a look of disappointment.

Birk glanced away, and Thalon hung his head. No one knew what to do with themselves; the energy in the room was still charged. An oppressive silence filled the air.

"I . . . uhm . . . I think I'm going to bathe," Thalon abruptly inserted.

Birk collapsed onto the bed and placed the pillow over his face.

After Thalon slipped out, Ravenshire checked to ensure the door was shut. He turned to his friend. "What was that about? Don't you think you were a little rough on him?"

Birk sat up, "You weren't there when I met Thalon. He's rude and antagonizing. I don't trust what will come out of his mouth."

"Sure, he's a little blunt and sharp around the edges, but maybe give him a break. It seems like he's trying. Remember, the rest of us have friends and family surrounding us. It has to be hard being the outsider."

Birk sighed, "You're right, I didn't think of that. I let him get under my skin. He has this issue with Grey, *which I don't understand.* And this thing happened today between us . . ."

"Something happened between you today? Another argument?"

Birk bit his cheek. "No—not an argument." He fidgeted, "I'd rather not talk about it."

Ravenshire searched his face, "Fair enough," he paused. "Perhaps you should give yourself a break, too. You've been dealing with a lot of new things all at once. That's a lot of pressure. It's normal to make mistakes and fall short. Don't be so hard on yourself; we can't be heroes every day."

Birk offered a grateful smile and nodded.

Rejoining his friend on the bed, they sat cross-legged and continued to chat, easing their nerves about the upcoming day.

When Thalon re-entered, he disrobed without interrupting them and crawled into the bed across the chamber. Birk's gaze kept wandering back to him, tossing and turning in the bed.

He felt guilty.

Thalon tried to bridge the gap between them, and Birk stomped all over it. Filled with conflicting emotions and anxiety over Grey, he hurt Thalon's feelings and resurrected the divide between them.

Hearing Ravenshire yawn, Birk acknowledged the mutual need for sleep. Giving his friend the room to stretch, he blew out the lamps and carefully slipped beside Thalon in the other bed. He stared at the ceiling.

"Thalon," he whispered to his back, "Are you still awake?"

Thalon remained silent, his eyes open, facing the opposite direction.

"I want you to know . . . I don't hate you."

FORTY-NINE

The Gauntlet

The White River Colosseum was built to honor the old world and celebrate the ingenuity of the new. Stretching across the raging river, the steel and white marbled structure rose twenty levels high. The Colosseum's majestic arcades and spectator seats spiraled around the central arena, offering the audience unparalleled views.

Thirteen imposing towers encircled the Colosseum, each with a statue depicting one of the Original Thirteen, an accolade to their legacy, or a salute to their myth, whichever a citizen believed. Under each statue, Azure archers stood sentinel, watching over the stadium. Royal blue banners fluttered and billowed against the spires emblazoned with the symbol of a white star encased inside a mechanical cog. The emblem represented progress and innovation.

The grandest tower at the stadium's heart stood in tribute to Lady Ironspire. It was positioned over a bridge connecting the Royal Citadel and the opulent Royal Box Theater. Zara stood at the box's edge, waiting impatiently for the competitors to arrive. Vincent clucked his tongue at her to take a seat.

An adolescent girl caught her eye, jumping and waving from the middle of the stands.

"It's Zara," Brynn pointed while Shayvonne ushered her to their seats. Talbot and Xavier trailed behind them, overwhelmed by the scale of the architecture and the size of the crowds.

"I assumed the floating palaces would be the grandest thing I'd ever see," Xavier remarked to Talbot.

"Agreed. It's much larger than I anticipated, which makes it more difficult to defend or reach the children if they need our help," Talbot worried.

"Let's pray to the Protector, it won't come to that," Shayvonne replied.

The crowd leaned forward as they filled the stands, gawking at the imposing gauntlet on the arena floor. On one end, a gigantic pendulum held four silver axes that swayed back and forth hypnotically inside it. Eight levels high, the glint of their razor-sharp blades caught the sunlight, casting a blinding gleam across the playing field. Beneath the swinging death trap, circular blades emerged from the ground with a menacing slice—rolling in a deadly rhythm.

Behind the pendulum, a massive wall rumbled and opened to reveal a fierce and mammoth mechanical dragon, positioned on its hind legs. Steam rose from its nostrils in a threatening plume. A roar echoed from its belly, magically engineered to mimic the legendary beast.

On the opposite side of the dragon, the tournament floor was covered with tiles, laid out in eight rows. Each tile was large and long enough to hold four soldiers at a time. An optical illusion, they pulsed and changed colors—a disorienting blue, silver, and white blanket.

The gauntlet finished with the last quarter of the tournament floor covered in sand, with something moving below the surface.

In the underground hypogeum, where all the competitors were now fitted into the Academy's gambesons, Birk heard the drums beat. Indigo had arrived early in the morning, rushing them through their routines and ushering them into the tunnels below the Colosseum. Now, they filled the space with restless energy.

Fear gnawed at the young contestants. Hyacinth kneeled against the

wall, praying to the Protector. Biddy's pale hands tremored uncontrollably. Ravenshire lost his breakfast for the second time, and Birk's pulse raced, watching his friends falter under the weight of their insecurities.

A familiar hand placed itself on Birk's shoulder, sending a shockwave of relief through him.

It wasn't the expected face of Grey, who stood behind him, but Thalon. "Don't worry, I've got your back," he assured, pushing aside any tension between them. Birk was grateful.

A booming voice echoed through the chambers, interrupting them and silencing the noise from above. Vincent stepped up to a giant silver conch positioned in the royal box, engineered with Sable's magic to amplify his voice across the city. "Please stand for your ruler, the Great Lady Ironspire," he announced to the sounds of horns, boisterous whistles, and cheers.

"Welcome to the seven hundredth anniversary of the Azure Trials," her voice rang out to more applause.

The Azure Captains soon drowned out her introductory speech, barking orders for the candidates to line up and grab their weapons. Keeping his hand on his hilt, Birk stood behind Ravenshire and scoured the room for Grey.

Indigo swept by them, tightening their straps and clapping them on their backs. "Remember, play as a team," they reminded, scooting them up the ramp toward the doors.

Suddenly, everything surrounding Birk decelerated to a crawl. It started as a subtle unease, a nagging feeling in his stomach. The world around him slowed, and his heart raced erratically, pounding against his chest.

Behind his shoulder, each inhale and exhale from Thalon was prolonged and exaggerated. Every tap from Biddy's fingers against his axe resonated like a hammer. Subtle creaks and cracks from Hyacinth's body were magnified when she drew out her crossbow in long, extended movements.

Ravenshire turned his head, initiating a sluggish nod. His muscles

tensed, and his torso pivoted. The wind tousled his friend's hair, and he broke into a languid run.

Someone was talking behind Birk, trying to get his attention; the words were out of focus, distorted.

"Birk!" Thalon shouted, shaking him. "We've got to go," he urged, motioning to the open doors at the end of the ramp.

Birk snapped to alertness.

The world around him slowly returned to focus. The screams and cheers from the audience, the contestants running past him, and Thalon's hand on his back forced him to the present. Closing the line, they ran onto the arena floor.

"It's Birk," screamed Brynn, jumping up in her seat, "and Thalon is next to him."

"I see Ravenshire and Thalon," Talbot squinted, "but where's your brother?"

"Before we begin the trials," Sable's voice boomed across the stadium, bringing the crowd to a hush, "I'm delighted to introduce an extraordinary competitor in today's events." The crowd grew silent in anticipation; a gate to Birk's right slid open, smoke curling from its sides. "The last of my beloved brother, the Protector's descendants, and my Royal Champion—Grey the Great!"

The smoke cleared, and Grey swaggered forth. He raised his arms to the people's applause and resounding stomps.

Zara eyed her mother with suspicion.

Shayvonne clutched Talbot's hand. "Something is off. How did she know he was the Protector's descendant?"

"Who cares? He looks amazing!" Brynn shouted. "That's my brother!" she squealed, jumping from her seat.

On the tournament floor, Birk's face lit. *He was safe. He was here.* Grey paraded back and forth, ramping the audience. Birk desperately tried to catch his attention.

"And you think I'm the arrogant one," Thalon mocked. "*Grey the Great?*"

Birk ignored him, but agreed; Grey's behavior was aberrant. *Maybe this was part of his strategy—playing the crowds, revealing his identity to Lady Ironspire to build trust?* It wasn't until Grey joined the candidates in line that Birk became concerned.

Standing a few soldiers away, Grey focused on the Gauntlet, refusing one assuring glance back at him or the others.

"Your focus is distracted," Thalon scolded. "Keep your head in the game; your teammates are counting on you."

Thalon was right. He didn't want to admit it, but his concerns about Birk's emotions for Grey were coming true. Birk's anxiety was taking over their mission. Ravenshire and the others were depending on him; whatever Grey was doing or not doing would have to wait.

"Weren't we relying on him to help us in the trials?" Ravenshire asked. "What'll we do now? It doesn't seem we'll be able to get his attention."

Birk swallowed hard, directing his attention forward. "We focus on the team we have; nothing has changed."

Everything changed.

The sound of trumpets blared, signaling the start of the competition. Grey exploded forward, a blur of motion, propelling toward the Gauntlet. Not far behind, Packington tried to catch up with him. With a glance upward, Grey took a quick assessment before launching into the air like a mountain lion, grabbing the middle of the swinging pendulum.

Wasting no time in his ascent, Grey climbed with the fluidity of a predator, scaling the massive machine with the same ease he did the trees of the forest. When he reached the top, the wind rushed through his hair, and the screaming crowd fueled him. Running across the top beam holding the monstrous machine together, a funnel of fire shot up at him, almost causing him to lose his balance. Leaping into the air, he disappeared—diving into the next layer of the gauntlet.

Packington swung back and forth on the pendulum, unable to maintain Grey's pace. Reaching behind his back, he pulled out one of the

Azure's crossbows and shot an arrow attached to a retractable leather cord—one of the engineer's inventions. The arrow looped around the top beam, anchoring into a knot, allowing him to swing from the first axe and pull himself to the top.

Another flame shot into the sky. Narrowly avoiding it, Packington slid down the back end of the structure.

Taking Packington's lead, several academy members shot their crossbows into the air, mimicking his approach. Twelve cords wrapped, crossed, and entangled around the beam, each other, and the axes, all at once, creating a catastrophe. Only a few lucky competitors in the lead were swift enough to swing out of harm's way—before the carnage started.

The pendulum snapped and sliced the remaining cords, sending the Academy trainees flying. Some collided in mid-air, and others were thrown into the stands. The majority plummeted to the ground, flailing, trying to grab hold of the swinging handles as they sped toward the rotating saws on the ground.

Birk raised his hand to summon a wind or have the ground rise to meet them. Thalon quickly pushed his arm down and stood in front of him. Blocking his view, Thalon held his wrists in place. They grimaced at the screams—the sound of bodies sliced and ripped apart.

"Why didn't you let me help them?" Birk yelled.

Thalon raised his eyes from the ground, "You wouldn't have been able to prevent it; they were falling too fast."

"I could have tried," Birk ripped his wrists from Thalon's grip and shoved him in the chest.

"You'd have been eliminated *and still unable to save them*. You have others to protect. They need you to get through this alive," Thalon reminded. "These deaths aren't on you."

Peeking down the line, only a few academy members remained. The majority were exiled elves, along with their party of five. Squaring his shoulders, Birk took a steadying breath.

Locking eyes with Thalon, they held each other's gaze. "I want you and Hyacinth to lead the elves through," Birk rallied.

Thalon shook his head, "I'm not leaving you behind."

"We both know you see a safe way through this; you and the elves have enhanced skills the rest of us don't. The three of us will hold you back," Birk ordered.

"Do you have a plan for the rest of you?" Thalon asked, concealing his concern.

"I'm working on it," Birk admitted.

Another long stare passed between them until Thalon gripped Birk's shoulder. "I'll wait for you on the other side of the wall. You have ten minutes, and then I'm coming back. No one gets left behind."

Emboldened, Thalon addressed the gathering elves. "Elves, follow me if you want to live."

The elves, encouraged, followed Thalon toward the base of the pendulum. "One at a time," he instructed, "slow and careful." Leaping, he landed on the flat base of the swaying blade, allowing it to carry him forward instead of resisting the motion. Holding onto its middle, he looked back at Birk, giving him one more reassuring glance.

Thalon's instincts kicked in, vaulting off the first blade, he seamlessly transitioned to the next as it swept toward him. Time slowed, and Thalon repeated this execution with each oncoming blade. The elves behind him emulated his every move, giving the crowd the illusion of a parade of switching dance partners. With precision, each landed safely on the other side.

"I can't do that," Biddy confided softly, the color draining from his face. Ravenshire nodded in agreement.

"I know. We have to pass through the hard way," Birk directed, leading them to the entrance.

"There's always the option to forfeit," Ravenshire suggested, motioning to the remaining players who made this choice. "Grey is still bound to win, with or without us."

"I don't think we can count on Grey right now," Birk said, hating himself for saying it aloud. "And we can't leave Thalon and Hyacinth alone."

"I'd rather die than let down my mum," Biddy admitted. "I'm not doing this for me."

The gauntlet grew more menacing with every step closer. Birk felt the pressure from his friends to find a way through; their lives were dependent on his decisions.

Even though the rules state you'll get eliminated if you use magic, that's only if they can detect it.

You have the potential to encompass the magic of all of the Thirteen.

Whose magic would be helpful? Whose powers were discreet and inconspicuous?

"*Everything has an order to it; you only have to figure out what makes it tick. Piecing it together becomes simple once you've accomplished this,*" Birk cited aloud.

Aunt Edi, of course!

"What?" Biddy asked.

"It's something my aunt used to say to me," Birk paced back and forth in front of the gauntlet. "I need a minute."

Birk didn't know how his aunt's powers worked, but he remembered she had the insight to assemble and deconstruct any object. If anyone wielded the ability to detect a pattern, it'd be her. However, he didn't know how to summon her sight.

He wrapped his hand around his mother's bracelet; it was the closest connection to his aunt on him. He hoped the bond between twins would be enough. *Aunt Edi, I need your help; please give me your vision.*

Whispering it repeatedly in his head, he willed her to hear his call.

Then he had an idea. Faunwood had shared that he was capable of communing with anyone or anything connected to the source.

Edi was connected. She was the first. *What if he could partner with Driftstone to channel his request to her?*

He kept one hand on the bracelet and the other on the earth, and tried again.

He sifted through his memories to strengthen his connection: her magic mothering, their bond over books, all the little intentional and thoughtful items she curated to make him smile. Suddenly—*Birk*—her voice was in his head—*Open your eyes!*

Birk gasped, and his eyes sprang open. Everything looked different.

A canvas of different-colored geometric shapes blanketed his vision, cataloging designs and archiving notes about each object, organic and man-made. Her sight allowed him to dissect mechanics and biology, outlining the operations of anything he inspected.

What a magnificent lens through which you view the world. "Thank you, Aunt Edi!"

Crouching onto his knees and jumping in the air, he ran the length of the gauntlet back and forth, looking like a lunatic. He examined every inch, laughing with delight. Able to detect each blade's speed, trajectory, and breadth of its swing—Birk solved the challenge.

"Should we be worried?" Biddy shared a concerned glance with Ravenshire.

"I can see the pattern," Birk laughed again, running over to them. "I've figured out how to pass the gauntlet."

"How?" Ravenshire asked.

"We're going to walk," he declared enthusiastically, prompting another concerned glance. "It sounds crazy, but I need you both to trust me."

Birk ripped his sleeve and tore off a long piece of cloth from his gambeson.

"Erm . . . what are you doing?" Biddy asked.

"Blindfolds for the both of you," he instructed, handing one to each of them.

"You want us to do this blindfolded?" Ravenshire pulled at his ear. "Birk, I trust you, but this asks a lot."

Placing a hand on each of their shoulders, Birk explained his plan. "I need you to concentrate on everything I tell you to do. We have to move together in tandem. If you see the dangers before you, you may hesitate, and even a second behind me is too late."

Blindfolds on, Birk walked them to the center entrance. The axe swung by them, causing their bodies to shake. Positioning between his teammates, Birk grabbed their clammy hands and squeezed them tight. "When I say forward, take one step forward, not two. If I say jump, it's straight up, not forward or back. Block everything out except my voice."

The crowd went silent. Everyone's eyes were on them. Birk studied the pendulum again; as the first blade swung past them, he shouted, "Forward." Progressing one step, they waited until the second blade glided clear of them, "Forward and Jump." With a slight push in the air to help them with their weight, they jumped in time to avoid two circular blades crossing the ground underneath them.

"Forward," Birk yelled, stepping behind the third blade.

The fourth blade sailed by them faster than the rest, grazing the tip of the gambeson where Biddy's belly stuck out, inducing a whimper. The fourth blade was the trickiest. It released a surprise fifth blade on its ascension when it zoomed upward—sending it hurtling back. They needed to wait for the fifth blade to pass, with only seconds to move forward before the third and fourth returned.

"This is the last one—when I shout, take two steps forward, as fast as you can—jump—and one more leap ahead to exit." Their palms sweated in his grip. "Are you ready?" he shouted when the fifth blade barreled toward them. "Forward, forward—jump—forward!"

They made it!

Stumbling to the ground in front of the wall, Biddy ripped his blindfold off and hugged Birk. Ravenshire vomited.

Birk leaned against the wall, not expecting it to slide open; he stumbled into the next room. Before he could blink, Thalon grabbed him around the waist, pulling him to the side. "Move carefully," he whispered.

Hyacinth slid against the inside wall and reached out to guide Ravenshire and Biddy inside, motioning them to stand with their backs against the entrance. A towering metal dragon hovered over them, steam pouring from its snout. At its base lie several burned bodies, some alive, all lying motionless.

"I'm glad you're still with us," Thalon said, "I believed in you."

"It's good to see you too," Birk replied, relieved. "You waited?"

"I told you I wasn't going to leave you."

"What is this?" Ravenshire asked, horrified.

Hyacinth pointed to a line on the floor, "The moment someone steps in front of this line, the dragon is activated. It's magically enhanced to detect any movement, unleashing a torrent of flames."

"It's fast, too. They tried distracting it by having multiple people cross simultaneously," Thalon motioned to the results on the ground.

"There has to be a way to pass it; otherwise, everyone would be trapped in here," stated a blonde female elf standing on the other side of Thalon.

To her right, an academy trainee chimed in, "Most of them bypassed it by going above," he motioned, prompting them to all look up. *That's how Grey and Packington made it across*, Birk thought. "Is anyone else coming? We don't have much room left in here."

"We're the last three," Birk confirmed, "the others forfeited."

"So, it's the seven of us," the elf observed. "How do we do this?"

"Can the dragon rotate its head backward?" Birk asked.

"Only right and left, up and down, and forward," Hyacinth replied. "Why?"

"If we can't go over and we can't pass through, what about going under?" Birk contemplated.

Thalon cocked his head, giving him a quizzical look. "What are you thinking?"

Birk grinned. "I have an idea, but, Ravenshire and Biddy, I'll need your help." Biddy groaned.

Since Ravenshire carried the only enchanted shield, he approached the dragon slowly with the armament over his head. Biddy followed him, his arms wrapped tight around Ravenshire's waist, shadowing his moves. The dwarf was required for the second part of the plan.

"Slow steps," Birk instructed. Ravenshire took a cautious step over the line.

The dragon's eyes clicked as soon as the sole of his boot touched the ground. Spinning its head rapidly, it pelted a stream of fire on Ravenshire's location. Thrown by its force, it took Ravenshire a minute to adjust and hold the shield steady. Like a wave of water, the flames repelled off the shield, splashing across the chamber walls.

"Everybody stay on the ground," Thalon shouted, ducking in time to avoid his head being singed.

After taking a quick moment to ensure everyone was ok, Birk encouraged Ravenshire to continue. Gradual and measured steps, Biddy followed him, cringing as the flames sparked around them. The room boiled. Everyone knelt against the walls, trying to avoid the relentless spout of fire drowning the shield.

Dripping with sweat, Ravenshire called Birk, "I'm not sure I can hold much longer; my hands are slipping."

"You're almost there; only two more steps," Birk encouraged. "Biddy, get ready."

Birk knelt on the ground, his hand to the floor, behind the line, ready to do his part. Ravenshire stopped a few feet away from the dragon. They were lucky, the only thing enchanted to move was his head. His arms, tiring, shook under the weight of the full force of the dragon's blast, his black curls matted to his head in sweat.

"Birk, it has to be now; I'm losing it!" he shouted.

"Biddy, Go!" On Birk's command, Biddy sat on the ground. Ravenshire spread his legs wide. Birk slapped the floor, sending a burst of wind to push Biddy between Ravenshire's stretched extremities. Grabbing the soldier by his ankles when he passed, Biddy flipped Ravenshire onto his back—pulling him with him—they slid under the dragon and slammed into the back wall.

The crowd erupted with cheers and laughter. From their view, it appeared the dwarf made an acrobatic move *without* the aid of magic.

Moving quickly, Ravenshire hoisted Biddy up the back of the dragon. Pulling himself to the top, the dwarf took out his axe and beheaded the monster with one mighty swing. The beast's metallic skull fell to the arena floor with a clang, moving the audience to hysterics.

Infused by the people's enthusiasm, Biddy raised his axe into the air, resulting in thunderous applause and laughter from his teammates.

"Biddy, the Dragon Slayer," Hyacinth yelled.

Thalon grinned, offering his hand to help Birk off the floor. "Ingenious! Impressive leadership."

Birk blushed.

They knelt by the burnt and moaning bodies of elves on the floor. "How do we help them?"

"The Azure will bring healers in once we pass," the academy trainee informed. "We have to keep moving; time is running out!"

"This is inhumane," Birk said aloud.

Thalon placed his hand on Birk's back.

"This is Driftstone," he replied in a lowered voice. "Right or wrong, this is what our mothers protected us from. Let us trust Ironspire's healers will know what to do. If we hope to make change, we must keep moving."

Birk placed his hand on Thalon's knee, and an understanding passed between them. Nodding, he stood and addressed the others, "We move forward with caution; no one else gets hurt."

The wall slid open, revealing the third portion of the gauntlet.

On the ground, where forty tiles once glowed with color, fifteen remained. Portions of the arena floor were missing, revealing a deadly fall into the rapids miles below. Their objective was to reach the other side by avoiding unsupported tiles.

"I guess the good news about being in the back is everyone else did the hard work for us." Ravenshire commented, kneeling, "We can now peek underneath the tiles."

Lying on their bellies, they could see hovering mechanical circles supporting ten of the tiles. Quickly memorizing a layout, Thalon turned to Birk. "I've mapped out a path, but it will require some jumping. Nothing we can't handle. We should move in three groups to help each other if one group gets into trouble."

Birk nodded. He didn't have any better ideas, and it appeared pretty straightforward. Hyacinth and Biddy would go first, allowing Thalon to guide them. He'd follow with the blonde elf and the academy trainee; Birk and Ravenshire would bring up the rear.

The first row was easy; they only needed to step onto it. From there, they'd need to do a diagonal jump to a tile on the second row, walk

forward two tiles to the fourth, and make another diagonal jump to the fifth—it became more complicated.

With no supporting tiles on the sixth row, their most significant jump would be to the seventh, followed by a walk-through to the eighth and a step onto firm ground.

"Right, let's get it over with," Birk said.

Making it to the fifth row without issue, Biddy and Hyacinth paused to assess the gap for the long jump. "You can do this, Biddy," Hyacinth encouraged, "all you need to do is get a running start. I'll show you how it's done first, then I'll be able to help you from the other side."

"Wait!" Birk shouted. "Let Ravenshire run through and join you. If Biddy jumps short, he's too big for you to pull him up on your own. He'll drag you over. No offense, Biddy."

"None taken. She's as light as a feather on a diet, and I'm a boulder in a cotton race," he teased, lightening the mood.

All in agreement, Ravenshire zipped by Thalon's group to catch up with Hyacinth. One by one, they were able to cross the distance, *including Biddy*, much to everyone's surprise. With everything going according to plan, Thalon moved his group forward.

Birk stepped onto the first tile. The support underneath the foundation shifted.

Tearing forward, Birk made the diagonal jump just in time to watch the tile he was standing on crumble into the river. Another vibrational shift. The tile in the second row cracked under his feet. Panicking, he shouted out to Thalon, "RUN!"

Thalon turned to his group, positioned in the fifth row, and yelled, "We have to move now! Go, Go, GO!"

The blonde elf didn't hesitate; leaping across the sixth row, she landed on the seventh and ran to join the others. The academy trainee jumped next, making it to the seventh row. Dashing across the eighth tile, it disappeared under his feet, sending him screaming and plummeting toward the river below.

"What's happening?" Ravenshire shouted over the chaos.

"We're the last ones; we've taken too long; they're trying to rush us," Hyacinth yelled back, hurrying away from the edge.

Ignoring the collapsing tiles, Birk attempted to reach Thalon, who had just leaped from the fifth row. Thalon's target, the tile in the seventh row, started fading. As Thalon's feet touched the surface, he catapulted back into the atmosphere. Spreading his arms wide, he caught the wind, flipped, and landed on all fours on the other side.

Scrambling back to his feet, Thalon rushed into action. There was no way Birk could clear three rows on his own. He grabbed Hyacinth's crossbow from her hands and shouted orders as he ran to the edge. "Biddy, wrap your arms around my waist; Ravenshire, wrap yours around him; I'll need you as my anchors."

Everyone jumped and mobilized to the orders.

Aiming his crossbow at Birk, their eyes locked across the chasm—they were out of time.

The foundation beneath Birk disappeared.

Yielding to gravity, the world around Birk blurred with speed. He hurtled downward, the air whistling, disorienting him and drowning out Thalon's screams. An arrow flew past his head.

From his peripheral, he spied something trailing the arrow.

There's a cord attached to it!

Thrusting his arm into the air, he nearly missed snagging it in time. Swiftly wrapping it around his forearm, he fell—and the cord reached the limit of its stretch.

The full accelerating force of his body coming to a halt yanked Thalon forward to the open rim and forcefully swung Birk back. The cord burned their skin as it rushed through their tightly gripped fingers. Hyacinth and the blond elf dived forward, throwing their arms around Biddy and Ravenshire, attempting to keep Thalon steady.

They braced themselves.

Swinging wildly in the air, Birk pulled the group with every oscillation, fighting to find a way to steady himself with the air currents. Arm

over arm, everyone worked as a team. Inch by inch, they pulled and hauled Birk up. Once within reach, Thalon snatched him under his arms and heaved him to safety.

Breathless, they collapsed, entangled on the ground.

"You've got to stop falling for me. People are talking," Thalon cheekily elbowed Birk.

Releasing a strained laugh, Birk collapsed his head against Thalon's chest.

"I hate to break this little reunion," the little blonde elf nudged, "but we've still got one challenge ahead of us."

The adrenaline of the moment slowly gave way to the enormity of the ordeal, leaving their minds bordering on fevered hilarity.

"Who is *she*?" Birk asked, snickering with exhaustion.

"I don't know," Thalon shrugged, tickled, "someone whose life I saved," inducing Birk to laugh even harder.

Helping each other off the ground, they turned around to the moving pit of sand. All six stared motionless into the pit. Lacking energy or will, no one wanted to make the first move.

"Sand vipers," Biddy noted.

Calmly retrieving her bow, Hyacinth loaded it in silence, aimed it at the moving sand, and released a flurry of arrows into anything that stirred.

"Defunct Vipers," she declared.

Everyone stood silent.

Ravenshire emitted the first snerk, followed by a snort from Biddy, until one by one, all of them succumbed to delirious howls of laughter. Doubling over, they toppled into each other's arms and onto the ground. Depleted of energy and amused with themselves, they were grateful to be alive. Clinging to one another, they made their way across the finish line, oblivious to the crowd surrounding them.

Including the little blonde elf—no one knew.

FIFTY

Primal Instincts

Brynn was distraught. She laughed when she witnessed her elder brother stride out into the arena, exuding an air of over-the-top bravado. Never one to take things too seriously, she assumed it was his flagrant attempt at mocking the trials. Now she wasn't so sure.

At the outset, she stood and cheered when her brother cleared the obstacles in record time—not realizing how deadly the gauntlet would be for everyone else. He'd made it appear simple. But when she watched other competitors lose their lives, a rotten pit grew in her stomach.

Why hadn't Grey helped them? His defining characteristic, *as annoying as it was sometimes*, was his instinct to protect. Her brother didn't abandon others. *Ever.*

Granted, Thalon wasn't their favorite person, but Grey wouldn't be so cruel or indifferent as to hold grudges. And he certainly would never, ever leave Birk behind. It would be like ignoring herself or Shayvonne—unimaginable.

Birk was the first person who achieved what she and her mother couldn't; he opened Grey's heart to a glimpse of what life could be like without solitude. Her brother's gentle spirit carried a weight of sadness through the years. Ashamed at running from his family's slaughter, he still blamed himself for surviving.

When he arrived home with Birk, he was different. The melancholy often stirring in his eyes was absent. His posture was more confident. His energy zealous. He was extra tender, doting, and full of life; his laugh had never been so loud.

There was nothing—not trials, enemies, or forces of nature—Grey wouldn't plow through to protect Birk.

Something was wrong.

"I want to see Grey," Brynn declared, interrupting Shayvonne, who was attempting to rationalize Grey's behavior to Talbot and Xavier.

They didn't know Grey, and they didn't understand how much Birk and her brother meant to each other. They were afraid and rightfully upset.

"I'd like to see him myself," Talbot snapped, his tone rising. "You don't leave a man behind, particularly if you claim to *have feelings* for this man. I wasn't expecting these trials to be the dangerous part of this mission; if I'd been made aware of how brutal they were, I would've never allowed it."

"We were wise to send Ravenshire in with him," Xavier added, "at least *they* have each other's backs."

"If I were in your place, I'd be as angry as you are, but you need to understand this is just as upsetting for us," Shayvonne pleaded. "I know my son, and this isn't him . . . Grey is gentle and kind and . . ."

Talbot took her hands. "Enough," he said, his voice softening. "I believe you. I apologize if we've drawn the wrong conclusions. I'm just concerned because if Grey is compromised—things are worse than expected."

Brynn lacked patience for adults' conversations. Everyone talked too much and in circles. Grey required their help *now*; she didn't have time to debate or argue. She knew exactly what to do. Slipping out behind them, she made her way back toward the exit. She was going to need reinforcements.

Beneath the stadium, Birk was also seeking Grey. Marching through the corridors, any joy and camaraderie that had existed minutes ago had faded. Desperation was taking its place. The gravity of almost losing his life compelled him to uncover what was going on with Grey. It didn't matter if he wasn't himself; confronting him was the only way to figure out what was happening.

Thalon and Ravenshire chased him, warning him to be careful and begging him to stop, but Grey's indifference to their well-being was consuming him, *again*. When they crossed the finish line and Grey wasn't there, something inside him snapped. The realization that Grey didn't care enough to watch or be concerned sent him over the edge.

Birk's rage wasn't directed at Grey, *not exactly*; he was furious at whoever did this to him. He wanted answers.

Rounding a corner, he braked abruptly. Grey stood over a basin, his back to him, washing with a cloth. Birk's temper immediately melted at the sight of him.

Birk softly tapped his shoulder. "Grey?"

Grey jerked away with a flash of contempt.

Birk stepped back. "Grey, are you okay?"

"Why wouldn't I be?" he scoffed. There was no sign of softness in his face or acknowledgment between them. "I'm surprised to see your lot survived."

His words slapped. "We almost didn't. We almost lost our lives," Birk tried to pull out the compassion he knew was inside him. "*I almost died.*"

"Well, there's always the second round." He pushed Birk to the side.

Grabbing his arm, Birk pulled him back. "What's going on? Did Vincent and Sable do something to you?" Birk searched his face. "Or is this an act? Are you trying to push me away to protect us from something? If you're in there, even a small part of you, please show me."

Grey hesitated for a moment. A cruel smile crept into the corners of his face. Forcefully taking Birk's hand off him, he narrowed his eyes. "I don't know who you are or what insane obsession you have with me, but the next time you touch me, I promise you it will be the last."

Birk visibly shook.

Thalon inserted himself between them, placing his hand on Birk's chest, forcing him to look at him. "Let's go. You have your answers. I promise we'll sort it out later."

Leading Birk around Grey until he was safe with Ravenshire, Thalon circled back. "It's clear you're not in there right now, so I'm going to take it easy on you, but don't you dare mess with him."

Grey stepped forward, growling in Thalon's face. "Are you threatening me? Are you afraid I'm going to hurt your little boyfriend?"

Thalon's nostrils flared. Clenching his fists, he held Grey's stare. After a long pause between them, Thalon stepped back. "You've already hurt him, you ass!" Backing away, he glared, "If I *were* his boyfriend, I'd be an improvement over his current one."

Grey stared at Thalon walking away. "Watch your back out there," he warned. "I'm coming for you."

Outside, Brynn was fighting against the flow of the crowd, excitedly making their way back into the Colosseum. Realizing the second challenge was about to begin, she knew she wouldn't make it in time. Undeterred, she sprinted to the forest's edge, where help would be waiting.

Scanning the area to make sure she was alone, she howled into the trees. "I know you're out there," she cried into the forest. "We need you—Grey needs you!" A rustle sounded in the trees. A patch of white fur darted out, howling back at her. Winter licked her face, Brunt trailing behind.

Indigo strapped armor onto Birk's party, preparing them for the next event. Their usual strong and stoic face appeared concerned.

"What's wrong, Indigo?" Birk drew the rest of his party's attention. "You're worried about something, aren't you?"

"The only thing I'm worried about is ensuring I keep all of you alive," Indigo dismissed.

"No," Thalon commented, "there's something else."

All eyes looked at the warrior, expectant and nervous. Sighing, Indigo shook their head, "Listen, these trials are different than any we've

held. They've always been dangerous, but not as deadly as today's games. Vincent was up all last night, ordering last-minute changes."

"Give me one good reason we shouldn't forfeit right now," Thalon demanded. "And please don't tell me because of Grey; he's proven he'll be fine."

"Hyacinth and I have no choice but to continue," Biddy confided, "our families are depending on it."

Ravenshire turned to Thalon, "We can't leave them on their own."

Thalon slumped his shoulders.

"We also need Lady Ironspire's help for the quest," Birk reminded him.

"*Do we?* We have Zara; she'll leave with us. As far as I can tell, Lady Ironspire is conspiring to kill us all," Thalon argued.

"You'll need Sable's help for your quest *and* her approval," Indigo inserted. "You don't want her as an enemy. If she views you as a threat, *which she will if you take her daughter*, she'll send the full power of the Azure army after you."

"Is there *one* sane original Magic-Born left? No wonder Driftstone is falling apart," Thalon vented.

"She may not be presenting her best self at the moment, but Lady Ironspire has more knowledge and experience than anyone. Only she can provide the answers you seek to continue your quest." Indigo shared, "There is a way to gain her influence—to do that, you *must* play her game."

"And what game is that? The trials?" Birk asked.

Indigo lowered their voice, "The trials are a part of it, yes, but she *is* testing you. If she identified Grey, you should assume she is aware of your identities. There is no one she trusts less than her siblings, and you're an extension of them. You need to prove you're not her enemies."

The sound of trumpets startled them, signaling it was time for their entrance. Indigo rushed them to line up. "Listen, we don't have much time. I wish I knew more, but I can only tell you the rest of the tourna-

ment has changed. Only twelve contestants are left, and the six of you need to work together to win this round, or you'll be eliminated."

When they stepped onto the tournament floor, the atmosphere was ripe with unease. On both sides of the arena, a three-tiered stone structure with a flag at its top was assembled in front of them. The challenge was straightforward: capture the opposing team's flag.

They positioned Hyacinth and Ingrid, *who they learned was the blond elf's name*, at the top to serve as their archers; Biddy stood at the base's center, hugging his axe. Fit with a thin layer of armor for this challenge, Thalon stood out front, surveying the opposition. Not far behind him, Birk and Ravenshire stood to his sides, their swords ready.

Across the tournament floor stood Grey, opposite Thalon, out front. Refusing the armor they offered, he carried only his spear. Beating his chest with one fist, he paced in circles, focused on Thalon. Behind him, Packington and a thick girl from the academy named Grilda flexed and stretched. Two bearded archers, appearing to be brothers, and a face-painted bald contestant from the academy completed their entourage.

Birk's team wore their apprehension. Their opponents' towering physicality outmatched them. "Remember, strength isn't everything," he shouted, attempting to rally their spirits. "They'll try to overpower us, but we have an advantage. We've already survived one challenge by working as a team, whereas they've yet to work as a unit. It'll be easy to pick them apart. Focus your energies on separating them, and they'll fall."

The ground beneath them shook. "What's happening?" Biddy yelled, steadying against the fortress wall.

Thalon and Grey both took a step back. The center of the Colosseum opened, revealing the ravine leading to the river underneath them. An open-air chasm now stood between the teams. Simultaneously, circles of sand swirled on both sides of the arena floor.

Rising from the ground in response to the trumpet's blare, mechanical replicas of Azure soldiers sprang into action, six on each side.

Distracted, both teams prioritized their new threat. Biddy, the crowd favorite, was the first to make a move. Kneeling to the ground, he flung his axe at the three sentinels closest to the base, severing them all at the ankles and sending them crashing into the sand. Retrieving his axe, he hacked and demolished their remaining bits to pieces, eliminating any chance of recovery.

The stands went wild, eliciting a raised eyebrow and nod from Lady Ironspire in the box.

Hyacinth and Ingrid, taking advantage of Biddy's opening, diverted their attention to the other team, who were still deciding their first move. Targeting one archer, the young women vaulted a line of arrows, piercing one of the brother's shoulders. Two other arrows perforated his arm and leg. Effective but not fatal. Falling from the opposing fortress wall, he was eliminated from the game.

His brother, alarmed at the speed and accuracy of the surprise attack, took cover. A second wave of arrows hurtled toward him.

On the ground, Birk, Ravenshire, and Thalon stood in a back-to-back formation, facing off against the three remaining advancing soldiers on their side. When the mechanical warriors charged, Ravenshire sliced his blade through the air. With a swift parry, he deflected a blow aimed at his side, countering it with a thrust that found its mark. Impaling the armor, he continued to charge it with his shield until the entity dislodged from his sword with a clang.

Birk transitioned from defense to offense, dancing around his opponent and exploiting his bulky frame with multiple quick strikes. Thrusting and slashing at every opening, he lanced and slit every enchanted limb until the Azure imposter toppled into a heap of metal and circuits.

Talbot and Xavier rose in the stands, screaming to their companions.

"Those are my boys!" Talbot beamed. "For Balincia!" Xavier cheered.

Thalon held his ground and honed in on the movements of their final threat. He waited, timing his final assault. Using the weight and strength of his body, he jumped in the air, swinging the sword above his head;

unleashing a cry of war, he landed a fatal blow, ripping through the fake Azure's neck and chest.

After exchanging a quick celebratory smile, they turned to see how their opponents were faring.

The three sentinels nearest Grey and Packington lay at their feet. Grilda had laid waste to the fourth. The painted-faced academy warrior was on the ground, overthrown by the remaining two metal Azure. Turning their attention toward the archer, they scaled the wall.

Rushing to his teammate's defense, Packington grabbed the enchanted opponents by their ankles and heaved them to the ground. Before the circuited sentinels could gain their footing—Grey pounced. In one savage and primitive movement, he ripped their arms and heads from their bodies, tossing them into the stands.

Down two team members, Grey raised his head. Intent on closing the gap, he locked eyes with Thalon and roared. With the speed and power of a snow tiger, he charged forward, preparing to jump the open expanse between them.

A humming and whirling sound interrupted him.

A wall of flying steel wyverns rose from the direction of the river, filling the air. Grey slid to a stop, catching himself on his back arm. Jumping to his feet, he hurled his spear before the blockade was complete—never losing sight of his target.

Distracted by the miniature flying dragons, Thalon didn't see the incoming spear broaching the Wyvern wall and flying directly toward his temple. Moments before impalement, the full weight of Ravenshire hit Thalon in the back, knocking him to the ground. The spear bounced off the Balincian's shield with such force it sent him flying backward.

Collecting themselves off the ground, Thalon's face flushed with anger. "He's trying to kill me!"

Birk's stomach dropped.

An axe flew above them, drawing their attention back to the battle. Biddy was attempting to take down the flying beasts. Smaller than the soldiers, the creatures made up for their size by swarming them in numbers. Their sharpened tails flicked in the air, curling and striking,

autonomous from the reptilian-circuited bodies to which they were attached. Ravenshire gripped his shield over his head.

Swatting and batting with swords, both teams attempted to fight off an aerial attack.

A scream came from behind them.

Ingrid fell from the defensive wall, gouged through the chest by a bladed tailpiece. Biddy redirected his attention and released a battle cry. Scrambling to Hyacinth's defense, he carved a path through the creatures in his ascent to her side.

With no room for error or space to retreat, the warrior's swords, spears, and arrows generated a deafening noise, knocking the threats from the sky.

Another scream, this time from the other end of the arena.

The remaining archer from the opposing team was pulled into the air, flailing and kicking. Grabbing several arrows at once, the bearded trainee reached up and stabbed his antagonist, causing it to whirl and spin out of control. Tumbling to the ground, too close to the edge, they slid over the precipice and into the ravine.

Plucking a wyvern from the air that had flown too close to him, Grey wrapped one hand around its throat and the other around its tail and ripped the creature in half. His unshackled bellow raised the hairs on every spectator's arm.

Two of the dragons remained. One dived toward Birk. Aiming her bow, Hyacinth released her final arrow, penetrating the vile thing through the eye and sending it crashing to the ground at his feet.

On the other side, with a boost from Grilda, Packington vaulted into the air, ending the final threat with one last decisive hit.

Reeling from the assault, no one was prepared for Grey. While their guard was down, he cleared the jump over the divide.

The sound of bones cracking whipped everyone to attention.

Grey had slammed into Thalon with the force of a raging, long-haired bull. Skipping across the hard dirt floor like a stone, Thalon slid without control, pummeling Biddy against the fortress wall.

Jeering and booing, the audience sprang to their feet.

Zara ran to the edge of the box and clutched the handrail. Vincent smiled.

Even Packington and Grilda froze—horrified by the sheer viciousness and brutality of the blow.

Bending to retrieve his spear, Grey failed to notice Ravenshire, closest to him, coming from behind. Sensing the shuffling of his boots against the sand, Grey rounded on the young soldier with the speed of a viper, grabbing both sides of the shield as he charged him. He lifted him off the ground in a deflective spin and flung Birk's childhood friend into the wall barricading the stands.

Grey was now channeling all of his powers and making no attempt to hide them.

Hyacinth was out of arrows. Ravenshire discarded. Biddy was holding a bleeding and broken Thalon. The only thing standing in Grey's way was Birk.

"Grey, Stop!" Birk pleaded. "Don't do this; I don't want to hurt you."

Grey paused, cracked his neck, and stared at Birk with amusement. "You think you can hurt me?"

"You may not remember, but I can put you down if necessary." Birk's voice wavered, shaking in its delivery. He wasn't sure it was true, but he wouldn't allow Grey to hurt anyone else.

Birk neither backed up nor retreated. He compelled Grey to face him, made him remember, and stayed still because he believed, with all his heart, Grey wouldn't hurt him.

When the spear closed in on his face, Birk realized his error.

This wasn't something words or hearts could fix. They weren't in a training exercise in the cave; Grey had taken off the gloves. With a quick flick of his fingers, Birk threw the spear back toward him, passing it swiftly over his head as a warning and dropping it into the river below.

"You really don't want to hurt me, do you?" Grey mocked.

"Not if I can help it."

"That's why you'll lose," Grey crouched low. His sights on Birk, his muscles rippled throughout his body, a wound spring. Exploding forward, he propelled from the arena floor.

With little time to react, Birk ripped a piece of ground from beneath them, flinging it between them and knocking Grey from the air. Summoning the winds, Birk shook the foundations of the Colosseum, stirring the crowd into a panicked frenzy. Rocks and debris circled him—a cyclone of elemental chaos. Extending his arms, he directed the forces of nature at Grey, who was already back on his feet and trying to attack Birk for the second time.

Please don't make me hurt you.

Birk knew he was holding back. He feared he'd push Grey over the edge and into the ravine if he lost control. The potential impact on bystanders compounded his worry. He considered calling down lightning, but Birk was concerned about the blast's damage. He was too inexperienced to harness such precise control.

Grey was right; I'm going to lose.

He would tire first; he was *already* exhausted. The moment he wavered, Grey would seize the opportunity. If Birk were unwilling to hurt him, they'd all fall.

Zara had witnessed enough. She could no longer stand there and do nothing. Something was wrong with the bear, and Birk's life was in imminent danger. This trial differed from prior competitions; she was terrified, she knew who was behind it. "Mother, you need to step in and stop this," she demanded.

"And why would I do that?" A small smile formed on Sable's lips. Vincent stood behind her, his ringed hand on her shoulder. "I think the people need to see this."

"They . . . they're using magic . . . it's explicitly against the rules," Zara pointed out, grounding her argument on her mother's legislation. "Intervene and eliminate them before things spiral out of control and they endanger our citizens. You're the only one who can."

Sable's face made a sharp turn toward her daughter. "If you were so concerned about everyone's safety, why did *you* bring them here?"

Zara swallowed, taking a step back. "You knew?"

"Did you think I wouldn't recognize the perfect likeness to my lost brother? He resembles Farren even more than you resemble me."

Studying the smug face on Vincent, things clicked inside Zara's mind. "Why did you sponsor him?"

Lifting her chin, Sable directed her gaze toward the trials. "What else was I to do after your little speech? You gave me the means necessary to prove to our people why we can't trust anyone's magic but mine." She paused and added, "I should thank you."

"It was you who put your friends in this position," Vincent reminded her. "Your mother won't appear a villain now when she recedes from your impulsive declarations. The unleashed beast and his terrified boyfriend will remind everyone what unchecked power can do."

Zara stared at Grey, horrified. "What did you do to him?"

"All it took was a little truth spell for Grey to reveal everything to me," she boasted. "I gave his feral abilities a little push, his memories a little wipe, and took away his conscience for good measure."

"It's fascinating. You're witnessing your friend's most primal instincts." Vincent said, running his slimy fingers down Sable's arm. "Imagine if our engineers duplicated him, adding our own blended concoction to ensure loyalty, of course. We'd not only have the largest army in Driftstone but an unconquerable one."

"This is why the Azure hasn't stepped in!" Zara exclaimed. "You've ordered them not to intervene. You made the trials deadlier at the cost of the young lives in *your* academy."

"One day, you'll learn the cost for the greater good," Sable dismissed. "I wanted to assess their full capabilities. The stakes needed to be high, so your friends felt threatened—bringing the audience along." Facing her daughter, she emphasized, "More importantly, I needed *you* to see how easy it was for them to turn on each other just as my siblings did to me. All it took was a little nudge."

"This isn't the same. You didn't nudge Grey; you *poisoned* him. You don't get to create lies to reinforce your conspiracies. They aren't your siblings *or your enemies*. If Grey revealed everything, you should know

they came to protect us. Didn't he share the visions of the arcanivores and Morvana?"

"Don't be a foolish child; you've been manipulated into believing that. These boys used their magics against you, convincing you that you have powers of your own," Sable laughed. "You've always been insecure about my gifts not being passed down to you. They used this to their advantage to infiltrate our city. Morvana is trapped in the Under; she can't hurt us from there."

Zara backed away from her mother. "It's you who have been manipulated by corrupting influences," she spat, glaring at Vincent. "If you don't intervene, I will."

Pushing Vincent out of the way, Zara rushed to exit the box. Two Azure attempted to follow her. Lady Ironspire shook her head. "Let her go. She can't do anything; let her face the consequences of truth. Our extended family is not to be trusted."

Circling outside the Colosseum, Brynn searched for the tunnels used by the contestants to enter the tournaments. Riding on the back of Brunt, she found a heavily guarded gate, with ten Azure posted at its entrance.

"Halt! You're traveling in the wrong direction," one of the Azure called out. "No one is allowed back here. Return to the forests."

Brynn sighed, "I need to see my brother. He's in the arena. I'm the only one who can stop what's happening inside."

The soldiers drew their swords, standing in defense. "Apologies, miss, but you've misunderstood. If you don't change direction, we'll be forced to take you into custody."

Brynn shrugged and leaned down into Winter's ear. "I tried to do this the easy way. Try not to hurt them too badly."

While Brynn and her animal companions paved their way through the soldiers, Birk was struggling for his life in the arena. Drenched in sweat, his power was waning. Grey, angrier with every step, resisted the forces

against him. Birk took a step back, trying to gain distance, and his heel landed on a rolling piece of debris.

He stumbled.

It was the briefest of moments. It was also the only opening Grey needed.

Using his massive frame to tackle Birk, he subdued him with his sheer size, knocking the breath from his lungs. Seizing his prey in a vice-like grip, Grey snatched Birk off the ground, suspended him in the air by his neck, and violently slammed him back down again.

Birk's ears rang after his head collided with the ground.

He couldn't think. He couldn't feel. He couldn't move. Pulled into the air again, he hung limp, his limbs unable to coordinate or respond to the velocity of the attack. Grey's hand circled his throat. Birk begged him to wake.

Thwip! An arrow sailed past them, diverting Grey's attention. *Thwip! Thwip! Thwip!* Three more flew in rapid succession from the opposite side of the playing field, all landing in the arm he was using to hold Birk aloft.

"Let him go!" Packington yelled. "This isn't the way of the Azure." Grilda stood beside him, their crossbows aimed and ready.

Grey released Birk, allowing him to drop to the ground with a thud. Turning to the threat, he ripped the arrows from his arms, unleashing another roar.

A swift flurry of white came zipping through the air behind him, grabbing Birk's attention. Thalon was awake—transformed into the Ashendrake. Popping into his human form, he landed on Grey's back. Wrapping his thighs around his waist, he boxed his ears repeatedly, sending Grey into a spinning mountain of rage.

Reaching behind him, Grey grabbed Thalon by the collar, flipping him into the air. Another POP! Thalon was back into Ashendrake's body, darting between Grey's legs. Snapping back and forth between his two forms, he zoomed in and out, landing punches and darting away.

Grey was in a frenzy, eluding arrows and frantically trying to grab

hold of Thalon. Ravenshire, recovering from his landing, pulled Birk away from the assault. Regaining their balance, the group kept Grey on his feet, swinging between opponents and alternating attacks; they infuriated him even more.

In the heat of the brawl, Thalon made a quick miscalculation, flipping the tides back in Grey's favor. Flying too close to his opponent, Thalon transformed, hoping to catch Grey off guard with a sweeping kick to his feet. Making the transition earlier than he should have, Grey grabbed his ankle and threw him to the ground.

Thalon quickly rolled, avoiding Grey's heel—stomping where his head should have been.

He tried to push off the ground. He wasn't fast enough. Grey landed his fist against his face. The impact created a thunderclap across the arena, a brutal connection of bone meeting bone. Blow after punishing blow, Grey demonstrated no mercy.

Birk screamed, rushing forward, sword in hand. Thalon grunted and grasped for an escape.

Another arrow flew past Birk, planting into Grey's shoulder. This one was white—glowing with electric energy. A second one, similar to the first, struck Grey in the thigh, driving him back from Thalon. The first signs of real pain etched across his face.

Zara had entered the trials.

Gasps escaped from the crowd. The warrior princess took to the floor, her body glowing with the same white electric aura. Stepping forward, she pulled a light-forged whip from the air. Cracking it across the arena's earth, she shouted, "This ends now!"

Lady Ironspire leaned forward from her throne, "Zara . . . no!" Vincent's eyes darted between the witch and her daughter. A quick betraying glance of concern.

A moment of clarity crossed Sable's face, her daughter's magic awakening something within her. "I need to get down there; this has gone too far. What was I thinking?"

Vincent touched her bare shoulder. The blue sapphire on his ring

emitted a soft glow. "Zara is a traitor; she seeks to dethrone you through this mayhem. Let the people see who she is."

His words dripped with persuasive venom.

Lady Ironspire slipped back into her seat and relaxed. "You're right. She's brought this upon herself."

On the floor, Biddy and Ravenshire sprinted forward, using Zara's arrival as a chance to retrieve Thalon and drag him back to safety. Jumping at the princess's snap of the whip, they were relieved to find she kept Grey pacing back and forth. "This is my mother's doing," she declared to Birk without losing focus, "but I don't know how to break his enchantment."

"Well, whatever your magic is made of, it's the first thing provoking a response," Birk stated. "He's treated the other arrows like bee stings; your weapons seem to burn. I've been trying not to hurt him."

"I know, Birk. That's why I'm here," she confessed with a steady face. "I don't want to hurt him either, but we have to put him down. You need someone who can make the decisions you can't. You're too emotional right now."

Birk's heart sank; once again, his connection to Grey was being tested. By putting him down, she meant permanently, if necessary. The trained warrior was speaking.

He couldn't hold it against her. Zara was only thinking about the safety of her people, and right now, regardless of how they got here, Grey was the most significant threat to everyone on the field.

"Can you buy me some time? I'm convinced there's a way out of this; I need time to think," Birk begged her.

The tail of her whip snapped across Grey's chest, triggering him to howl in pain.

Zara nodded. She'd do what she could. "Figure it out, quick," she instructed. Pushing her palms into the air, she summoned a barrier between them and Grey, a white shield of protection.

Charging the shield, Grey bounced back from its vibration, causing Birk to flinch. Zara stood her ground. Shaking his head, Grey charged it again, *and again and again*, pushing them backward toward the others.

Waving her arms, Zara expanded the shield, covering the makeshift fortress and their companions. Huddled inside, they all trembled at every inflicted blow against the white wall of magic.

Ravenshire and Biddy clutched their weapons with their backs against the fort—shaking with each vibrating crash of Grey's arms. Thalon lay unconscious across Hyacinth's lap.

Zara's endurance was straining.

"Birk, I need a solution fast!" Zara yelled, stretching and tightening her arms to hold their position. "I can't hold out much longer."

Walking to the edge of the barrier, Birk placed his hand upon it, trying to find the face of the man he knew. "*Help me,*" he whispered. "*Help me find you.*" Slamming his fists against the white shield, Grey sent a ripple of energy back to Birk, causing his dragon-winged pendant to jump against his chest.

His pendant—the Protection of Truth— tied to his neck with a leather strap so he'd never forget it was there.

Gripping Talbot's gift, he knew what he had to do. "I've got a solution," he shouted.

"Great!" Zara shouted back, cringing when Grey beat on the barrier again. "Let's hear it."

Removing the jewelry, he held it out to Zara. "I have to place this around his neck."

"How are you going to get close enough? He'll snap your wrists before you get the chance."

A loud, sharp crack exploded behind them.

The massive gates guarding the entrance to the competitors burst open with a crash, bringing the crowd to a hush. Everyone turned to watch three shadowy figures emerge from the tunnel.

Striding confidently onto the tournament floor, a girl, riding a grizzly bear and accompanied by a giant white wolf, assessed the scene before her. Behind her, Indigo, Kodalt, and Alezander rushed in, keeping their

distance from the girl and Grey. Sliding off the bear, she commanded her brother's attention.

Birk's face broke into a grin. "I think we have our answer."

Abandoning his efforts with the wall, Grey shifted his attention to the new arrivals. Hypnotized, the animals and the girl drew him to them. Moving with caution, he centered in front of them. Winter howled into the air, immobilizing him.

"It's going to be ok, bear butt," Brynn assured her brother. "We're here now."

Brunt and Winter's eyes radiated green with the colors of the forest. A soft breeze blew through Grey's hair. Carried within it were the voices of his ancestors—the Protector, and his parents—guiding his spirit home. The wind sang to him, soothing his inner beast.

His familiar walked closer and lay on both sides of him, comforting him.

His resistance wavered. His eyes transformed and mirrored the beasts. His fierce demeanor softened. His shoulders slumped. Dropping to his knees, the last crumbs of his wildness swept away.

Approaching her brother, Brynn traced her fingers across his face, searching for a sign. He stared back, confused and afraid. He didn't recognize her. She placed her hands on his shoulders; her tears silently trickled onto him. He was subdued, but his mind was still lost to her.

Taking advantage of the quiet moment between them, Zara lowered her shield, allowing Birk to join them.

Kneeling before Grey, he hung the pendant around his neck with a trembling hand and kissed him softly on his cheek.

Its magic weaved through Grey's tangled memories and emotions—overwhelming his fractured mind. Grabbing Birk's hands for comfort, the warrior became a child.

Memories of loss, love, and longing were pulled from his consciousness. Candles drowning out the dark. His past unfolded before him: his parents' tragic demise, hunting with Brunt, running with Winter—his

little sister's laugh. He remembered Everglenn, his home, and the warmth of a new mother. And slowly his mind found its way to Birk.

These were his anchors, his family, his reason to live.

Gasping for air, his eyes returned to beautiful hues of brown. He greeted Birk with a dampened smile. Crumpling into his arms, Grey sobbed and heaved into his chest. He was finally his true self again.

FIFTY-ONE

VINCENT

Tearing through the crowds, Shayvonne and Talbot desperately tried to make their way to their family. Under Kodalt's orders, the Azure attempted to move an unwilling crowd out of the Colosseum. Alezander and Indigo tended to the wounded on the arena floor.

The trials were a disaster for everyone except Vincent, who watched from the box with glee. Everything was going according to plan, *his plans.*

Within a day, Zara accomplished everything Vincent conspired to do since the day she was born. Until her arrival, Vincent was the only one Lady Ironspire confided in and trusted. Working one's way to Royal Advisor had been no easy task; nothing was gained without patience.

Lady Ironspire was a powerful witch, but her scars blinded her.

Recognizing this early on, Vincent validated and played to her conspiracies and fears whenever she was in a room. It started small, complimenting her foresight in building a military or creating rumors of threats that would reach her ears. Whenever she aired her grievances aloud or shared her concerns with the court—he was there to confirm her thinking.

When others raised questions or doubts, Vincent challenged their loyalty to her. Sure, he made enemies along the way, but this was a small price to pay. Flattery, lies, and unquestioning loyalty to the ideas of the arrogant were a requirement for longevity as a Royal Advisor.

Then Zara was born.

Her conception surprised him, as did the quick bond Sable formed with her. Holding the baby in her arms, Sable's war with her past faded, as did her ideology. The child renewed her mother's faith in people, spawning a new approach to the future that didn't require Vincent's influence.

With his future positioning threatened, Vincent moved to regain control of the situation. An apt pupil, he studied Sable's methods of magic. It was genius to condense it for the engineers to use in their weapons and inventions. His favorite: the small amount of persuasive magic she utilized in the Azure ceremony. It wasn't enough to change or possess a mind, but it still carried the right amount to bolster one's loyalty.

Stealing one of the sapphires used in the Azure's spears, he tucked it away and fashioned it into a ring. He wasn't foolish enough to believe he could overthrow or control her; however, a small dose of daily influence went a long way. The best part was that he used her own magic against her; she'd have detected anyone else's.

The first time he wore the ring, he brushed his hands against her when he poured her a glass of tea. A subtle hint to test its limits. He suggested she take an afternoon off to relax and offered to watch Zara. Yawning, she agreed that a break would be nice.

After offering small hints and recommendations for a week, he noticed she was receptive to most of his ideas. She only pushed back when the suggestions didn't benefit her. Learning from this, he framed everything within a narrative that aligned with her own perspective. Playing on her deep-seated fears and past experiences, he planted and nurtured the ideas she'd previously rejected when her daughter arrived.

Using this method, he distanced Zara from her mother. Taking over as her caretaker in her youth, he passed along worrisome stories about her conception, leaving them to percolate in Sable's mind. Progressing bolder day by day, his persuasion gained strength.

Fearing his schemes would be uncovered, he fueled the Queen's suspicion of others with magic. This not only reinforced *her* beliefs but also

eliminated anyone who might have realized what he was doing. Granted, at the time, he'd no idea Zara was born with magic, but it *was* a pleasant surprise to find out.

When Sable recognized the boy, Grey, and he spilled his truths under her spell, she was already angry with Zara, assuming she'd been betrayed again by family. Using this resurfaced distrust, it wasn't hard to convince her of treason. Her siblings' children, finally emerging from the shadows, were here to finish the war they started years ago.

He suspected Grey's revelation of Zara's magic was true, but Sable resisted it. There was still an unbreakable thread with her daughter; Sable preferred to see her as a victim. So, he let it play out, counting on Zara to out herself. Her secrets would bury any remaining trust with her mother.

It was cruel to push the boy to the brink, but subtlety wouldn't work at the trials. The descendants needed to be seen as ruthless and savage.

Vincent wanted the people to fear Grey—fear could easily be transferred to hate.

Flashing his yellow teeth, he rested his hand on Lady Ironspire's shoulder, stared down at the chaos, and grinned. Yes, everything was going according to plan.

Until it didn't.

FIFTY TWO

DARKNESS DESCENDS

No one agreed on what came first when they spoke of that day. For Xavier, it was the shift in the sky. Dark clouds rolled in from the horizon, eclipsing the Colosseum from the sun. Brynn would say the haunting screams first grabbed her attention—rising from the river below. She covered her sensitive ears and watched Winter leap to attention, the wolf's muzzle searching the wind.

If Birk hadn't been distracted, he might have noticed both warning signs, but his mind and heart were occupied.

When the first wave hit, they were still recovering from the trials. Picking themselves off the tournament floor, they weren't aware dark creatures were flowing in from the gates—slinking over the walls of the arcades, sliding in through the tunnels.

It happened so fast.

No one realized—arcanivores were crawling everywhere.

To her credit, whether centuries of survival instincts kicked in or it was the imminent threat to her people, Lady Ironspire responded first. She witnessed the culmination of dark magic from the box from every angle.

She prioritized protecting the unarmed citizens, trusting the Azure and contestants to handle themselves.

Barking orders out to the Azure, she abandoned Vincent and catapulted from the balcony of the Royal Box into the crowds. Not a ruler to hide behind her army, she'd lead from the front, solidifying her reputation, built over generations as the fiercest fighter of the Thirteen. Drawing her wand from her side, she extended it into a lethal double-bladed bow, calling her citizens to get behind her.

Advancing on a creature conjured from the imaginations of the wicked, she retched at its putrid smell. Feasting on an elf, it rotated its oily black bull-shaped head, catching the scent of her power. Howling into the air, it charged toward her.

With reflexes polished over millennia, she dodged its slashing claws with her bow. It pressed closer. The beast was stronger than anticipated, forcing her backward. Step by step, she blocked each blow, seeking an advantage. Turning, she positioned to counterattack with a downward thrust of her bow and sliced open the arcanivore's throat, releasing a spray of black acidic goo.

Arrows flew past her, prompting her to whip around and find their target. A clump of decaying flesh and wet foliage shaped like a human snuck from behind her. Glowing red pupils peered beneath a tangle of writhing vines and fungal growths. Filled with arrows, it swayed and tottered until a final shot exploded through its open jaw, reducing it to a melted slough of boiling slime.

Raising her head to find the soldier who helped her, Xavier's eyes connected with hers. Offering him a quick nod of appreciation, both returned to the threats flooding the crowds. In tribute to the falcons he raised, Xavier honed in with clarity on his targets amid the battlefield. He calculated distance and trajectory with a hunter's instinct, cutting through the distractions. Every arrow from his quiver hit its mark.

Talbot and Shayvonne raced toward their family in the faint, cramped tunnels below. An Azure soldier hurtled past them, savagely thrown

against the wall, blocking the entry path into the arena. Placing his arm out as a protective sheath, Talbot stalled them.

An excruciating, inhuman roar came from around the corner. The silhouette of a four-legged beast with a bristling mane launched against the soldier and into view. Its massive paws ripped through the armor of the Azure, pinning the panicking soldier against the wall.

Talbot shouted, attempting to distract it from its prey and save the young Azure's life. "Get away from him," Talbot yelled, drawing his sword, gifted with Pan's magic. "Come and fight me instead." The lupine beast cocked its head, turning its sleek midnight-black body toward them.

The wolf-like beast snarled and bared its teeth, accepting the retired Captain's challenge. Lunging toward them, Talbot braced. The middle-aged soldier lifted his weapon. His once-strong limbs, now tested, felt the familiar burn of exertion when he swung his sword. Making contact with the creature's flank, he scratched the surface of its underbelly and slid underneath it.

Moving to the side, in time with Talbot, Shayvonne forced the beast behind them, avoiding the creature's claws. The arcanivore pressed another attack with a ferocious turn, cramping the already tight tunnel. Motivated to reach their children, a surge of adrenaline filled them. Synchronizing their assault, the duo charged back, coordinating strikes and evasive maneuvers until Talbot impaled its vile head with one last merciless strike.

With no time to waste, they rushed to the arena floor, already bursting with monsters, and packed with Azure.

Kodalt and Indigo led the charge, struggling to build momentum. Without magical protection or runes on the soldiers' weapons, the creatures reformed into larger, more hostile beasts. Biddy and Hyacinth learned the same lesson, needing Ravenshire to shield them from a fae-infused arcanivore, attacking them with acidic spit.

Not far from them, Birk propped Grey, who was still regaining his footing, against Brunt. Positioning in front of them, he was struggling to defend

them against an attack. A nightmarish hybrid of centaur and centipede circled them on sharp, chitinous legs. Its human torso melded with the segmented body of a monstrous arthropod—a tangle of twisted horns mounted its head. It clicked its jaws in hunger, snapping at them.

Birk, exhausted with rage, conjured forth a blazing twister from the torches in the stadium, engulfing the foul abomination. Writhing and screeching, ooze slipped from its charred flesh, creating a grotesque and unsettling sight. Gripping his sword, he swooped forward, driving his blade into the heart of the enflamed defilement.

Out of the corner of his eye, he spotted Talbot and Shayvonne entering through the tunnels and shouted to them, "Help the soldiers! We'll be fine." With a nod, they joined forces with the Azure, helping to turn the tide with their enchanted weapons.

Satisfied the Azure were receiving aid, Birk circled and set his sights on Zara. About to advance to her side, a strong hand pulled him back.

"Let me help," Grey implored, now standing without aid. "My mind is clear; after everything I did, I *need* to help."

Birk shook his head, having flashbacks from his vision. "Your spear is gone; even with Brunt at your side, it's too dangerous. I can't lose you again. I need you somewhere safe."

Brynn interrupted, landing next to them, riding atop Winter. Leaning down, reading her brother's intent, she passed him her bow and quiver of arrows, "Take these and keep your distance; I have the dagger."

Sweeping his eyes across the battlefield, Birk leaned into Brynn, "Can you and Winter retrieve Thalon and get him somewhere safe? He's still lying unconscious on the floor. I'll take care of Grey."

A quick nod and an exchange of appreciation passed between them.

The wolf bounded forward.

Grey grabbed Birk's face with both hands, "I know I've scared you, and despite our promises, we keep finding ourselves fighting alone or against each other. Let's see what we can do together, as we always intended."

A fleeting moment of trepidation crossed Birk's face.

The thought of almost being torn apart still haunted him, as did his

nightmare. If it were up to Birk, he'd raise the ground around them and trap Grey, isolating him from any further threats. Still, choosing to stand together against an uncertain future strengthened his resolve, *along with the fact that Grey had already demonstrated his ability to break through any barrier Birk built.*

"Together," he agreed.

Grabbing his hand, they rushed headlong into the fight with Brunt behind them.

As their enemies closed in, Birk and Grey worked together, relying on the training and trust they had built over the past several weeks. They combined Birk's agility with Grey's marksmanship to break through a group of arcanivores, trapping Alezander and Indigo. Covering each other's blind spots and responding to each other's moves instinctively, they quickly defeated the foul magic beasts, freeing the Azure warriors.

In the Royal Box, Vincent focused on Zara. Like her mother, she exhibited the skills of a warrior. Soon, she'd surpass the best of the Azure. Obsessed with her, he followed her every move in the battle, studying the magic she summoned and noting her vulnerabilities.

Getting rid of her now would be perfect. He could use the villainous changelings as cover. The dark clouds of arcanivores were swarming her from all sides. Her light-based weapons, however, were a threat, proving to be the most effective against them for permanent defeat. Switching from swords to spears to arrows, she was forced to fight without a break.

She had distanced herself from her allies, trying to protect the wobbling dwarf and the elf waif by luring the arcane creatures away. Her empathy would be to her detriment. If one weren't looking down, as he was, she could easily be lost among the moving walls of darkness. Her presence was only signaled by an occasional splash of white light bursting through the pitch when she used her weapons.

He grinned. Maybe he wouldn't need to intervene after all. Abandoned by her peers and consumed by her enemies, she'd exhaust herself.

Tapping his fingers on his protruding waistline, he waited patiently—unable to hear the approaching slithering sound over his scheming.

An arcanivore shaped like a giant serpent slinked inside the box, leaving a trail of putrid black slime across the polished floors. Vincent, who was leaning against the balcony, spun in alarm when the creature tipped over the throne with a flick of its tail. The elf backed into the handrail, gripping it with his tubby hands and opened his mouth to scream.

Springing with uncanny speed, the serpentine arcanivore slid into his gaping jowls with a sickening slurp.

Vincent's three chins and bloated belly expanded while the snake writhed down his gullet. His eyes turned a soulless black. A faucet of oily ooze seeped from every orifice, turning him into a visage of rot. And when it seemed he'd burst, the last remains of his body melted into the recesses of the dark, globby mound. All that was left was a rounded worm wearing Vincent's face.

Across the Colosseum, Sable and Xavier cleared the crowds in the stands after removing all the arcanivores from the arcades. Lady Ironspire addressed her new ally, "You'd make a good Azure if you're ever interested."

"I'm honored, but here to help as a loyal Balincian," he smiled.

Giving him a curious look, a wave of pain shot through her, and she winced, grabbing Xavier's arm to steady herself and mouthed, "Vincent."

Consumed by the arcanivore, his influence no longer clouded her mind. Free of fear, she was more awake and alive than she had been in centuries. Scanning the Colosseum, she found her daughter struggling and surrounded. Every doubt or conspiracy plaguing her over the years now was irrelevant; Her daughter's life took precedence.

"Balincian, would you be so kind as to follow me to the arena floor? The princess needs our assistance."

"It would be my privilege," he bowed.

Brynn knelt on the ground, pleading with Thalon. "Hey, Fox-Face, wake up," she ordered, shaking his shoulders. "Winter left me to help

Ravenshire, and you're too heavy for me to carry," she grunted. Straining at his weight, she attempted to move him again. "I know we're not close or anything, but I saw what you did for our friends, and I'd rather not leave you as an arcanivore snack."

Thalon's chin fell to his chest.

An encroaching shadow covered the unsuspecting pair. A liquid bomb of black acid splashed against the stone wall behind Thalon's head, eating through the granite on contact. Redirecting her focus to the air, Brynn shoved him to the ground, facing the creepy fae hovering above them.

It was an unnerving entity, around the size of Brynn, with shredded wings. Thorny protrusions decorated its slender form, and little jagged teeth filled its mouth. Flittering above them, it appeared more despondent than the others. For a fleeting moment, Brynn was sad she had to kill it—until it unhinged its jaw, spitting another round of acidic bile at her face.

"I'm going to rip those wings from your body," she hissed, dodging the projectile vomit.

Another shadow crept around the corner, sliding its fingers around the curve of the fortress wall. Brynn covered Thalon's body with her own. An amalgam of goblin and sprite scrambled toward them. Grabbing her dagger, she crouched to the ground, resembling a cornered cub. She thrashed the small blade before her, temporarily keeping it at bay.

"Now would be a perfect time for you to get up, Thalon," Brynn nudged his leg. "I need your help. I understand my brother hurt you, but he didn't know what he was doing. I don't want you to die, and I hope you don't want me to die. We pain in the asses have to stick together."

"I'm not—a pain in the ass!" a voice groaned, rousing from behind her. Sitting up, Thalon quickly appraised the situation. The monsters recognized the awakening threat and reacted quickly. The goblin jumped, and the fae dived forward, leaving Thalon seconds to respond.

Summoning his mother's elemental magic, he jutted an arm toward each of their incoming foes. A pillar rose from the earth underneath the

goblin, catapulting the fiendish creature into the air. With his other hand, he summoned the strength of the winds and sent the fae backflipping in the opposite direction.

When the goblin came flailing back toward the earth, Brynn was ready for him. Pouncing—her dagger collided with it mid-air, scattering its form into pieces.

The fae barreled back, her arms extended, and a shrill screech filled the air. Thalon gave it a repugnant look before summoning a lightning bolt and striking it from the sky, reducing her frame to ash.

"Centaur's balls! You've been holding back!" Brynn's face lit in admiration.

Thalon offered a weak smirk of confidence, "Help me stand," he groaned.

Across the arena, Birk and Grey were helping Zara clear the mountain of arcanivores around her. "I'm sorry it's taken so long for us to get to you," Birk shouted over the noise of the battle.

"You've both been fighting all day; I was happy to fill in for a while," she grunted, throwing a spear of light into a troll-figured arcanivore. "But I'm glad you're here now," she smiled with relief.

Grey studied the arcanivores, trying to deconstruct their motives and appetites. Their behavior was different from the variations he'd faced before. They weren't driven out of the need to feed; they were coordinated this time.

They avoided some confrontations, and when they did engage, they were more strategic in their approach. They had intended to overwhelm and scatter the crowds, but not kill them. *Why?*

Because those arcanivores were a distraction!

Every time they were killed by anyone without magic, it made them stronger. *They were building numbers.* They were planning something bigger.

And if his eyes didn't deceive him, they were gathering around Zara.

"Zara, something about you attracts them!" Grey shouted over the fighting, shooting a rune-carved arrow at a charging black stag.

"I know," she yelled, exasperated, slicing through an impish fiend, "Despite the volume, I've evaded every attempt at contact. I don't understand it. I can't be this lucky."

Flying between Grey and Birk as the Ashendrake, Thalon surprised them when he switched back to human form and landed on his feet. "They're not attacking you. *They're keeping you busy,*" he informed, jumping into the conversation.

Birk's face lit at Thalon's arrival. Relieved to see him standing, he reached out to touch his arm. "Thalon, I was worried. Are you sure you're okay to be on your feet?"

Thalon swallowed, "I promised you at the start of the trials, I'd have your back. A few broken ribs and a concussion won't keep me down."

Grey lowered his head, "Thalon . . . I'm . . ."

Thalon cut him off sharply, "Save it—not now." Raising his palm, he shot a flame over Grey's shoulder, hitting an arcanivore coming from behind him. "I'm glad you aren't trying to rip us apart anymore."

"What do you mean they're keeping me busy?" Zara interrupted, growing impatient.

"*You're* the bridge from the Dreamscape to Driftstone. They don't want to hurt you; they need you. If you fall, Morvana loses her ability to reach us." Thalon yelled. Switching to his Ashendrake form, he flew over behind her. "They're swarming you because every time you use your magic against them, they multiply and pull others through. You aren't just opening doors; *you've become the door.*"

"He's right; they appeared after you conjured the shield," Birk affirmed. "Consider the amount of energy you employed to maintain it."

Thalon took her hand, "Morvana has found a way to use you as a conduit. They'll keep coming until your connection with the Dreamscape is severed."

Zara pulled her hand away; she didn't want to be touched. She stared at the carnage and destruction surrounding them. "*All of this is my fault?*"

"No, my love, it's my sister's fault," Lady Ironspire corrected, arriving behind them. "And *mine* for keeping you at a distance. If I didn't

outlaw magic, you would've felt safe to come to me, and we wouldn't be in this mess."

Zara's lips trembled, "You look . . . different."

"I feel different." She paused. Walking over, she wiped the tears forming in Zara's eyes, a tender gesture that surprised her daughter. "We've much to discuss—" Sable's words were cut short. Leaning forward, she clutched her daughter's arm. A sharpened black tentacle pierced her shoulder. "Zara—" Another thicker appendage slapped around her waist, yanking her into the air.

"Mother!" Zara lunged forward too late.

"It's coming from below the Colosseum," Birk shouted, pointing at the imposing beast emerging.

The whole arena lurched forward, sending them all to the ground.

A titanic dark fist punched through the arena floor, sending Zara and Thalon flying backward.

Another hand rose from the waters below, followed by an army of tentacles. A gruesome combination of a giant and a kraken pulled itself into the stadium. Its gnarly dripping head came into view and emitted a piercing cry.

The towers atop the ancient structure crumbled.

Gripping their ears, everyone fell to the ground. Glass, marble, and steel rained from the sky.

The monster's shriek called to the remains and puddles of its defeated brethren, pooling them together. Their dark slime slid in from the tunnels and over the walls of the stands. Mangled, charred, and dismembered bodies rolled toward their new host, joining the alpha, helping it to grow and expand.

One by one, they were torn from the air. Dragged across the ground. Kodalt was dropped headfirst to the floor; the troll holding him ripped toward the magic vortex. Ravenshire lowered his shield and Biddy his axe when the winged arcanivores chasing them followed suit.

The monster's torso and misshapen head bloated. The faces of every

consumed being and beast of magic stretched out from its inky skin, wailing in unison.

Two tentacles shot toward them, one grabbing Winter, who yelped at the surprise of being yanked into the air, and the other grabbing Birk.

Grey quickly grabbed the appendage, struggling to loosen its hold on Birk's waist. A huge hand suddenly intervened, forcefully grabbing the young protector and lifting him into the air.

Talbot and Shayvonne raced toward the beast and were swatted away like pests. Biddy's axe, Xavier's arrows, and Ravenshire's sword did nothing; this arcanivore was impenetrable, stronger than the rest.

Ignoring the Azure and Non-Magic-Born, the arcanivore's tentacles hunted the witches and their familiars. Snatching Brunt, it chased Thalon across the battlefield. He switched to his Ashendrake form and darted in and out of the reaching limbs, eluding its every attempt to grab hold of him.

Grey was trapped and suffocated in the giant's grasp; his irises turned black. Sable hung, choking opposite him. The creature was feeding on them.

Gritting his teeth, Birk fought against the tentacles' constriction. His muscles strained as he tried to channel his magic. Like unseen chains, an oppressive force held him back, stifling his connection.

"Zara! You have to do something!" Birk shouted. "Grey and your mother are dying! This thing is canceling our magic; it'll kill us all if you don't do something!"

Time stood still for Zara.

Staring at her mother, she watched the life slowly drain from her face. She'd never seen her so still, silent, almost statuesque.

It was odd to have these thoughts with her body shaking inside.

When Azure froze in battle, she often wondered what they were thinking about. She assumed panic made the mind freeze, never considering it might wander. Maybe it was a distraction technique, the mind helping the body to accept the inevitable.

She heard Birk in the distance. She was aware of the urgency, but she

didn't know what to do. She feared she'd only feed and strengthen the creature if she used her powers again.

And because of that, she resented her mother. She resented her for not being there to help her and train her, and for now leaving her in this position.

"Tell me what to do," she raged at her mother, tears flooding her face. "You've never held your opinions before. Why are you silent now? When I need you the most?"

She didn't scream because her mother could hear; she screamed because she was angry. She screamed because she felt helpless. She *screamed* because she was tired of fighting alone.

A hand touched her shoulder.

"You know what you have to do," Thalon said softly, appearing behind her. "You have to sever the connection."

"I'm the connection," she swallowed.

He lowered his head. "You make the calls no one else can."

"What will happen?" she asked with a quiet voice.

He took her hand, "I'm not sure. Your powers are light-based, unlike any I've seen. Trust your magic. Trust your instincts."

"I'm scared," she confessed.

"I'll be here with you."

A soul-wrenching cry to her right made them both turn.

Shayvonne.

The beast held Brynn in its grip. The girl kicked and pounded the massive monster with her tiny fists, demanding release as it whisked her into the sky. Her mother lunged at her daughter's legs, falling face-first to the ground, helpless, like Zara.

The white wolf, Brynn's guardian, hung limp. Unable to lift its head in response to her charge's cries.

It was Brynn who broke Zara's trance.

Small and fierce—the girl commanded the world to see her. She wouldn't allow the child's future to be snuffed out by the sinister aspirations of the wicked.

She deserved her voice.

Fighting the paralysis in her body, Zara ordered herself to move.

Staring down the beast, Zara opened the palm of her hand, pulling out a sword steeled in golden white light. The creature's embedded faces in the giant's swollen belly, keened and shrieked in reaction.

Good, she had their attention.

She clenched her fist. *Is this the price for redemption?* Forced to pay with her own life for a mistake inflicted upon her? Relegated to a pawn in someone else's cruel game.

It was unfair.

Scouring the lost faces in the clotted clump of deformed corruption, she searched for an outlet to channel her fuming indignation, someone or something to replace her grief and grant her the fortitude to do what needed to be done.

And she found him. Drowning in the sewage where he belonged.

His caustic eyes. His wobbly chins. His sardonic smile. The embodiment of every crushed dream and every ruined ambition. Yes, he'd do.

"BURN IN THE NETHER, VINCENT!" she bellowed defiantly. Lifting her golden sword, she looked toward the heavens and plunged the blade deep into her heart.

Rushing forward, Thalon scooped her into his arms and slowly lowered her to the ground. Her mouth foamed, and her eyes clouded. He cushioned her when her body lapsed into seizures and drew back when her skin sizzled with light.

There was a spark near her chest. A small orb housing a key. Floating upward, it expanded and grew, forcing him to divert his eyes.

A blinding light filled the sky—followed by an explosive blast.

The light, infused with her essence, tore through the malignant entity, shredding its shadowed existence with an unforgiving fury. An army of wails vaporized against the walls of the ravine.

The monster's hostages, lifeless, fell from the sky—no longer held aloft by their vanquished captor.

With the celerity of a hummingbird's wingbeat, Thalon summoned a gale of cyclone winds and blew their bodies over the breach. His final gambit before he and the others—unable to avoid the shockwaves—were expelled through the air, forcefully colliding with the ground.

The clink of a dull brass key, void of magic or light, hit the earth.

Everything faded to white.

FIFTY THREE

THE BRIGHTEST STAR

When Thalon regained consciousness, the skies were blue. Birds sang in the trees outside the Colosseum, and the clouds were soft and white. Lying on his back, the taste of blood still soured his mouth. Attempting to prop himself on one shoulder, he winced from the pain. His other arm was lame, and he was pretty sure his ribs were broken.

The giant arcanivore was gone, along with the darkness—leaving no trace, they were ever there.

Indigo and Ravenshire stirred to his right. Others were waking. Scanning the area, he found Zara not far from him.

Pushing over to her, he gently pressed his fingers against her neck. Checking her pulse, he was relieved to find her breathing. Rolling her over, he scanned her body, shocked at the absence of any wound.

Her eyelids squinted open, and she forced a lazy smile. "I did it," her voice strained. "I severed the connection."

"Yeah, you did. You made the call; no one else could have," Thalon grinned at her.

"Thank you for pushing me," she said, sitting and painfully hugging him, "and staying with me. I don't think I could've done it alone."

"You never have to fight anything alone again, Zara," he said, and hugged her back. "How did you know what to do?"

"When you told me to trust my magic, I realized something. Only the dark should be frightened by the light."

"And you're the brightest among us all," he said in her ear.

Leaning against Thalon, relief washed over her, releasing the doubts and fears plaguing her for so long. In the still aftermath, she remembered her box in the Dreamscape, filled with color and potential. A new light kindled within her. One, she was eager to explore.

Standing, she helped Thalon to his feet and noticed him frantically searching the bodies strewn across the ground. "He's over there," she said, motioning to Birk, who was stirring. "Go to him; be there when he wakes."

Thalon's face flushed, "How did you—"

"I saw how you fought for him at the trials, the way you look at him. It's clear you care for him."

"He's my teammate, of course; I—" he paused, unable or unwilling to pretend any longer, "He's not . . . mine."

Encouraging him with a soft touch on his arm, she reminded him of his words, "Trust your magic."

FIFTY-FOUR

CULPABILITY

"Zara!" Sable shouted; her chest heaved.

Zara grabbed her hands. "I'm here, mother. You're okay," she soothed.

Lady Ironspire squeezed her daughter's fingers until her knuckles were white. "What happened? All I remember is suffocating darkness."

Zara sat at her mother's bedside and recounted the events. She spoke of facing her fears head-on and emerging victorious against their threat. She caught her up on her dreams, visions, stumbles, and falls—and most importantly, a voice she'd found and would never hide again.

Sable looked upon her daughter with new eyes, no longer a girl but a warrior in her own right.

"There is something else you should know," Zara stood and crossed the room. She picked up a ring from her mother's vanity and handed it to her. "The Azure found this in the Royal Box."

"Vincent." Sable's eyes raged. "My own magic used against me. Where's the traitor now?"

"Let's just say . . . we never have to worry about him bothering us again," Zara didn't expand.

"For how long have I been played the fool?" Sable threw the sheets from her bed, indignant for being made to look weak. She moved to stand.

"Does it matter?" Zara straightened her face. Drawing the curtains open, she let the light in. "It wasn't all Vincent, mother. His influence wouldn't have worked if some part of you wasn't willing."

Sable sat back, rearing her head back at the admonition.

"I've sat here and replayed this conversation in my mind all day—all the things I wanted to say to you and all the things I needed to hear," Zara said, turning to her mother and straightening her posture. "And while *we will* have those conversations in the upcoming days, I don't have the stomach to hear your excuses now. You owe me more than explanations. You owe more to your people and to those who saved your life. You owe us change."

"Is my daughter telling me to sit and think about what I've done?"

Zara stood over her. "I'm asking you to reflect on our future. I love you, but we . . . I . . . need more from you."

Zara exited the room. The sound of the closing door resonated like a closing chapter, a stark reminder of their unresolved distance. Left to face the consequences of centuries of her bitter resentment, Sable sat alone once again.

FIFTY-FIVE

SWIMMING IN CIRCLES

The Azure Academy healing wing remained full after a week. Having escaped with only bruises and a mild concussion, Birk wandered the halls, trying to find Thalon.

Grey was busy recovering in a private suite in the Royal Wing. Lady Ironspire considered this one of the many reparations she owed. Having his mind, body, and magic picked and pulled apart the same day left him brittle *and a little ornery*. Birk thought that had less to do with any pain he was in and more to do with everyone's insistence on his staying in bed.

The healers assured them he'd recover in full. However, he still required days, if not weeks, of rest before he'd feel whole again, *and that was only what his body needed*. Birk wished they were near the healing springs so he and his family could care for him there. A selfish part of him longed to go back to the comfort of Grey's home in Everglenn.

Taking the opportunity for fresh air, he left Grey sleeping, surrounded by his family. After checking his old room at the academy, Birk peeked into the dining hall, finding Ravenshire and Biddy playing cards at a table. "Have you seen Thalon?"

"I think he's out by the reflecting pool," Ravenshire answered, his wrists bandaged. "Any idea what we can expect from Lady Ironspire's summons tomorrow?"

Birk shook his head; Sable was avoiding Grey and himself.

"I wonder if she'll hand out medals to us," Biddy grinned. "My mum would be so proud."

"I'm confident she's already proud of you," Birk said, clapping his shoulders. "You're the Dragon Slayer!"

Biddy glowed. "Did you hear? Lady Ironspire kept her word; our families were moved into the elite housing level yesterday. *And* she's offered us a formal position on the Azure, *if we still want it*. She even invited Ravenshire."

Birk raised an eyebrow at his childhood friend.

"I thanked her but told her I have a family waiting for me," Ravenshire smiled.

Hyacinth came in from behind Birk, hugging him. "It's good to see you; how is Grey?"

"Physically, he's fine. He's built sturdy," Birk jested.

"And the rest of the bits?"

"It'll take some time, but we'll get there." Eager to change the subject, he shared the latest news from Zara with them. "I'm not sure if you heard, but your families aren't the only ones being housed. Sable reversed her position on the Magic-Born. They're moving back into the city today."

"Zara did it," Ravenshire beamed, "she influenced her mother. This is a win, after all."

"She and her mother are healing, too. Apparently, Lady Ironspire wasn't under the best of influences either," Birk mentioned. He'd let Zara elaborate on Vincent.

"She's open to helping us, now?" Ravenshire asked.

"Zara's implied as much. We'll learn more tomorrow." Eyeing Thalon in the courtyard, he gave quick goodbyes to his friends, promising to catch up later.

Thalon sat alone by the reflection pool. Birk laughed to himself. When they first met, he hadn't seemed like the type of guy who meditated on much of anything.

Birk realized now that was probably not true, even then. There was a lot he misunderstood about Thalon.

This revelation brought him here today.

Thalon winced in pain, standing to greet Birk. "I thought you'd be busy enjoying the royal life upstairs," he teased. He carried his right arm in a sling, bandages were wrapped around his rib cage, and his face was covered in bruises. He was tougher than Birk gave him credit for; he'd expected to find him in worse shape, considering the blows he endured.

The other reason for his visit today.

"I missed slumming it with my mates," Birk replied. "Besides, we promised we'd never leave each other behind, remember?"

"I remember," his voice caught in his throat. "Walk with me. I need to stretch my legs, and you appear to have something on your mind."

Birk nodded, jumping in, "Grey will want to share this with you, but—"

"But you're running interference for him?" Thalon gently cut him off. "Listen, I know that overthinking brain of yours wants to mediate this, but I'll be fine . . . we'll be fine."

"Will you, though? Because I'm not sure I'd be if I were you." Birk hesitated. Thalon was being Thalon, brushing it off—building another wall between them.

"It's my fault anyway. I was always provoking the bear; it's no surprise he finally bit back."

Birk stopped Thalon carefully with his hand.

"This isn't your fault." He paused, locking eyes for a brief moment. "And . . . it's not Grey's, either. I imagine that may be difficult to believe when you're recovering from the injuries he inflicted upon you."

"He hit you, too," Thalon reminded, rubbing the nape of his neck.

Birk looked away.

"I'm not having trouble moving past Grey's assault. I understand possession and enchantments. I don't hold him accountable for his actions

during the trial." His voice lowered, and his defensiveness retreated. "Is that what you want to hear? Because it's the truth, and I'd rather move on. If the reason for your visit is to discuss your boyfriend, I don't have the constitution."

It's not what Birk wanted to hear, and he didn't want to move on. There was more lying underneath the surface.

He nodded anyway.

Thalon kicked the ground, aggravated with himself for shutting down and holding back.

Standing shoulder to shoulder, they stared at the Golden Koi gliding beneath the water. A barrier was erected between them. So many of their interactions had been fraught with friction and misunderstanding. Words left unsaid. Emotions buried deep.

Birk's gaze lingered on the Koi. The fish mirrored his emotions, swimming in circles, hunting for an escape from the enclosure.

"I remembered something the other night," he began, his voice barely above a whisper, "the night we slept beside each other at the Academy."

Thalon raised his brow, "That you snore?"

Birk cracked a small smile. "I finally remembered you . . . from my dreams . . . the ones in the Dreamscape."

Thalon shot a quick sideways glance. "Well, that's not news; you stated as much at the Living Forest. You recalled glimpses of me."

"Yes, but not vividly, and I didn't understand." He paused, tracing Thalon with his eyes. Placing his hand into his pocket, he resisted the urge to reach out and touch him. "You did more than observe me; you helped me. You kept me from following Zara into danger—you guided me to the hallway of doors. You navigated me to Driftstone. You were leading me to you, weren't you?"

"You had the most magnificent dreams," Thalon reflected, a wistful smile crossed his face. "I was fascinated by you. It was the first time I encountered someone similar to me. When your nightmares started, I wanted to help. I felt a connection. You were trapped, lied to, and had your potential hidden. I was experiencing something similar—we've more in common than I've had the chance to share."

A pang of guilt gnawed at Birk's conscience. His assumptions of Thalon being spoiled and entitled had colored his interactions with him, preventing him from probing deeper.

"I . . . should have asked," Birk confessed.

"I was overconfident in thinking you'd pick the door leading to me." Thalon paused, uncomfortable with his confession.

"I almost did," Birk reflected. *Enchanted wood whispers its sweet plea, a door where kindred spirits will be.*

"I wanted you to find me. I envisioned us changing things together, finding *our* truth. I was elated when you arrived at my doorstep." Thalon hung his head. "Then I realized you were with him. I was jealous." Thalon took another step back, turning his head from Birk. "Grey found you before I was even given a chance. I felt . . . threatened . . . and I made an ass of myself. Pushing you away in the process."

"Thalon . . . I didn't know," Birk said, caught off guard.

"Would it have changed anything if you did?" Silence. Thalon regretted asking the question as soon as it came out of his mouth.

Birk hesitated longer than he should have. "Maybe . . . I . . . don't know what to say."

"You don't need to say anything." Thalon lowered his voice, "I know you care for him."

"Yes . . . but—"

Thalon looked at him, masking the hope in his eyes, "But what?"

Birk wasn't sure what he intended to say. There was no, *but*—he didn't think there was—it had been a slip of the tongue. He was trying to process Thalon's emotions, grappling with his own.

From the start, they clashed like bulls. He wondered if their differences fueled their underlying conflict or if their similarities were the root.

Thalon's insights into the arcane arts and education of the Thirteen had been invaluable to the group. Yet, his sharp tongue and unfiltered opinions grated and exasperated Birk.

Thalon was infuriating one moment and—something else—the next.

During the trials, Thalon demonstrated a side Birk hadn't foreseen.

Beneath his brusqueness lay a well of empathy for others, a tender heart, and an unwavering loyalty to their cause. He changed everything between them when he saved Birk's life at great personal risk.

Thalon witnessed Birk's fears and insecurities under stress. Instead of judging him or considering him weak, Thalon showed compassion, encouraging and rallying him when he needed it the most. He never stopped seeing him as a leader.

And then, there was—the other day.

A moment. A reaction. An accident. A mistake. Something more?

"But what, Birk?" Thalon repeated, pulling him back into the moment.

"Nothing . . . I'm grateful you're in my life. I'm grateful you brought me here. I'm grateful you found me. I don't want things to return to how they were between us."

Thalon shifted his weight.

"I need you, Thalon. On this quest, and in my life. Can we build on that?" Birk placed his hand on Thalon's shoulder.

Thalon bit his lip and inhaled. "I'm not going anywhere. I'm here to see it through to the end. Wherever our paths lead us."

Thalon's words stayed with Birk when he climbed the stairs to the Royal Tower, wondering what lay in store for them all. When he approached the top, he found Zara's mother on the balcony, gazing down at the migration of exiles back into the city. Reluctant, he joined her when she acknowledged him with a quiet nod.

Together, they stood in silence for a while, watching the city below them.

"It's not easy to lead, Birk," she ruminated. "I come out here sometimes to remind myself to look out at everything I'm responsible for. It humbles me. No matter how powerful or how long we walk this earth, we'll always neglect something."

Birk considered her words before replying, "I hope that's when we can lean on others to show us what we've missed."

Sable considered him. "If you're to lead this quest with my daughter, you'll learn that others will let you down, even those you love."

"I'm sure that's true, as I will disappoint others. All we can do is trust someone else will always be there to pick us up."

"My sister's kin came to the aid of Ironspire, but it also begs the question—what of your mothers?" she asked, pressing her point. "They were aware of Zara's vision and Morvana's intentions, yet it was you who showed up at my doorstep."

"I'm not sure I'm the person to answer," Birk admitted. "I believe Edi, Faunwood, and my mother would've been here if they could. You preside over the largest city in Driftstone; I'm sure you can appreciate the nuances of responsibilities and timing. Isn't it enough we came?"

She laughed dismissively, turning her face back to the land. "It is as it was. Each protects their interests. Nothing's changed."

"You misunderstand," Birk leaned forward. "Mistakes were made ten thousand years ago. My mother has carried those mistakes with her every day since—never recovering from that loss. It was her grief for her past that bore your daughter, and the reason her son stands before you today. We all have an opportunity to build a new future together, to tear down the walls dividing us. Allow us to prove that to you."

"I pray you're right, and our path is different this time. You may see me as cynical or blind, but the young often forget we have walked in your shoes."

He paused. "I was angry at my mother when I started this journey. Her deceptions hurt me. She asked me when I left to find grace for her when I learned of her past."

"And have you?"

"It's easy for me to say I would've done things differently, but I'm not sure that's true." Birk paused again, reflecting on the truth of that statement. "I wasn't faced with the decisions she was forced to make. I don't have insights into the fears or pain that motivated her at the time. What matters to me are the choices she's making now *and* the peace she is attempting to make with her past. Shouldn't that be all that matters when we love someone?"

"I'm not sure Zara will be as forgiving when she considers me," Sable admitted, reflecting on her conversation with her daughter. "I apologize . . . I'm not in a position to judge your mother when my choices have cost lives."

"I can't predict your daughter's actions, but I'm confident that if you focus on the relationship you want to have with Zara in the future, those will be the memories she holds."

Sable closed her eyes. "I hear you, son of Chaos. You have shown me the value of your heart." She paused, "I regret what we did to Grey. Whether influenced or not, I invited my demons to your door. My actions are unforgivable, and you've only shown kindness to me in return."

"I'm who your sisters raised me to be," Birk reminded her.

She offered a sad smile, "We'll talk more tomorrow. I haven't forgotten my debt."

By the time Birk returned to Grey's room, his family had retired to bed. Sneaking in, he tried not to disturb him. Sitting on the edge of the bed, he ran his fingers lightly through his hair. Opening his eyes, Grey took Birk's hand and kissed it.

"How are you feeling?" Birk asked.

"Better now that you're here," Grey said, grabbing Birk around the waist and pulling him into his arms.

"I missed you," he said, nuzzling against him.

A silence passed between them.

"Birk, I—"

Birk pressed his lips against Grey's mouth to hush him. "I know what you want to say, Grey, but it wasn't you, and it wasn't your fault. You were under an enchantment; out of everyone here, I understand how that feels."

"It may not have been me on the inside, but it was *still* me...or my body that did those things. I can sense how others view me has changed; they're more cautious, frightened."

Birk shook his head. "We never forgot who *you* were. Do you feel I'm treating you differently?"

"No. I don't think my heart could take it if you did, even though I'd understand."

"Has your perception of Zara changed? It was her magic conjuring the arcanivores." Birk reminded him.

Grey sat up. "Of course not. Morvana used her as a vessel." Upon hearing the words, he stopped. "Oh . . . I see your point." He looked down, "I'm not sure everyone sees it that way, though. Zara didn't attack any of you directly."

"If you're referring to Thalon, allow him the time and space to heal. He recognizes the truth; it's . . . a little more personal for him."

"I'm indebted to him. He saved your life when I abandoned you."

"I'm sure you'll have plenty more opportunities to save my life," he nudged.

Grey cracked a smile, "I do believe this to be true. You find yourself in a lot of predicaments."

Birk shrugged, "That's what you get for falling for a child of Chaos."

FIFTY-SIX

A New Tomorrow

The following day, Grey almost tripped when Birk pulled him by his hand, running to the Royal Reception Hall. "Aren't you supposed to be the agile one?" Birk teased.

"It's these boots," Grey complained, tugging at one of them while jumping on one foot. "My oversized feet weren't made for shoes. Not to mention, it's the first time I've been allowed to be out of bed. I'm a little wobbly."

Rounding the corner, Grey burst into a laugh when they ran into Shayvonne, who was doing her best to usher Brynn and her rat-nest of hair along. "This family needs a better system of waking up in the morning," she sighed.

When they burst through the door, all eyes turned to them. The Reception Hall, currently housing a few hundred audience members, was a lot larger than they'd expected. Zara raised her brow at Birk, hiding her amusement. Sitting on the throne beside her mother, she faced the audience.

"So much for sneaking in back," Brynn side-mouthed to her brother.

Saving them from further embarrassment, Indigo escorted them to their line of friends, assembled front and center of the crowd. Brynn, pleased to be standing next to Thalon, elbowed him. He winced.

Sable smiled, unfazed by their punctuality, and stood to address them.

"My brave and noble citizens, esteemed guests, and honored heroes, today we stand united in the aftermath of a challenge that tested Ironspire at its core." Stepping down, she walked the floor. Admitting her failures as a ruler to her people, she humbly spoke of accountability and change. Turning her attention to the youth before her, she paid tribute to their bravery and determination.

"Today is a new day where we will reclaim our title as a City of Innovation. My daughter and her friends have shown me our future can't be defined by our pasts. We need new ideas and alliances to move forward and each of your minds to contribute to our success."

Erupting into a thunderous applause, the crowd stood and cheered—chants of "Long Live Ironspire" sung across the room.

"I will no longer rely on my old counsel or that of a royal advisor, ensuring we stay committed to our new path. The old ways were built to validate *my* thinking, and if we are to grow, I must evolve, too. Experience has its place, but I've forgotten that to be innovative, one can't be afraid of new ideas and fresh voices. If there is no one to challenge me, I've become stagnant, immobilizing you with me. In the coming weeks, each community—Azure, engineer, elf, dwarf, human, and Magic-Born—will all have a voice in the future of our home. To lead this new council, I have appointed a familiar face you all trust—Ironspire's warrior, Indigo."

Zara leaped from her throne, leading another round of cheers. The Azure stomped their feet in celebration. Kodalt, taking his child's hand, led Indigo to the front, where they bowed and joined the hero's procession.

"Finally, in Ironspire tradition, we honor those who prioritized our kingdom's safety. May their nobility and service always be remembered."

Walking to the stage, Sable took Zara's hand, leading her to the center of the procession line, standing her between Birk and Thalon. Kneeling

before her daughter, every Azure and audience member followed suit, bowing their heads in respect.

"Foremost, I pay respect to my daughter, your princess—the heart of our people. It is through her actions our nation stands today. Partnering with my siblings' children, she will take her rightful place in leading us to our future. She will represent us as our banner against the rising threats to our realm. Our brightest light—may you never dim."

"May you never dim," the audience repeated.

Kodalt rotated the line to face the assembly; the champions were instructed to kneel.

Ironspire's citizens stood and placed their hands on their hearts. The Azure thumped their feet and spears on the ground—humming an honored tune for soldiers. Walking behind the defenders, Lady Ironspire hung a medal around each of their necks, blessing each of them as she passed.

Biddy and his mother sobbed, moving Ravenshire to throw his arms around him. Thalon looked forward, handsome and regal, instigating Brynn to snort at his pensive composure.

"Son of Faunwood, you stood by my daughter in her darkest hour. Your gallant showing in the trials would make your mother proud. Let your example rekindle the old alliances. Today, we reunite our mighty kingdoms—the Living Forest will always have a friend in Ironspire."

Zara grabbed his hand and squeezed it.

"Son of Chaos, disruptor of Order," Sable continued, reaching Birk. "Prophet and instigator, a foreigner to these lands—without pause, you came to aid strangers—rallying and rounding up this small army of champions to rebalance a world you held no stake in. After ten thousand years, you've led the charge of uniting us again. I give you the full support of Ironspire in your quest—we are forever in your debt."

Saving Grey for last, Sable stood behind him and placed her hand on his shoulders.

"Grey, the descendant of my beloved brother, Farren, you've suffered most at my hands. I have defiled the legacy of my brother, the Protector,

the gentlest among us. I've committed the gravest of atrocities for a witch. I invaded your mind and corrupted your spirit."

Walking around him, she turned her back on the audience to face him and knelt.

"I forced you to bare your soul to me, and so I offer mine—willingly in return. In all my years, I've only communed with one other, my brother, Cyrus. It's the only thing I can offer to heal the wounds between us—if you accept it."

Grey hesitated; he looked to Birk and took his hand. They spoke to each other through their eyes. Turning back to Sable, he offered a slight bow of his head.

She took his face in her hands and placed her forehead against his. An aura of soft blue surrounded them. The room went silent. No one, other than a witch, had witnessed a ritual of soul-sharing.

They found a kindred spark within each other. Both carried loss and unhealed wounds from their pasts. Both were haunted by loved ones who departed. Both held regrets, building walls around their hearts.

There was strength in their connection. Fragile pieces coming together to form a whole. Unhealed scars faded. Doubt swept away.

Pulling back, Sable's eyes widened. She didn't mask her streaming tears. Grey exhaled; his full health returned. A smile passed between them.

"From this day forward, you and I are bonded. Your connection to the Thirteen—your rightful birthright—is restored." She hung a dragon's fang around his neck. "This talisman was Farren's. I have condensed a piece of myself within it. Wherever you are, whoever you protect, my gifts will be added to yours."

Upon request, Birk stayed behind before joining the festivities, eagerly awaiting Lady Ironspire to finish clearing the room. After Kodalt closed the door, giving them privacy, she invited him to join her.

"I understand you arrived at Driftstone through my brother Cyrus's

portals," she stated. "And this is what's keeping you from finding a way home?"

Birk nodded.

Walking behind the thrones, she pressed her hand against a wall. Sliding open at her touch, it revealed a hidden chamber. "I can help with that."

Inviting him in, Birk recognized the hallway of doors, similar to the ones inside Pan's pantry.

On the far wall, a blue curtain hung out of place.

"If you've heard my story, you may recognize this space. It's where my brother Cyrus and I held our last stand against Morvana. This is where, with his dying breath, he forced her into the Under."

She stood at a door made of rotting, singed wood and ran her finger along its frame before turning to Birk with a proud glint in her eyes. "Cyrus's magic was always underestimated. He put in a failsafe in case Morvana or the others figured out how to copy his magic: No one could use a portal unless it were created by him to escape the Under. You're lucky the door you chose led you to the Over; otherwise, you too would've been trapped."

"I'm aware of the story," Birk's heart raced.

"What history leaves out, as it often does with women, is the fact that I helped engineer their magic and am also capable of building them." Ripping the curtain from the wall, she revealed another frame, except this one held no door. "I've built this portal for you as part of my gratitude and amends. All it needs to operate is your touch and intention. I'm unable to bring it to life since I've never been to Balincia nor aware of its location."

"But I can?" he asked, walking over and touching the cold frame.

"Yes, all it needs is your vision and intent."

Birk turned to Sable, "Do you hear their voices too?"

"No." She eyed him with concern. "Only Cyrus heard them. I'd caution you to remember that while all energy is sentient, it can evolve beyond a creator's intent; you need to be careful before you take stock in what they have to say."

"I was initially scared of them, only because they were unfamiliar, but they guided me to the door I selected, which brought me here; that must mean something." He ran his palm across the empty space.

"You sound like my brother," she said with a sad smile. "I don't question their resourcefulness or necessity. However, I'll share the advice I gave Cyrus: What happens when their intentions no longer align with ours?"

Birk paused and studied the frame.

"Continue to pay them the respect you would in any communion, but, I'll repeat myself, be wary of their whispers. Your decisions should always be your own."

"What of the quest?"

"I hope you don't abandon it, but, speaking as a mother, I know my siblings would be heartbroken if you didn't visit them before you left. As a leader, I'd also advise your friends need time to rest and recuperate. There's no better place to gain your footing than home."

"Will you join us? I know my mother would love to see you."

Sable touched her heart, "I was hoping you'd ask." She wrapped her arm around his shoulders and guided him toward his friends. "There's still much for us to discuss, and I promise I'll share everything you need to know before the next leg of your journey. For today, however, be with your companions and enjoy the festivities. Tomorrow, we'll take you home."

FIFTY-SEVEN

A KNOCK AT THE DOOR

Pan nearly fell off her chair in the kitchen when she felt the warning signal. Someone breached Balincia's protective wards. Edi, who sat across from her, sprang to her feet, wand in hand.

A crashing sound came from the pantry, alarming them both. "Someone's entered through the doors," Edi braced herself.

"It's impossible; I've been so careful," Pan quickly checked her magic in her mind. "Not only would they have to know our location, but you helped me to enchant it to ensure no one without an invitation could pass through."

"And the only one we left the door open for was—" Edi was interrupted by a knock on the pantry door.

A familiar voice called from the other side. "In case Aunt Edi is standing there with her wand, I wanted to announce ourselves." The door creaked open slowly, first a hand waving, followed by the red hair of a Storyteller. "I'm home," Birk beamed.

Flinging the rest of the door open, Pan threw herself into her son's arms. They held each other, tears flowing freely as they experienced the catharsis of finally finding peace in each other's embrace. "I've missed you, Mom." Pan sobbed and squeezed tighter.

Gently pulling her to the side, he motioned behind him. "I hope it's okay, but I've brought some friends home I'd like you to meet."

Pan's face lit in surprise when she peeked behind him. A line of people tentatively followed him up the stairs. While she made room for them to pile into the kitchen, Birk grabbed Edi by the hand, pulling her in for a hug.

Her lips quivering, she pulled back, placing her hand on his chest. "Birk, the way we left things—"

"Doesn't matter now. I understand a lot more than I once did." Leaning forward, he planted forgiving kisses on her cheeks. "You saved our lives in the trials, Aunt Edi. I know you'll always be there when I need you."

Weeping at her nephew's words, Edi backed into something large and furry, sending everyone into hysterics at her reaction. Clutching her chest, she turned, finding herself face-to-face with the perpetrator of her alarm and the crash below. Edi scratched behind his ears, "Brunt, you silly old fool, you scared me to death."

"And Winter, too," Pan squealed with delight as the wolf affectionately circled her upon entering the room. "You were a mere pup when we last saw you."

Talbot and his men entered the room next, raising the spirits of the overcrowded kitchen. "Our Balincian Heroes!" Pan exclaimed, spoiling them with affection.

Edi grabbed Ravenshire. In a rare show of tenderness, she hugged him tight. "And our sons," she declared.

Taking his mother by the hand, Birk led Pan to the others for introductions. Seeing Grey and Thalon, her eyes welled with tears. "You need no presentation; I recognize you both," she choked.

Spreading her arms wide, she wrapped one hand around both necks and pulled them into her. She stepped back and slid her hand down one side of their faces and to their hearts. Assessing them both with a long and meaningful smile, she whispered, "My son's protectors."

Taking them both by the hands, her eyes twinkled. "I see my siblings

in both of you. I'm so grateful my son has found you. Thank you for taking care of him."

Greeting Shayvonne, Pan took hold of both her hands. "I knew you were a mother from the moment I saw you in the mirror. I'll never forget how you cared for my son as if he were your own."

"I hope, like him, you'll find our family to be an extension of yours," Shayvonne bowed.

"Is this the palace he grew up in?" Brynn eyed the kitchen slack-jawed.

"The same. I promise I'll give you a tour later of all Birk's favorite hiding places," Pan winked, squeezing her nose.

"I told you he was a prince," Brynn shouted to Grey.

Pan laughed, squeezing Brynn's hand. Shifting her attention to Zara, she smiled, "And you are the spitting image of—"

"Me?" asked an apprehensive voice, entering the room.

All three sisters locked eyes—years of emotions crashed between them. Grief for lost time, nostalgia for the moments they missed, lingering aches of past mistakes, but, above all, a reminder of love—lost but not forgotten. Rushing to Sable's side, the three siblings circled in a long, overdue embrace.

"Sable, we've missed you so. Do we have you to thank for reuniting us?" Edi held her sister's hand.

Sable looked across the room at Birk and smiled. "No, we have our children to thank for that."

Everyone desired to stay close, so they were provided temporary housing on the Royal Isle. Grey stayed with Birk in his cottage, while Ravenshire, *thrilled to finally be gifted his own place by Edi*, invited Biddy and Thalon to bunk with him. Talbot generously offered his home to Shayvonne and Brynn while he lodged with Xavier in the interim.

Over the next couple of weeks, building their small family and community helped them heal. Zara and Hyacinth were doted on by Saffrona.

Never having daughters of her own, she relished their company and opened her home to them.

Sable stayed with Edi at her palace, enjoying long strolls in the gardens with her sisters and catching them up on the events since the war.

Birk's heart brimmed with pride. He loved seeing everyone's enthusiasm for exploring Balincia's islands and borderlands. He appreciated its beauty and charm more than he did when he left. Now, through new eyes, he could see all the love and energy Edi and Pan had poured into it over the years.

Spending their days sailing on the lake's calm waters and exploring the local markets, everyone found their place.

Birk was thrilled to find Thalon and Zara shared his mutual love for books. Spending hours curled up in the library together, Edi allowed them to explore the once-forbidden recesses with her and Shayvonne. Crashing into each other on the couch, they learned of their mothers' histories and became educated on the magics growing inside them.

Outside the palace walls, Talbot developed a relationship with Grey, who missed the father figures from his past. Traveling with him and Xavier by boat, Grey and Brynn were fascinated with the dragon-sized manta rays and wildlife circling the land. Teaching them to sail and tie knots, Talbot helped the two siblings appreciate and thrive in an environment outside the mountains.

Indigo found new mentees in Hyacinth and Ravenshire, spending hours with them on the beaches, honing their skills, and teaching them the ways of the Azure. Even Grey and Thalon found a way to connect through Brynn, who served as a bridge. Her growing affection for Thalon after the trials and their shared sarcastic wit opened the doors to a hesitant friendship.

Perhaps the most surprising of duos, much to everyone's delight, was between Biddy and Saffrona. Learning his love for food translated into a niche for cooking, the short, dwarf toddled around after the giant chef in Edi's kitchens. The two became inseparable. Sharing her culinary recipes, she delighted in watching him present his creations to his friends.

The Balincians, in turn, were enthralled with their first visitors.

Brunt always attracted attention in the marketplaces, as did Grey, often followed by a group of swooning young women. Biddy would tumble and perform in the outdoor amphitheater to entertain the children, while Zara always found herself in long, curious conversations with strangers, telling them about the lands beyond their borders.

Birk and Grey also found time for each other. Mornings watching the sunrise and long walks in Pan's garden healed any insecurities or feelings of displacement. Holding hands under the table, they laughed while their mothers shared stories of their childhoods over afternoon tea.

One afternoon, Edi walked into her back garden and found Sable sitting at the infinity pool.

"One of the things I've missed is our ability to never mince words with one another. Pan, as you know, always requires a bit of handling," Edi said, joining her sister on the lawn. "I know there's something you want to ask me, Sable. It's written all over your face."

Her sister turned, her eyes lost in the past. "Why did you leave the war?" she asked, toneless.

Edi stared into the horizon and lifted her chin. "We left to give you a chance," she replied quietly.

"You left to give *yourselves* a chance. Both of you knew you were the most powerful of us. Without you, we fell apart."

"No—you won," Edi corrected, turning to look into her sister's eyes.

"At what cost? Countless people lost their lives. Faunwood always took Pan's lead; she disappeared soon after you did, costing us another ally. Feyluna tore herself in two to give us an edge, and Cyrus . . ." She paused; her throat grew heavy. "We only won because of him—and a part of me can never forgive you for his death."

Edi wrung her hands. "I know you don't want to hear this, but Cyrus is the one who convinced us to leave. He created this space for Balincia. Deep down, when you look around, I think you know we couldn't have

achieved this alone. He's the one who helped us escape and protected us in this paradise."

"I don't believe you," she said, shaking her head in denial. "He'd never willingly put so many lives at risk."

"You're right. He did what it took to save as many lives as possible," she paused. "Cyrus and Farren uncovered a plot to weaponize Pan's powers during the war. As our prime creator, you're aware she is connected to all the hearts of Driftstone. The results would've been catastrophic if she'd been compromised or pushed over the edge."

"That's ridiculous! That could never have happened, your powers would neutralize—" Sable stopped. Her mouth parted, and she turned slowly to meet her sister's gaze. "Morvana aimed to kill *you*."

Edi offered a tight nod. "Farren didn't die protecting Pan in the Battle for the Valley—he died protecting me." Sable took her sister's hand. "It was then that Cyrus concocted his plan to send us away. Pan had to be removed from the war for all our sakes."

"Why didn't he share this with me? We shared everything," Sable grieved.

"He wanted us to be martyrs. If you held any hope we were alive, you would've spent your efforts distracted—trying to find us. He believed *you* were the only one who could win the war. He promised he'd return for us once it was over, to let us know it was safe to come home. When we heard nothing . . . we assumed the worst."

Sable laughed and looked into the sky, blinking away her tears. "Optimistic fool, he didn't count on his own death." She shook her head and leaned in to hug her sister, "All this time—had I known."

"We've all wasted too much time regretting or running from our past," Edi said, holding her sister's arms. "Stealing a cue from my nephew, I think it's time we write a new story."

After two weeks, it was time for Sable and her newly appointed Royal Advisor to return to Ironspire.

Standing amid the hallway of doors, she held her daughter's hands. "I'm so proud of you and the woman you're evolving into. Don't break trust with your new friends or make the same mistakes I did with my sisters. Our chosen family is important."

Zara hugged her mother. "I'm proud of you, too. We're finally building a relationship—I feel torn to leave you now."

"The path you're on will ensure we have years ahead of us to enjoy together. I have faith in you, my daughter."

Edi and Pan embraced their sister as Indigo and Zara exchanged goodbyes.

"Our door will never be locked to you again," Edi squeezed her sister's hand.

"And when you need us, we will come running," Pan assured her.

Sable stood tall. "We will see each other soon."

"We'll bring them to Ironspire before they head back out again," shared Pan.

Sable glanced around the room before pulling her sisters in close.

"The children will need to travel across the Over to Feyluna. She's the only one who can guarantee safe passage into the Under," Sable reminded them.

"Are we sure we shouldn't be joining them?" Pan asked again, "There's still so much we haven't shared. They're still learning to use their powers."

"Don't underestimate them. I've witnessed them in action." Sable squeezed her sister's arm.

"Pandi, we don't want to tempt Fate. The prophecy is clear: this is a quest for the children. We'd only resurface our old grudges and mistakes." Edi tempered. "It doesn't mean we can't help them along the way." She winked at her sister.

"We're aligned?" Sable confirmed.

With a nod, the sisters embraced again.

In the evening, everyone gathered on Birk's lawn for a picnic to watch the suns set. The yard was filled with laughter. Leaning against Grey, Birk rested his head on his shoulder. Closing his eyes, he listened to the waves lap against the shore.

"May I sit with you?" Pan asked Thalon, sitting behind the group on a bench.

Scooting over, he smiled at Pan; she reminded him of Birk. "Please, I could use the company."

"Yet, you're surrounded by friends," she motioned. Sitting beside him, she placed her hand on his leg. "I see my chaos within you," she commented softly.

Thalon blinked, "Pardon?"

"Just as my son draws on your mother's connection to the earth, I see my storms of chaos brewing inside you."

"Should I be worried?"

Pan gave him a gentle maternal smile. "No, chaos magic shouldn't frighten you. It's fueled by love . . . and grief. It indicates you have a huge heart. You have to be careful you don't try to contain it." Directing her gaze to the lake, she reflected for a moment. "I've made this mistake many times—it will always spill over if you don't learn how to release it."

"I'm not sure I know how to do that," he confessed. "What if my emotions hurt others?"

Pan shook her head. "Our emotions don't hurt others; what causes damage is our approach and method of sharing them. How else can we determine if our feelings are true and accurate if we don't explore them and leave them open to examination? Baring one's soul can be terrifying, but imprisoning it will destroy you."

Thalon searched Pan's face; she knew. "I . . . tried."

"And in doing so, you learned you hold a special place in my son's heart." She noticed his gaze fall on Grey and Birk. "Don't make the mis-

take of comparing your place in someone's heart with anyone else. The heart will always surprise you with its capacity. Let it soothe you to know you're in there. Treasure what you have now; love always shifts and grows."

Rubbing his back, she encouraged him to join his friends. When he walked down, she watched Zara pat the blanket beside her—her son smiled, welcoming Thalon between them. They'd find their way.

Sitting beside her sister, Edi took Thalon's place. Watching in silence, the twins drank in the purple, pink, and orange hues painting the sky. Listening to the children's laughter—their hearts grew full.

Edi took her sister's hand. "We've shared many beautiful sunsets, haven't we?"

"This one may be my favorite."

Epilogue

Morvana brooded over her cauldron. Biting off and spitting her nails into the boiling black brew, she contemplated her thwarted plans with the arcanivores. Despite the loss, she reminded herself she was playing the long game. Besides, there was still a lot to celebrate.

Tiny cracks were forming among this new generation, and if she'd learned anything from her brother, Discord, small cracks could become large fissures. They were still young and naïve, and even if they wielded power stronger than their parents, they lacked the years of experience to control it. She could play with this. They'd need to descend into the Under to fulfill the prophecy, and she'd be prepared and waiting.

The princess was headstrong, Faunwood's son insecure, and due to Sable's interference, they were all now afraid of Farren's kin, who demonstrated his true savage colors in the arena. Only two pesky details concerned her: the little girl and the binding of the Ashendrake to that pretentious prince. She couldn't find their strings with her fate magic. She'd need to deal with them first; she'd waited too long for this moment to leave anything to chance.

Chaos's son, however, would be the linchpin to her liberation—the weapon she'd need to exact her revenge. Armed with the knowledge of

Balincia, she'd use him to burn his home to the ground. She wasn't worried about the twins; they wouldn't be able to defeat her once she finished her other project in the In-Between—even Chaos and Order can't escape Fate.

NOTE FROM AUTHOR

Appendices have always been my favorite part of a book. While a story shouldn't rely on an appendix, it can enhance the full immersive experience, opening the door for deeper context and exploration.

I've gone to great lengths to avoid spoilers while still laying delicious cake crumbs to entice curious readers with clues. Every appendix included in the *Driftstone series* only has information set before the book's timeline, revealing characters, events and locations solely referenced or relevant to the current book. I want my readers to experience the world through Birk's eyes and enjoy the journey of discovery with him.

I would offer three alternative approaches to diving into the appendix for tentative readers worried about uncovering information not yet revealed in the story.

1. Read the appendix at the end. The story is complete and whole, with all the information needed to enjoy without the use of an appendix. When you're hungry for more, the appendix will add color to your experience and provide more depth when revisiting the book or series.

2. My personal preference is to hold off on the temptation to dip into the appendix until *after* you've finished Part One. This method minimizes minor spoilers and keeps you on track with Birk's journey.

3. Careful navigators may prefer to look up references as they are mentioned. Just be forewarned; some details foreshadow certain events.

There's no right or wrong way to enjoy a book. I hope, however you navigate your exploration, it sparks creativity and imagination. We're all creators, and a good story requires the love and nurturing of the Storyteller *and* their audience.

Trust your magic, my friends!

S.W. Kent

The World You Know So Far

DRIFTSTONE

MAP OF THE OVER

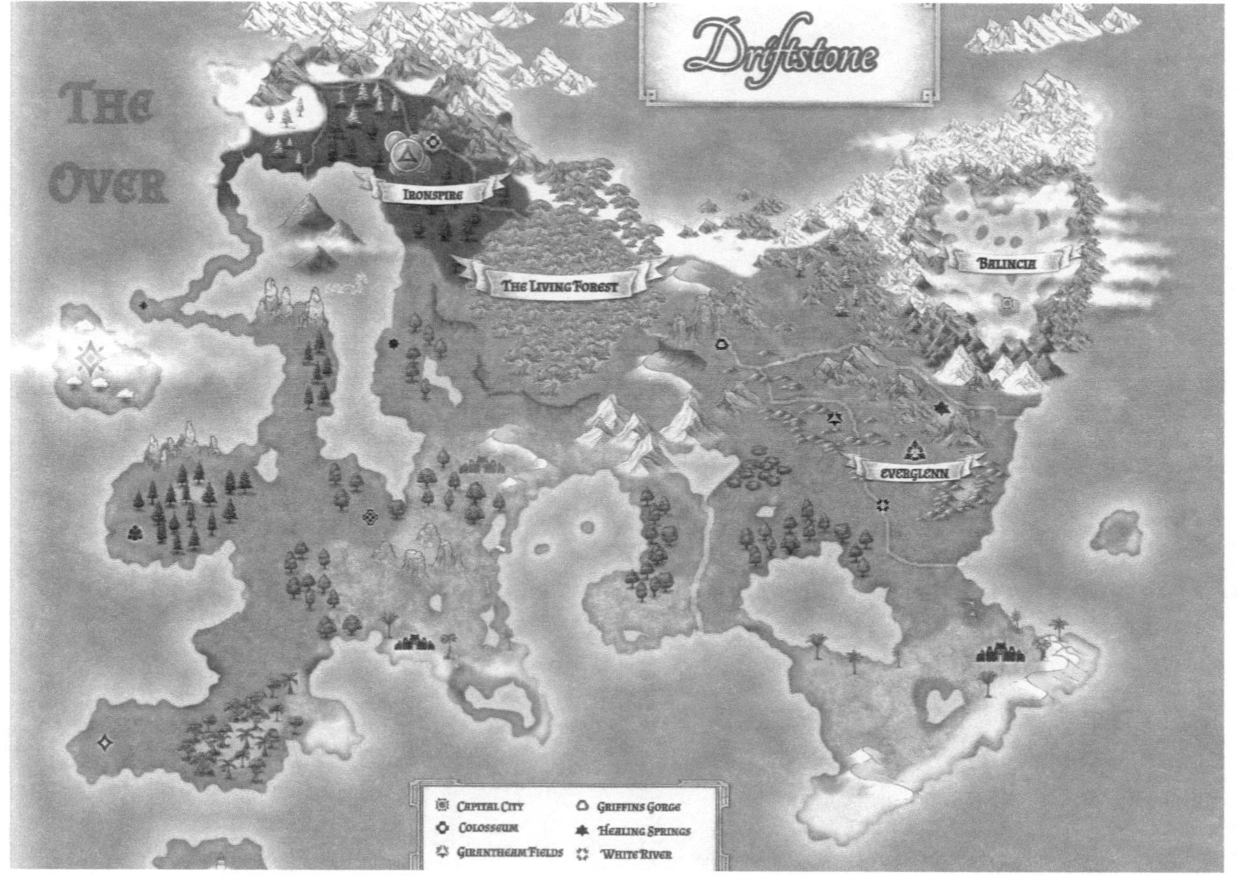

Driftstone
The Over
Ironspire
The Living Forest
Balincia
Everglenn
Capital City
Colosseum
Greantheam Fields
Griffins Gorge
Healing Springs
White River

PROMINENT LOCATIONS

Balincia

Laws of Governance:

1. Every Citizen Has A Purpose
2. Every Citizen Will Have All They Need
3. Every Citizen Is Gifted With A Talent
4. Reading And Writing Is Prohibited
5. When One Soul Departs, Another is Born
6. The Scales Must Always Remain Balanced

Rulers: Edi (Practitioner of Order) and Pan (Practitioner of Chaos)

Additional Governance: Township Leader Council, The Royal Guardians

Significant Landmarks

Capital City: It is the land's main center for trade, celebration, and entertainment. Due to its distance from other towns, most citizens need more than a day to reach the city. The largest island stands out as one of only two that lack a traditional township. Its only permanent residents are innkeepers, a healer, a falconer, and four guardians trusted by the witches.

To accommodate travelers, the inn extends along the entire northern coast of the island, featuring two grand halls, a kitchen, stables, and enchanted sleeping chambers that multiply and expand based on the number of guests. A circular cobblestone entrance leads inn lodgers into the lantern-lit streets of the town square. Adjacent to the square is an open market where visiting townships set up vacant storefronts to sell their goods and services.

At the center of the town, a large fountain honors the witches, surrounded by a descending outdoor amphitheater where crowds gather to watch the performances of the Storyteller and other visiting artisans. Beyond the town limits, scenic gardens and walking paths lead to white-sanded beaches.

Crystaline Lake: Fed by the pristine waters flowing down from the Cosimo Mountains, the lake is an essential lifeline for Balincians. Citizens rely on the lake for freshwater and as a route for trade and travel. Its crystal-clear waters support a diverse ecosystem of aquatic life, which helps sustain the livelihoods of fishermen and traders.

Cosimo Mountains: A range of massive, snow-capped peaks that surround and dominate Balincia's landscape. The mountain's incredible heights and unfathomable depths have prevented anyone from carving a path through or over them.

Dense Forest—At the base of the Cosimo Mountains, the Dense Forest covers the northern and eastern borders of Balincia. The forest offers a sustainable supply of timber combined with ideal grounds for hunting within its regenerative groves. Despite the brave efforts of its explorers, the forest seems endless and unconquerable. The deeper one journeys toward the mountains, the thicker the trees become, slowing travelers and giving the forest its dull name. It is home to a variety of wildlife, including stags, tusked wild boars, and wolves.

Faerie Mines: The mines form a maze of endless caverns buried deep within the caves and foothills along the southern border. Each contains a variety of precious stones, metals, and minerals vital for the forges and artisans of Balincia. The mines undergo the same cyclical regeneration of bounty as the forest and lake.

Border Townships

The **Fisher's village** is situated on the western border, featuring a shallow aquamarine coastline. Freshwater manta rays, as large as boats, patrol the waters alongside fishermen, aiding in catching fish and casting nets around the coastal bedrock caves. Citrus fruits are plentiful in the lush jungles beyond the coast, which are also home to puffed-belly parrots and blue-horned iguanas. The Fisher's Township is the largest community and plays a vital role in trade and transportation. Most residents here excel in shipbuilding and rope weaving.

The **Farmer's village** is located on the eastern border and is surrounded by green hill country. The land here is fertile and supports the harvest of potatoes, root vegetables, greens, and gourds. Downy cattle are raised for both meat and milk, roaming the hills alongside sheep and horses. Eastern citizens are known for their husbandry, mastery of irrigation, leather tanning, and textiles. They supply most of the land's blankets, rugs, and materials for the tailors.

To the north, near the Dense Forest, is Balincia's **Lumber Township**. The village provides all the harvested timber, which is made into furniture, barrels, and bowls, and also serves as fuel for cooking and heating homes during winter nights. Wood pulp is produced at the sawmill to help insulate cottages and to produce paper for the witch's books, scrolls, and the falconer's messages. Three-tusked boars and herds of wild elk inhabit the forest where Huntsmen are trained.

The lake's southern border is marked by the **Mining Township,** who manage the faerie caverns. An abundance of gems and coal fills the mines, providing full-time work for *jewelers (and ornate furniture designers for Edi)*. To the left of the mines are the Iron Hills, which supply blacksmiths with everything they need to forge steel, craft ship hulls, build surgical instruments for healers, and mold cutlery for the people.

Island Townships

Smaller than the border towns, the islands focus on niche but essential trades. There is an island dedicated to beekeepers who curate Balincia's dark golden floral honey and another that farms lavender moon moths for their silk. One island only grows wheat and is connected to a smaller island that houses the flour mill. The loudest isle is the **Township of Poultry,** home to hundreds of free-roaming chickens and roosters, who crow relentlessly at the rise of each of the three suns.

Everglenn

Nestled in the Protector's Valley, **Everglenn** is a village built on the faith of its people and their respect for the land. This settlement features stone cottages, sheep farms, and sturdy stables, and was established as a welcoming sanctuary for migrants, nomads, and travelers seeking a peaceful place to settle. Influenced by the Church of the Protector, its citizens follow the principles of life taught by Farren, one of the Original Thirteen. Protected by runes and buried standing stones, the village and its surrounding valley are considered sacred.

Significant Landmark
The Church of the Protector: The church serves as a place for prayer, meditation, and town gatherings. Its massive stone walls and stained-glass windows are sculpted and crafted with scenes from Farren's life. The church's bell tower functions as the town alarm, warning villagers of invaders or predators.

Ironspire

Rulers: Lady Ironspire

Additional Governance: Council of the Elite, The Azure, The Princess of Ironspire. The Royal Advisor

The Eight Rotational Levels of Ironspire:

1. **Citadel Tower:** The crown atop Ironspire City, the Citadel Tower contains the Throne Room, where decrees are issued, the Great Hall, where exclusive gatherings occur, and Lady Ironspire's Private Chambers. A retractable bridge connects the tower to the Royal Box in the White River Colosseum.

2. **Royal Housing:** The Royal Housing level hosts the Princess of Ironspire, the Royal Advisor, and the Captain of the Azure Guard. It includes key chambers such as the military planning room, the council chamber, the Royal Dining Hall, and the Royal Armory.

3. **The Academy:** The Academy houses the Azure soldiers and their trainees. The facility includes training grounds, meditative gardens, housing barracks, dining halls, and heated bathing pools.

4. **Engineering:** The Engineering level contains the mystical forges, laboratories, and libraries that support Ironspire's progress in technology and defense. Here, engineers combine magic and science in daring projects covering defense systems, housing solutions, transportation advances, and the devices used in the Colosseum games.

5. **Elite Housing:** The Elite Housing level is for the families of the Azure and Royal Council. It includes private gardens and reflection pools as additional benefits for those who serve Ironspire.

6. **Market and Storefronts:** The market and storefronts level was built for artisans and merchants who exclusively cater to the upper five levels.

7. **General Population:** Ironspire's foundation, the General Population level, houses most of its inhabitants. Here, the city expands into markets, villages, and communal areas.

8. **Border Walls:** The Border Walls of Ironspire are mobile fortifications that adapt and grow with the city's population. The walls also serve as temporary accommodations for the Azure guards on duty. There are secret tunnels built beneath the Border Walls that connect every area of the city, except for the Citadel Tower and Royal Housing. These clandestine passages serve as express pathways for the Azure to respond to emergencies.

The Living Forest

Rulers: Faunwood

Additional Governance: The Chamber of Roots; The Prince of the Living Forest

Significant Landmarks:

Aeruvia, the Treetop Village
Aeruvia is the Capital of the Living Forest. This village, built from arched trees and swinging bridges, is home to various magical races, such as centaurs, sprites, and elves. Other residents of the Living Forest often travel here to trade goods and share stories.

Burrowed Hollows

The Burrowed Hollows is a vast tunnel system underneath the forest floor. Foxfire Beetles often light the paths, which Bramble Badgers maintain.

Eternal Thicket

 A valley filled with brambles and thorns, the Eternal Thicket serves as a protected entrance to the Nether Realm. It is the only part of the Living Forest that is avoided and neglected.

Glade of Lumaroel

The Glade of Lumaroel is an enchanted pool for lovers. The waters of Lumaroel possess the power to open hearts and connect soulmates. Those who swim or bathe here will find themselves more receptive to following their desires. If the Moonhorn Moose appears to a couple in the Glade, it's a signal that Driftstone has blessed their union, and he'll lead them to the sacred realm of Elysiamore.

Shallow Gardens

Near the northwest borders, the water from the White River pours into the Living Forest, creating the Shallow Gardens. A system of gradually sloping falls that generate cascading pools and gardens. These pools are often a gathering place for Satyrs and River Nymphs.

Sporewood

A section of the living forest made entirely of fungi. Fungus of varying sizes, from caps no larger than a dewdrop to mushrooms as big as trees, carpets the forest floor. Gnomes, Pixies, and Faunerbils call this area home.

Verdant Nexus

Home to the Chamber of Roots. Here, Faunwood and the guardians of the forest commune with gleamers, seeking guidance on issues threatening the Living Forest and Driftstone.

The Hearts of Driftstone

The Seven Hearts of Driftstone

- Heart of Vitality: Connected to Sylvanethia.
- Heart of Wisdom: Connected to Omniscora.
- Heart of Balance: (Destroyed in the war) Disconnected from the Chronoscape.
- Heart of Essence: Connected to the Nether.
- Heart of Tranquility: (Corrupted after the war) Connected to the Spirit Realm.
- Heart of Creativity: Connected to the Dreamscape.
- Heart of Connection: Connected to Elysiamore.

Strength of Hearts

The Heart of Vitality and the Heart of Connection are the two strongest hearts. They're directly tied to the world's magic and sentience.

Consequences of Heart Destruction

If all seven hearts of Driftstone are destroyed or corrupted, the land's magic will collapse. Driftstone will lose its sentience and connection to the prime creator and its stewards. This event would cause the decay and imbalance of Driftstone, affecting all life forms on it.

A corrupted heart's influence can spread like decay, permeating the land with dark energy. Plants will wither or perish, waters will become stagnant, and animals will fall ill or become aggressive. The ecosystem will become unstable, leading to natural disasters and magical anomalies.

Driftstone Stewards and Communion

- The Driftstone communes solely with the prime creator (Pan) and its chosen stewards (Farren, Faunwood), who are responsible for protecting its seven hearts.
- The stewards of Driftstone can relocate, shield, or transplant the hearts to protect them.
- The stewards of Driftstone share a deep, empathic bond with the land. They can feel its pain and its distress.

Celestial Body Influence

Influence of the Suns
In Driftstone, the three suns—red, yellow, and orange—influence the growth and development of plants and animals in different ways:

Red Sun

Longevity: The energy of the red sun enhances the physical endurance and health of plants and animals, promoting flourishing ecosystems.

Yellow Sun:

Adaptation: The yellow sun's energy promotes mental acuity in animals and adaptability in plants when faced with changing environmental conditions.

Orange Sun Influence:

Diversity: The orange sun's influence amplifies the ability for species to birth varieties both within and outside of an animal or plant's inherent biology.

Influence of the Moons
In Driftstone, the presence of two moons, one blue and one lavender, exerts influences on the laws and usage of magic.

Tides of Magic
Magical currents surge when both moons are full and aligned, enhancing spellcasting, enchantments, and rituals. Conversely, during new moons or when the moons are in opposition, magic may wane or act unpredictably, leading to fluctuations in the potency and reliability of spells.

Lunar Rituals and Ceremonies

During the blue moon's ascent, ceremonies focused on wisdom, knowledge, and divination are most effective. In contrast, the lavender moon's cycle is associated with intuition, dreams, and spiritual communion.

Luminous Flora and Fauna

Plants that bloom under the blue moon's light may possess healing, illusory, or empathic ingredients for potions. Those that grow under the lavender moon are more likely to induce dreams, enhance perception, or stimulate creativity.

Animals connected to the moons' magic may exhibit greater intelligence.

Laws and Sciences of Aging

Celestial Influences

Driftstone is governed by three suns (red, yellow, orange) and two moons (blue, lavender) that emit unique energies which affect the aging process. Ages are defined by cycles around the suns.

Prime Life Cycles

In youth, individuals age rapidly, experiencing accelerated aging, particularly during puberty, and the process decelerates when individuals hit their early prime. The balance of the celestial influences and Driftstone's magic keeps the majority of the population in three prime life cycles— early prime, mid-prime, and late prime. These cycles help sentient life to remain at its strongest and most fertile, thereby maximizing adaptation and evolution.

An example of a **Non-Magic Born** Life Cycle:
- Youth: 0-22 Cycles Around the Suns
- Early Prime: 23-300 Cycles Around the Suns
- Mid-Prime: 300-800 Cycles Around the Suns
- Late Prime: 800-970 Cycles Around the Suns
- Old Age: 970+ Cycles Around the Suns

Lifespan Variations by Species or Race:
- Non-Maic Born: 1,000-1,500 Cycles Around the Suns
- Magical Races: 3,000-5,000 Cycles Around the Suns
- Dragons and Fae*: 15,000-40,000 Cycles Around the Suns
- Original Thirteen**: 100,000-500,000 Cycles Around the Suns (*Hypothesized*)
- Sacred Creatures and Familiars: Unlimited

*After completing puberty and reaching 23 cycles around the suns, fae cease to display physical signs of aging. Their perpetual youth is a result of being created from light magic; their physical bodies reflect their spirits' invulnerability, which protects them from the effects of aging. The Aging Process, however, is dependent on their time spent in the Spirit Realm. If their exposure is disrupted, their aging will progress, and their lifespans will be similar to those of dwarves and elves.

Witches (also known as Magic-Born) possess the ability to suspend or slow down their aging process using time magic and controlled atmospheres. However, strenuous magic, essence drainage, dark magic attacks, transference, loss of both familiars or magical exertion without adequate restoration may accelerate a witch's aging process.

Children of Driftstone

Sacred Species
Sacred species are born directly from the magic and energy of Driftstone, including two distinct groups: Sacred Creatures and the Original Thirteen Magic-Born. They are the first inhabitants, creators, and guardians of the world, and are considered Driftstone's Children.

Sacred Creatures
Sacred creatures predate the Original Thirteen and were created to protect the Sacred Realms and Driftstone's adjacent hearts.

While magical creatures, created by Magic-Born, derive their abilities from various sources of magic, including celestial bodies, sacred creatures are considered magic-incarnate and tied to Driftstone's life force, also known as the divine source. Their fate and success are directly connected to the Magic-Born, requiring an invested partnership between them.

The Ashendrake

The Ashendrake is a harbinger of hope and restoration during or after great upheaval. Its appearance heralds an era of potential transformation and renewal. This sacred creature is the only biological entity able to travel into each sacred realm without aid and remain undetected if warranted.

The Chamber of Roots

The Chamber of Roots is the eldest of the sacred creatures; a mystical multi-entity connected to the living essence of Driftstone and Sylvan-ethia. These sentient roots also serve as the council to Faunwood and protectors of the Living Forest, and are often considered the direct mouthpiece of Driftstone.

Moonhorn Moose

The Moonhorn Moose is Elysiamore's guardian. When Driftstone senses the presence of two lovers whose destinies are fated, it summons the Moonhorn Moose to guide them to Elysiamore. Many lovers in the Living Forest flock to the glade hoping for the moose's blessing, often leaving disappointed. The beast's appearances are so rare throughout history that the Moose and Elysiamore have become stories of myth and legend.

Sagebeak

The Great Owl was the guardian of Omniscora before Goetfeather killed it. A majestic creature of immense size, its wings could span a single valley. Due to its unfortunate extinction, historians do not know much about this sacred creature.

Shadow-wing

Shadow-wing, a giant raven, is the only creature able to navigate the pathways connecting the realms of the living and the dead. Shadow-wing is one of the few sacred creatures to applaud the arrival of the Magic-Born, due to his own self-interests in their creations.

The Unicorn

The Unicorn is the guardian of the temporal flow, entrusted with protecting the past, present, and future in the Chronoscape. She is the only sacred creature to become a familiar to one of the Magic-Born. With the ability to walk in several timelines at once, she often gets confused about where she is at any given moment.

The White Mane

This albino sacred creature, standing taller than most mountains, has the face of a lion and the body of a gorilla. Its flowing beard contains strands of pure magic, capable of healing wounds, dispelling curses, and mending shattered souls. Elusive, the White Mane only grants audience to those whom he believes have the purest of hearts, and was the most prominent objector to Driftstone's decision to create the Magic-Born.

The Original Thirteen

The Magic-Born, *named Witches and Warlocks by those who came after*, were created from the energy and magic of Driftstone. Born and shaped with purpose, each of the Thirteen was given a gift: the power to design, develop, and protect the land they call home.

Recognizing the balance required to keep such powerful forces in check, Driftstone formed a partner for each Magic-Born—a kindred spirit to complement and temper their sibling. This balance of power was designed to ensure creation and preservation would always walk hand in hand.

Until they didn't . . .

Historians still argue whether the Original Thirteen are myths and legends used to explain the creation of Driftstone, or if they're story has been exaggerated over time.

Calder (Brother Ocean, the Tidewalker)

Master of the Oceans and the Winds, Calder was an aid to travelers and critical in the evolution of trade and transportation. Seen as a friend to man, he was once revered as much as Faunwood, with consistent offerings made to him from sailors, anglers and fishing towns.

Prior to the war, he freely roamed the lands and was known for his volatile temper against those who abused the oceans. Despite his angry countenance, his alliance with his darker siblings, Goetfeather and Morvana, still shocked his followers. With his mastery over the water, he turned the literal tides for a greater part of the war and was directly responsible for the largest number of casualties.

Historians still do not understand his motivations for turning against Driftstone. Now banished to the Oceans in the Under, he cannot set foot on land.

Cyrus (Brother Architect)

Blessed with the innate ability to fold and expand the dimensions of space, Cyrus was often referred to as an Architect. Considered eccentric, he was always experimenting and pushing the boundaries of the overlap of magic and science. The inventor of sentient portals, he formed the world's greatest library from his research and discoveries. The library vanished when he died in the war, and rumors of its existence in a pocket dimension persist today.

Discord (Brother Influence)

Discord was born under the moniker *Influence*, but his name changed when he caused division among his siblings. The youngest of the original siblings, he is the least known to historians outside of his role as the catalyst in the Witches' War. He is the only member of the Magic-Born created without a partner, which has generated several theories around his intended purpose.

Edi (Edict, Sister Order)

Eldest of the Thirteen by a few seconds, Edict is Pandora's twin sister and plays a critical role in maintaining the 'Scales of Balance' as the Mistress of Order. Known for her intelligence and directness, she and her sister disappeared during the war. Historians believe the twins were killed in the Battle of the Valley of the Protector.

Farren (Brother Protector, The Great Protector)

Farren was the eldest brother of the Original Thirteen, whose duties included protecting the land and its inhabitants. His bond and fascination with wildlife made him a powerful primary creator for many of Driftstone's magical creatures. Caretaker of the land, a steward to Driftstone's hearts and a voice for the beasts, Farren's life and death were revered as sacred and noble, leading to a faith-based practice in his name.

Faunwood (Sister Earth, the Elven Witch)

Known to many as the Elven Witch, Faunwood is a secondary creator and mother to half of Driftstone's magical races. Along with Farren, she is a steward to its seven hearts. Before the war, she was celebrated for her contributions to the earth and one of the more popular patroned of the Magic-Born in the Sacred Grove. After her brother Farren died in the Witches' War, Faunwood retreated to the Living Forest. In partnership with the Chamber of Roots, she has separated herself and her children from the rest of Driftstone for ten thousand years.

Feyluna (Sister Soul, The Witch Fairy, Mother of Fae)

Feyluna is a secondary creator and mother to the fae and steward of the Spirit Realm. Considered the purest of the Original Thirteen, Feyluna is the only sibling able to harness spirit magic, a special form of light magic. Like her brother, Farren, she actively avoided the temples and patrons in the Sacred Grove, preferring her mission to be untainted or influenced by humans. Feyluna's essence was split in two during the Witches' War when she was forced to banish her brother Calder from the land. Retreating to the Spirit Realm, she hasn't been seen or heard from since.

Goetfeather (Brother Wisdom, Alvis)

Gifted with mental prowess, Alvis was a glutton for knowledge, especially the forbidden kind. Instead of using his gifts to advance society, he hoarded his insights and collected them as weapons. It took little persuasion from Discord to goad him into hunting his darker pursuits, including necromancy, earning him the name Goetfeather. He is infamous for the unforgivable crime of killing a sacred creature, the Sagebeak, to absorb its knowledge and gain access to the Omniscora.

Morvana (Sister Fate, The Bog Witch, The Dark Witch, Queen of Decay)

Once popular among humankind for her abilities to unravel fate, Morvana has transformed into the symbol of Dark Magic and the definition of an evil witch used to frighten children. Ten thousand years after the Witches' War, Driftstone is still healing from the poison and rage she embedded into the land. Trapped in the Under, she has been no less idle or threatening; taking over the Dreamscape, she monitors the halls for opportunities to escape and strike revenge.

Nazeem (Brother Dream)

Nazeem is the only sibling to accomplish the creation of a realm, *the Dreamscape*, and the only Magic-Born to receive a transference of power from a sacred creature, *the Ashendrake*. After the Witches' War, Nazeem was trapped in the Under, where he continues to battle Morvana in the Dreamscape and attempts to keep Calder and Goetfeather from reforming an alliance. The weight of these wars and the potency of magic required to sustain his defenses have accelerated his aging beyond that of his siblings. Fearing corruption or forced transference in his weakened state, he gave the Ashendrake back its form once he was banished from the Dreamscape. Without allies or aid, the future of Nazeem is uncertain.

Pan (Pandora, Sister Chaos)

Twin sister to Edi, Pan is considered the most powerful and unpredictable of the Original Thirteen. As a prime creator, she is responsible for dragons and humans, the bio-prints for all future life. Connected to the Divine Source of the Driftstone and wielding the innate magics of Chaos, she is the most fluid in her power and holds a special connection to all sentient life. Vulnerable to deep emotions, her sister Edi keeps her grounded and balanced.

Pan was accused of killing her brother Discord and initiating the Witches' War. Like her sister, Edi, she is thought to have been a casualty of the war after the Battle of the Valley.

Sable (Lady Ironspire, Sister Innovation)

Sable, the most prominent and recognizable member of the Original Thirteen, not only survived the Witches' War but has raised Driftstone's largest army and most innovative city. A brilliant engineer and fearsome warrior, she is a polarizing figure who represents the Magic-Born's haunted past and Driftstone's future. When she won the war, at the cost of losing her brother and best friend, Cyrus, she felt abandoned by her surviving siblings, who'd retreated.

Sable is the only active and visible Magic-Born left, guarding the Over, which has left her anxious, conspiratorial, and paranoid. Many of Driftstone's inhabitants no longer believe in the existence of the Original Thirteen, and they view Sable's narrative of her past as a method to manipulate and control a divided populace.

Selene (Sister Body)

Beautiful but vain, Selene ignored her innate gifts of regenerative and transformative magic to pursue youth and immortality. Despite forsaking her purpose, she's the only member of the Original Thirteen to have accomplished communing and connecting with a sacred creature, the Unicorn, and forming a bond with it as her familiar.

MAGICAL RACES

Primary Creations

Primary creations are lifeforms created by magic from pure energy. They are the bioprint for secondary creations.

Dragons

Created by Pan, dragons were initially intended to help protect mankind alongside the Original Thirteen. Gifted with language, they once bonded with their Magic-Born riders. Over millennia, a faction of dragons fell from grace, seeking to challenge and overthrow the Original Thirteen. Their betrayal led to the creation of the uncontrollable Wyverns and the dragon's subsequent banishment to Fang Fell.

Non-Magic-Born

According to lore, the Magic-Born gazed upon creation and longed for companionship. Driven by a desire to explore the full spectrum of existence, Pan channeled her energies into a form like their own. Pan gave humanity the gift of curiosity, the flame of inspiration, and the will to shape their destinies.

Secondary Creations (Magical Races)

Magic-Born, who are secondary creators, designed Magical Races from the bioprint of humans. They typically exhibit human-like intelligence, emotions, and social structures. Each race has its own language, traditions, and culture, often living in communities. Some magical races were gifted with enhancements and special abilities, even limited amounts of magic, but unlike their creators, they don't possess innate magic beyond their assigned gifts.

Centaurs

Centaurs are considered noble beings with a human upper body and a horse's lower body. Known for their speed and archery skills, they are often depicted as wise and proud guardians of the forests and plains. Centaurs rarely engage in interspecies mating and believe in keeping the purity of their bloodline.

Dwarves

Dwarves are stout, sturdy folk renowned for their craftsmanship in metalwork and stonemasonry. They excel in creating intricate and durable items, from weapons and armor to elaborate underground cities. Dwarves are often characterized by their love of mining and a strong sense of honor and tradition. They are extremely loyal and the most family-focused of all the magical races.

Due to the nature of their work, dwarves are often subjected to loud and explosive noises that are amplified within caverns. Over the years, the impact of their exposure led to many dwarves being born deaf or developing hearing loss in their later years. Thar'Keal, a sign language invented and used exclusively by dwarves, is utilized both by the hearing impaired and as a method of communication in the mines and on the battlefield.

Elves

Elves were the first magical race created by Faunwood from the bio-prints of humans. Elegant and long-lived beings, they are known for their beauty, grace, and deep connection to nature. Their bodies are more enhanced than humans, making them quicker, stronger, and more agile. Their visual and auditory senses are on par with those of hawks and eagles. These evolutionary advantages make them skilled rangers and soldiers, and one of the most capable races on Driftstone.

Fae

The Fae are a magical race who inhabit the sacred Spirit Realm beyond Driftstone. Children and secondary creations of Feyluna and the White Mane, the fae have developed a reputation for being arrogant and youth-obsessed. Only the original fae have physical wings; the generations that followed can manifest wings of light at will, which take the shape and color of their spiritual aura. They are also the only race gifted with light magic. After the Witches' War, the Fae withdrew from Driftstone and set up borders to avoid engagement with other magical races.

Giants

Giants are colossal beings known for their immense strength and size. Often depicted as living in remote mountain ranges or secluded valleys, they blend in with the natural landscapes. Despite their intimidating appearance, giants actively avoid confrontations or engagement with other magical races and encourage rumors that exaggerate their dangerous reputation.

Goblins

Goblins are cunning creatures known for their love of tricks and traps. Although smaller in stature than other magical races, goblins make up for it with their resourcefulness and skill in crafting devious inventions. They are often found in dark forests, underground tunnels, or abandoned ruins.

Gnomes

Gnomes are clever and industrious beings with a deep affinity for nature and technology. They are skilled inventors and engineers, creating intricate devices and mechanisms that blend magic and craftsmanship. Gnomes, smaller than dwarves, are often depicted as cheerful and curious folk who dwell in hidden burrows or forest glades.

Hydrosylphs

Hydrosylphs are an aquatic magical race, created by Calder. Humanoid, but adapted for the deep, they can breathe in any environment, swim swifter than any ship, and are one of the stronger magical races due to their ability to handle the deep pressure of the oceans. Hydrosylphs communicate through pulses of sound and light when underwater, and are also well-versed in most sylphic languages. Exiled to the Under after the Witches' War for their role in the massacre of human civilians, they've been forbidden to ever again set foot on land.

Kobolds

Kobolds are small, reptilian creatures known for their cunning and territorial nature, crafted from the bio-prints of dragon and human. Kobolds are skilled miners and trap-makers, often found in underground caverns or ancient ruins. They are one of the more advanced races in utilizing schooled magic by studying the flora and fauna used for ingredients in healing and potions. They hold a deep spiritual connection to dragons, given their biological bond, and pray for their return to Driftstone.

Nymphs

Nymphs are an elemental race known for their beauty. Unlike Sprites, Nymphs are only female; they are parthenogenic, and their host forms are made from the bio-prints of humans and nature's elements. While they do not need mates to reproduce, they are still an amorous and playful race, often drawn to music.

Satyrs

Satyrs are half-human, half-goat beings known for their love of revelry, music, and dance. With their jovial personalities and natural charm, Satyrs are often associated with celebrations and feasts in enchanted forests and meadows. They are skilled musicians and hedonists who enjoy life to the fullest and are usually surrounded by Nymphs.

Sprites

Sprites are closely tied to the natural world and its elements. Guardians of the forests, rivers, and meadows, they are masters of camouflage and often go unseen by mortal eyes. Sprites possess magical abilities that allow them to manipulate plants and water. Varying in size, they can be as tall as humans or as small as pixies.

Taurothians

The Taurothians are a dying race, created by Farren, who are hybrids of a human and a bull, with four arms, known for their immense strength and stubborn persistence. They are independent and self-reliant, preferring solitude and introspection over society. They are fiercely loyal to those they trust, but slow to warm to new acquaintances. Due to their isolated lifestyle, their race is becoming extinct because they refuse to couple and mate.

Trolls

Trolls are large and fearsome creatures known for their strength, regenerative abilities, and sometimes dim-witted nature. Often residing in remote and desolate regions like mountains or swamps, Trolls live in small communities that can threaten unwary travelers. Despite their intimidating appearance, Trolls vary in temperament, with some being more aggressive while others are more reclusive. Driven by hunger and primal urges, it is rare for them to be interested in politics or forming lasting alliances.

MAGICAL BEASTS

Magical Creatures

Magical creatures have abilities, appearances, or characteristics that set them apart from humanoid societies or regular wildlife. Often hybrids of different animals, they are connected to the magic of Driftstone, the sacred realms, and the celestial bodies. Each magical beast was created with a purpose to aid or support the land and its inhabitants.

Bramble Burrow Badgers

Benevolent creatures with fur that appear as thorny brambles, they are expert tunnelers that maintain the passageways in the Burrowed Hallways of the Living Forest. Able to dig through any material, rock or soil, they are also favored pets for mining dwarves.

Emberback Deer

This majestic deer species thrives in the red sun's energy, exhibiting robust antlers and a fiery coat. Emberback Deer are more swift and agile than regular deer. They are often considered messengers of the animal kingdom, warning other species of approaching predators or incoming natural disasters.

Familiars

Animals that form sacred bonds with the Original Thirteen. Guided by the *Law of Familiars*, these animals supersede their original animal biology and purpose, and their essence becomes tied to the Magic-Born who connected with them.

Faunerbil

Standing at about ankle height, the Faunerbil has the slender, agile body of a gerbil, covered in soft fur of varying earthy tones. Its face combines a gnome's pointed ears with a faun's gentle eyes and small, curling antlers. Gnomes often use them as a quick mode of travel in the forest, and can usually be found frolicking with pixies.

Foxfire Beetles

Bioluminescent insects that thrive in the Living Forest and draw energy from the Orange Sun. More resilient and adaptable to environments than fireflies, Foxfire Beetles are often kept in lanterns as a safe alternative to fire and are easily trained to occupy and dwell in smaller spaces.

Giant Crickets

Natural pruners, these insects grow to the size of small children and help keep the land from becoming overgrown. They are also considered delicacies and a high source of protein for nomadic tribes and centaurs.

Girantheam

Gentle behemoths with six towering legs, shaggy hair and the face of a water buffalo. Girantheam roam fields and plains, feeding off apricot and mimosa trees. Their saliva is often used by roaming tribes as a salve to help accelerate the healing of wounds. Their skin is considered impenetrable, and during the Witches' War, elves used them to mount attacks.

Golden-wing Hawk

A majestic bird of prey that absorbs energy from the yellow sun. Known for their intellect and sharp vision, Golden-wing Hawks were often used by Witches as links, serving as scouts and spies during the war.

Griffins

Griffins are legendary beasts that combine a lion's body with an eagle's wings and head. Fierce predators often use gorges and canyons as their hunting grounds. Griffins do not interact or engage well with other species, preferring isolation. They are extremely territorial. It is rumored that Faunwood placed Griffins outside the Living Forest to help patrol unwanted visitors.

Lunar Horse

Farren created lunar horses as gifts for the centaurs. Their pelts glow under the blue and lavender moons. Stronger and faster than regular horses, lunar horses can be domesticated but are often found in wild roaming packs. The male equine pelts represent the colors of the sun, and the female pelts represent the moons. Spotting lunar horses and centaurs together is considered a sign of good luck.

Lunar Moths

A mesmerizing insect with the ability to produce silk of pure light, a material that radiates a gentle, silver glow under the moon's beams when woven into blankets and garments. These textiles are soft, durable, and offer warmth in the coldest of climates.

Manta Rays

Larger than most ships, manta rays are found in freshwater and saltwater varieties. A gift from Calder to humans, they are gentle and intelligent beasts that help herd fish for anglers, pull boats, and radiate light in the evenings to help sailors safely navigate storms and dark waters. When utilizing their light form, they can glide in the air for short periods of time.

Kraken

A sea monster known for its massive size and destructive power. Krakens can manipulate water, creating powerful currents and whirlpools to trap their prey. Calder utilized the beasts during the Witches' War as part of his oceanic army to ensnare and sink enemy ships.

Pixies

Diminutive magical beings that are known for being pests and pranksters due to their playful antics. Residing in forests and meadows, they are guardians of the magical flora and fauna in Driftstone. A pixie can mislead or guide a traveler in their pursuits based on their offerings and intentions. They are often mistaken for small fae due to their humanoid appearance and wings, but they are classified as magical creatures because they are more feral and resistant to societal norms.

Wizwart

Known for their colorful hues and patterns, these frogs can live in almost any water source. The potent oil in their skin serves as an antidote to most poisons and toxins. When carefully harvested and distilled, this oil can neutralize even the deadliest venoms, including Nightshade. Wizwart oil is highly sought after by healers and alchemists.

Wyverns

The first and only magical beasts created by Dragons, Wyverns, were a catastrophic plague on the land. Smaller in nature, with two feet instead of four, Wyverns lacked their creators' intelligence and language skills. Driven only by appetite and instinct, these vicious predators bred and multiplied at an alarming rate, swarming and terrorizing Driftstone's inhabitants. Dragons and Witches partnered to wipe out the predatory pests and drove them to extinction. While Wyverns do not exist today, they are still represented in stories and artisan symbols.

SACRED REALMS

Chronoscape

In the Chronoscape realm, time is a river flowing through Driftstone's past, present, and future. Not much is known about the realm because no one but Selene and the Unicorn has breached its borders. According to Cyrus's record-keeping, if you can find a way into the realm, there are only three laws to follow:

- You can watch the past.
- You can freeze the present.
- You can jump ahead into the future.

Dreamscape

The Dreamscape is a realm shaped by sentient beings' subconscious thoughts and emotions. Dreams take on a tangible form in this realm, creating shifting landscapes, from tranquil meadows to towering mountains of pure imagination. Time flows differently in the Dreamscape, where moments can stretch into eternity or pass in the blink of an eye. Created by Nazeem as a gift to inspire all sentient beings, the realm is currently under siege by Morvana, who is fighting for control of it.

Driftstone

Driftstone is not merely a geographical entity but a sentient and magical earth connected to five celestial bodies and the seven sacred realms. Home to the mortal realm, Driftstone supports and sustains all biological life and serves as the original and central realm. Within Driftstone's core reside seven hearts, each representing a distinct connection to one of the sacred realms. These hearts are not only a source of power; they beat with Driftstone's life force and are a critical component in ensuring its magic stays in balance.

Elysiamore

In this realm of love, soul mates are free to explore the depths of their hearts, confront their fears and doubts, and ultimately reaffirm the strength of their connection. Elysiamore offers them a safe place to feed and test their love while preparing them to emerge even stronger. Only those who are destined to be together, and whose relationship will help shape Driftstone, are invited by the Moonhorn Moose to enter.

Fairy Realm (The Spirit Realm)

Known by many names in different cultures, the Fairy Realm can only be accessed through the city of Faerielithia. This realm is unlike others; created by the White Mane, it's a spiritual haven, where Feyluna raised the original fae. Also known as the Spirit Realm, the time spent inside its borders helps each visitor to reach a state of nirvana within themselves and evolve into their highest state of being. Each of the beasts that dwell within the realm serves as a different spirit guide, based on the needs of the traveler.

Nether Realm

The Nether Realm is the bridge between the living and the dead, serving as a transient station for a soul's ultimate destination. While it is a depository for some, it serves as a waiting place for others who may move on to Sylvanethia.

Omniscora

Omniscora is a realm of infinite knowledge and enlightenment where seekers of wisdom come to solve mysteries and expand their understanding of the universe. Celestial libraries soar to impossible heights, filled with volumes of esoteric lore and maps that chart Driftstone and the sacred realms.

Sylvanethia

Sylvanethia is a realm built by the Chamber of Roots, where many of the spirits of the Living Forest go to retire. The rumor is that this sacred space serves as an alternative to the Nether for those who prove themselves worth; however, it also serves as a guard to many of Driftstone's secrets. It is the only realm that a Magic-Born has never set foot in.

THE DREAMSCAPE

The Dreamscape

Rulers: Morvana (Dream Creator), Nazeem (Exiled, Realm Creator)

Government Support: Dreamwalkers (Currently Vacant)

Laws of Governance

Dreamwalkers

- Only dreamwalkers possess full access to the entirety of the Dreamscape and hold the ability to unlock any door within its realm, navigating non-magic dream chambers at will.

- Only fae dreamwalkers can reveal hidden or locked dream chambers.

- Dreamwalkers cannot enter the locked chambers of Magic-Born; however, they can project their astral essence into the dreams or visions of the dreamer.

- Verbal communication is prohibited in chambers to avoid disrupting or influencing a Magic-Born's dream.

Magic-Born

- Magic-Born can enter the Dreamscape through their designated dreamchamber when asleep.

- Magic-Born cannot open other doors in the Dreamscape unless accompanied by a dreamwalker.

- Magic-Born with prophetic abilities who use their dreamchamber for visions risk exposure of their revelations to other entities within the Dreamscape unless their chamber is concealed. Otherwise, transparency is required to avoid corrupt practices.

- Magic-Born who exit their chambers into the Dreamscape should use protective measures to shield themselves from possession.

Dream and Realm Creators

- A Dream Creator can create, shape, and mold nocturnians and the surrounding landscape within the Dreamscape.

- Dream Creators can inspire, influence, and implant dreams in Non-Magic Born dreamers but are bound by the limitations set by Nazeem, the original Realm Creator.

- A Dream Creator cannot unbind the laws designed by the Realm Creator.

- Dream Creators are blocked from possessing non-magic dreamers or opening locked doors without a dreamwalker's key to ensure a balance of governance.

- Dream and Realm Creators must exit the Dreamscape through their chamber and point of entry.

Nocturnians

- Nocturnians feed on dreams, deriving sustenance from the vivid imaginings of dreamers within the Dreamscape.

- Nocturnians may influence and nurture thoughts, but are prohibited from possession or direct control over dreamers.

- Nocturnians are confined to the Dreamscape unless a Dream or Realm Creator grants explicit permission to exit the realm. Shadebinders are the only exception to this law, but require a deal of exchange with a dreamer and all liabilities included.

- Nocturnians, if granted exit permissions, can only depart through doors unlocked by dreamwalkers, ensuring their presence in the physical realm is regulated and authorized.

- Nocturnians who enter Driftstone require biological changes, including physical transformations and a shift in sustenance to survive. They must rely on a Dream or Realm Creator for alterations.

Nocturnians

Dreamweaver
Artisans who craft and build the landscapes of dreams. Weaving together a dreamer's unconscious thoughts, memories, desires and fears, they construct and tear down the settings for nocturnal experiences.

Echoflight
Creatures with butterfly-like wings that serve as messengers in the Dreamscape. Carrying messages and memories to dreamwalkers and dream creators, they represent the fleeting nature of dreams.

Shadebinder
These manipulative creatures can interact with any dreamer and propose an agreement to bring their dreams to reality. Forced to take on the form and shape of a dreamer's request, a Shadebinder can live in the real world under the assignment of the narrative provided to them. If they are recognized in the real world as a shadebinder, they will vanish and can no longer hold shape. The illusion is broken. If the dreamer dies of

causes uninfluenced by the shadebinder before their contract is finished, the shadebinder is free to live in any form they choose for their remaining days.

Shadowmire

These elusive beings manifest from the darkest corners of the subconscious mind, taking on the form of a dreamer's fears and nightmares. Appearing as shadow figures with glowing red eyes, they feed on negative emotions, insecurities and anxiety. Shadowmires partnered with Morvana in the Dream Wars against Nazeem and are eager to escape the Dreamscape.

Sorrowkindler

An entity whose presence evokes tears and heartache. These gentle, sad beings have a bittersweet beauty; their translucent forms are curtained with tears. Sorrowkindlers feed off grief and help release the burdens carried by dreamers.

Whispervine

These nocturnal entities are formed from strands of light that twine together like vines. Whispervines create a calming aura and atmosphere that encourages comforting dreams.

THE MAGIC OF DRIFTSTONE

Definitions and Terminology

Magic-Born

"Magic-Born" encompasses many lineages and origins, each bearing different characteristics and powers. Although they are sometimes used interchangeably, distinct differences set these categories apart.

Magic-Born (Witches, Warlocks, The Original Thirteen, Sacred Creatures)

Authentic Magic-Born individuals are sentient beings born from the energy and magic of Driftstone. They are defined as magic incarnate. They are infused with potent magical abilities from birth, surpassing other magic users and secondary creations in both power and potential. Only Magic-Born are gifted with the powers to create.

Born with Magic

Individuals born with magic are the result of a union between a Magic-Born and a Non-Magic-Born. Though they inherit magical abilities, their human lineage limits their magical potential. The potency of their abilities may diminish with each generation unless acts like transference or familiar bonding occur, enhancing their connection to their ancestor's source of magic.

Created by Magic

Races created through magic-wielding, whether through energy (primary creations) or bio-prints (secondary creations), exhibit varying levels of assigned magical abilities.

Beings such as dragons, elves, fae, nymphs, or sprites possess limited inherent magic or enhanced biological traits gifted by their creators. Unlike authentic Magic-Born, they are not born from Driftstone's divine source but fashioned by skilled magic wielders. Their potential with magic often extends only as far as the abilities gifted to them.

Schooled Magic

Alchemists, healers, soothsayers, and spellmakers are practitioners without inherent magical abilities. They specialize in the theoretical and practical study of magic without being Magic-Born. These non-magic users rely on acquired knowledge and skills to practice magic, such as healing, divination, spellcraft, and alchemy. Though their abilities may be comparatively low-level, they provide essential support in fields like agriculture and medicine.

Levels of Magic

Innate Magic

Innate magic refers to the type of magical ability that an individual is born with, which is inherently part of their biology. This form of magic requires the least amount of external energy to manipulate and often manifests instinctively or unconsciously. Those with innate magic possess a natural affinity for certain magical skills or elements. Innate powers tend to be connected to a Magic-Born's essence, personality, or lineage. Individuals with innate magic might not be aware of their abilities until puberty or a particular event triggers them.

Primary Magic

Primary magic is a type of magical practice that involves creating or shaping magic from raw energy sources. Practitioners of primary magic can manipulate the fundamental forces of magic themselves. This type of magic enables users to craft spells, conjure illusions, and create life by channeling and molding pure magical energy.

Secondary Magic

Secondary magic users require a tangible source or bio-print to wield their magic, as opposed to being able to draw it from pure energy. This magic often requires study, discipline, or established tools, forms, or bases. Users of secondary magic typically rely on external sources, such as spellbooks, enchanted artifacts, or magical runes. This type of magic often involves rituals and incantations to reconstruct, modify, or replicate primary magic.

Scales of Magic

Magic is a force defined and governed by a delicate balance of opposing elements and energies. Each pair of opposing forces is interconnected and relies on the other to create a balanced and healthy magic ecosystem. Just as a set of scales must be in equilibrium to function properly, the magical scales must also be balanced to prevent symptoms and consequences of overexposure to any one energy.

THE LAWS OF MAGIC

Theory of Sentient Energy
In Driftstone, all energy is imbued with sentience, granting consciousness and awareness. Everything in Driftstone and its adjacent realms possesses thoughts, feelings, and language, though often incomprehensible to human understanding. Sentience drives the laws and ethics of magic.

Laws of Sentient Energy

- Law of Energy: Energy is the essence of life and consciousness.

- Law of Language: Every sentient being can communicate through vibrations, frequencies, or patterns that convey emotions, intentions, and knowledge.

- Law of Portal Sentience: Portals, an extension of space and dimension, exhibit their own form of sentience as conduits between different realms or dimensions. They can be cooperative or resistant, opening or closing based on their own will or the intentions of those seeking to traverse them.

- Law of Respect: Sentient beings must approach each other with respect, empathy, and an open mind. Establishing a respectful communion is essential for cooperation. Demanding or forcing sentient energy to respond or act in opposition to their nature may result in unpredictable and destructive outcomes.

- Law of Intention: Intentions and emotions influence the behavior of sentient energy. Positive intentions, clarity of purpose, and alignment with the inherent qualities of the sentient beings' natural energy increase the chance of productive communion.

Laws of Familiars

- Bond of Essence: Familiars are sacred bonds formed between the spirit of an animal and an Original Magic-Born.

- Law of Protection: During their ceremonial bonding, familiars are sworn to act as protectors and representatives of their host's body and essence, at all costs.

- Exchange of Strength: In exchange for their allegiance, familiars grow larger and stronger than their original biological form. They are equipped with enhanced regenerative abilities for rapid healing and the ability to channel limited extensions of the host's magic.

- Law of Immortality: Although familiars can be killed, they are gifted with the potential to live forever. Upon the death of their original Magic-Born host, the familiar's connection will pass to the next of kin.

- Law of Legacy: If the bloodline of an Original Magic-Born ceases to exist, familiars lose their connection to the source of their magic and longevity. Unless chosen by a descendant of another Magic-Born, a familiar will revert to its original form and life expectancy.

- Law of Immunity: Familiars are immune to possession, transformative, and illusionary magic. They can break enchantments to restore their hosts to their true selves.

- Law of Autonomy: If their host's essence is corrupted and they resist returning to their true nature, familiars possess the free will to break the ceremonial bonding.

- Law of Bonds: A Magic-Born may only bond with two familiars throughout their life cycle, emphasizing the significance and sanctity of their choices.

Laws and Risks of Transference

- Loss of Personal Power: When transferring magic permanently or temporarily, the host may experience a depletion of their magical reserves and/or a weakening of their abilities. This loss of energy can impact their spellcasting, skills, and magical proficiency.

- Imbalance in Power: The transfer of magic from one individual to another can create an imbalance in power dynamics, especially if the recipient gains significantly more magical strength or abilities than the giver. This imbalance may lead to conflicts, dependencies, or misuse of powers.

- Bonded Fates: Permanently transferring magic can create an unexpected connection between the giver and the recipient, tying their destinies together in ways that may have unforeseen consequences. Changes in one's magical path or choices may affect the other, leading to shared fates.

- Law of Dependency: The recipient of transferred magic may become vulnerable to attacks, manipulations, or unwanted influences that are attracted to their new energy. Dependency on the giver for magical support or guidance may arise, potentially leading to relationship strains or power struggles.

- Ethical Considerations: The permanent transfer of magic raises ethical questions about consent, autonomy, and the responsible use of shared magical abilities. Issues of ownership, control, and the ethical implications of altering one's inherent magical nature come into play when magic is permanently passed on.

- Law of Biology: Transference may have unexpected, positive or negative consequences on a recipient's physical, mental, or spiritual well-being.

- Law of Identity: The permanent transfer of magic can alter the recipient's sense of self, identity, or purpose, changing their essence.

Magical Items, Places and Properties

Azure Weapons

Azure weapons are imbued with condensed magical energy, allowing them to transform according to the wielder's will. Azure weapons are coveted for their versatility and will not operate for anyone who is not bonded in allegiance to Lady Ironspire's court.

Enchanted Weapons

Enchanted weapons are ordinary arms and armor that have been magically enhanced to combat or resist magical forces. They are strengthened through rituals, spells, or the infusion of magic, granting them enhanced durability, potency, or the ability to disrupt opposing magical elements.

Regenerative Elements

Regenerative places and properties are items or locations blessed with protective or healing energies that aid in the restoration and renewal of body, mind, and spirit. These sanctified objects and locations (healing springs, sacred groves, wizwart oil, girantheam saliva) can mend wounds, remove toxins from the body, or rejuvenate the recipient.

Runes

Runes are magical sigils used to craft spells, enchantments, or protective wards. Runes are often carved or inscribed onto objects. Runes amplify magical effects and imbue items with specific powers. They are commonly used in divinations or to convey messages.

Standing Stones

Standing stones serve as conduits to help amplify rituals or communions. The rocks allow practitioners to draw power from the land and commune with spirits. They can also be used to serve as a defensive barrier against dark magic.

Talismans

A talisman is a mundane object infused with energy from a Magic-Born. A talisman may provide magical protection, luck, or specific benefits to the person who possesses or wears it. Talismans can take any form the wielder chooses; among the most popular are stones, pendants, rings, and charms.

Wands

Wands are magical instruments crafted to help practitioners focus and control magical spells with precision. These slender rods are infused with magical cores, enchanted woods, or mystical gems that amplify the wielder's magic.

Pages from the Driftstone

The Hallway of Doors

Break or bend, please or implore,
You can't unlock a witch's door.
There is an oath to which it's sworn,
To only open for Magic-Born.

To identify a friend or enemy
You must introduce your energy.
Magic hands that mean no harm,
Will be given access without alarm.

Carried by the Wings of Dragons
Wisdom takes Flight
For in the Grip of the Protector
The Truth is Guarded Tight

Acknowledgments

Professional
Belquis and Martel Publishing
Miles Smart
Yornelys Zambrano
Mayfly book design

Personal
D&D: My Anchors and Hearts
The Great Eight: My Chosen Family
The Eatonton Mary Faeries
Sweet Baby Girl from Heaven
Queen B & Wren
I&A
Duh, Amy and T
Joan, Tav, and Trav
Aussie, Aussie, Aussie!
My Nieces and Nephews
In-Laws in Brazil
Miami Mama
Bruce, Clark, and Diana
Briscoe, Garbus, Redd, and Talley

About the Author

S.W. Kent lives with his husband and his familiar in the Pacific Northwest. Outside of being an author, he has enjoyed a twenty-year career as a coach, counselor, and leader, focused on equity and human rights. He desires to inspire and create worlds where anyone can be the hero, where love knows no limits, and where magic thrives unrestricted by prejudice.

About the Cover Illustrator

Miles Smart lives in San Francisco, where he spends his free time hiking, off-roading, and dreaming up new places to explore. Inspired by stories of brave heroes, monstrous creatures, and far-off lands, he brings each illustration to life with a sense of wonder and adventure.

About the Appendix Illustrator

Yornelys Zambrano is a Venezuelan illustrator specializing in inks. She is a freelance artist who loves botany and fantasy. Follow Yornelys's Instagram (@missyozart) for her full portfolio.

TRUST
YOUR
MAGIC